TREASURE COAST

TREASURE COAST

TOM KAKONIS

This is a work of fiction. Names, characters, places, and incidents either are the product of the author's imagination or are used fictitiously. Any resemblance to actual events or persons, living or dead, is entirely coincidental.

The time setting for this novel is the late 1990s, and as a consequence many of the actual venues cited have changed dramatically or, in some cases, vanished altogether. Other anachronisms (e.g., uses of cell and pay phones) may also be attributed to the passage of time.

ISBN: 194129801X
ISBN 13: 9781941298015

Published by Brash Books, LLC

12120 State Line, #253

Leawood, Kansas 66209

www.brash-books.com

ALSO BY TOM KAKONIS

Criss Cross
Flawless
Blind Spot

The Waverly Series
Michigan Roll
Double Down
Shadow Counter

For Kayla and Jill, two points of light in the gathering dark. Also for Lee Goldberg, who may have rescued me.

The road to gold is long and cold,
and few there are who mind it.
Come search for treasure while ye may,
for gold is where you find it.

—Anonymous

PART ONE

ONE

LIKE MOST MEN CLOSING IN ON THE BENCHMARK forty, Jim Merriman made far more promises—to others mainly, a dwindling few yet to himself—than he knew, heart of hearts, he ever intended to keep. It was a habit by now so deeply entrenched, so much a part of him, that he wore it like a second skin: Generate an earnest pledge today; effortlessly shuck it off tomorrow. Mostly it was harmless, this habitual shortfall between oath and execution, deed and good intention. A commonplace human failing, to his thinking, small and forgivable. A way of getting by in this sorry world.

But the vow exacted from him by a dying sister—that now was giving him serious pause. Better make that acute discomfort. (If he were going to be honest with himself, for a switch, figuring—trying to figure—how to squirrel out of this one. Very unsettling.)

From across the continent, he'd been summoned to her bed of pain, where eventually, floating up out of a narcotized fog, she found the strength to peel back crusted eyelids, fix him with a fluttery gaze, and in a voice fainter than a whisper, feebler than a gasp, murmur, "Jim? That you?"

"None other," he affirmed, putting some of that fraudulent deathwatch heartiness into it.

"You came."

"Said I would."

"Been here long?"

"Not long," he lied. In fact he'd been sitting there for the better part of the afternoon, studying her sleep, marveling at the relentless progress of this formidable malady, its curious manifestations. Her face, in sleep, was sunken, sallow with a greenish tint, the color of mold-infested cheese. The sockets of the eyes, hollow and dark, looked to be rimmed with a dusting of soot. A limp hand, its flesh withered and veined as a dry leaf, seemed to sprout from a forearm grotesquely swollen to Popeye proportions and out of which coiled an IV vine that leaked some colorless, powerless anodyne into her blood. Now that hand moved in an effort at a sweeping gesture. "No, *here*, I mean. Florida."

"I got in this morning. Leon picked me up at the airport."

"Leon?"

"Yes."

"Where is he?"

"Your place. I told him to go back and crash. He looked pretty wasted."

"It's been hard for him," she said.

"He'll be OK."

"You think so?"

"Sure."

"I wonder."

"How about you?" he asked. "They treating you right here?"

"They do what they can."

"Well, you need anything, you just let me know," he said, more confidently than he felt—as if he had a direct hotline to the nerve center of the AMA and could make the quacks jump at his barked command. Hotline to nowhere was what he had.

She nodded dismally, said nothing.

To put something into the oppressive silence, he launched a wandering monologue, picking his topics cautiously, from the security of the distant past mostly, skirting that phantom third presence in the room, Lord Death, with his constrictive time horizons. "Remember that time..." he'd begin a tale, lifted from their shared heartland childhood, and through the malleable prism of inventive memory, he'd mutate some perfectly ordinary incident into an adventure antic. Outrageously the tales grew in the telling, spinning the sunny *Leave It to Beaver* mythology of a tight, joyous, loving family life. Pure fabrication of course. All of it. The sorry truth was that, apart from the accident of birth, they'd never had much in common, never been particularly close. Nevertheless he wore on, mouth running tirelessly, until at last the grab bag of hilarious anecdotes was depleted, the memory-lane tour exhausted, and again a desolate silence settled over the room.

The somber interval lengthened. After a while she filled it. "Jim?"

"Yeah?"

Eyes tearing over, she said, not as a question, "There's not much time left, is there."

"Oh, I don't know about that. Nurse out there says you're holding your own."

"Will you do something for me?" she asked, ignoring the blatant falsehood.

"Whatever I can."

"It's Leon. He's all alone now. So helpless. Like a child. Will you watch out for him?"

"Sure, I'll give the kid a hand" is what he told her. Another in that legion of empty pledges. Slippery, purposely vague. The kind of thing you search for to say. Should have been enough.

Except she couldn't leave it alone. "Promise?"

"Hey, you can count on me," he said lightly, conscious of the sickly smile tacked on his face.

"Need to hear you say it, Jim."

"Uh, what's that?" he asked, stalling, averting his eyes from that pleading, miseried gaze, unblinking now, insistent.

"You promise."

So, cornered, he heard his voice utter that one too, the "p" word, figuring, Why not? What's the damage? Whatever it took to help her exit gracefully, or as graceful as anyone riddled by outlaw cells, wildly multiplying even as they spoke, could ever exit. It was only words. Nothing lost, no one really hurt.

His first mistake. First of many.

Ten minutes later he stood outside the entrance to the Palm Beach Gardens Medical Center, idly puffing a cigarette. A nurse, briskly efficient, professionally cheery, her smile as starched as her uniform, had appeared only a moment after the vow-taking ceremony (nice timing, those mercy angels) and shooed him out of the room, chirping something about "Time for meds" and whatever other ghoulish things they did to keep the croakee wheezing and earn their pay. OK by him. Welcome break from the white world of the hospital and its clash of pungent perfumes, its soiled bedsheets, lemony cleansing solutions, acrid antiseptics, hothouse flowers, rank festering flesh.

The slanting rays of the sun, still fierce on an immense slate of bleached sky, steamed the hospital lawn, glued the parking-lot tar. The dank air resonated with the atonal hum of insect energy. *Symphony of famished worms,* he thought ruefully, *gathering for the feast waiting just on the other side of this door.*

A sudden mournful ache, hollow and unfocused, overtook him. But whom did he really mourn? An expiring sister in there, seldom seen, scarcely known, barely recognizable anymore, soon to be floating out of herself? No, it was himself he sorrowed for, himself, a couple of weeks short of a milestone birthday, half a lifetime squandered, pissed away, and dying just as surely as she, only daily, increment by increment, puff by puff. Conducting his own requiem in advance, dirge supplied courtesy of an invisible swarm of bugs.

What they're doing, these crusading nicotine zealots, by banishing us from their haloed presence, he further reflected, dourly now, *is creating a breed of solitary, morbid philosophers. Seekers of occult mystery in wisps of smoke.*

His cigarette had grown a tail of ash. He ground it under a heel, defiantly lit another. And just as he put a flame to it, a most handsome woman clad in a satiny blouse and designer jeans came through the door, paused, fished a pack of Capris from a Gucci bag slung over her shoulder, and shook one loose. The flame in his hand still flickered, and so in that wordless bond that links a renegade fraternity, he offered it to her. She favored him with a small smile and ever so lightly touched his hand in a steadying gesture. Fetching gesture, fetching smile. Up close this way, he could see she wasn't young but not yet old either, a ripened thirtyish somewhere; by his best estimate, forty tops. Around a plume of smoke, she said, "Another second-class citizen?"

"Afraid so."

"They're turning us into a bunch of sneaks."

"Or worse yet, wimps. Where's Bogie when we need him?"

"Who?" she asked.

"Humphrey Bogart. Remember him? Tough as nails, and he always had a weed stuck in his face."

"How about Bette Davis? Nobody crossed her."

"There you are."

One thing you had to give your habit—it was an instant icebreaker. Something to be said for that, particularly when your commiserator comes equipped with a dizzying cascade of platinum curls; good bone geometry; skin lacquered to a high sheen; a generous crimson-glossed mouth; eyes a cool blue but with a glint of worldly mischief in them; and pliant, slightly plumpish curves under a fashion-statement outfit. Like this one did. All of which he assimilated in a sly sidelong glance, as he no longer pondered his own mortality but rather the enduring quality of lust, how it occasionally nods but never really sleeps.

"You visiting somebody?" she asked him, turning the talk elsewhere, extending it. Promising signal.

"A sister," Jim said.

"Is it serious?"

"It's cancer."

"Bad?"

"Terminal variety."

"That's a shame."

He shrugged. "Yeah, well, cancer always wins."

She took a long, meditative pull on her Capri. The third finger of the cigarette-bearing hand, he noticed, was bedecked with a gaudy rock the size of a boulder. Generally—though not absolutely, in his experience—a bad signal. In a stagy, breathy voice, she said, "I'm real sorry."

"No need to be," he said with mock solemnity. "Doctors determined it wasn't your fault."

For a sliver of an instant, she looked perplexed. Then, as she got it, her smile widened, displaying an abundance of teeth, dazzling as neon and much too perfect to be anything but orthodontist enhanced. Jim gave her back his player smile, oblique, distant, hint of evasiveness in it. Dueling grins.

Hers departed first, displaced by an earnest expression. "Is she centered?"

"Centered?"

"Centered," she repeated, as though the echo explained itself.

"Afraid I don't follow," he said, baffled by the corkscrew twist in the conversation and wondering if maybe this time the joke wasn't on him.

"Like, in tune with her spiritual center."

Evidently no joke. "Well," he said, "we've never been what you'd call God-fearing people. She taught math, some community college down here. Numbers are—*were*—her religion."

"Got nothing to do with religion," she declared, a little impatiently.

"No? What then?"

"Energy. Strictly energy. See, I read this book by this Indian guy—from India, I mean, not your American kind—where he shows how we're all a part of this one big spirit. Only he calls it energy. Cosmic energy. And it's, like, steady. Never changes, never dies. What we call 'dying' is just trading energies."

"That's a comfort."

"And what you got to do," she plowed on, voice elevating urgently, "when your body's ready to pass, is zero in on it, your place in this energy field. That's what centering is. Sort of like finding your way home."

"Interesting theory," Jim allowed, thinking they all have to come with some wart, physical or otherwise. Even the best of them, like this dumpling of sex here, with the loopy-energy hair up her sweet apple ass. Too bad. Terrible waste.

"Changed my life, I can tell you."

"Bet it did at that."

"What I do now," she said, "is try and help people get in touch with it. Their energy center. That's why I'm here. My best girlfriend's mother—she's about to pass too."

Sounded to him like some spiritual fart cutting, with her being the therapeutic Gas-X. But what he said was, "Sounds sort of like volunteer work."

"Guess you could call it that. See, growing up, I wanted to be a nurse. Never did make it, so this is the next best thing."

"You? A nurse?"

"I always wanted to help people."

Yeah, right. "I see," he said cautiously, radar suddenly alert for a scam coming on.

"So you think she's centered yet?"

"Who's that?"

"Who we're talking about here...your sis."

"You got me."

"If you want, I could speak to her."

Finally the pitch. Everybody peddling something. Pretty prosperous clip too, by the looks of that stone weighting her finger. Unless, of course, it was fake. "Appreciate the offer," Jim said, "but I don't think she'd be very receptive." Figured that'd be the end of it. Any good fleecer knows when it's time to book.

Figured wrong. "OK," she said breezily and, in yet another of those bootleg turns, added, "You're not from around here, are you?"

"How could you tell?"

"Wild guess."

"You guessed right."

"Whereabouts then?"

"Nevada."

"Vegas?"

"Reno."

"Reno, Vegas—they're like Florida," she said. "Nobody's *from* there."

"Right again."

"So? Originally where?"

"South Dakota."

"No kidding!" she exclaimed. "Me too. I'm from Bismark."

"That's in North Dakota."

"Same thing."

"I expect maybe it is. There's not all that many of us, either province."

"Hey, don't I know? That's why we got to stick together. What I always say is, 'When you're from Dakota, you got to be good.' "

Jim regarded her narrowly. A corner of her wide mouth was lifted once again in a suggestion of a smile, artful, provocative, faintly amused. The naughty mischief he'd seen earlier, thought he'd seen, all but given up on during the energy drone, shimmered behind her eyes. "By that," he said, choosing his words carefully (for if four decades had taught him any lesson at all, it was that a man never knew when he was going to get lucky), "do you mean 'nice good'? Or oh, say, 'skillful good,' 'accomplished'?"

Before she could reply, a sleek silver Porsche swung into the lot and lurched to an idling stop twenty or so yards from where they stood. A head—male, jowly, squinty eyed, round, and hairless as a billiard ball—poked out of the driver's-side window like a wary turtle emerging from its shell. She gave it a high-handed wave, a big theatrical welcoming grin, calling, "Hi, honey. Be right with you." To Jim she stage-whispered, "The big doolie arrives."

"Doolie?"

"The worse half."

"Oh."

She lowered the waving hand, abruptly thrust it at him. "Been real nice talking to you."

Jim took the offered hand. Grip was surprisingly firm; the shake snappy, businesslike. "Same here," he said.

"My name's Billie. Billie Swett."

"Swett?"

"You got it. Like in the perspiration, only with an 'e' and two 't's. Cute, huh?"

"Well, everybody's got to be named something."

"And you are?"

"Jim Merriman."

"Merriman," she repeated, the tantalizing shimmer not quite gone out of her eyes. "You don't look so merry to me."

"Inside I'm laughing."

"Listen, you change your mind—about your sister, I mean—I'll be at the hospital here. Next couple days anyway. Ask around. They know me in there."

"I'll be watching."

The Porsche's horn bleated. The turtle head squawked, "C'mon, honey. We're runnin' late."

"I'm coming, hon," she called back sweetly, but under her breath, softly, though not so soft as to be inaudible, she muttered, "Asshole."

Across lawn and lot, she sauntered, loose easy stride, studied sway in the shapely hips. Into the Porsche she climbed, pecked the turtle on the cheek, checked her reflection in the rearview, patted and primped the cotton candy ringlets. And with that the two honeys were gone, sped away, leaving Jim to speculate now on the quirky nature of luck, which, he suspected, like gold, was where you found it.

For the next seventy-two hours, he and Leon took turns: six on, six off. Bedside sentinels. *Or boneyard vultures*, Jim caught himself thinking during one of his on shifts, with an effort to push the grisly image from his head. Mostly his sister slept, though now and again, she'd drift out of a morphine-induced stupor long enough to mumble incoherently. Something about snow. Luckily for him, the Leon promise seemed to be buried in dying dreams dominated by snow.

As for that other category of luck, it proved fickle. The lush Billie Swett, mistress of assorted energies, was nowhere to be found. Not that he didn't search. On the occasional (well, frequent actually, as the days plodded on) break in a tedious watch, he'd scout the hospital corridors, peering into rooms, feigning confusion. Or plant himself outside the entrance again, chaining smokes on the off chance of another accidental encounter. Or stop by the nurses' station to remark, elaborately casual, "I don't suppose you've seen Mrs. Swett today," a transparent query that invariably got him either a negative head bob or helpless shrug, both often as not accompanied by a knowing smirk. No Mrs. Swett in evidence. Toward the end of the long vigil, he'd pretty much resigned himself to the harsh proposition that, for him anyway, luck and gold forever would remain equally elusive.

Shortly after midnight on the final day, he was sitting at the kitchen table in his sister's cramped, cluttered apartment (shared for years with an untidy son, chronic fuckup), sipping a beer and nibbling stale Doritos and salsa, the closest thing to food he could find in the place. Seriously dragging ass. Wondering when it was all going to come to a merciful wrap, for all concerned. And as if in answer to that uncharitable question, the cell phone now habitually kept by his side rattled, and down the line came his nephew's voice, trembling on the edge of tears. "Uncle Jim? That you?"

Like there'd be anybody else here. "Yeah, it's me, Leon," he said wearily. "What's up?"

"It's Mom. Nurse says she's about ready to go. Can you come back?"

"Sure. Be right over."

"She's asking for you."

"For me?"

"Yeah."

"She, uh, say why?"

"No."

"OK. I'll be there."

"Better hurry."

"I'll do that."

He did too, more or less. Left the beer unfinished, took a leak, switched off the lights, locked the door behind him, hopped into Leon's restored shark-finned Caddie (outlandish relic, drew chute-jawed stares when driven in the daylight), and pointed it in the direction of the hospital. On the short drive, he was careful to observe the speed limit, scrupulously obey all the traffic signals. Wasn't stalling exactly, just exercising normal cautions. Who needed trouble?

He found Leon standing braced against a wall outside the room, eyes flooded over, thin shoulders quaking. "She's gone, Uncle Jim. Mom's dead."

"When?" Jim felt compelled to ask, even though he wasn't sure he wanted to know.

"Right after I called you."

So it made no real difference how fast he had, or hadn't, hurried. Some things, at least, worked out for the best. And that's about what he told Leon, for something to say. Words of comfort never came easily to him.

"She's still in there. You want to see her one last time? Say good-bye?"

He hesitated. Cinematic farewells weren't among his stronger suits. "She's dead, Leon."

"I know it. But she cared an awful lot about you, Uncle Jim. She told me so."

Maybe the kid was right. Maybe he did owe her that much. Wasn't easy anymore, sorting out a battery of tangled emotions: sorrow from relief, guilt from grief. He sighed, stepped into the room, barely illuminated now by a small lamp on a corner table. He came up alongside the bed, gazed at her ashen, rigid face, whose features bore an expression neither peaceful nor distressed but more, in his perception, puzzled, as though she wrestled with some particularly knotty mathematical equation. The sum of zero maybe.

TWO

EARLIER THAT SAME DAY, SOME SEVEN HUNDRED miles to the north, in a weathered doublewide set in a stand of towering pines off a dirt road that snaked tortuously up a mountain near a western North Carolina hamlet that went by the quaint name of Maggie Valley, the topic of death was also under discussion by a foursome gathered in the trailer's shabby living room. More accurately it was the focus of a windy monologue delivered with solemn intensity by a portly, paunchy man dressed all in black. Suit (slightly frayed at the collar and sleeves), nylon shirt (produced in Taiwan), tie (also crafted by busy oriental hands), socks, patent leather shoes—all black. Like some memento mori materialized ominously out of the late-afternoon shadows that slanted across the room. An impression only partly relieved by the shock of hair, arctic white; the pinkish flush to the chipmunk cheeks; and trace of a sparkly twinkle in eyes otherwise wintry gray. Exactly the effect he sought to create at the onset of a game.

"Yes, as my card you hold there indicates, I'm still very much a man of the cloth," he was saying, winding down a lengthy verbalized résumé, the preamble to the burn. "But I like to believe I've found an even higher calling," he concluded, eyes piously shuttered now.

Seated directly opposite him on a sofa whose springs here and there penetrated its tattered fabric, an elderly couple, Dwiggins by name, Homer and Selma, squinted at the alluded-to card. It identified the speaker as B. Noble Bott, DD, and somewhat murkily, described his present vocation as prebereavement services counselor. The man of the trailer cupped a vein-tunneled hand behind an obscenely furry ear plugged by the half-shell of a hearing aid and bellowed, “You wanna speak up little? Found what, you say?”

“A higher calling.”

“That mean you ain’t preachin’ no more?”

“Not in the traditional sense. That is to say, I no longer minister to a single congregation. My flock, so to speak, has widened. Multiplied many times over.” A sweep of a pudgy arm testified to its vast breadth, incalculable numbers.

“Just what biness you in anyways, Mr....” A glance at the card still clutched in a gnarly claw supplied the surname. “... Bott, is it?”

“Please. Bryce. My Christian name, for which the ‘B’ signifies.”

“I’m askin’ what biness you in. It ain’t preachin’.”

“The business, my friend—may I call you Homer?” A nod all but imperceptible seemed to grant consent. “The business, Homer, of hallowed memories.”

The Dwigginses gawked at him, thoroughly bewildered.

“Allow me to explain. One fine Sunday morning, not so many years gone by, squarely in the midst of a routine sermon, I was struck by...by—how best to put this?—nothing less than a vision. A truly blinding vision. Not unlike Paul on the road to Damascus.”

“Say who?” Homer demanded. Whether from deafness or ignorance it was impossible to tell.

“The Apostle Paul,” he said, jacking up the volume and adding, to cover both bases, “From the Good Book, you’ll recall.”

“So what it show you, this vision?”

“What it revealed to me, Homer, was the essence of that calling I spoke of a moment ago.” He paused long enough to lean forward in his chair, thereby establishing a Dwiggins-Bott confidential zone. On he plunged. “How, I asked myself, do we differ from the apes and other brute beasts? The answer, I discovered, is simplicity itself: foresight. Our ability to foresee that most awesome, mysterious, dreaded event we all must one day confront."

"Which one's that?" Homer wanted to know.

"The day of our passing, my friend. Our final reckoning. Oh, many the funeral service had I presided over in my pastoral capacity, searching vainly for words of solace to offer grieving loved ones left behind. None were adequate. Something more, my vision told me, was required. Something tangible, solid, lasting. Something more...concrete, if you will."

How smoothly he spoke, how creamy the words. Plainly he was possessed of the natural-born gasbag's passionate enchantment with the orotund peal of his own voice.

Homer, however, was as yet unmoved. "Yeah," he grunted skeptically. "What'd that be?"

On cue the fourth party in the room, a reedy young woman, scant of flesh, slight of bone, pallid of complexion, reached down and produced a colorful brochure from a satchel at her feet. Without a word she handed it to Bryce, who said, "Thank you so much, Waneta."

She smiled thinly. Like the putative Reverend Bott, she was outfitted in black—filmy blouse, ankle-length skirt, pumps—but unlike him she remained silent, seemingly attentive to the oily flow of words.

Which resumed, once he had laid the brochure on a rickety coffee table set between him and the marks, in grandly intoned pronouncement: "*Here* is where my vision has led me."

For a long moment, the Dwigginses gaped at it. Finally it was Homer who said doubtfully, "Tombstones? You sellin' tombstones?"

"Monuments, my good friend. Testaments to the unbreakable bond forged between us and our dear departeds. Quarried from the finest Italian marble and guaranteed to endure 'til that sublime moment of scriptural prophecy when the last trumpet shall sound, and believers like ourselves shall be plucked bodily from the blackness of the grave and lifted up to an eternity of heavenly bliss."

"I dunno," Homer muttered, leafing through the brochure. "Mail-order tombstones..."

"Among the many virtues of purchase via post," Bryce put in quickly, his manner shifting easily from inspired visionary to supple huckster, "is the abundant selection of styles. Notice, for example, on page seven the angels available in a variety of postures and shapes, from innocent cherub to imposing guardian. All of them masterfully crafted, I think you'll agree."

Homer found the cited page. Frowned at it. Said nothing.

So Bryce cast another line. "Not least of those virtues is the cost factor. No small concern," he added with a sly wink, the soul of good common horse sense now, "to those of us on a tight budget."

Homer stabbed a finger at the page. "You sayin' them is cheaper'n what I could get over in town?"

"You'll find our products, even the designer models, come in at well below anything the local competition can offer."

"Huh. Don't look so cheap to me. 'Course I ain't been doin' much tombstone shoppin' lately either."

"Precisely the purpose of our chat," Bryce said gently. "To spare you and Mrs. Dwiggins..." Here he flashed a mushy smile at Selma, the lady of the trailer, a jumbo oinker of a woman who filled out a flowery-print housedress big as a feed sack and who, like his own female companion, had contributed not a word to the man-talk parley. "...that melancholy task. Furthermore," he went on, the smile gradually enlarging, "were we to act today, I've been specially empowered to discount all our listed prices by a full fifty percent."

Homer's jaw dropped. "How much, you say?"

"Half off anything you see in the catalog," repeated the beaming Bryce, "in commemoration of our firm's seventy-five years of dedicated family service. The date of which, by happy coincidence, falls on this very day. But only today can I make this offer."

Homer tucked his thumbs under the straps of his bib overalls, moved his head side to side slowly. "Still lotta money for a hunk a rock."

Bryce smothered a sigh. "A small down payment would secure you and Mrs. Dwiggins the monuments of your choice and at truly remarkable savings."

"How small we talkin'?"

"Twenty percent would do nicely," Bryce said, narrowing in on the close. All he wanted was to get their John Q. Corndogs on the dotted line, pocket the plunder, and get into the wind.

Homer pondered, stroking his scraggly chin as though it were a favored house pet.

Sensing a kill, Bryce struck a magnanimous note on the sonorous organ of his voice. "My friend, I can see you're a man of good faith. That being so, ten percent will suffice." With a wallet dipping perilously near to empty, even a five-and-dime take would help out.

Homer turned to his wife. "Mother?"

To Bryce's plummeting dismay, Mother Dwiggins responded to her spouse's simple query by bursting into anguished tears. More times than a few had the old boohoos, sparked by a helpmeet overcome by the thought of her lovey duck's demise, cost him a nice cut of change. "There, there, ma'am," he murmured. "Better than most do I realize just how painful these deliberations must be. I too have suffered great personal loss." Like those bills, he was thinking, headed straight down the Chinese toilet if he didn't get a lock on this pitch and soon. To that end he added wisely, "The contemplation of death is never easy. Nonetheless it's only prudent we prepare ourselves—"

"Ain't *us*!" she wailed. "It's LuJean! Our poor little LuJean!"

Homer, slick eyed himself, explained, "LuJean's our daughter. She's all fulla the tumor. Doctors can't do nothin' more, so they sent her on home here to die."

"You have my deepest sympathies," said Bryce, putting on a suitably doleful face behind which a calculator tallied numbers revised to reflect a possible hat trick in the making.

"Appreciate that," Homer said. "Her time is short."

His last observation generated a fresh round of waterworks from the stricken Mother Dwiggins. Great shuddery sobs this time. Like some honking hippo. Bryce figured his only hope of turning the potential double play into a three-bagger was to get Pa Kettle out of the room, so he said to him, "Perhaps you would permit me to pay my respects."

"S'pose it can't hurt none. She always likes to see company, LuJean."

Homer led the way down a hall to a bedroom in the back. Outside the door he hesitated, said, "Uh, be better you don't tell her what biness you in."

Bryce made a "not to worry" wiggle with a hand. In they went, into a closet-size room shrouded in darkness by a drawn shade at the single window. Two steps and they were bedside. Bryce blinked furiously, adjusting his eyes to the gloom. And when at last they came into focus, what he saw (worse yet, smelled—big-time downtown stink) was a wasted facsimile of a human shape lying motionless under a malodorous urine- and fecal-stained sheet pulled up to the chin, exposing only a head bald as an egg and with the putty-gray features of a waxwork figure miraculously, albeit briefly, endowed with breath. A share of which dwindling supply she expended on a plaintive greeting. "Papa? That you?"

Homer stooped over and tenderly stroked the hairless skull. "Sure is, sweetie. An' I brung you a visitor."

"Visitor?"

"This here's Mr. Bryce Bott. He stopped by to say hello."

"Such a pleasure, not to say privilege, it is, meeting you..." Bryce began, blowing his usual quota of smoke, which, under the durable gaze fastened on him by eyes luminous as beacons in that caved-in face, unexpectedly and for him quite uncharacteristically, faltered, trailed away altogether. For it was as though she stared not so much *at* him as *through* him, through flesh and bone and spongy innards, straight to the bottom of his wicked heart. And out of that dry slit of a mouth, slightly ajar, came the feeble, whispery, enigmatic words, "What shall I tell them, Mr. Bott?"

"I beg your pardon?"

"The other side. What do you want me to tell them?"

"I'm afraid I don't—"

Homer nudged him, made a windmilling gesture around an ear. To LuJean he said, "Now, now, daughter. You don't wanna go troublin' this fine genemun with your fool notions."

"What shall I tell them, Mr. Bott?" she asked again, oblivious to her father's caution, voice lifting urgently now, unflinching gaze still sealing the visitor.

A queasy twitch of a smile was the most Bryce could manage.

Homer to the rescue. "You need your rest, sweetie. Anyhow, Mr. Bott got to be goin' now."

He gripped Bryce at an elbow, guided him to the door. Out in the hall, he said, "Don't pay her no mind. She got it in her head she can take messages over to the other side with her."

"Other side?"

"Yeah, y'know, spirits passed on."

"She believes she can communicate with the dead?"

"Y'mean talk to 'em? Like you 'n' me doin' here?"

"Yes."

"Nope. Just carry messages."

"In both, ah, directions?"

"Sometimes. Mostly, though, it's just from here over to there. Either way a blasphemy."

"You think so?" Bryce said absently. In a remote chamber of his busy head, something strange was gathering. A thought? Impression? Strategy? Scheme? Impossible to tell. Something blurry, shapeless, yet ill defined but gradually assuming a willful substance of its own.

"Why, sure, it's blasphemy," Homer declared. "Goes against your Bible. Worst part is she got other folks believin' she can actual' do it. They been comin' from all over with their messages they want delivered."

"From *all* over?"

"Far as up to Asheville we get 'em. Had one fella drive down from Johnson City even. Said he got something real important to tell his missus, been gone ten years or better."

"Really. And how is it these people learn of your daughter's, uh, gift?"

"Ain't a gift. It's the Devil's work. Preacher like yourself oughta know that."

"Yes, of course. Yet somehow these poor, deluded souls must hear of it."

"Word gets out quick. Lotta loonies out there. Some of 'em, after they talk to her, even wanna leave money. Like a church donation. You imagine that?"

"Indeed I can."

"Mother, she think we oughta take it, help out on the cleanup costs when LuJean's time come. Me, I say no. That's Satan money."

"I see," said Bryce, and he did too, and with all the stunning clarity of one of those extemporized, wholly fictional visions that tripped so easily from his pitchman's tongue.

He made no effort to close on any slabs that day. Much too wired to clutter his head with trifles. Broad new vistas, fruitful and vast, opened behind his eyes. Back in the living room, he bade the woodchucks an airy farewell, motioned the astonished Waneta to her feet, and hustled her out the door.

"You don't wanna talk no more 'bout them tombstones?" the fuddled Homer called after them.

"Another time," Bryce called back.

Coming down the mountain, Bryce was oddly silent, absorbed in a mind life crowded with soaring dreams. Waneta piloted their rust-cankered, decade-old Seville, yellow-knuckling its wheel on the hairpin curves, herself silently seething. 'Til at last she said grimly, "OK, Bryce. You gonna tell me what's up?"

"Up?" he echoed, brought suddenly, thuddingly to earth.

"What went on back there? What's shakin' down?"

"Down, up—your grasp of direction seems a bit confused, my dear."

"Don't go playin' no mind-fuck word games with me. This is Waneta Jean Pease you're talkin' at. Remember?"

"You make it difficult to forget," he replied mildly.

"So? How come we didn't close them two major hicks? While you was in the back, I got Miss Piggy there quieted down and all primed to pop for one a' them baby angels."

"Cherubs, they're called."

"Whatever."

Up to then, Bryce had been gazing abstractedly out his window, watching the branches of the pines shiver under a faint breeze, the sky go violet with dusk. Now he turned and scrutinized his partner closely. The naturally cadaverous body, frail as a twig; the Niagara of hair, tar black, falling below the spindly shoulder blades; the arrowhead symmetry to a face (even in petulance, as now) of almost somber beauty, with its chalky skin innocent of paint, its cheekbones so prominent and regally elevated that they seemed to cast long shadows under the deep-set forest-green eyes, its thin bloodless lips, narrow jaw with a cleft carved in it...perfect!—all of it perfect—as if it had been expressly crafted to fit his inventive new conception of her, embryonic, still budding. And as he studied her this way, it was hard for him to believe he'd discovered so delicate-seeming a creature in some rude bugspeck off in the Tennessee hills. Until, that is, she spoke, as she was doing just then. More on the order of haranguing actually. "You hadn't fucked up back there, we'd be sportin' two, maybe three bills for all our time and trouble, 'steada zip."

Came with a hard mouth, this girl. On the slabs scam, that hadn't been a problem: Like a magician's assistant, her mere presence, silent, competent, serene, had added just the proper dimension, a tranquil contrast to his blustery torrent of words. Now, however, it posed a problem. Going to require some serious coaching. "Waneta," he said reflectively, "how long have we teamed, you and I?"

"Huh? What's that got to do with anything?"

"Indulge me. How many years has it been?"

"Beats me. Couple, I guess…three."

"Closer to four," he corrected. "And in all that time, have I ever once failed you?"

"Depends."

"On what?"

"On what you call 'fail.' Ain't like we ever been on top of the happy jack."

"True enough," he conceded. "But perhaps we're about to be. And sooner than you may think."

"What's that suppose to mean?"

Bryce loosened his tie, made a thoughtful steeple of his hands, thumbs supporting a suety secondary chin. "What it means," he announced portentously, "is that I believe I've had a revelation of sorts."

"A *what*?"

"An inspiration. Vision, some might say."

She lifted a hand off the wheel, reached over, and snapped a finger in front of his eyes. "C'mon, Bryce. Save that pigeon poop for the bubbleheads."

"What I've stumbled on," he continued, quite unruffled, "purely by happenstance, is a bold new design guaranteed to put us in possession of what you're pleased to call the 'happy jack.'"

Waneta snorted. "Bet I'm gonna be the first to hear about it too, this new design."

"That you are," he said, and, steeple suddenly collapsed, hands excitedly rending the air now, he outlined it for her, elaborately fleshing out details, adding refinements as they came to him. And when he was finished, he clasped his hands over his portly middle and said simply, "Well?"

"Jeez, I dunno. Pretendin' like I'm carryin' some flapdoodle shit over to ghosts..."

"Messages, Waneta. Vital personalized messages. And to spirits, never ghosts."

"Yeah," she said dubiously, "an' I'm the one gets to play mailman."

"Who better qualified than yourself?"

"I'm twenty-seven years old, f'chrissake. Who's gonna believe I'm croakin'?"

"Even the young can be visited by the Angel of Death. I'll see to it you're thoroughly rehearsed, properly prepared to bring it off. Trust me."

"You think it'll fly?"

"Soar, my dear, soar. Who among us doesn't long to believe in a great beyond peopled by the vaporous souls of our vanished loved ones? Who doesn't yearn to communicate with them one more time? Therein lies the artless beauty of this venture."

"So where'bouts we takin' it, this big venture?"

"South," Bryce said vaguely.

"This *is* the South. We're already here. I'm askin' where you want me to point this banger."

After a meditative pause, he said, "Florida," smacking his lips over the strung-out syllables of the word and thinking how the Lord does indeed work in mysterious ways, his wonders to perform, the thought of which compelled him to declaim, "That earthly paradise, bounteous land overflowing with milk and honey. And bottomless store of marks."

THREE

AT ABOUT THE SAME TIME REVEREND BOTT AND his confederate were headed in the direction of Florida, two men could be found sitting in a back booth of a dingy eatery located in a coastal community of that state. Unknown to each other until now, they were exchanging identities, backgrounds, and it might be said, credentials in a wary, cryptic code.

"You here on receivables?"

"Tha's correct."

"Berkowitz send you?"

"You got it, man."

"You sure about that?"

"Hey, you can give him a call, you not feelin' comfortable."

"Outta where?"

"Huh? Pay phone right up front there."

"I know where they keep the phone at. Inquirin' where you hail from."

"Miami. Big M. Where else?"

"Figures. You ever done any scufflin', this part of the world?"

"Boca's far north as I worked."

"So how come super Jew sends *you*? Still Anglo country up here, last I looked."

A shrug. "He just tell me tool on up there, and take this slugger's back." Plus a whole lot more, none of which seemed, at the moment, needful of mention.

This nonexplanation was greeted with an utterance somewhere between a grunt and a sniff. "That's a hoot. Wetback takin' Junior Biggs's back."

"Ain't no wetback, man. I got papers."

"Yeah, right. Fresh printed."

A crafty, toothy grin. "They pretty fresh. Anyhow, you don't got to worry. I know how to carry myself."

"Terror a Chihuahua, huh?" The initial syllable emerged a slushy *shee.*

"I'm from Tampico, man. And that's *Chee*-huahua. *Chee.*"

"Tampico, Sheewawa—either place, you still a big *bandolero,* right? Real desperado?"

"Tha's the word on the street."

"Street don't mean dick. What's your blue card say?"

"Say nickel bid, Marion. Strapped robbery."

This intelligence, proudly asserted, generated nothing more than a sneer. "How I hear it, Marion's a Girl Scout camp. Myself, I done a straight eight, Jacktown. Gladiator school."

"On what?"

"Murder two. Accessory to."

"Jacktown, that's way the fuck up north someplace. What bring you down here?"

"Sun and fun," he said, though the sour expression on a somewhat pasty, wide-margined face speckled with tiny black acne holes seemed to suggest not much of either.

"Well, you in the right spot for both of 'em."

"OK," he said grudgingly, "might as well trade names. We gotta eat off the same plate awhile. Mine's Biggs. Morris Biggs."

"Yeah, Mr. Berkowitz—he already tol' me that much," said the other dryly.

"I go by 'Junior.' On account a' 'Morris' was my daddy's name too."

"No kiddin'. I'd've figured it for a little joke, like, for your size." Which, in his eyes, was of truly Godzilla dimensions. Easy six four; couple hundred and a half; keg of a chest sloping into a battering-ram belly on him; guns dangling out the sleeves of a canary-yellow sport shirt like a couple of tattooed ham hocks, swastikas on them mostly, some Brotherhood *scheize*, a heart with "Mother" across it by an elbow.

"Some a' that too," he said complacently, baring mottled teeth in a slant of a smile that elevated a vertical scar at a corner of the mouth, half a parentheses. "And you'd be?"

"Hector Pasadena."

One shag-rug brow arched over eyes chilly as black marbles punched into clay. "Fuck kinda name's that?"

"Latino."

"Sounds wop. An' you for sure ain't no wop."

"You got that right, man. Pureblood Spanish."

"Fuck, 'Pasadena' ain't a name, even. It's a place. Out in California."

"Can be a name," Hector insisted. "Like, y'know, this town we in right here. Stuart. That's both too."

Junior had to ponder this for a moment. Even in the face of its irresistible logic, he looked unpersuaded. Finally he declared, with questionable relevance, "Comes to wiggy names, you bean dips gettin' bad as the spades," an observation triggered less by bigotry than a sweeping, scattergun malice toward everyone indiscriminately, though perhaps with keener focus on those of duskier hue.

Which his table mate surely was. A wiry little man, this Hector Pasadena, lean as a licorice whip; skin the color of polished walnut under a helmet of sable hair, glossy with oils natural and applied, slicked back off a low shelf of brow and knotted into a bulb at the base of a skull bracketed by the tiny, pointy ears of a bat. Eyes bird-bright glittered out of the angular face, and the mobile mouth had a way of opening easily in a big disarming smile. As it was doing just now. "Fact is," he confided, "I took it off a map, Pasadena."

"So what's your real one?"

"Name?"

"Fuck're we talkin' about here? Yeah, your name."

Already Hector was regretting the shared confidence. A little sheepishly he said, "Jesus Morales," the given name delivered in precise Spanish pronunciation.

"That 'Hay-soose' spelled like the Bible Jesus?"

"Yeah."

"So why you people say it funny?"

"Tha's how we do."

"Don't seem right, callin' yourself Jesus."

"Why's that?"

"Ain't like you is exactly holy."

"So? Lotta names come from them Bible dudes. Y'got your Matt, Mark, Luke, John," he enumerated, ticking off the Gospels on the fingers of a hand, warming to the topic, "an' none a' the guys I ever seen wearin' them tags walkin' on water either. How about your Jew names? They all come outta there. Like Mr. Berkowitz. Sol, that's for 'Solomon,' I think. Look at them, Jews. They the ones snuffed Jesus."

Junior, swamped by this flood of indisputable evidence, put a stop-signal paw in the air. "Awright, awright. I got your meaning."

"The 'Hector,'" said the vindicated Hector, "I got off a sign I seen someplace. Hector's Hardware."

Junior glanced at his watch. "OK, Hector, Hay-soose, whoever the fuck you are," he said in a low, get-to-business growl. "Tune-up time."

"What I'd like you to do for me," Mr. Berkowitz had told Hector earlier that day, speaking in that slow, even, untroubled tone all your heavy wallets seemed to have, "is spend a week or two with this Biggs fellow. Keep your eyes open. The word I'm getting on him—on his style, I should say—is not, well, encouraging. A certain amount of force, where indicated, is acceptable. That's only business. But we can't have any loose cannons in our ranks, even part-timers. That's bad business. Don't you agree, Hector?"

Hector was quick to assure him he agreed. From experience he knew Mr. B liked harmony, agreement. Hector had been with him since right out of Marion, seven years now, the better part of his twenties, which he was going to be looking at in the rearview a week or so down the line. Worked his way up from mule to certified collector, Hector had. Done real good with the Cubans, where most of the Miami trade came from, mainly because he had this nice, easy way about him: mellow, kicked back, cool. Talked reason, not smack. That's how you collected your receivables. The razor-edged shank he kept Velcro-taped to a slender ankle (wore it all the time—sleeping, doing a nasty, you name it) hardly ever got used. No more'n—what?—half dozen times maybe, all them years. He drove a snazzy red Mustang, got his share of gash (senoritas mostly, but gash is gash), had some pesos in the bank. So he was doing OK for himself.

Except every time he had a face-to-face with the chief there, like the one this morning, he came away feeling...feeling...fuck, he didn't know. Not unhappy exactly but not so rosy either. Restless, like. Anglos in general, Jews particular, could make you feel that way, like you just stepped off the back of the bus. How come you don't got what Mr. B got? High-backed leather chair; big mahogany desk; big glassed-in office with a view of the cruise ships steaming out of Dodge Island; tall blond Bambi for a secretary with skirt riding up near the honeypot and sleek legs going straight on up to the ass, Miss Hide the Burrito on open call—how come you got none of that, Hector? Huh, how come? Past time for his wedge of that American dream pie they're always yapping about, this country. Someday he was going to get it too.

But for now, slouched in the passenger seat of a van that would do the scrapyard proud, parked in a trash-littered empty lot across the street from a goddamn Speedway station, sitting next to a knuckle dragger sucking a wad of tobacco and firing black globs of it out the window—back in the mean and drab here and now of his ordinary life—that someday was looking as far off as the dark side of the moon. Out of reach almost. So partly to see if he could jack himself up a little, partly to fill a silence broken only by the periodic bursts of spittle, but mostly just to kill time, Hector said, "So when this mooch suppose to show?"

"Seven."

"Tha's another quarter hour yet."

"So? You got someplace to be?"

"Just remarkin' the time, man."

"The time I got. You ride with me, you go by my clock."

Touchy gringo, this one. No wonder Mr. B wanted to keep him scoped. "This dude named Marvin?" he asked incuriously.

"Marvin? Fuck you get that?"

"Sign over there say, 'Starvin' Marvin.' "

"Where you been, dick brain? All them Speedways got that sign. It's a, y'know, slogan."

Hector shrugged. "Me, I use the Shell."

"Jesus fuck," Junior muttered disgustedly. Then a thought seemed to come to him. "Maybe I oughta be sayin' it 'Hay-soose fuck,' way you border jumpers do," he said, chuckling at his excellent wit.

"Hey, you a real comedian, man. You oughta try out for the TV."

"How that sign should read," Junior went on, disregarding the zinger, "is 'Starvin' Abdullah.' Somethin' like that."

"Yeah? Why's that?"

" 'Cuz he's a raghead, this punk we lookin' to crowd."

"Raghead?"

"Yeah. Y'know, sand nigger, camel commando, A-rab."

"No shit. Never knew them people was into sportin'."

"This one ain't no sport. Way I hear it, pussy's his blindside."

"Whose ain't it?" said Hector tolerantly.

"Well, sure," Junior conceded, "every man need a knob polishin' now and then. But your ragheads, they ain't normal about it."

"How you figure normal?" Hector asked innocently, yanking his chain a little. Something to do, tick off the time.

"What I just said, that's normal. Porkin' anything in sight, anytime, anyplace—that ain't. Ragheads, they fuck a rock pile, they thought there was a snake in it. Which is why they won't let 'em into your zoos."

"Zoos? Where you get that?"

"Tellin' you how it is."

"You sayin' a A-rab can't get into a zoo?"

"That's right. Least not your American ones. You let 'em in, they put the brown eye to all the animals. Next thing y'know, y'got a zoo fulla red-ass monkeys."

Hector rolled his eyes wondrously, fresh out of contributions to this squirrely conversation. Fortunately none were needed, for at just that moment, a lank, bony, brown-faced man came marching down the street, occasionally tossing a furtive glance over a scrawny shoulder. "That's our boy," Junior said, and at his direction, they waited until the Arab was behind the cash register inside and all the pumps were clear. While they waited, Hector, remembering his charge, inquired, "You ain't, uh, packin' no ordnance, this gig?" saying it real casual-like, more an off-the-cuff comment than a question.

Didn't fly. Junior turned and looked at him narrowly. "Why you ask?"

"No reason special. Just figure this one for a walkover. Baby food."

"Will be. But I'm still wearing a throw-down piece on my hip, double deuce. Insurance. That meet with your OK?"

"Whatever you want, man. You the boss."

"Right now all's I want," Junior said, climbing out of the car, squaring his shoulders, and drenching a luckless palmetto bug at his feet with a juicy spray, "is to get busy."

This was the part, coming up here, Junior always liked best. He'd been feeling out of sorts lately; why, he couldn't say. Fucking climate maybe. Like living inside a steam bath. Been down here a year now, and he still wasn't used to it. Missed the seasons. Missed Detroit. He got on with the Miami Jew boy through some Brotherhood connections (helped out, being a ranking member, SPSM chapter), and even if it wasn't steady, he wasn't bagging groceries either. Was a living.

So Junior was determined to enjoy himself tonight, even if he did have the little greaser looking over his shoulder, watching his moves. Kikeowitz for sure sent him up to play snitch; that much was plain as a pile of pig shit on a sofa. What a world it was getting to be—him working for a Hebe, spic for a partner. OK, they wanted moves, he'd show them moves. Nothing like laying on some hurts to bring a man around.

"Hey, Abdullah" was how he began, leaning into the register, a corner of his thin seam of mouth tucked back in a threat of a smile. "How they hangin'?"

A-rab looked startled. "Ahmed my name."

"That a fact. Well, that's a good name too, Ahmed. Mine's Mecca. An' my friend over there..." He wagged a thumb at Hector, who stood sentinel at the door, watching the pumps. "He's Chico."

A-rab tried out a squirmy grin, like he was in on the joke. "I help you with something?"

"Unh-uh," Junior said, glaring fixedly at him, thinking how pus ugly your sand spooks had to be, all of 'em, with their beak snouts and undershot chins and big sheepdog eyes. This one probably had to pay for any boinking he ever got. Gonna find out tonight if it was worth it.

"What I do for you then?"

"You don't gotta do nothin'. Other way around. Me 'n' Chico there, we come by to help *you*."

"Me?"

"That's right. Sorta like the mountain comin' to Ahmed," Junior said with a snigger. His day for the knee slappers.

"How you help me?"

"By joggin' your memory little." Junior removed a small notebook from his shirt pocket, flipped some pages, laid a finger on one of them. "See, it says right here you got a heavy marker out with a gentleman from down in Miami. Nice fella. Jewish."

"Mr. Berkowitz."

"There ya go. Your memory's improvin' already."

"Mr. Berkowitz send you?"

A-rab's eyes went swampy with dread. Finally getting the news. 'Bout time. Not quick, this raghead. "He asked would we look in on you," Junior said. "See what your thoughts was. On that marker, I mean. You remember it now, that marker?"

"Yes, yes, yes," Ahmed sputtered, hysteric edge to what was left of the grin. "I don't forget. I call him up on phone last week only. This one right here." As if in evidence, he pointed to a telephone tacked to a wall by the cash register.

"Yeah? What'd he say?"

"He say, 'Ahmed, is OK. Everything fine now. We work out new pay times, and you start in—' "

"Said that, did he?" Junior broke in on him.

The head bobbed vigorously. "That what he say. You call him, he tell you."

"Funny, don't recollect him sayin' nothin' like that to me. Chico? You?"

"Not to me," Hector said, adding quickly, "Maybe you oughta give him a jingle. Can't hurt."

Junior pulled at his prow of a jaw. Like he was giving the idea some serious thought. Buying into this dribble shit.

"You use my phone here," Ahmed insisted.

"I dunno. Be a charge call."

"Is OK. You don't worry."

"Well, you say so." Junior came around the counter and picked up the receiver, hesitated. "You sure now?" he asked, stringing it out a little, having some fun with it.

"You call him. He tell you what I tell you true."

In a looping backhand Junior swung the receiver into the brown face, simultaneously balling the other hand into a fist and driving it squarely into the soft midsection, buttering the knees. Down goes Ahmed, face-first. Over by the door the greaser's jaw drops and he takes a step toward the counter. Junior motions him back, growling, "Street, street. Cover the street." Then he squats down, rolls the fallen figure over, straddles it. Ahmed's still conscious, more or less, spittin' blood, makin' some gurgly noises, no words in 'em. Don't need none. The eyes, eloquent with pure terror, say it all. Junior, he says, "You been eatin' Berkowitz's lunch, camel-fucker, an' that ain't real smart, seein' how you A-rabs and Jews never could get along. Guess what it takes is a good ol' Aryan boy, keep the peace."

He grips the limp right arm, expertly crimps it at a tortuous angle human limbs were never intended to assume. Gives it a wrench. Hears the gratifying pop of bone fracturing, followed closely by an astonished piercing howl, more squeal than scream, like the vic can't believe what's happening to him, even when it's happening. Junior knew the difference. Heard 'em both before, many a time. He swivels around, does essentially the same thing to a leg. Left one this time, in the interest of symmetry.

Junior comes to his feet. Stands over him, waiting for the howl to dwindle to a whimper, like it always does. Takes awhile, this sissy. When finally he's sure he'll be heard, Junior says, "See what happen when you stain your sheet? Can get worse. Stiffer can get to be a stiff real quick. You follow what I'm tellin' you, Ahmed?"

Gets a groan for answer. 'Bout what he expects. Glaze of shock bleaching some of the shit-brown out of the face. Snap a couple more bones and you maybe get a regular white guy.

"Forty-eight hours," Junior tells him. "That's what your Miami shy givin' you, make good on that marker. Forty-eight. Or we hafta pay you another visit."

As a kind of inventive punctuation to this intelligence, Junior ejects the last of his tobacco sauce, winging it with unerring accuracy and in perfect arc onto Ahmed's brow where, like an inkblot, it slowly seeps into his eyes and the roots of his hair.

Driving away, Junior chortled, "That's one raghead ain't gonna be enterin' no ass-kickin' contests for a while."

Hector said nothing.

So Junior shot him a chilly sideways glance and said, "You got a problem, what went on back there?"

Hector put up a defensive palm. "Got no problems, man."

"That ain't how you do it in Miami?"

"Sometimes. When you got to. Me, what I like to do is make nice first. Have a little conversation. Friendly chat. Sometimes talk do it too."

"Talk," Junior snorted. "Talk gets you a handful of smoke. Or a spike in the back."

"You think he woofin' you, this Ahmed?"

"Woofin' how?"

"That call to Mr. B."

"Fuckin' A. They all try 'n' use that dodge come hurt time."

"Suppose he did though? Make that call?"

Junior shrugged. "If he did, then the Yid would get his loot express mail is all. After tonight Ahmed there, he gonna come up with it. Sell the family tent, he got to. An' that's a Junior Biggs guaranfuckintee."

Hector started to say something, thought better of it. Letting it go, he asked instead, "Who's next?"

Steering with one hand, Junior consulted his notebook again. "Dude name a' 'Cody.' 'Leon Cody.' "

"Do him tonight?"

Junior deliberated for a moment. He was still stoked, from the tune-up back there, but he also wanted to stretch out this assignment a little, sweeten the expense sheet. He made his decision. "Nah, says here he's clear down in Palm Beach Gardens someplace. Catch him tomorrow, next day."

"Your call, man."

"That's my call. Pack it in. One a night's plenty."

"So what now?"

"Whaddya mean, what now?"

"Mean, what's up now? For, y'know, little R & R."

"You, I dunno. Me, I'm headin' up to Avenue D. Smoke a bone, get loose, get laid maybe."

"Wha's that?"

"What?"

"That avenue you said."

"D, fuck nuts. Avenue D. Fort Pierce. Where the action is, this vicinity."

"How 'bout I ride along?" Hector said, his interest escalating. Visions of blond gash, like Mr. B's secretary, danced behind his eyes.

"That one's your call."

"I'll ride along."

Junior swung the van north on Highway One, and they drove that way.

FOUR

AMONG THE MANY THRIVING COMMERCIAL enterprises the northbound pair passed en route to their rendezvous with illicit pleasures was a place called Gentleman Jim's, one of the community of Stuart's finer dining establishments. Inside, seated by design at the head of a long rectangular table (though anywhere he chose to sit always had a way of becoming a table's head), specially prepared for a party of ten and strategically located near the sumptuous buffet board, Lon (known familiarly to an intimate circle of family and friends as "Big Lonnie") Swett presided grandly over his own birthday festivities. He was, at that moment, regaling the assembled company with the account of how he had amassed his fortune, a tale told so many times it had by now the ring of a theatrical monologue or pulpit sermon, conscientiously rehearsed and exuberantly delivered.

"So there I am," he was saying, establishing the scene, building dramatic tension, "streets a' Chicago, nineteen years old, married, wife with a bun in the oven, fresh outta the service, no skills, no school diploma. Tryin' to rub two nickels together, I come up one short."

Big Lonnie's voice had a wheezy, preemphysemic quality to it, and there was a breath-sucking pause here, a series of shallow pants taken in through the mouth like a snared fish gasping for air. To his immediate right, the current Mrs. Swett, number five in the succession, hung on doggedly to a tight, anticipatory, yawn-smothering smile. The woman on his left seized this opportunity to erupt in a shrill laugh, as though he'd reached the punch line of a particularly hilarious joke. "Joy" was her name, one half of the Kroll couple, friends and sometime associates of that now risen and ripened bun, son Howard, who anchored the other end of the table and who attended, somewhat glassy eyed, to his father's recital. Like everyone else present this evening, the Krolls not excepted, he had heard the story before, many times, and in the secrecy of his skull, he silently shaped the predictable words of its next installment, which resumed once the appreciative peal of mirth expired.

"So I gotta do some scramblin', right? Take the first job I can land—only one—which is haulin' trash for an outfit works the suburbs. Goddamn garbageman is what I am. Future not lookin' so hot for your Lonnie Swett, right?" He quickly supplied an answer to the purely rhetorical question. "Wrong! See, them rich suburb people throw out stuff anybody else, your average grunt, try 'n' sell secondhand. So what I done, once I get a peek at these goods, is start squirrelin' 'em away. Old tire here, set a' pots and pans there—I cart 'em on home and peddle 'em to the neighbors. Pocket coin, but the profit margin's nifty. Hard to beat hunnert percent, am I right?"

Because Lonnie had lately fallen into the habit of occasionally straying from his chronicle, Troy Kroll made the colossal blunder of interpreting this last remark as a genuine question. "Can't top that," he allowed, adding with a buttery smirk, "'Course, we come mighty close sometimes, the construction business."

Big mistake. Lonnie, unaccustomed to interruption or, worse, any attempted departure from the squarely centered universe he inhabited, scowled into his martini glass. The bristly nostrils of his pickle nose twitched slightly, as if from the unexpected intake of some noxious odor. The liverish lips tightened. He snuffed out his cigarette, lit another. A hush descended over the table.

The lickspittle Krolls, who up to now had been absorbing the drone with rapt, gee-boss-you're-great expressions etched on their sun-leathered Florida faces, squirmed uneasily. Billie Swett watched them with about an equal mix of pity and contempt. The Krolls were here tonight in honor of their friend's father's passage into certifiable old age but also and not incidentally in pursuit of their own transparent agenda.

Troy was a big-shouldered man with a thick swag of soot-colored hair and the sort of square-cut features some might call ruggedly handsome were it not for a mouthful of jack-o'-lantern fangs for teeth. He wore a silk sport shirt patterned with tropical birds suspended in altitudes of flight against a milky-blue sky; looked to Billie like it came off a Walmart rack. Joy was outfitted more formally, if not more tastefully, in a bilious-green cocktail dress of some indeterminate shiny material (that one Billie pegged for a Blue Light Special, for sure). Her hair was styled—to put it charitably—in an altogether too youthful mop of curls as wiry and springy as a Brillo pad and tinted an improbable tangerine. Billie, herself a relatively recent refugee from the beauty business, had a keen professional eye for such details. She wondered idly whether the rhyme of their given names was the magnetizing force that had first brought and now held the Krolls together. Troy and Joy. Unbearably cute.

"So then what happened, Dad?"

This gentle prompting rose from daughter-in-law Darlene, a dishwater blonde with the pinched, nettled face of a woman who suffers from an assortment of female complaints, which she did, and the washed-out indoor pallor of a librarian, which she certainly was not. "Darlene the Baby Machine" Lonnie liked to call her, an only half-joking reference to the four young Swetts, males all, stepladdered in ages from seventeen to eleven and spotted around the table. The eldest (and in truth the only one of the decidedly unlovable quartet Billie could readily identify)—a sullen, lumpish youth with greased hair and a spray of pimples—had been calculatedly named after his grandfather and dubbed, inevitably, "Little Lonnie." Also terribly cute.

"What happens is," Big Lonnie resumed, "I pretty quick scrapes the gelt together to buy my own truck, hire some grunts, go into business for myself. 'Lonnie's Trash Removal: No-Swett Service' I put on the truck. Spelled it like my name, for a little joke," he explained with a dry bark of a laugh.

His audience dutifully chuckled, the Krolls perhaps a bit louder than the rest.

"'We haul any and everything' was my motto. We did too. All the heavy stuff your regular garbage goober won't touch. Stoves, sofas, TVs don't work no more, general junk—you name it, we hauled it, free of charge. Only not to the dump. 'Stead I'm takin' it into the city, where I open up my first discount store, hustle all the fat cats' throwaways. This was down on the South Side, where your jigaboos just startin' to move in, them days."

He paused long enough to drag in some sustaining breaths, and Joy recklessly ventured a question: "Wasn't that awfully dangerous for you?" Troy shot her an alarmed glance. The others studied their drinks.

Amazingly it proved to be a shrewd stratagem. For second only to an ostentatious show of wealth was the pleasure Lonnie took in displaying the valorous side of his nature. "Sure, there gonna be some risks involved, that kinda customer," he said bravely, a corner of his mouth tucked back in swashbuckler grin. "More times'n a few, you'd get a coon come stormin' through the door not happy with his merchandise, want his money back."

"Whatever did you do?" Joy asked breathlessly.

"Point 'em to a sign I kept on the wall behind the register. 'See that sign?' I sez to 'em," he said, toughly now, catching the spirit of the dramatized encounter. "'All sales final. That goes for you too,'" he growled, jabbing a sausagey finger at a phantom black.

"Did any of them ever get, well..." said Joy, with a little quake in her voice.

"Yeah, I had some blades flashed on me," Lonnie said, completing the unutterable thought for her. "That was the chance you took, doin' business that part a' town. You gonna make a buck, you gotta be willin' to take some risks."

"You're lucky you weren't killed."

Lonnie shrugged.

"What a fascinating story!" Joy gushed.

Billie's eyes spun in their sockets, and the fascinating story wore on. Two drinks and a superabundance of numbing, self-aggrandizing, often wandering detail later, it was at last mounting to a merciful climax. "Yeah, by the time I sold out, I had me a fleet a' trucks coverin' the burbs and a chain a' forty stores in the city."

"*Forty* stores!" Joy squealed worshipfully. "Imagine that!"

"'Swett Shops,' I called 'em. Put my brand on everything I owned."

"What a marvelous success story!"

"Tell ya what I learned," Lonnie told them all, assuming now the mentor role and concluding, as he always did, with the linchpin of the Lon Swett success formula. "What I learned, all them years, is you wanna make it in business, you gotta have stroke."

"Stroke?" Joy echoed, doggedly playing at straight woman.

Lonnie lifted a hand and rubbed thumb and forefinger together in a gesture of crafty greed. "Juice, palm oil," he explained, and with a sweeping proprietary glance around the table, barest hint of a threat in it, he declared, "Yeah, only thing money can't buy is poverty."

Troy shook his head in vigorous assent. "Man, that's the truth. Why, I found that out just last week, when I had to make that pitch to the zoning board."

Lonnie looked blank.

"On that project I was telling you about," Troy said expectantly.

Lonnie said nothing; his expression remained unchanged.

From the other end of the table rose a timid, deferential voice. "That apartment complex we're—Troy's—trying to get off the ground. Remember, Dad?" Howard to the rescue.

"Oh. Yeah. That one."

Troy started over. But early on in his anecdote, custom designed to underscore the wisdom of the Swett business philosophy, Lonnie grew fidgety, and turning to his wife, he broke in on the narrative with, "I'm gettin' hungry. How 'bout you, honey?"

"Whenever you're ready, hon," said the compliant spouse.

"Let's order up."

Everyone (even the crestfallen Troy, his story rudely aborted) agreed, and at the snap of a finger, a waitress materialized. Orders were placed, buffet plates heaped, and soon the steaming entrées arrived.

Big Lonnie was a focused eater, assaulting his food with the single-minded intensity of a famine victim. His fixity of purpose in no way slowed his prattling speech, for even as he forked in his dinner, he contrived somehow, around mouthfuls of it, to keep in motion a rambling monologue centered on the minutiae of his day—whom he saw, what he said, where he went, what he ate for breakfast, what for lunch, how his investments were prospering, his assorted aches and pains—a string of non sequiturs with no discernible connections or transitions. Like a child, whatever bubbled up into his consciousness he gave instant voice to.

Near the end of the feast, Joy and Darlene exchanged conspiratorial glances, excused themselves, and disappeared. Billie, schooled by now at feigning entrancement with her husband's nonstop babble while conducting her own busy inner life, followed them with her eyes, watched them huddling with the hostess. She had a pretty good idea what was coming next: a birthday-boy salute from which she had been deliberately excluded. Cunning bit of one-upmanship. Didn't matter. She still held all the aces, sat on top of a world-class persuader.

Sure enough, no sooner had the giggly pair returned to their seats than a troop of beaming waitresses appeared, one bearing an ice bucket out of which two champagne bottles projected like missiles, another a gigantic pink-frosted cake adorned with three flickering candles. Immediately the assembled company burst into a warbly, seriously off-key rendition of the traditional birthday ditty, including the second verse's "How *old* are you?" refrain, which seemed, to Billie's ear, delivered less as query than stark declaration of the honoree's antiquity. A polite ripple of applause rose from onlookers at adjacent tables. Bottles were uncorked, glasses filled. The cake was set before Lonnie, who frowned at it puzzledly. "Look like you come up sixty-two short in the candle department," he muttered.

"Those three stand for past, present, and future," explained Troy, the ebullient, entirely self-appointed master of ceremonies. He lifted his glass in a toast. "Here's to that future!"

Glasses were clinked all around.

"Blow them out," Joy urged. "But first you got to make a wish."

"Whaddya gonna wish for when you already got it all?" Lonnie snorted. But in grudging deference to the spirit of the celebration, he extinguished the three candles with an anemic, labored wheeze.

"I'm betting here's one thing you don't have," said a hugely grinning Troy, producing a square box gift-wrapped and ribboned, and handing it to Lonnie.

"Now what'd this be?"

"Open 'er up and see."

Lonnie ripped away the paper, lifted the lid of the box, stared at its contents. "Cigars," he said flatly.

"Not just any cigars," Troy put in quickly. "Those are *Cuban*."

"Cuban," Lonnie repeated, sounding slightly more impressed. "How'd you come by 'em?"

"Oh, little of that stroke you were talking about before."

Lonnie rewarded him with a thin, if somewhat guarded, smile. "Yeah, well, thanks."

"Enjoy," said Troy with a magnanimous toss of a hand.

More presents were carried to the head of the table, gag gifts most of them (for what indeed do you give the man who has it all?), accepted with impassive grunts and only the scantiest of acknowledgments. Then came the ceremonial carving and consuming of the cake, Joy wielding the knife and passing the plates, while Lonnie, who waited for no one, shoveled a jumbo-size wedge into the widening hole in his age-and-indulgence-thickened face.

Billie nibbled at hers indifferently, taking in all these ritual proceedings with a suspicion of a smile playing over crimson-lacquered lips. Her own gift, delivered earlier, was a simple pair of L.L.Bean Trailblazer hiking shorts (like he was going to hike any farther than the fridge), elastic banded to accommodate the swell of Swett belly. Like so many Florida fossils, Lonnie lived in short pants, was in fact wearing them now, and there were times when Billie wondered whether this favored and decidedly unflattering choice of outfit weren't merely the first symptom of senility's advance, childhood's resurfacing. Of course the Trailblazers represented only half of her contribution. The second half was coming up shortly and guaranteed to put a smile on the birthday boy's face (her own smile turned inward now at the unintended pun).

The check, like the gifts, was presented to Lonnie routinely and as a matter of course, a conclusion foregone. They knew him at Gentleman Jim's. He extracted a fat wad of bills from a pocket, peeled off an appropriate number of Ben Franklins, and handed one to the hovering waitress, saying, "This honeybee's for you, sweetheart. Top-drawer service."

"Oh, thank you so much, Mr. Swett," she burbled ecstatically.

The display of generosity elicited an idolatrous murmur around the table, but Lonnie wasn't listening anymore. He hauled himself up out of his chair, signaling the party's end. Farewells out in the lot took the form of a protracted round of hugging, back-thumping, hand-pumping, jocular well-wishing. Troy, last in line to clutch Lonnie's hand, suggested casually, as though the idea had just come to him, "Y'know, Lon, we got to get together for lunch one of these days."

"Yeah, we'll do that," Lonnie said vaguely.

"Maybe talk some more about that project."

"Gimme a call sometime," said Lonnie, forcibly recovering his hand. He spun on his heels and stalked away, moving with the stiff, back-slanting gait of a man balanced precariously on stilts (which his exposed legs—spindly, bony—resembled) or, in his case, as if in counterweight to a truly enormous eclipse of loose flesh whose ominous gravitational sag seemed to threaten at any moment a plunge through the seams of his shorts in a chromatic, visceral splash at his feet.

Slumped on a cushy sofa in the sprawling living room of his mansion, bloated, burping, periodically spicing the air with the rankest of flatus, Big Lonnie groaned to his wife, "Think maybe I ate too much tonight, honey."

Billie sat directly opposite him, languidly puffing a Capri, bracing herself with brandy. "Well, it was a special occasion," she said tolerantly.

"Gut don't know that," he said, thumping it.

"Would you like me to get you some Maalox?"

"Nah, I drop one more thing down the ol' chute, and the whole business'll likely blow."

Billie tactfully refrained from any reference to the booming backdoor eruptions ("My house, I fart where I please" was his standard justification for a particularly volcanic blast). He reached for one of the cigars from the box on a coffee table heaped with gifts, stuck it in his mouth, and set it afire. "Ain't half bad," he allowed around a gust of smoke.

"Very thoughtful of Troy," she said carefully.

"You think so?"

"Don't you?"

"You wanna know what I think?"

"What's that, honey?"

"Think that sleazeball slipperier'n a greased hog. Lookin' to stroke me with some fancy cigars."

"Oh, I don't know. They seem like a nice couple, the Krolls." It was Billie's verbal strategy never to utter a word critical of either the Swett family or any of its acquaintances. She left that to Lonnie, and he seldom disappointed her.

"Nice like a couple scorpions nice. Both of 'em. They figurin' to get next to me through Howie and Darlene, who ain't either one got the brains God give a mule. Tell ya this much," he said vehemently, rolling the turd of a cigar from one corner of his mouth to the other, "young Mr. Kroll there—he's in for the surprise of his life."

"You're not interested in his apartment project then?"

"Project!" he sneered. "Punk like that wouldn't know a moneymakin' project if it snuck right up and pronged him in the ass."

Nobody's fool, Lonnie. A boor, yes; appetite-driven lout, no argument; but ever the shrewd player when it came to money.

"Well, I'm sure you know best, hon," Billie said sweetly.

"'Cept when it comes to packin' in the groceries," he said with yet another groan. "Never could seem to learn in that department."

Billie sensed it was time. She had an instinct for such matters. She took a last fortifying sip of brandy, stubbed out the cigarette, came to her feet, and glided over to him. "Here, let me see if I can help."

Lonnie laid the smoldering rope in an ashtray and, at her direction, removed his shirt and stretched himself out flat (or flat as the parabolic arc of tummy allowed for) across the sofa, face buried in a cushion. Gently, expertly, she massaged his manifold distresses away, starting at the neck and working slowly, tantalizingly slow, down the lardy back, like a master pastry chef artfully kneading dough, now and then brushing her fingertips, as if by accident, over the gorge between his flaccid mounds of buttocks. Some pleasured purring sounds escaped his slackening lips. Signal to move on.

"Now the other side," she said in a voice at once silky and husky, a blend perfected by years of practice.

Obediently and without a word, he rolled onto his back. Billie knelt alongside the sofa and moved her palms in feathery, circular motions over his blubbery chest, where they paused long enough to flick at the nipples before proceeding upward over the globe of belly then down, down, through layers of marbled meat, to their ultimate destination. She undid his belt buckle, unzippered his fly. Fished the slithery little eel from its nest of wiry hair, pumped some life into it, and slid it through the brandy-moistened gates of paradise.

"That's the ticket," Lonnie gasped. "That's it right there."

After a few preliminary passes, she gradually picked up the tempo. What had begun as soft purring rapidly amplified into a string of staccato, raptured yips, and as it did, Billie was thinking, with some regret, that as accomplished as she was at imparting pleasure, which was, after all, nothing more than the flip side of easing pain, she could certainly have been a nurse.

And Big Lonnie, in the instant before giving way to an orgasmic moan, was for his part of it thinking how after the five times he'd stepped up to the marital plate (not to mention an incalculable number of side trips), he finally had hit a homer and how this one was a keeper, for sure.

FIVE

IN THE DARKNESS AND SOMBER STILLNESS THAT had fallen over his dead sister's apartment, a pajama-clad Jim Merriman sat on the scruffy living-room couch that served as his makeshift bed, smoking steadily, now and then absently pulling from a can of beer, last one in the twelve-pack he and Leon had sailed through after returning from the hospital. Nothing more they could do there, or so a bustling nurse, seemingly energized by the spectacle of death, had assured them. "Stop by first thing in the morning," she'd advised, for what she'd called "arrangements." First thing. Sure. Easy for her.

The luminous dial on his watch read three bells; morning, by her construction, only a scant few hours off. And yet, beer-fogged, bone-weary, drained of unsettling and alien emotions, the balm of sleep perversely eluded him. He knew why. The confounding riddle of deathbed promises, their slippery nature—that was why. How strictly was their language to be interpreted? The "watching out" he'd agreed to—what exactly did that cover? Were such oaths in fact binding? If so, for how long? A week? Year? Lifetime? Hadn't he listened with a proper show of sympathy while, for the past two hours, Leon poured out his grief, capriciously pendulating between sunny, fanciful memories of his mother and a powerless sense of loss, swiping tears from his eyes, voice gradually slurring 'til finally, exhausted of sorrow, he'd staggered off to bed? Hadn't he done that? Had to count for something, didn't it?

Fuck if he knew anymore. Only thing he knew for sure was that however you labeled it, whatever diagnosis you assigned it, however vainly you undertook to treat it, the mysterious affliction commonly called "conscience" had to be the most crippling, most paralyzing of them all. No contest.

An affliction considerably more palpable and urgent issued from his bladder. He came to his feet, made his way by cautious feel to the john, blissfully relieved himself. Blissful but for the ceiling bulb that flooded the tiny room with harsh yellow light and stung his eyes. Its fixture, he noticed, supplied a luminous tomb for a cluster of expired flies. Surrounded everywhere by death. He studied the lineaments of his face in the mirror for portents of it in himself. Saw nothing too alarming except eyes a little smeary, but that could be written off to sleeplessness and drink; couple of vertical lines stitched into the brow above a noble Anglo-Saxon nose; some threads of gray streaking the thick black hair like trails of smoke. But otherwise everything looked pretty much intact: the lean, bladed features of the record-setting (in his small corner of the world) middle-distance runner (too short on persistence for the longer hauls, too slow for sprints) he had once upon a time been. Nevertheless the reflection gave him back that disquieting question all mirrors ask: *Who am I?*

Who indeed? Back on the couch, he pondered the question. Arrived at no firm conclusions. He had come down here on this errand of obligation laden with the burden of half a lifetime's (or was it two-thirds now?) personal baggage but never had learned to unpack his heart. And petrified or not, the heart, he was discovering, had its own logic and its own memories, not always consistent with the truth perhaps but no less wistful, no less nagging.

The glowing tip of another cigarette pierced a hole in the night. His thoughts went spiraling through a maelstrom of memory pictures, eventually blurring, tailspinning into the deepening dark of a merciful sleep.

While Jim Merriman slept, his nephew, in an adjacent room, tossed and thrashed about the bed, his slumber riddled by bizarre, baleful dreams, not all of them of his mother, whose remains, rapidly chilling, reclined in a vault in the hospital morgue. Whether or not she dreamed, no one could say.

Some ninety miles to the south, in an elegantly appointed apartment one floor up from his offices (where phones still jangled, computers hummed, and sedulous clerks still kept meticulous tallies, for the churning of money was a round-the-clock affair and knew no sleep), Solomon Berkowitz, another chronic insomniac, lay awake in bed, deliberating on the knotty problem of how best to cope with one of his more troublesome employees, considering the shrinking alternatives, weighing his options. Coming to terms with the issue. Last thing you needed in business was trouble.

Approximately one hundred and fifty miles to the north, two of those employees were, at that moment, in the colorful words of Junior Biggs, "wettin' the ol' whacker" with a pair of Avenue D's finer pavement princesses in a Fort Pierce no-tell (it was Junior's inspired idea to share a room, hit the Jew boy for the expense of two, and split the difference) of such monumental squalor it sickened even Hector, who had seen some pretty scummy cribs in his time but never anything like this. Nor was he much taken with their choice of companions, squat fleshy black girls, both of them (also was it Junior's contention that "y'ain't a man 'til y'split dark oak"), whose services were engaged only after considerable squawky haggling over price—a long way from the tall, cool, sleek, foxy, blond squish Hector hankered after and so richly deserved (like that one he'd scoped in Mr. B's office—when was it? only this morning?; seemed a thousand years ago), but he thumped away at his all the same, operating on the eminently reasonable proposition that you never say no to a slice of boom-boom: black, brown, yellow, white (you was lucky), green—you name it. And not long after he got the job done and was sinking into a stoned sleep, Junior's slushy guttural voice hailed him from the other bed: "Hey, cholo, wake the fuck up. Party's just gettin' started. Time for a little switch meat." *Gonna be a long night* was Hector's joyless thought.

For Billie Swett, only a few miles south, it also was proving to be a long, sleepless night. Just why, she couldn't say, for apart from the birthday bash, it wasn't much different from any other night of her married life. Earlier she had slipped quietly out of bed, taking exquisite pains not to wake the Big Lumpie, whose appetite-sated sleep was always fitful and whose honking snores trailed her into the living room, where now she sat curled up in a massive chair and enveloped in darkness, gazing through a wall of glass past a huge rectangular pool and across an expanse of manicured lawn at the St. Lucie River, the back boundary to the concrete-walled and iron-gated mansion, thinking how she'd traveled a goodly distance from Bismark, North Dakota, but wondering at what cost. Wasn't like she was dissatisfied with her lot, exactly, or disliked her husband. How you going to dislike a magician who waves the money wand, and good things appear, problems vanish? Was just another job, really, being a rich man's wife, an occupation a whole lot easier (not to mention more rewarding) than painting nails and trimming cuticles in a corner of a shop that went under the not-so-subtle name "Get Nailed." Which was where Lonnie had found her and exactly what he'd done, in every sense of that stark, suggestive command. And yet, for all his magic, there was still something absent in her life, something missing. She, who had everything now, felt a vague longing for something, well, spiritual, you might call it. Like that centering work she'd gotten into lately (much to Lonnie's disgust), helping others pass over gently and serenely, the way she'd done with her girlfriend's withered mother, who only yesterday had joined that numberless legion of souls floating somewhere out there in an immensity of darkness.

In another, considerably less affluent part of the community of Stuart, Troy Kroll was at that late hour pacing the floor of a room he chose to call an office in his modest and heavily mortgaged bungalow, gulping a beer and fretfully turning over in his head the disturbing and entirely unsatisfying events of the evening. Immediately on returning home, he'd thrown a duty fuck into his wife, who'd gotten all sexy squirmy from the bubbly and who now slept soundly on the other side of the wall, secure in the perfect faith that she'd charmed the guest of honor, the party was a smashing success, and the big bucks were dead ahead. Troy wished he could share her confidence, but he didn't. Didn't like the way the Big Swettball dodged the topic every time he'd tried to swing the talk around to the project, or the way those froggy eyes slid scornfully over him when he'd dropped the lunch hint. Fucking wimp Howie, spooked out of his skull in the presence of the old man, was no help. Troy had a suspicion it was the uppity new wife getting in the Swett ear, souring him on the venture. Fucking nail polisher. What he ought to do is bang the bitch, bring her over to his way of thinking. Make an ally. It was a thought. Another thought was simply to wait it out (like she was for sure doing), wait for the shit sack to eat and drink and smoke and boff himself to death and the bulk of the loot to pass to a peanut-brained son; this happy ending had to be just around the corner. By rights anyway. If Troy had the time and resources, that's exactly what he'd do—hang tight, stay the course. Sadly he had neither. Which meant something was going to have to give, and on the quickstep.

In the master bedroom of a somewhat larger home (though by no means lavish, for the livelihood of its occupants depended entirely on the largess of a temperamental patron) located in a slightly more upscale Stuart neighborhood, Howard Swett lay next to his wife, both of them sleeping peacefully. If they dreamed at all, it was doubtless of magnificent pots heaped with gold at the end of a distant rainbow.

Not far away the punished sedated body of a swarthy gentleman of Arabic descent, Ahmed Awal by name, twitched and shuddered in a glaze of shock, one arm and one leg sheathed in tubes of plaster and suspended at curious angles above the hospital bed. What he might or might not have been dreaming was anybody's guess.

No question what waking dreams pranced in gaudy imagery behind the eyes of B. Noble (an artful rendering of the more prosaic "Norbert") Bott, as just then their rattly Seville, chugging south on Interstate 95, crossed the invisible line demarcating the states of Georgia and Florida. Occasionally he was rudely yanked back into the reality of the moment by the growly throb of a sixteen-wheeler barreling past them, plunging ahead into the night. Occasionally the otherwise silent Waneta muttered something, complaints mostly: her mounting fatigue, stiffening back, numbing hands, the inequitable division of labor that saddled her with all the driving. To which Bryce murmured soft words of commiseration or encouragement or exculpation (depending on the nature of the grievance) then promptly resuscitated his inventive inner life. In his mind he cataloged all those things he loved: bulging wallet, luxury accommodations, gourmet foods, fine wines, edifying texts (a relentless self-improver, wherever his travels took him, he carried a Bible, *Bartlett's Familiar Quotations*, and a collection of well-thumbed vocabulary builders), and when he was young, the pleasures of the flesh. But what he loved most dearly, and with a passion approaching religious zealotry, was the swindle, the game. And now all those elusive treasures, bundled in a single package, were about to be gifted to him and miraculously, by the most unlikely and happiest of chances. A quote, long ago filed in a vault of memory, its source long forgotten, returned to him now: "Chance makes a plaything of a man's life." How true, how true.

PART TWO

SIX

ON THE AFTERNOON OF AUGUST 10, NARROWLY inside the forty-eight hours required by law for the disposition of unembalmed corpses, Jim and Leon strolled along the Singer Island beach, trying without much success to appear inconspicuous in their street clothes as they scattered the ashes of Elizabeth Merriman Cody (who, tightfisted and unsentimental in death as in life, had insisted on a frugal cremation) in surreptitiously strewn handfuls and in blatant violation of a local ordinance. More accurately, they were aerating them, for a sultry breeze lifted off the shore and wafted them out to sea on a ghostly cushion of air. Jim carried the container, a flimsy paperboard carton grudgingly provided by the funeral home as part of the budget package, remarkably small. It was hard for him to believe it held all that remained of a once big-boned, heavy-hipped, thick-waisted woman, plagued by poundage all her life, or right on up to its final weeks, 'til death supplied the ultimate miracle diet. When the last handful was flung, he said, "Well, that does it, kid."

A brutal sun hung in a sky scorched white. Leon made a visor of a hand and stood for a moment, gazing out at the blinding dazzle of ocean, its horizon lost in a shimmery heat haze. Finally, sniffling a little, he said, "She's gone, Uncle Jim. Now Mom's really gone."

Jim laid a comradely arm over his nephew's scrawny shoulders. "Better not to think about it. C'mon. I'll buy you a beer."

The two survivors, their duty done, threaded through a recumbent mass of sun worshipers strung like sizzled slabs of meat across the blistering sand. On the street that fronted a cluster of connected shops known as the Ocean Mall, Jim chucked the empty container into a trash can, and they elbowed their way through a lazily sauntering, straw-sucking, chili-dog-devouring, Slurpee-slurping crowd clad either in the skimpiest of swimwear (exposing a range of shapes, from obscene corpulence at one extreme to lush curves and chiseled muscularity at the other) or shorts and T-shirts bearing all manner of messages: innocuous geographic place names, determinedly cute aphorisms, coarsely vulgar proclamations, urgent calls to action ("Save the manatees!"—Jim wondering silently what the fuck manatees were). Aloud he wondered irritably, "Who *are* all these assholes? Can't all be tourists this time of year."

"Just your local folks," Leon said. "This is a popular beach."

"Why the hell aren't they at work?"

"It's Sunday, Uncle Jim."

"Oh. Right. So it is. I seem to have lost track of the days."

Moments later they sank into chairs at a canopied table on the deck of a tavern that overlooked the beach, a couple of Buds in front of them. Jim, for his part of it, was thoroughly cashed. The blurry procession of deathwatch days, the nights of ruptured sleep, the enervating flurry of final arrangements, not least of which entailed resisting the aggressive efforts of a professionally melancholy funeral director to pitch them a bells-and-whistles service at triple the cost—all of it had taken its toll, and it felt good to unwind, kick back. Except of course there was still that nagging problem embodied in the person of the youth seated opposite him, this stranger only tenuously linked by a diluted stream of blood, pale of complexion, lank, almost gaunt of frame, the bones of his face angular and sharply defined under a wild scramble of hair, the myopic eyes perpetually blinking behind glasses thick as thumbs. Twenty-one by the calendar but gawky and fidgety as an adolescent. And what do you say to an adolescent? Jim had no experience with that level of dialogue, so he lifted his bottle, touched it lightly to Leon's, and because it seemed fitting, a closure of sorts, said, "Here's to your mother."

Leon nodded, took a small obligatory swallow, set the bottle down, and stared morosely into his lap while the fingers of one hand drummed the table.

Jim glanced at him covertly, fearing the worst. Up to now there'd been no serious waterworks, and in the hope of forestalling any, he said quickly, "Life goes by, kid. For all of us. That's just how it is." In the way of condolences, it was the best he could do.

Leon, addressing his lap, said, or tried to say, "It was right, wasn't it, what we did with her, y'know, out there on...?"

A child of television, all his cerebration seemed to come in images, and he had a habit of ending a half-completed thought with a vague gesture, as though the image that generated it were dissolving in his head. The gesture in this case was a toss of the finger-drumming hand in the direction of the ocean. Jim interpreted the question as a reference to their ritual on the beach. Just to be sure, he asked, "You mean with her ashes?"

"Well, yeah, that part too. All of it. Whole thing."

"The cremation?"

"Yeah."

"It's what she wanted," Jim said. "She told you that. Remember?"

Curiously his own memory served up the unwelcome image of a long-forgotten acquaintance, a scuzzy Vegas funeral director with a fever for the dice. This prince of sleaze (name long since lost) once had confided that in the sardonic argot of his trade, a cremation stiff was known as a "shake and bake" (which sparked yet another image, his sister's corpse, popping and spitting). Last he'd heard, this addict had blown a potful of his clients' preneed loot on a roll of the cubes gone wrong and was currently doing cannery time for his indiscretion and wicked luck. Which only proved that once in a great while, some things turned out OK. And thinking that way, he said, "She wanted it done on the cheap, Leon. Leave more money for you."

"I know. Just seems there oughta be a...some...well, place, like."

"Grave, you mean? Casket, flowers, formal service, stone with her name on it? All that takes dinero, boy. Hard dollars. We brought this thing in for under a dime. If there's a way to cheat the undertaker, your mom found it."

"S'pose you're right."

"Bet your ass, right," Jim affirmed, trying to put some cheery bounce in it, elevate the somber mood.

Didn't work too well. Leon lifted his gaze, fixed it on him, and said earnestly, "Anyway, I'm sure glad you came, Uncle Jim. Don't think I could've, y'know, got through it without you."

Behind the goggle glasses, his eyelids batted like an owl's in a harsh noonday light. All that furious blinking gave the impression of a certain shiftiness, which Leon, while many things, was most surely not. Unable to meet the fluttery gaze, Jim fumbled for a cigarette, went through the lighting motions, mumbled something noncommittal.

"Was almost like the old days," Leon went on. "Like when you used to come and visit."

Which couldn't have been more than half a dozen times in all the kid's twenty-one years and only when there was some action in the vicinity. Nevertheless Jim said, "Yeah, almost like them."

"Except we didn't play any gin. Remember how you taught me that game?"

"Did I?"

"Sure did," he said, seeming to brighten some at the memory. "You used to take all my lunch money. Remember?"

Jim shrugged. "Well, everybody's got to learn how to lose."

"Maybe we can have a game sometime while you're here. I'm better at it now."

"Want to recover your losses, do you?"

"Couldn't hurt."

"It's a good thought, Leon, but I don't play cards much anymore."

Leon blinked at him quizzically. "You don't?"

"No."

"How come?"

"It's a long story."

"I got time."

"Some other time."

"So what're you doing then these days? For a...y'know...?"

"Living?"

"Yeah. Living."

Jim hesitated for a moment. Assistant in charge of the sports and games section of a bookstore was an honorable enough vocation but a long slide down from hard-rock player, pro. No matter how you cut it, he was still a clerk. And he still had some pride left, pinch of it anyway. So he said, extemporizing, "I'm what you might call a gaming consultant."

Now Leon looked baffled.

"What you do is share your expertise with the cousins," Jim explained (thinking, Yeah, like in directing them to books with such deceitful titles as *How to Beat the Casinos, The Science of Roulette, Professional's Guide to Winning Blackjack).* "For a fee."

"What's a cousin?" Leon wanted to know.

"Amateur, wannabe. World's full of them. Gambling's a growth industry; people come to you. I got more clients than I can service."

On he went, spinning a wholly fabricated yarn, authenticating it with jargon and a wealth of detail, spicing it with anecdotes wholly imagined. Like most practitioners of his former profession, Jim was an accomplished—pathological, some might say—liar. You had to be if you hoped to step up from a table winners. Went with the territory. But in the midst of his tale, it occurred to him to wonder which came first: Was it the cards that taught him to lie or a genetic predisposition to duplicity that foreordained him to the gaming life? Damned if he knew. He let the fantasy run down.

Leon regarded him doubtfully. "Sounds like you're doing, uh, pretty good for yourself."

"It's steady work," Jim said, and hearing in his words the potential for a segue into a considerably touchier topic, he added with an air of studied nonchalance, "Won't be, though, if I don't shag ass back to it soon."

A flash of alarm streaked across his nephew's pallid face. "You got to go back?"

Jim took a deep drag on his cigarette and exhaled a mighty gust of smoke, as though he hoped somehow to disappear in it. " 'Fraid so, Leon."

"Jeez, I hate to see you leave."

Wasn't hard to figure why. All his life somebody was leaving him. Father ducked out when he was still an infant; wife and a kid flew the coop after eighteen months of a disastrous and, by all reports, evil-starred union; a mother, his last anchor, vanished by death. *And now*, Jim thought ruefully, *it's your turn to skip out.* To soften the news some, he said lamely, "I can maybe hang around a couple more days…'til you get squared away."

Leon shifted his gaze out to sea, said nothing.

"Anyway, you got a job to get back to yourself, right?"

"At the garage?"

"Yeah, garage," Jim said. Or wherever it was he worked. A high-school dropout and natural-born gearhead with an unaccountable artistic flair, Leon had found a calling in the restoration of antique vehicles. Or so he often, in happier times, claimed. Now, however, he said dismally, "Things been pretty slow there lately."

"You're *not* working?"

"Sorta part-time."

"Well, least your mother left you a pretty healthy nut," Jim reminded him, determined to find the silver lining somewhere.

"Nut?"

"A stake. That bank CD you were telling me about."

"Oh. That one."

"What'd you say it's worth?"

"Twenty-five thousand."

Jim gave an appreciative whistle and, with a heartiness only partly forced, said what was inarguably true. "There you are. Twenty-five long covers a lot of downtime. Oughta keep you in style 'til you get back on your feet."

"Feet?" Leon echoed, seemingly puzzled by the figure of speech.

"Get things back in order again. Put some direction in your life." Even as he passed along this bromidic advice, Jim wasn't entirely insensitive to his own shameless hypocrisy. Some sour joke, coming as it did from the master of disorder, misdirection.

Leon squirmed in his chair. Somewhat sheepishly he mumbled, "See, thing of it is, Uncle Jim, I owe forty-five."

Slowly, as the ponderous weight of the number sank in, an attitude of stunned disbelief settled over Jim's face. "Forty-five *thousand*?" he said.

"Plus interest."

"Who to?"

"A bookie."

"You lost forty-five thou gambling?"

Leon nodded glumly.

"On what?"

"Y'know, sports, things like that." The gesturing hand swept the air, vague as ever.

Jim threw up his own hands, signaling an infinite disgust. "Fuck do you know about sports betting?"

"Remember how you showed me how to do middling? Y'know, kinda hedging your bets? Last time you were here?"

"*I* did?"

"Yeah, and I was doing good with them too. Breaking even anyway. Then I tried some of those proposition bets they got. You know how they work?"

"I know what a prop bet is, Leon. Custom-built for pigeons. Or suicide players."

"Well, they're the ones brought me down."

Jim felt a splenetic storm, at once impotent and turbulent, gathering in his chest, clotting his throat, but at what or whom, he could no longer be sure. Containing it, he asked, "How long you had these markers out?"

"You mean owed the money?"

"Yeah, Leon, that's what I mean."

"Oh, been quite a while now."

"I'm asking you how long."

"Four, five months. Maybe a little longer."

"And nobody's crowded you yet?"

"What do you mean?"

"Come to collect."

"Not yet. But I been getting some, like, unfriendly calls lately."

"From your bookie?"

"No, somebody else. Sounds real pissed off, whoever he is. Real, y'know, tough."

"That'd be the *shtarker*."

"What's a starker?"

Jim laid his head in the palm of a hand. All the anger was gone now, replaced by a dull throbbing at his temples and a bitter black bile in his stomach. "Enforcer," he explained. "Slugger, goon. You got any idea just how mean those people can get?"

"Pretty mean, I s'pose."

"Head-cracking mean. Bone-busting mean. That's how mean. They don't dick around."

"I was thinking maybe the twenty-five would help out some."

"Won't mean shit if you been in the glue that long."

"Well," Leon said timidly, casting a pleading glance at his uncle out of the corner of a wildly flickering eye, "I was also hoping maybe you could advance me the rest."

"Advance? Me?"

"Just a loan, like. 'Til I...y'know, get on my feet. Like you was saying."

"You think I'm carrying twenty large on my hip?"

"I dunno. Seem like you always used to have a lot of money."

"Not anymore."

"Not even with that new job you got?"

"Doesn't pay that much," Jim said, regretting his fantastic story.

"You can't help me out then?"

"Not that way."

"Sure wish Mom was here," Leon whimpered, plaintive as a child. "She'd know what to do."

"Your mom can't bail you out anymore, Leon."

"What *am* I gonna do, Uncle Jim?"

For that he had no ready answer.

Leon anxiously scanned the ocean, as if awaiting the appearance of a mystic vision on its murky horizon, a deliverance. Jim looked up at the sun-bleached sky. In the near distance, a flock of sea gulls dipped and looped and soared; far off a jet climbed steeply, banked, and pointed west, trailing a plume of smoke, white on white. Up there birds frolicked, and aboard the plane, voyagers chatted affably or dozed peacefully or settled back with cool drinks in their hands. Down here, earthbound, such elementary amenities were outside his reach. The specter of his sister floated behind his eyes, and the words of his expedient, imprudent pledge, echoing dimly in his ears, returned to haunt him. "I don't know," he said at last. "But we'll think of something."

SEVEN

"HOLY MOLY!" EXCLAIMED THE REVEREND BOTT, recradling the phone and breaking spontaneously into an exultant, if a trifle stiff, little dance step on the pumpkin-colored linoleum. Having at one point or another in the bizarre odyssey of a long life gone through every conceivable variation on all the commonplace obscenities and profanities, Bryce nowadays, in the acquired decorum of his golden years (which numbered somewhere upward of sixty, though he never admitted to more than fifty-five), permitted himself only those quaintly anachronistic expletives resurrected from a vanished boyhood. Another of which, slightly less euphoric, a bit more alarmed, sprang unbidden to his lips at a glance at his watch and the sudden recognition of the urgency of time. "Jeez-o-Pete," he muttered, rounding the stained, pitted counter that divided grimy kitchenette from shabby sitting room, striding down a short hallway bisecting the apartment's two bedrooms, and charging unannounced through the door of the one presently occupied by his comatose partner. He stepped over to the window, opened the blinds, and stood waiting expectantly while shafts of brilliant midday sunlight fell across the unstirring figure sprawled across the bed. *Sleeping the proverbial sleep of the dead*, thought Bryce, chuckling at the felicity of the cliché. He gave it a moment, and when still there was no sign of life, he recited in hortatory tones, "'Awake! For morning in the bowl of night hath flung the'...ah..." The concluding line of the quote escaped him, so he improvised nimbly, "darkness into light."

Waneta groaned and pulled a pillow over her head.

"Time to arise, my pet. And it gives me no end of pleasure to be able to waken you to the most inspiriting news."

"The fuck...?" he heard her mumble.

The remainder of the thought, muffled by the pillow, was indistinguishable, so Bryce came over and settled his fleshy buttocks on the edge of the bed. "Scarcely a single day have we been here," he boomed triumphantly, "and already our first client has surfaced."

Waneta lay motionless on her stomach, the fine straight filaments of hair splayed out over her bare back like black lace. She made no reply.

"Do you hear what I'm saying?" Bryce demanded. "We have pressing business to attend to."

From beneath the pillow came the peevish plea, "You wanna hold it down little? I ain't on the beach over there, y'know. An' I got a head out to here."

Small wonder, given the jug of Gallo she'd drained immediately upon their arrival, ostensibly to bring herself down from the tension of the long hours behind the wheel, help her sleep. But Bryce, his patience exhausted, yanked the pillow away and said firmly, "You *must* get up. Now. Time is fleeting."

One of her arms dangled over the side of the bed. With an enormous effort, she lifted it to shield eyes rudely exposed to the light. "Fuck time *is* it, anyways?"

"Three o'clock."

"What day?"

"Sunday. You've slept over twenty-four hours. More than enough for anyone."

"Yeah, you try drivin' that heap seven hundred miles without a break. See how long you crap out."

Bryce expelled a sigh. Reminded himself that partnering with the intellectually impoverished was always a daunting task. Said gently, "Be that as it may, in less than four hours, there'll be a mark at the door. And we're woefully unprepared, Waneta. Even you must recognize that hard truth. Which is why I solicit your cooperation in this most promising endeavor."

She craned her neck enough to gaze at him. Anxious, bleary gaze. "Mark's comin' tonight?"

"Around seven, she said."

"Holy shit, I *better* get movin'."

In stages painfully slow, she hauled herself into sitting posture, scratched her armpits, stretched her frail limbs, wobbled to her feet, and buck naked, stumbled off to the john. The casual display of nudity was artless, thoughtless, a product of her Dogpatch upbringing. Indeed, early on in their alliance, she had offered him ready access to her bony body, offhandedly and as a matter of course, an offer Bryce declined, albeit reluctantly, on the sober grounds of impropriety in a business relationship (omitting any mortifying mention of a time-smothered libido); the demurral was greeted with an indifferent shrug. Now, however, catching a glimpse of the tiny, pointy breasts; fuzzy crotch; smooth, if pinched, haunches, he experienced an unfamiliar and all but forgotten thaw in his chilly loins, and he had to wonder whether money, even the mere anticipation of it, possessed a magical power to rekindle the ashes of lust, charm the slumbering serpent. Who could say?

He heard the toilet's flush, shower's splash. He waited. And as he did, his thoughts vaulted forward in time to the crucial test just ahead then pirouetted and waltzed backward, swirling in the mind's eye all the previous day's strenuous activity and lively scheming.

Fail to plan, plan to fail—a caution taken from a bank marquee somewhere but no less pertinent to the manifold challenges of their present circumstance. And while Bryce was guilty of many things, absence of methodic planning never had been among them. Accordingly (and in response to Waneta's incessant on-the-road nagging: "So where'bouts in Florida we takin' this boss scam of yours?"), he'd settled on the West Palm Beach vicinity generally and, as they neared it, Singer Island specifically (years back Bryce had hustled the area, recalled it dimly), reasoning that its central location and proximity to wealth provided an initial base of operation close to ideal. Later, if the swindle proved as rewarding as he devoutly hoped, they could gradually swing south to the peninsula's tip then up its western coast, blitzing every pocket of affluence along the way and absconding with righteous plunder.

They found lodging in a stucco-sided, single-storied fourplex known as the Surf and Shore, a misnomer on both counts inasmuch as a tarred parking lot, paved road, and an easy half mile separated the structure from the nearest beach. Considerably short on elegance the Surf and Shore was, and with all the architectural allure of a barracks. No matter. For now it would have to do. FURNISHED APARTMENTS WEEKLY OR MONTHLY, the sign out front announced, and Bryce engaged a unit for the former, discovering the off-season rates for even so brief a stay effectively emptied his wallet. "Towels and linens included in the price," an oily manager had informed him, evidently reading the culture shock on his face.

"Most generous," said Bryce, smiling feebly as he handed over the last of the bills.

No sooner were they inside than Waneta offered her blunt assessment. "Jesus, what a dump. I seen hog wallows got a leg up on this."

"Nothing a little tidying up can't remedy," said Bryce, ever the buoyant optimist.

"Yeah, well, you wanna get on the wrong end of a mop, be my guest. Me, I'm gonna crash."

"As well you should, my dear. It's been a long, arduous journey."

"Hope to shit, long. My ass feels like it turned to stone." She'd ransacked her bag, produced a bottle, and sank into one of the

Goodwill-special chairs, explaining, "First I gotta have a little dance with Dr. Gallo."

"At ten in the morning?"

"Mellow me out. You wanna hit?"

"None for me, thank you. I have some serious deliberating to do."

"Yeah, I seen what the tab on this sty done to our bankroll. You damn well better do some deliberatin'. Deliberate us up some mean green. An' quicker'n cat shit."

Sound advice, however crudely put. And so while she drank herself senseless, eventually tottering off to a bedroom, Bryce paced the worn carpet, narrowing in all his not inconsiderable deliberative powers on the knotty problem at hand. Because they had neither time nor wherewithal to wait for the news to leak slowly (unlike the Carolina hayseeds), he had to find a way to get the word out, make things happen. And in her vernacular, cat-shit quick. Question was how.

In past ventures a scatter-gun approach always had served him well, carried the day. Perhaps it would again. Fire off enough rounds, and one or more is bound to find a target. The murky outline of a plan, extrapolated from that reliable principle, gradually began to take shape in his head. He put a pattern to it, substance, order, design. Then he swung into action, unpacking, one by one, his bountiful bag of tricks.

First he copied a number of addresses from the phone directory. Next he secured an area map from the manager. By now Waneta was unconscious, and so, much as he disliked piloting a vehicle, he got behind the wheel of the Seville and steered it cautiously out of the lot and into the stream of Saturday traffic that zoomed down the street. He drove to an establishment in Riviera Beach called InstaPrint, which fulfilled the extravagant promise of its name by producing a stack of flyers bearing a cryptic, studiedly ambiguous message of his own fertile invention, holding out the possibility of new hope for restored dialogue with the dead and inviting inquiries at the Surf and Shore number. Payment for this and all subsequent goods and services was accomplished via a risky skating of a credit card deftly, not to say fortuitously, nicked by Waneta only the day before yesterday and as yet—knock on plasticized wood—still cold.

From there Bryce made the rounds of distribution sites with the greatest potential for generating the sort of business he sought: health-food stores (notorious for their credulous clientele), a spiritual healing center, some upscale retirement homes (your freeze-drys being, in his experience, the easiest of marks). A pleasant word and ingratiating smile invariably gained him permission to tack a flyer to a bulletin board or place it in the hands of a like-minded soul. Dupes were dupes, the world over.

That task completed, he dropped by several funeral chapels, assembled a confused mournful face, spun a glib tale casting himself as a bereaved bumpkin relative lost in an urban wilderness, thereby obtaining names and addresses of recent crowbaits. Within the hour his flyers appeared in their survivors' mailboxes.

One stop remained. At a Palm Beach Gardens Mall, he purchased several small but, to his thinking, significant items that could prove useful in preparing Waneta for the role she was, with any luck, soon to assume. In this, as in all swindles, success turned on meticulous attention to detail.

Making his way back to Singer Island, Bryce chanced to find himself on a street named, of all things, Prosperity Farms. As an omen it seemed decidedly auspicious, and he clung to that thought as, exhausted from the frantic intensity of his labors, he stretched out on a bed in the Surf and Shore, offered up a silent prayer to all the capricious gods that roved the spheres, and floated off into a dreamless sleep.

His prayers had not gone unanswered, Bryce reflected now, regrounded in the present by the sudden appearance of a towel-swathed Waneta, hair damp and shining, eyes clear, her normally waxen skin pinkened from the steamy water, padding into the room and announcing, "Man, did that ever hit the spot. Feel like I'm back in the human race again."

Ah, the resiliency of youth, thought Bryce wistfully, dealing her a smile indulgent and benign.

"I'm starved. Whadda we got to eat?"

"For now we must defer dining."

"Huh?"

"After the performance we'll eat."

"But it's *now* I'm hungry," she whined.

"And it's precisely that starved, ravaged look we want to project. In this little playlet we'll be staging, fidelity to fact is of paramount importance."

"Fuck you talkin' about, Bryce?"

"Credibility, my sweet. A willingness to believe the unbelievable, which is the foundation of all successful scams and which can only emerge from exhaustive rehearsal. I think you'll agree we have a great deal to master in the next four hours."

She made a vinegary face and, with a mix of petulance and resignation, sighed. "OK, so what's the drill?"

"That's the spirit," said Bryce, chuckling softly at the quite unintended pun.

As with all good theatrics, the drill commenced with makeup and costume. The former consisted of a chalky dusting powder liberally applied to every surface of her skin (with particular attention paid to face, neck, and shoulders), followed by the application of eye shadow the color of soot; the latter was simply a thin cotton nightie, shapeless and floppy (the nearest to a hospital gown Bryce's search of the mall could uncover), its gauzy fabric revealing the contours of her skeletal frame, loose-fitting top exposing a stark ridge of collarbone. Inspecting her image in the bureau mirror, Waneta remarked disgustedly, "I look like fuckin' Vampira."

"Exactly the effect we're after," Bryce assured her. "And now on to phase two of our preparations. Assume a supine position on the bed, please."

"A *what* position?" she said dubiously.

"Lie on your back. Under the sheet."

Like a temperamental director—gentle, fussy, tyrannic by abrupt turns, coaxing, badgering, goading, cajoling, pleading—Bryce coached her in his gradually enlarging conception of the character she was about to portray, its every nuance, subtlest shading.

Vocal pitch: "A dullish monotone. Faint, distant, labored. Soft, softer. It's rather a hoarse whisper I'm looking for. There, that's much better."

Choice of words: Borrowing from LuJean, Bryce gave her that eerily intoned opening line, "'What shall I tell them?'" To it he added a few terse transitional phrases, simple, direct, easily committed to memory, concluding with the stern admonition, "Above all else, you must—repeat, *must*!—lose the gutter language. No curses, no vulgarities. Strike them from your vocabulary."

Posture, bearing, expression: "Limp, motionless, too weak to stir, though from time to time, allow a small wince of pain to crease your otherwise blank features. Yes, that's good, very good. A nice touch."

Eye contact: "The eyes are the key," Bryce lectured her, once again drawing his inspiration from LuJean. "You'll of course be staring fixedly at the mark, a kind of zombie stare, but to get it right, you've got to imagine yourself gazing *through* her, *beyond* her, past death's forbidding gates, and on, on into the blackest abyss," he rhapsodized, not at all displeased with the lyrical quality of his description.

Messages: "Remember, you have the power to carry them in both directions. Those dispatched from here should pose no problem, but any that you bring back from the other side must be vague, blurry. Nothing too specific just yet. Teasers, so to say. If we hope to generate repeat business, we've got to keep our fish on the line."

Like many simple people, Waneta was an accomplished thespian, possessing the chameleonic talent to glide effortlessly into a new and altogether different persona, burrow herself beneath the skin of her character. The transformation from coarse, ignorant, foul-tongued mountain girl to tragically expiring waif was nothing short of miraculous, an act of artless beauty. By six o'clock she had it down perfectly, so flawless a portrayal that Bryce was all but persuaded she was indeed fresh worm food. Praise was in order, and he laid some on. "Superb performance, my dear. Absolutely compelling."

"So what do I do if this broad throws me some kinda curve?" Waneta inquired, lapsing into her natural self.

"Grieving daughter," Bryce corrected. "Keep in mind the mother has just passed over after a long, painful illness. Planted this very afternoon, as a matter of fact."

"Yeah, yeah, yeah. Still askin' what I do."

"You'll have to extemporize."

"You wanna talk English?"

"Wing it," Bryce translated. "Not to worry. I'll be here to help you field any awkward questions."

"Yeah, easy for you. I'm the one gotta come up with the words."

No disputing that. Bryce tugged at his shelf of secondary chin and slipped into deliberative gear. Another inspiration arrived. "Give me your hand," he said. "Left one."

"What for?"

"Just do as I say."

He removed a pen from his shirt pocket, took the extended hand, and filled its palm with as many words as the wafer-thin flesh could accommodate. "Prompts," he explained. "Signal terms designed to spark your memory."

Waneta examined her palm. "Hey, that's pretty slick. Sorta like a cheat sheet."

"Exactly. What you do, if cornered, is draw your arm out from under the sheet, cup your hand, and lay it over your eyes. A stiff motion, painfully slow. Thusly."

He demonstrated. She imitated the movement. Tried again. Improved on it.

"Excellent," said Bryce, beaming. When he checked his watch, the smile faded. "Time grows short," he declared, "and I've a few final touches yet to apply."

"What am I suppose to do?"

"Relax," he advised her, exiting the room. "Empty your head of negative thoughts. Give yourself over to the comforting embrace of the spirits."

"Yeah, right."

His final touches included a thorough hands-and-knees scrubbing of the grease-streaked kitchenette floor with an industrial-strength, ammonia-based cleanser (another mall purchase), whose pungent perfumes induced a sanitized, sick-room fragrance into the air. The involuntary twitch of his nostrils confirmed the desired effect. Next he swiped a damp cloth over the counter and the sitting-room furniture. He found a vacuum and gave the carpet a quick sweep. In the bathroom he scoured the sink and stool. Grunting and sweating from the unaccustomed and less than agreeable physical exertions, conscious of time's relentless advance, he showered, ran a blade over his face, and dressed in his black suit.

It was ten minutes short of the appointed hour. He went into Waneta's room and closed the blind, further dimming what remained of dusk's falling light. On the bureau he arranged a pair of slender candles, put a flame to their wicks. Shadows danced across the walls and ceiling. His last touch, easily the finest.

He pulled a chair up alongside the bed, settled into it, said, "I do believe we're ready." Waneta didn't say a word. Evidently his advice had registered, for she lay with her head cushioned in its nest of hair, eyes open but inward turning, as though peering deep into the heart of her character, submersing herself in the part. Her gaunt, lovely, powder-blanched face displayed an ethereal quality, scarcely of this world.

They waited.

Punctually at seven the doorbell's harsh screak pierced the silence. Waneta shuddered. Bryce came to his feet, found her hand beneath the sheet, gave it a squeeze, and murmured, "Curtain time. Break a leg, as they say."

Out in the sitting room, he paused long enough to arrange his features in suitably woebegone attitude. Again the bell sounded. He swung open the door and discovered, to his surprise, not one but two females, handsome shapely women, stylishly coiffed, both outfitted in mourning black and sporting expressions compounded of sorrow and a perceptible apprehension on their comely, painted faces.

"Mr. Bott?" said the one nearest him.

"Reverend," Bryce purred unctuously.

"Oh. Right. Sorry."

"And you are?" Bryce asked, projecting a kindly, fuddled innocence.

"Courtney? Courtney Cleland? I called you this afternoon? About my mother?"

Like so many Floridians, she had the distressing habit of casting every utterance as a query. The sort of annoyance one could learn to overlook if the money was right. "Cleland, Cleland," Bryce repeated, like some harmless coot conducting a confused search of his memory. Pacing was all. He gave a recollective finger snap. "Ms. Cleland, of course," he said, motioning them in with a waiterly flourish. "My niece and I have been expecting you. The poor girl hopes to be of some small help in easing the pain of your tragic loss."

"Same here," allowed the one called Courtney, and catching his inquiring glance at her companion, she added, "Oh, and this is my dearest friend, Billie Swett? It was her idea we come see you?"

EIGHT

"Y'KNOW SOMETHIN', *CHICO*?"

"Name's Hector."

"Y'know what, Hay-soose?"

"Yeah, wha's that?"

"Your eyes look like a couple piss holes in the snow."

"Florida got no snow. Where you been?"

"That ain't the point."

"What is?"

"Way you look. Which is like a goddamn warmed-over burrito."

"Yeah, well, you not lookin' so hot neither."

"Least I can see my hand in front a' my face." As proof, Junior lifted one, middle digit extended. "How many fingers you count?"

"How 'bout you get down and eat this wet burrito?" said Hector, clutching his crotch.

Junior made a short barking laugh. "Hey, you're OK, Soosie. Don't care what the rest of the world say."

In this fashion their conversation, such as it was, lurched forward, long silences interspersed with little bursts of bickering. They were sitting at a booth in the Stuart Denny's, that same Sunday morning, Junior with a Grand Slam breakfast special laid out before him, while Hector, battered and wasted from thirty-six hours of nonstop partying, tried to revivify himself with bitter black coffee, for the most part vainly. His head throbbed. His tongue felt as if it had been varnished with shellac. Now and then his gut produced the ominous creaky rumble of ancient plumbing. Not so Junior, who, apart from his own scarlet-veined eyes, appeared to be in fine form, and who allowed around a forkful of spattery eggs, “We really had us a hoo-ha, right, cholo? Real fiesta.”

“Tha’s your idea of a fiesta?”

“Bet your jingleberries. Calls to mind my first pruno party, in the keep.”

The condiment-rich, we-never-close stink in the air stung Hector’s nostrils, dizzied his punished head. He sensed a story coming on. He was right.

“Got myself so swacked I was trippin’ over spider webs,” Junior declared proudly. “Took two a’ them SWAT teams to do a cell extraction on me. That’s twelve hacks, full storm-trooper gear. Still busted a few heads before they took me down. Cost me a month-in-the-hole holiday. Was worth it, though. Yeah,” he concluded dreamily, “them was the times.”

“How about these ones?”

“What ones that?”

“Times.”

Junior shrugged. “They’re OK too.”

“Tha’s not what I’m askin’, man.”

“So spit it out.”

“Askin’ your thoughts on what we oughta be doin’,” Hector said peevishly. “Here in the now times.”

Junior looked baffled. “Doin’? Scarfin’ eggs, sloppin’ coffee, gettin’ straight. What we’re doin’.”

“It don’t bother you we pissed away half the weekend?”

“Why should it? Man’s entitle’ to a little honky-tonkin’. This is America. By rights we shouldn’t even be workin’ today, it bein’ Sunday. That’s in your Bible someplace.”

“Mr. B maybe don’t see it that way.”

“That’s ’cuz he’s a Yid. They ain’t got no Sunday, your Yids. Too busy reamin’ us goys.”

“Yeah, well, he still the one payin’ the freight.”

"So?"

"So I'm thinkin' he not gonna be too cranked, us dickin' off like we done here."

"Fuck 'im. Stiffers ain't goin' no place. We'll see he collects his pound."

The sandpaper rasp that was Junior's voice this morning carried an unmistakable note of finality, so Hector, for all his fretful anxiety, thought better of pursuing the topic. Another of the silences, broken only by the lip-smacking sounds of mastication, settled over the booth. Junior, his appetite unimpaired by prolonged dissipation, sat hunch shouldered, fork moving with robotic precision from plate to mouth, shoveling in his breakfast with heroic gusto. When the last crumb was consumed, he leaned back, thumped his keg of belly contentedly, and said, "Them Grand Slams, they eat good."

"So maybe now we go to work, huh?"

Junior made a little squirmy motion, like he was polishing the seat with his buttocks. "First I got me a forty-pound rat to shit," he said, and heaved himself up and lumbered to the john.

Hector shook his head defeatedly, watched him disappear behind the door. He sighed, fidgeted. The golden glow inspired by booze and tea and tail had long since faded, displaced by blurry memories of Avenue D, the soiled ugliness of it all. That wasn't what he wanted, not at all. What he wanted was to make something of himself, be somebody someday. And as he thought that way, it occurred to him he could count on a good quarter-hour wait, time enough to put in a call to Mr. B, fill him in, explain things, stay right with him. He got to his feet, hurried to a pay phone in the entry, pecked out a number.

"Yes?" came a coolly neutral voice down the line.

"Mr. Berkowitz?"

"Speaking."

"This is Hector. Hope I didn't wake you up or nothin'."

"Not at all. I've been working for several hours now."

So Biggs got it right about the Jews. Score one for the numbnuts. "Figured I better punch in," Hector said, "let you know how things shakin'."

"I'm pleased you did. Where are you?"

"Up in Stuart."

"Stuart?"

"Yeah, Stuart."

"Why?"

"Why?" Hector repeated, confused, wondering, *Fuck we got here anyway, echo chamber?*

"I'm asking what you're doing in Stuart."

"'Cuz that's where the first receivable on the list at. A-rab name of 'Ahmed.'"

"Ahmed Awal?"

"Didn't catch his last name."

"Have you, ah, contacted this person yet?"

"Yeah, we had a word with him."

Silence filled the line.

"Mr. Berkowitz? You there?"

"Still here, Hector."

Maybe so, but Hector was sure he detected a slight alteration in the pitch of the voice, like a chilly distancing had come into it. Guardedly he said, "Somethin' wrong?"

"Yes. Very wrong."

Uh-oh. Hector had a pretty good idea what that meant. "You didn't want him touched up, this A-rab?" he asked anyway, hoping the fuck he might be mistaken.

"I specifically instructed that imbecile Biggs to strike Mr. Awal's name from the list. We'd arrived at an agreement satisfactory to both parties."

Hector's turn for silence.

"This is not cheering news," Berkowitz said.

"No way I could know," said Hector weakly, trying to put some space between himself and the bad news, all the while booting himself in the ass for not stepping up the other night, insisting they check out the jerk-off A-rab's pleading story.

Berkowitz didn't seem to be listening. "This kind of bungling is simply not acceptable," he murmured, barely audible, like a man consulting with himself, thinking out loud. "Not acceptable. Not in business. We're going to have to work out a new arrangement with our Mr. Biggs. Something entirely different."

"You think I oughta tell him about this, y'know..." "Fuckup," he was about to say, but remembering that wasn't the kind of language you used around a fine gentleman like Mr. B, he softened it to "mix-up? With the A-rab? See if I can maybe shape him up little?"

"No, that would be very unwise. We wouldn't want to alert him to what may soon...transpire."

Hector didn't much like the ring of that *we*. Or that *transpire* either, even though he wasn't exactly sure he knew what it meant. If it meant what he thought it did, he could put a figure on who the *we* was and get tapped to do the transpiring.

"In any case," Berkowitz went on, "I need time to evaluate the situation, assess the damages. What were they, by the way?"

"On the A-rab?"

"Yes."

"One arm, one leg."

Berkowitz made an exasperated huffing sound. "Bad business."

"So what you want me to do?"

"For now, nothing. Proceed with the list. Phone in periodically, and update me on your progress. I'll let you know when I've settled on a course of action."

"Rest a' them names on the list, they all OK? For crowdin' purposes, I mean."

"They're all delinquent, Hector. Do whatever needs be done. But watch Biggs. See that he exercises reasonable restraint. One blunder is more than enough to have to deal with."

Easy for him to say. You oughta try it sometime, restrainin' an ape like that. Find out quick about "easy." That's what Hector wanted to tell him, but instead he said simply, "Do what I can."

"I'm relying on you, Hector."

Funny how the Jews, ones he knew anyway, could make the plainest words, innocent ones, names even, sound like a sneer. Or a threat. "Be in touch," Hector said, and put up the phone.

In the nick of fucking time too. Here came Biggs gliding through the tables, ghost of a relieved smile on his face, Mr. Lighter'n Air now that he got that rat squeezed out of him. He stopped by the register to pay, looked around, spotted Hector, big-shouldered his way through the crowd of citizens waiting their turn for seats, stepped over, and said, "I tell ya, *chico*, y'get my age, good dump beat a piece a' ass, hands down."

"How old's that?" Hector inquired conversationally, thinking the best thing to do was to keep him yapping while he tried to sort out in his head the slippery signals coming down from Mr. B.

"Be forty-four next month," Junior said, fitting a plug of tobacco between lip and gum, bulging a cheek.

"Tha's pretty old, forty-four."

Wrong thing to say. Junior glowered at him, fired an opening salvo of juice onto the tiled floor, growled, "Not so old I can't administer a primo whuppin' anytime the mood takes me. Anytime, anywheres, anybody."

Now Hector was thinking, uneasily, about the corner he was getting himself backed into, quiet-talking badass Jew boy on one side of him, King Kong here on the other. Not a good place to be. "Hey, nobody sayin' you can't, man," he said from behind an elevated, placatory palm. "All's I'm sayin' is we both of us gettin' along in years for all that thrashin' and diddlin' we been doin'. Both of us."

The explanation seemed to pacify Junior. "Yeah, you prolly right. Other hand, life's short. You gotta suck it up while you can."

"We done our share suckin', last couple nights."

"That one you for sure got right," Junior allowed with a broad, lewd grin.

"So you ready to hit it now?"

"Might as well. Nothin' better to do."

On their stroll across the steaming, sun-drenched parking lot, something occurred to Junior, and he stopped, thrust out a gimme hand and said, "Oh, yeah, almost slip my mind. You owe me a buck."

"Buck? What for?"

"The coffee."

"They charge a buck for coffee in there?"

"Give or take a couple coins. Y'got your tip too."

"Fuckin' thieves," Hector grouched, but he laid a bill on the upturned palm.

"Takes one to spot one," said the grinning Junior, and finances properly settled, they hopped into his van, and off they went.

Junior was one of those persons who took vast pleasure in reprising his debaucheries, and tooling south on Highway 95, he anatomized this latest one in exhaustive detail, tirelessly reconstructing scenes, re-creating "I sez, she sez" dialogues, guffawing at seriously warped recollections of his rapier wit; while Hector, preoccupied with his own mounting worries and sick of the subject, occasionally nodded or offered a seconding remark but mostly kept silent. Eventually even Junior noticed the lopsided quality of the conversation and said, "You ain't got much to say for yourself, *chico*. Somethin' eatin' on you?"

Hector batted the air irritably. "Nah, nothin'. Still a little tweaked."

"Comes a' peelin' the ol' banana with them chocolate drops. Your coloreds, they all of 'em pokin' machines. Wear you down."

"Tha's the goddamn truth."

"Hope you was wearin' a raincoat, all that wick dippin'."

"'Course I was. With your flatbacks, you better."

"Good thing. Avenue D, that's Package City."

"Wha's that? Package?"

Junior snorted derisively. "You never heard a' the package? Big Marion grad-u-ate like yourself?"

"Am I askin' here, or what?"

"Just that AIDS shit is all."

"You tellin' me them two *putas* got the AIDS?" Hector said, his voice lifting in alarm.

"Ain't sayin' *them* two for sure got it. Sayin' your boogies up there famous for it."

Holy mother of fuck, thought Hector, ransacking his memory for assurances he'd in fact kept his dagger sheathed through all that boinking that had gone on. Praying to sweet baby Jesus he had. Like he didn't have enough worries already.

"Chill out, *chico*," Junior advised him, reading his thoughts off the distress in his face. "You wore your fish skin, you got nothin' to sweat."

"That don't mean you couldn'ta said somethin' before."

"Which *before* we talkin'? Now, or when you got it wet?"

"Wet."

"Figured you knew," Junior drawled around a pitiless smile that only served to harden his square, pocked face. "Way I heard it, you homies suppose to be street."

"Tha's real thoughtful a' you, man, puttin' me at risk like that," said Hector bitterly.

Junior shrugged. "No risk, no reward."

They rode for a few miles in silence, 'til Junior saw fit to fill it with the pensive observation, "Y'know, you think about it, though, it's a fuckin' shame a man can't get his nuts cracked without havin' to worry about coppin' it off some punker disease. Ain't like AIDS was the clap or the crabs, somethin' candy-ass like that."

"Hey, tell me about it."

"You got your spades to thank for that."

"For what?"

"What're we talkin' about here?"

"Why them? Anybody can get it. You Anglos too."

"I *know* that, knob drip," Junior said disgustedly. "What I'm sayin' is they the ones started it, first place."

"Spooks started AIDS?"

"Sure. Everybody know that."

"How you figure?"

"See, what happen was some rump-ranger jungle bunny over in Africa gets a hankering for a monkey an'—"

"Whoa," Hector broke in on him. "You sayin' this swisher humped a monkey?"

"That's exactly what I'm sayin'."

"Why'd he wanna do that? Gotta be plenty other faggots around. Even in Africa."

"Fuck would I know? Maybe he's ugly or somethin'. Lookin' for a tighter fit. Maybe it's love. Anyways, he jumps the chimp—only it turns out the wrong one, seein' how it got an assful a' AIDS germs. So now he's passin' 'em along to every blue-gummer he packs, which, your queens bein' hornier'n a three-peckered goat, way all them dick licks are, got to be more'n a few. Next thing is some fruit-bar bro from America comes over, prolly lookin' for a little Africa strange, an' that's what he gets, some heavy-duty strange. Like in full-package strange. Carries it back home with him," he concluded with a resigned sigh, "an' the rest is history."

Hector regarded him skeptically. "You jobbin' me here, man?"

"Listen," said Junior, heatedly defending his proposition, "that's in medical science. Look it up."

"Yeah, I'll be sure'n do that. Next time I'm in a li-bary."

But there would be neither time nor opportunity for medical research that day, for just then the PGA Boulevard exit loomed in the near distance. "Think this the one we lookin' for," Junior said, and swung the van onto the westbound ramp, drove about a quarter of a mile, then abruptly pulled over in a shopping plaza. He took a street map from the glove compartment, dug his notebook out of a hip pocket, and flipped through its pages, mumbling, "Cody, Cody...Fuck's Cody? OK, here."

"Where's *here*?" Hector asked, patience dwindling. All he wanted to do now was go to work, get his mind off his multiplying troubles.

"Be them apartments right over there." A toss of the head indicated a sprawling collection of identical buildings directly to the south of the plaza. "Number one six six, says here."

"Piece a dumb luck. I figured us for lost."

"Luck got nothin' to do with it. You ridin' with the ol' pathfinder, boy."

Nevertheless it required another twenty minutes or more before the pathfinder, steering his van through the maze of streets and squinting at apartment numbers, came across 166, located in a unit near the back of the complex. He switched off the engine, gave his head a few limbering rotations on the bullish neck, and said, "You set?" Hector nodded, and simultaneously they came out their respective doors, Junior vigorously working his jaws around the last of the tobacco wad. When no insect target presented itself, he splattered the sidewalk that led to the entrance with a gigantic burst of blackened spittle. "OK," he said, "let's go bust some bones."

About halfway down the hall, they found their number. Junior rapped on the door, got only silence in response. He knocked again. Same story.

"You s'pose he seen us comin'?" Hector said.

"Might've."

"Could be he's hidin' in a closet, hopin' we go away."

"Yeah, could be that too."

Hector tested the knob. Predictably the door was securely bolted. "Maybe we oughta crack it, take a quick peek inside."

Junior glanced up and down the hall. Empty, both directions. "I dunno," he said, frowning. "I ain't lookin' to get nailed on a B and E. Not for the wages that clipped-dick Berkowitz payin'."

"We gotta do *somethin'*, man."

Junior tried once more, hammering with his fist this time. More of the same, but behind them another door creaked open, and a pair of watery, prying eyes peered out at them from the tiny notch. "You lookin' for Mrs. Cody?" a croaky granny voice inquired.

They both turned, and Junior, natural spokesman, replied politely, "Was Mr. Cody we hopin' to speak with, ma'am."

"That's her boy. Leon."

"That a fact. Well, he's the party we lookin' for. Wouldn't be you seen him around?"

"Today?"

"Yeah, today."

"No, can't say I have."

Junior, still affable and with a deference bordering on courtly, said, "Don't s'pose you happen to know where we could find him?"

"Services, more'n likely."

"Church?"

"Funeral. His mother passed away. Just the other day."

Junior shook his head sadly. "That's a shame, his mom dyin' like that," he said, the normally growly voice softening to a pitch of woe remarkably convincing.

"Friday, I think it was."

"What was?"

"Mrs. Cody passin' on."

"But her boy, he's stayin' at the apartment here?"

"Lives here. He ought to be back before long. Tonight for sure."

Junior touched a finger to a brow in grateful salute. "Wanna thank you, ma'am, all your help."

"I could give him a message. Tell him who it was stopped by."

"That's OK. You done enough already."

"Be no trouble," she said hopefully.

"No, this not a good time, him feelin' bad about his mom and all. We'll catch up to him later." He signaled Hector, and they started away, Junior calling over his shoulder in parting well-wishing, "Hey, you have yourself a super day now, y'hear?"

Out in the van, Hector sniggered. "You got quite a touch with the old ladies. Couple more minutes there, you mighta got yourself some blue-head head."

"Fuck you mean by that?" Junior demanded, glowering at him.

"Just makin' a little joke, man. Lighten up."

"Lighten up your bunghole with a hot poker, you don't show them elderly ladies the respect they got comin'."

"OK, OK," said Hector, backing off, startled at the vehemence of the reaction, and to change the subject, bring it back to the safer ground of business, he asked, "So what we do now? Wait for him?"

"No."

"No? What're you sayin', no?"

"You got shit in your ears? They got a different way say no in spic?"

Hector looked at him puzzledly. Now the crazy gringo was doing the thousand-yard stare out the windshield, mouth twitching, eyes misted over, like he any minute was gonna bust out bawling, f'chrissake. Something weird was going on here.

"I remember when my mom croaked," Junior said dolorously. "Took me a month, easy, to get over it. Couldn't eat, sleep, work, get laid even. Finest woman you ever gonna meet, Mom was. We was close."

"That happen lately?" Hector asked, trying without much success to put some sympathy in his voice.

"'Bout ten years back."

Ten years? Fuck you say to that? "Oh," was all Hector could think of.

"That don't make it any easier. You never really get over somethin' like that."

"Bet you don't, at that," Hector said cautiously. " 'Course, we don't exactly got a whole month to wait on this Cody dude."

"No, but we'll give him a day or so, get past his grief. An' then," Junior added with a trace of a wicked, recovering smile, "we'll stop back 'n' give him another kind a grievin' to do."

NINE

NUMBERS NEVER LIE. JIM MERRIMAN SAT STORK shouldered and scowling at the numbers that filled a sheet of paper laid out before him on the kitchen table. No matter how you crunched and juggled them or how long you stared at them, they always added up the same. A long way off that 45K (plus some unspecified interest he didn't even want to think about). He went over them again, one more time. OK, you start with your base twenty-five thou from the CD, tack on the three that remained in his sister's checking account, include the two or thereabouts he might (or might not...he had no clear idea how much he had stashed in a Reno bank...not much) be able to kick in—still came up fifteen (or more) lame. Numbers don't lie.

The latest in a chain of smokes dangled from his lips. He crushed it out in a butts-heaped ashtray, glanced across the table at his nephew noisily munching Doritos and idly sorting through the mail like he'd removed himself from the problem...wasn't his to solve anymore. "I don't suppose your mother had any life insurance," Jim said, not bothering to phrase it as a question, so desolate were his hopes.

"No, she didn't believe in insurance."

"How about rings, jewelry? Anything like that?"

"Mom never bought any of that stuff. She was pretty tight, Uncle Jim."

Jesus, forty-six years on the planet, and this is what the poor woman had to show for it. And gazing at this helpless little dink, forever in a zone of his own, Jim could guess where it all had gone these past two decades.

"Doctor bills starting to come in," Leon remarked casually, like it was another problem he was handing over to Mr. Fix-It.

"Fuck the quacks," Jim snapped. "We got deeper troubles right here." To indicate the *here*, he stabbed a finger at the intractable numbers on the paper.

"You, uh, got any ideas on that yet?" Leon asked timidly, a chastened appeal in his fluttery eyes.

"Not unless the change in our pockets comes to fifteen long. Otherwise I'm fresh out." And then one suddenly came to him. "That Caddie of yours," he said. "It's got to be something of a classic, right?"

"Dunno if you'd call it classic. There's people collect 'em."

"What's it worth?"

"Y'got me, Uncle Jim. All's I do is restore 'em."

"Take a guess."

"Depends on the shape of the vehicle. Mine's no hundred percenter."

"Meaning?"

"Means it's not in mint condition. Needs a lot more work."

"So help me out here, Leon. What're we looking at? Ten thou? Fifteen? Give me a figure."

First the kid had to give it a moment's brow-furrowing thought. Finally he said, "Well, ten maybe, if you found the right buyer."

"Ten," Jim repeated, thinking ten would put them in spitting distance. If only he had some credit cards, he could kite the balance easy. Forget that. No plastic anymore. Maybe he'd get lucky, get the fifteen.

"You not planning to sell the car?" Leon broke in on this last, cheering thought.

"Damn right, sell it," Jim said exasperatedly. "We got to raise the money somewhere."

"But how'm I gonna get around?"

"How? Hoof it. That is, if we can keep your legs out of plaster casts."

Leon looked more crestfallen than scared, like the imminent loss of his wheels was the greater disaster. Jim was about to set him straight on that score when a most unwelcome sound, a thumping on the apartment door, silenced them both. He stiffened, shot a searching glance at Leon, who responded with lifted shoulders, a shrugged bewilderment. Jim motioned toward the bedroom. "Get in there. Keep down." Leon crept off on tiptoe.

Once he was out of sight, Jim slipped soundlessly through the living room, positioned himself behind the door, waited. Maybe whoever it was on the other side would give it up, go away.

Another knock, more urgent this time. Nobody was going away. "Yeah, who's there?" he growled toughly, considerably tougher than he felt just then.

"Irma Gath," came a female voice, squawky with age. "Your neighbor from across the hall."

Cautiously he pulled the door back no more than the width of the tautened chain lock, peeked out the narrow crack. True to the pitch of her voice, a dumpy little gnome of a woman with a puff of white hair and an osteoporotic hump stood there squinting back at him, a glass-topped serving dish of some sort clutched in her liver-splotched hands.

"Leon? That you? Open up."

"Leon's asleep," Jim told her, but he obeyed the sharp command, unhooked the chain, and opened up. Nobody else in evidence, either end of the hall.

"You relation?" she demanded.

"His uncle."

"Brother to Mrs. Cody, are you?"

"That's right."

"Sorry for your loss."

"Thanks."

"Funeral was today?"

"Yes."

"How's Leon takin' it?"

"He's holding up," Jim said, thinking, *What is this, fuckin' interrogation night?*

"He's a good boy, Leon. Always liked him." Perhaps as proof, she thrust the serving dish. "This is for him."

He took it, saying, "That's very thoughtful of you. Thanks."

"It's a casserole," she explained. "Tuna Helper. Just heat and eat."

"We'll do that. Now if you'll—"

"Y'gotta eat. Even in grief times. 'Specially then."

"That's the truth," he affirmed with a tight smile. "Now I really better go, Mrs. . . ."

"Gath," she filled in for him. "From across the hall. Your name is?"

Jim told her his name. Whatever it took to get her gone.

"Pleased to make your acquaintance, Mr. Merriman."

"Yeah, likewise," he allowed, the casserole precariously balanced in one hand, the other on the door. "And thanks again. I'll tell Leon you stopped by."

"Maybe you oughta tell him a couple gentlemen did too."

He caught the door midswing. "What's that?"

"Couple fellas come by today lookin' for Leon," she said, voice elevating to accommodate a presumed hearing impairment on his part. "I told 'em he wasn't home."

"Did they, uh, mention what it was about?" he asked, struggling to hold his voice steady, flat.

"Not to me. Said they'd talk to him later."

"Later today?"

"'Later's' what they said."

"You don't happen to remember what they looked like?"

"Sure do. One was a big fella, husky. Other one looked Mexican. Both of 'em real mannerly, though. Even the Mexican. You know 'em?"

"No," he mumbled to himself, and then, remembering she was still there, amended it to, "Yes, I mean."

"Well, which is it? Yes or no?"

"What?"

She gave her head an exasperated shake, let it go. "Hope Leon's not in some kinda trouble," she said hopefully.

"No, there's no trouble. Good night, Mrs. Gath."

From behind the closed and bolted door, he heard the bawled instructions, "Y'heat that casserole 'bout forty-five minutes, three hundred degrees."

"Leon," he called, "throw some things in a bag. For both of us. We gotta book. Fast."

Leon poked his head around the bedroom door. "Book?"

"Scoot, scat, split, sprint, run, flee. That plain enough?"

"How come, Uncle Jim?"

"Never mind. I'll explain later."

"Who was that at the door?"

"What'd I just tell you? Move. Quick time."

Out in the car, Jim said, "You know a motel where we can get down?"

"Hide, y'mean?"

"Yeah, Leon. Hide. Someplace out of the way. And cheap. Heavy on that cheap."

"Some like that over on Singer Island. Where we were today."

"Go!"

On the short drive, Jim kept glancing over his shoulder, scanning the street. Nobody tracking them, far as he could tell. Maybe, by the providential appearance of a cranky nosy old woman, they'd bought themselves another day of grace. God watching over drunks and fools.

Leon steered his antiquated Caddie, their last—their *only*—hope of deliverance, south on Military Trail then swung it west on Blue Heron. Crossing the bridge, he ventured a timorous question: "What's that you got there, Uncle Jim?"

"Where?"

"In your lap there."

Jim looked down, discovered the serving dish, forgotten in the panicked flight, still gripped in his trembling hands. "It's a casserole," he said. "Tuna Helper, I think."

While Jim and Leon were searching for a safe, if temporary (and cheap) harbor, Billie Swett was also, at that moment, behind the wheel of a car, a Jaguar XK8 in her case, easily her favorite of the six luxury vehicles in the Swett fleet lined up like a gallery of very pricy ducks and at her disposal. That's what being rich was all about: What's your pleasure?—take your pick. Invariably she picked this one, black as midnight, sinewy and feral as its animal namesake. She liked the way it seemed almost to float along on a cushion of air, smooth and sensuous as silk against the skin, its engine purring secrets in your ear, dreamy and strange and not of this world.

And that's how she felt, driving home under a moon-splashed sky, moonstruck herself, tranced by the tangle of images of all she'd borne witness to tonight: that pale bird-boned girl facing earthly extinction with a patient, eerie calm; the flickering candles casting long shadows over her bed of suffering; the luminous sheen that came into those hollow caverns of eyes as she combed the teeming ranks of the dead, stumbling at last on the departed soul of Mrs. Cleland; the message of love and loss and grief she selflessly and at the cost of visible pain carried from daughter to mother; the faint reply—confused, frightened, garbled—she tried desperately and without success to decipher and carry back, protesting in a genuine anguish of frustration ("Please...I know I can reach her...Let me try again...She has so much to tell us... Please.") the heartsick uncle's urgent call for rest.

All that and more, so much more. And for Billie, leery at first, watchful, it was as if she were drawn gradually, helplessly into a world of wonder, an outlander summoned to a remote frontier and offered a privileged glimpse of the alien, unmappable country of the other side. And it was that dazzling vision she brought home with her, only to have it rudely shattered by her husband's snappish greeting: "It's ten o'fuckin' clock, Billie. Where you been?"

"At the funeral. Like I told you."

"How long's it take to plant a stiff?"

"That's not very kind, Lonnie."

"Fuck kind. Ain't like she was the goddamn pope or somethin'."

He sat in a living room chair as massive as a throne, sag of belly drooping over his belt, glaring at her like a squat judgmental Buddha run out of charity. Itching for argument. Billie sank into a facing chair, said quietly, "No, but she was a good woman who died in terrible pain. It's been hard for Courtney, so I stuck around for a while to try and comfort her. She's my friend."

It was an innocent enough evasion, not even a fib actually, and she figured it couldn't hurt to couch it in a tone slightly aggrieved. Figured wrong, for he fired right back, "Yeah, and I'm your husband. Remember?"

Billie sighed. Like she was ever going to be allowed to forget. "I'm sorry, honey," she said, mustering a counterfeit contrition. "It was just something I felt I ought to do. Won't happen again."

"Better not," he muttered darkly. "I didn't get married to hang around waitin' on a wife thinks she's Florence fuckin' whatever her name was."

"Nightingale."

"Huh?"

"Florence Nightingale."

Now he looked at her narrowly. "You bein' wise ass here?"

"Come on, hon. I said I was sorry."

"Sorry don't cut shit. Not when you're sittin' home wonderin' where your wife's at, thinkin' maybe she been robbed or mugged.

Or worse even. It ain't safe for a woman to be drivin' alone, all hours a' the night. This ain't North Dakota down here, y'know."

Billie detected just the slightest softening in the peevish wheeze. Being spliced to someone like Lonnie Swett, you learned to listen for such subtle tonal gradations. "I think it's sweet of you to worry about me," she cooed, drawing from her arsenal of perfected smiles one ruefully penitent. Marriage to money required a lot of smiling. It was another of those things you learned.

"Didn't seem so sweet to me," he grouched, weakening some more but unwilling to let it go altogether, let her off too lightly.

Still was enough to reduce the spleen to a surly pout, buy her a shred of time to find a way to pacify him. Balling was out. After that birthday knobber she'd administered less than forty-eight hours back, there wasn't a hope in hell he could get it airborne again. Food, however, was always a reliable tranquilizer. She'd try food. "What did you do for dinner?" she asked in a tone of wifely concern.

"Hadda get my own," he said resentfully. "Nobody else around."

Billie knew, of course, that Sunday was the housekeeper's day off. Part of her oblique approach. With him you couldn't be too obvious. Or too careful. "Poor baby," she said. "You must be starved. Let me fix you a snack."

"Dunno what it'd be," he grumbled. "Fridge about cleaned out."

"Bet I can find something you'll like."

She went into the kitchen and, a few moments later, returned bearing a dinner plate covered with an enormous wedge of strawberry cheesecake and laced with a colorful spray of assorted cookies. The Big Lonnie conception of a snack. Among the dwindling fleshly pleasures available to a man of his mounting years and accumulated indulgences, sugary treats ran a dead heat with sex for first place, ordinarily capturing the prize through sheer constancy of gratification. He had a craving for them that bordered on the obscene. Certainly the infantile. By now Billie was a keen student of his appetites.

Lonnie had little tolerance for silence, so he soon came out of his sulk, talking tirelessly as he scooped in the cheesecake, exposing crimson-ribbed chunks of it between the chomping teeth while alternately plying his wife with probing questions on the details of the funeral (like all cheats, he suspected everyone of scheming to cheat him in return) and reminding her of all the anxiety and distress she'd put him through with her protracted absence. The questions she fielded expertly, and to the distress complaint, she replied docilely, "Like I told you, hon. It won't happen again. I promise."

He responded with a grunt, signal of his grudging acceptance of the peace offering.

What Billie didn't bother to tell him was anything about the meeting with that strange stricken girl, death's appointed messenger, or the next audience with her, coming up the day after tomorrow. Firmly grounded as he was in the visible, graspable, consumable things of this world, there was no way he could ever understand. Not that it mattered. Not tonight anyway. For Lonnie, sedated by food, had a habit of falling asleep, and predictably enough, once the plate was emptied, his jaws parted in a fly-catcher yawn, and midsentence he slumped back in his cushioned throne, head lolling forward on his chest, mouth ajar and out of which periodically issued spasmed piggy snorts.

Billie came cautiously to her feet, glided out of the room, and returned with a water glass full of brandy. She sat there for a while, sipping her drink, watching her husband's slack, bloated face ruined by greed and gluttony and suspicion, scowly even in sleep. Thinking how, after a certain number of years, everyone is accountable for his own face. Herself not excluded. To be charitable about it. And after forty-one years of living, what did hers reflect? All that scrupulous attention, all those creams and lotions and potions and surgical tucks failed to erase the guilt shadowing it all those years, the unburied memory of an innocent child brutally Hoovered out of her and carelessly discarded like some chilled gelatinous pudding. So long ago. And still so painfully remembered.

But maybe, just maybe, that other face—serene, generous, sanctified, doomed—possessed the magical power to absorb and transmit her remorse and bring back a message of forgiveness, absolution. And thinking so, flushed with hope and the golden warmth brandy kindled in her, Billie vowed to speak with the girl again, before it was too late. For both of them. Regardless of the risk. Or the cost.

No more than a few short blocks from the seedy Singer Island motel where Jim and Leon eventually found refuge for the night, the two bold guides through the pathless country of the other side were celebrating the extraordinary success of their initial foray into that shadowy territory. Or at least one of them was. "Six bills," Bryce gloated, snapping them between stubby fingers in broad caricature of the avaricious merchant. "A lucrative take, I must say, for an hour's work. Most auspicious beginning."

Waneta nodded but offered nothing in reply.

He pocketed the plunder and dug into one of the several cartons of takeout Chinese spread across the sitting-room coffee table, eating with the gusto that comes of a satisfying day's labor and washing it down with hearty gulps of Jack Daniels, a special treat for a special occasion. She, slouched at the other end of the tacky sofa, still in baggy nightie and ashen makeup, merely picked at her food. Which was all right with him, since her role required a suitably gaunt, haggard look, but which, on reflection, struck him as a trifle odd. Normally Waneta's appetite was uncommonly robust for so frail a creature, and earlier she'd been complaining of hunger. Perhaps she was still coming down from what had been, in his objective professional judgment, a truly masterful performance. Perhaps suffering the curtain-fall *tristesse* of the naturally gifted actress. So on a swallow of mustard-slathered eggroll, he said brightly, "You were magnificent tonight, my dear. As if you were born to the part." A little stroking now and again never hurt.

"You think so?"

"More than magnificent—superlative. Spellbinding."

She shrugged listlessly.

"For example that whole struggle to pluck poor dead Mother Cleland's words out of the fog—that, now, was inspired. I especially liked your 'She has so much to tell us' line."

"That one just come to me. Outta nowhere."

"And a brilliant improvisation it was. The perfect bait. The very fact they're coming back for more is testament to your boundless talent. You should be proud of yourself, Waneta."

She shook her head slowly. "I dunno. Couple times in there I felt kinda, oh, weird, like."

"In what way weird?" he inquired indulgently.

"Creepy weird. Wiggy almost. Like I was, well, on the edge of losin' it. Goin' off the deep end myself. Y'know what I'm sayin' here?"

"No, I'm afraid I don't. Losing *what* exactly?"

"Dunno that either," she said helplessly.

Vaguely disquieting, the direction this talk was taking. Bryce set aside the carton of soy-drenched rice he'd been spooning in and turned and faced her, projecting his best paternal attitude. "Something's troubling you, my dear. What is it? You can tell me."

She hesitated, staring into her lap, avoiding his eyes.

"Waneta?"

"It's just that," she mumbled haltingly, "well, all them other scams we run, they was about, y'know, *things*."

"You have misgivings over the product we're offering?"

"Yeah, I do. Fake tombstones, that's one thing. But it don't seem right, pitchin' the dead."

"Not the dead," he corrected gently. "What we're selling is the wind."

"Huh?"

"Something intensely felt but never seen."

She cuffed the air impatiently. "Dunno nothin' about that. All's I know is we're messin' with shit we oughtn't to be. Got no business in."

Bryce gave his chin a thoughtful tug. "Let me see if I understand," he said, understanding only too well what was going on here. Weaned as he knew she was on hillbilly revivalist voodoo, her long-buried conscience threatened now, at this least opportune of moments, to resurface. Also did he understand, better than most, that in their line of work, conscience could cancel all one's finest efforts, snatch a proverbial defeat from the jaws of victory. "You're troubled by the spiritual aspect of our venture?"

"Maybe that. I'm tellin' ya, Bryce, all that talkin' with dead folks—playin' at talkin' to 'em—it gets spooky."

"Put your fears to rest, my dear. What we bring for sale is that most precious of all commodities."

"Wind?"

"Hope."

"Hope, wind," she said dismally. "Same thing."

"You're absolutely right. We're the bearers of the winds of hope. Think about it, Waneta. Who among us has not regretted bitterly and too late the sentiment unuttered, the endearment left unspoken? We offer our clients hope's very essence, a second chance."

Now she fixed him with a beseeching gaze. "You really think it's OK then, this number? It's not a, like, sin or somethin', what we're doin' here?"

"Sin? Hardly. You must think of yourself as a heavenly postal service," he advised, adding with a sanctimonious leer, "And if, in the performance of that valuable service, we turn a tidy profit, where's the harm?"

"S'pose you're right," Waneta allowed but glumly and without a flake of enthusiasm.

"Of course I'm right," he averred, with a confidence notably larger than he was feeling just then. Squeamish doubts, potentially crippling scruples—these were a side of his tough little partner new to him, foreign, utterly out of character and altogether unforeseen. And not cheering. She was the linchpin of this swindle; everything turned on her. *Tread lightly, Bryce!*

"Speaking of profit," he said in a conversational move calculated to lift her dampened spirits, coax her back on course, "did you happen to take notice of the daughter's companion?"

"Unh-uh. I was keepin' my eyes on the one wanted to talk with her mom. Like you said to do."

"And rightly so, since she was the primary target tonight. At our next session, however, I suspect that focus will shift to the other, Ms. Billie Swett by name."

"Why you think that?"

"Why? A number of reasons. For one there's someone on the other side she desperately yearns to contact."

"She tell ya that?"

"Not in so many words. But I have an intuition about such things."

"Yeah, I seen how far that intuition yours gets us," she sniffed.

This was better. A marked improvement. This was the fractious, ornery Waneta he knew. Nothing like strategy talk to bring her around, get her grounded again, and his head was teeming with strategies tonight. He pushed on. "Also, and more to the point, there's the sweet perfume of money about her."

"I didn't smell nothin' special."

"A figure of speech, my dear," said Bryce patronizingly. "What I meant was all the signals are promising. Certainly those clothes came off no dog rack. Or that gargantuan rock from a cut-rate jeweler. And when they left, she was the one piloting the Jaguar."

"Don't prove nothin'. Lots a people put up a big front ain't got squat. You oughta know that."

"Would it surprise you to learn that five of that six hundred we collected this evening came from her?"

Waneta looked at him skeptically. "You jivin' me?"

"Jiving? Not at all. A most generous donor, our Ms. Swett."

"So how come she done that? I didn't take no messages for her."

"Because she can. She handed over those bills as casually as you and I would drop a coin in a beggar's hat."

"That's one I'd've never figured," Waneta grudgingly conceded.

"And there's more where that came from. Considerably more. Of that I'm convinced."

"How's it you're so sure?"

"Because as with so many worldly-seeming persons, hers is a mind open to marvels. And that's what we supply. I'm going to do some research on this fine lady, but unless I'm seriously mistaken, we may have stumbled, by happy accident, on our cash cow."

"Sure as hell hope so. Be about time."

Bryce's lips parted in a wizard smile. "Listen to yourself. The virus of hope infects us all. All of us." He grasped the bottle, reached over and filled their glasses, lifted his in toast, and with a long, ironic wink said, "Here's to realized hopes."

A few miles to the south, in a shared (at Junior's frugal, if self-serving, insistence) room in a Lake Worth sleep cheap, the two receivables specialists were, like Bryce and Waneta, unwinding after a day that had been, on balance, relatively successful. Not that it had produced anything in the way of money. But then that wasn't their primary purpose either. Though they thought of and often referred to themselves as collectors, it would be more accurate to call them consultants, or perhaps agents of reckoning, for the nature of their work was such that only rarely did it result in the immediate recovery of tardy debts, and seldom did they handle any actual cash. By the time their services were enlisted, the laggard debtors of Solomon Berkowitz had long since been consigned to a back page of his ledger that went under the heading "Delinquencies," a label that, in this business, carried with it particularly ominous overtones.

"Two outta three ain't a bad day's work" was Junior's satisfied assessment of their efforts, a reference to the would-be stiffers they'd tracked down during the remainder of that day. Neither of those two had a recently deceased mother, worse luck for them. The first, a professional musician, piano plinker, was left with one finger unbroken on each hand and with Junior's parting words of consolation: "You're gettin' off easy. Least you can still pound out a mean 'Chopsticks.'" The second didn't fare so well. A slim, attractive hostess at a fashionable Palm Beach dining spot, she emerged from the consultation with a flattened nose, fractured jaw, some bloodied roots where teeth had had been, and a number of ugly burns on her face, neck, and breasts. Hector reluctantly supplied the lit cigarette, for Junior prudently had given up the habit, though he hadn't forgotten the inventive uses smoking could be put to.

Didn't seem to bother him in the slightest, touching up a woman. In an age of equal opportunity, Junior stoutly maintained, in his words, "Twats entitle' to the same dingin' as a man." Also was it his contention that the penalty should fit the size of the debt. The musician's was under ten thou, so his punishment was commensurately light, more on the order of a nudge. The hostess's obligations were, sadly for her, well into the five-figure range, which accounted for the sterner measures applied in her case.

Hector, he didn't see it that way. It was one thing, after you run out of words, to deliver a final warning underscored with some swatting around or even, when the situation called for it, some selective cutting. Like Mr. B always said, that was only business. But what he had seen today and with the A-rab the other night, that had nothing to do with business. That was plain meanness. Dog-ass meanness. But he wasn't about to argue either. Not with this loco gringo. Not during the crowdings, not now. So all he said in reply to his unwelcome partner's smug assessment was a guarded, "S'pose so."

"Don't sound like you so sure."

"Whaddya mean?"

"That 's'pose' in there."

"OK, it was a primo day. World-class. That float your boat?"

"You jerkin' me off here?"

"Hey, man. I'm stomped is all. Whatever kinda day it been was a long one too."

They were stretched out on twin beds, the remnants of their thrifty dinner, a bucket of extra-crispy KFC, chilling on the nightstand between them. Hector stared at the water-stained ceiling. Junior swigged from a pint of Old Crow, noisily and steadily. "What you need's a squirt a' big bird," he said, extending the bottle in generous offering.

"Lineup a' things I need, that'd be 'bout dead last."

"That's where you're wrong. Little hair a' the pooch that nip ya in the ass tighten you right up. Works for me every time."

"Tha's you."

"Ain't just me. Works for everybody. Even you tostadas. Ask around, you don't believe. Ask a quack."

"You count sauce doctorin' among your many accomplishments?"

"Fuckin'-A. I popped back my share, my time. Woke up with more'n a few balloon heads."

"Yeah, well, tonight I'm gonna give mine a rest," Hector said, hoping maybe Junior would take the hint, give the gum flapping a timeout.

No such luck. "Big mistake, *chico*," Junior warned him.

"If it is," Hector said snappishly, "be me makin' it."

"Take it cool, cholo. What I'm tryin' to do is help you out here."

It was hopeless. Buttlicker wasn't gonna leave him be. And all that *chico*-cholo shit was getting on his nerves. Coming up off the bed, he announced, "What I'm gonna take is a long, hot shower."

"Shower? Now?"

"Yeah. That meet with your OK?"

"It's night. Mornin's when you scrub off. Everybody know that."

"Everybody 'cept me," said Hector, stepping into a john fit for a pygmy, trailed by the taunting question, "That how they do it down ol' Meh-hee-co way?" He didn't dignify it with a reply.

Thirty minutes later he emerged, towel wrapped around his trim middle, skin steamed a rich caramel. Feeling repaired, restored. Like he inhabited his body again. Feeling good.

He stood before the dresser mirror, running a comb through his shampooed and pomaded hair. If Hector had one vanity, it was his hair. Thick as moss, lustrous as freshly laid tar, it reached all the way to his shoulders when he chose to wear it unknotted in the back, as now. He stuck his head in close to the glass, tilting it left and right, the better to conduct the loving examination.

Which Junior had been watching critically and which prompted the sour remark, "Fuck don't you get yourself a haircut? Look like some goddamn jailhouse lady."

"Them as has it grows it," Hector retorted in caustic swipe at Junior's lank, mouse-colored, rapidly departing locks, twilighting as they were at the temples and laced over a bald spot as ragged as a crater at the crown.

"Least I don't part mine with a grease gun," he shot back. "No wonder they call you people greasers."

Hector figured he'd had just about enough. What he oughta do is take his blade and spill some gringo guts. Except it wasn't on his ankle now; it was back there in the shitter with the rest of his clothes. Or he could jump him, pound some respect into that cast-iron redneck skull. Except that wouldn't do either, seeing as how he'd for sure be the one to take the pounding off a biffer like that. So what he did was turn and give him a challenging stare, saying coldly, "How come you all'a time raggin' on me, man?"

"Just funnin' ya, *chico*. You ain't got nothin' bad to say about somebody, don't say nothin' at all. That's my motto." He flashed a big smirky grin, as though he'd just authored a most hilarious joke.

"Funnin's one thing," said an unamused Hector. "Dissin's another."

"Nobody dissin' you, Soosie. Long as we partnerin' here, we slidin' down the same pole."

"Tha's not how I'm hearin' it. Whole lot a Brotherhood ball bustin' is what I'm hearin'. What you vanilla milkshakes got against us Latinos anyway?"

"Got nothin' against you," Junior said mildly. "Nothin' personal anyhow. You're the oilers. We're the Aryans. That's just how it is."

"So how about we leave it there, OK? Don't need you to tell me the difference."

"That's cool. Like I say, ain't nothin' personal. Matter a' fact, one a' my better sidekicks back in the joint was a homey. Name a' Ramon. Standup spic. He was a pistol, Ramon. Doin' second degree, same as me. Only how he bought his bid you ain't never gonna believe."

"Jesus," Hector groaned. "Not another story."

"This one you'll like. Got one a' them—whaddya call it?—morals to it."

"I want moral, I'll see a priest."

"Ain't that kind. More like, y'know, inspirin'. Give ya hope."

"Either way, bet I'm gonna hear it," Hector said resignedly, sinking into a chair and wondering what had become of the verbal showdown, where it had gotten lost.

Junior launched into his tale. "See, before he took his fall, Ramon was a regular citizen, family man, never had no beefs with the heat. Clean jacket. One day him and the wife and kid was in a mall someplace. Was right around Christmas, and they was takin' the little chili pepper to see Santa, tell him what he wants for presents. Line stretched way the fuckin' gone, so they waitin' in it when word comes down Santa's splittin' five bells sharp, taking his elfs with him. Oh, yeah, forgot to tell ya, they got these midgets decked out in elf duds, passin' out your Christmas goodies to the squirrels."

"So what they got to do with anything, them elfs?"

"Got everything to do with the point a' what I'm tryin' to get across here."

"You wanna get to it, then, that point?"

"I will soon's you quit cuttin' in on me."

Hector spun his eyes, and the story resumed.

"OK, Ramon and the senora, they starts gettin' antsy. Also workin' up a slow burn. Been a long time coolin' their heels for Santa, and baby Ramon, he's by God gonna sit on that fat lap and speak his piece or it's '*Ay, caramba!*' time tonight. You got the picture?"

"Clear as glass. Only thing is I can't see nothin' the other side."

"It's comin'. Ramon looks at his watch, looks at the line, figures they gonna make it easy. So he holds down that south-a'-the border temper his 'til he gets the little pepper two crumb snatchers shy a' Santa. Everything lookin' to be copacetic, right? Wrong! Know what happens?"

"Fuckin' suspense killin' me."

"What happens is Santa starts packin' up his gear. Ramon checks his Timex, says five to five. 'Hold the fuck up,' he says but all's he's talkin' at is Santa's blubber butt waddlin' down the hall. He collars an elf, tells him, 'You can't leave yet. Ain't five. There's kids here.' Elf wiggles away, flips him the bird. Ramon goes wacko, chases the elf into a Radio Shack, and brains him with a boom box. Take the whole goddamn mall security to pull him off, and when they do, elf's wearin' a toe tag. And that's how Ramon got his ticket to Jacktown."

Junior took a gurgly chug of Old Crow, set the bottle aside, and clasped his hands behind his neck, evidently signaling tale's end.

Hector looked at him blankly. "Yeah, so?"

"What?"

"Tha's it?"

"That's it. Some story, huh?"

"Seem to remember you sayin' somethin' about a moral in there."

"You don't get it?"

"'Fraid not."

"I dunno 'bout you, *chico*." Junior sighed. And then, like a wise mentor interpreting the message of his uplifting fable, he said patiently, "Christmas come anyway that year. So he waxed the elf. So what? That don't prove there ain't a Santa."

"So what *does* it prove?"

"Ramon got his second degree, didn't he? Prolly back on the street by now. Proves there's hope for everybody, this gnarly world. Even you bean dips."

TEN

IT WAS JIM MERRIMAN'S EVIL LUCK THAT, AT THE moment of surfacing from a troubled sleep, his head was instantly flooded with all the distressing thoughts, doubts, and fears he wanted least to entertain. So he lay there for a time, eyes clamped shut against the gradually lifting dark, while behind them a troop of dreads assembled and passed in review. The shred of hope that had briefly animated him the night before seemed, in the advancing light of morning, crumbly and wafer thin and not at all sustaining.

But then an axiom from his gaming days (that other life of his that appeared now, in contrast, orderly and serene) came back to him: You play the cards dealt to you, however lame they may be. And in this present game, the Caddie was the nearest to a spot card in his hand, so there was nothing to do but see how it played, what it could produce. He rolled out of the lumpy bed, got himself shaved and showered and swanked out in his best—and only—linen suit. Ready to ante up, rough it up. Like in the old days, swaggering up to a table with only the skimpiest of banks but centered all the same, focused, energized by risk and sunny visions of reward. In a perverse way, it was almost exhilarating, like a trinket of a memory salvaged from the wreckage of that abandoned other life. 'Til he was struck with the sobering thought that by no stretch could this be likened to a game. Too much at peril here, too much to lose.

From the Yellow Pages, he compiled a list of all the dealers advertising an interest in antique and classic cars. Bunch of them in the immediate vicinity, which was a break; it narrowed the geography of the search. He considered rousing Leon (who'd been slumbering peacefully on his side of the shoebox of a room), bringing him along, but soon rejected that idea. By the kid's own admission, he knew nothing about the value of these relics, and the last thing Jim needed today was a nonstop babble in his ear. Better to let him sleep. Better for both of them. He scribbled a note of stern and cryptic warning: Stay in the room, keep down, speak to no one, wait for his return. Then he slipped quietly out the door and was gone.

First stop was a Riviera Beach auto laundry where he got the deluxe special: wash, wax, polishing, interior vacuuming, the works. Caddie emerged like a glittery jewel, and the grunt toweling it off drawled, a little ambiguously, "Quite a boat ya got here. Don't see many a' them no more."

"It's a classic," Jim said, choosing to interpret the remark as compliment, and he toked him a buck, for luck, and sped away.

It was not yet 9:00 a.m. Wouldn't do to be the first one in the door. Just as with cards, you never wanted to look too eager, telegraph your hand. So he pulled into an eatery on Highway 1 and sucked up an hour's worth of coffee and cigarettes, rehearsing opening lines in his head and scripting possible scenarios, each with its quota of snares and pitfalls but all with happy endings. Might as well think positive, and the caffeine-nicotine jolt helped steer him in that direction.

He paid the bill, left the slinger a generous tip (for some more of that luck), pointed his ace in the hole south to West Palm, and punctually at ten, sauntered into the showroom of the first dealership on his list.

Leon, at that same moment, was drifting up out of a sleep battered by fearsome dreams and nowhere near as tranquil as it had appeared to his uncle. It took him a while to get past that bewildering sensation that comes of waking in a strange place, but when he did, he discovered that, for him, wakefulness was no better than sleep. Reality was more terrifying than dreams. For the other bed was empty, the room silent, his last lifeline surely gone.

A bolt of panic surged through him. He stumbled over to the window, peered around the drawn drape. No car. No uncle. No hope. He felt like a castaway swamped in a vast, stormy sea. He paced the floor frantically, numb with misery and foreboding. Sluggers, bone busters, head crackers—that's what Uncle Jim had called them, and they were coming for him. And sooner or later, they were bound to find him.

If only Mom were here. Mom you could always depend on. She always knew what to do. No more Mom either. No help anywhere.

Except there was still that money she'd left him. That ought to count for something. Buy him some goodwill. Some time. He rummaged through his bag, found the bank CD and her checkbook. Both had his name on them now, one of the last things Mom had arranged before they took her off to the hospital. Always looking ahead, she was, planning for the worst.

Which was what he was going to have to learn to do himself, now that he was alone in the world. He threw on some clothes and set out on foot for Ocean Boulevard and the Riviera Bridge. It was a long hike under a blistering sun, and it did nothing to soften the bitterness hardening his heart against this latest in the parade of deserters in his life, a treacherous uncle who had absconded with the Caddie and fled for his life.

Of course had Leon bothered to glance at the nightstand, he would have discovered a message that might have restored his sense of charity, canceled this desperate errand, and perhaps altered the course of his life, not to mention his uncle's. But he hadn't, so he trudged purposefully on.

Three hours and six dealers later, all Jim's swagger was gone, and with it all the ersatz exhilaration he'd felt, or thought he'd felt, at the outset of this venture. So much for positive thinking. Called to mind a cautionary graffito he'd seen somewhere, forgot where, Vegas most likely, that went, "They told him it couldn't be done, so he tackled it with a smile—and he couldn't do it."

That's how he'd approached these sleazeballs, sporting the easy smile of the comfortable man of means who'd dropped by on a whim, maybe or maybe not interested in unloading this prized toy of his. It was a persona that fit him about as well as a Salvation Army suit of clothes, and by the time the verbal waltz cut to the hard-numbers chase, he was spanked, and he knew it. Operating off the reasonable assumption that you come in high, leave yourself some wiggle room, Jim allowed he might be willing to part with the Caddie for, oh, say, 20K, an offer consistently met with a look of pity and countered, if at all, with something closer to a quarter of that figure. They must have read the desperation in his eyes. No chumping your vehicle hustlers; they were the masters of the double shuffle. Any jobbing got done, they were the ones to do it. Dealer number three, after tapping out a prolonged symphony on his calculator, reluctantly consented to "take it off your hands for seven thou."

"I was born at night," Jim scoffed, stalking away, "but not last night."

Only now he wasn't scoffing anymore. The seven long looked to be top dollar, a stick-in-the-eye steal but better than what he had, which was zip. Better maybe to go back there hat in hand, before the shit heel changed his mind.

Except there was one place left on his list, an outfit up in North Palm that went under the name Arlo's Antique Auto Appraisals. Jim remembered a directory display ad featuring a photo of a kindly-looking coot, Arlo presumably, flashing a brace of tombstone teeth, and with the initial letters of the alliterative name done up in bold red, like a hand of killer aces. Maybe it was an omen. He'd try Arlo.

Unlike your machine-stamped brick-and-glass dealerships, Arlo's was a grubby pole barn flanked by an acre or so of ancient heaps in assorted states of disrepair, more on the order of an auto graveyard with a few of the corpses patiently awaiting resurrection. And unlike his photo, the proprietor himself was a solemn, taciturn, work-weathered man in grease-smeared coveralls (welcome change from all those hustlers in their cut-rate suits) who plainly took his vehicles seriously. While Jim looked on, silently offering up a prayer to any deity listening, Arlo subjected the Caddie to a thorough inspection, concluding finally, "Body needs some work, good lump under the hood. Whoever done the rebuildin' knows his business."

Score one for Leon. "He's an expert," Jim affirmed, assuming "lump" referred to the engine. Gearheads spoke a tongue of their own.

"What're you askin'?"

That was a language he understood. "Fifteen," he said after a small hesitation, his expectations humbled by the experiences of the day.

"Little high. I could go thirteen, but that'd be it."

"I'll take it," said Jim jubilantly, all pretense of shrewd negotiator abandoned. Thirteen was close. Thirteen might just turn the corner for them.

A deal was struck and sealed by a handshake. Jim agreed to bring in the car and the necessary papers first thing in the morning; Arlo would have the money waiting. In cash. No questions asked, no explanations offered, no contracts required. And driving away, Jim had to wonder if his decision to give up the gaming life hadn't been a little hasty or at least premature. After all, the same hand of Fortune that guides you safely through a hail of bullets also deals the cards, a thought that took some effort to force from his head.

Coincidentally somewhat similar ruminations on the vagaries of fate were dominating Leon's thoughts just then, though in his case those musings mostly took the form of an intense self-pity, a *Why me, O Lord?* lament. Because he could think of nowhere else to go, he'd returned to the Singer Island motel room; and even though his pockets bulged with banded wads of bills, more money than he'd ever seen (never mind handled), he still hadn't the foggiest idea what to do next. Also was he overtaken by both hunger and fatigue, so to ease these immediate discomforts, he plopped onto the unmade bed, propped a pillow behind his back, and nibbled at the cold Tuna Helper casserole supplied by Mrs. Gath. Since no utensils were available, he was obliged to eat with his fingers, yet another in the mounting catalog of distresses.

But with two of them more or less alleviated, his attention narrowed in again on that most urgent issue of all—where to go. Sioux Falls was the only other place he was remotely familiar with, but they'd left seven years ago, he and Mom, and hadn't been back but a couple times since. No family or friends there anymore. Scratch Sioux Falls. He could try his luck in Las Vegas, become a professional gambler like Uncle Jim was, or claimed he was, or used to be, whatever (probably lying about that too, Leon thought sourly, same way he lied about sticking around to help). Except he'd never been in a casino in his life, wasn't really all that good at card games, and seeing it was betting got him into this glue, that was probably the first place they'd come looking for him. No, Vegas was out.

Maybe he could head north, the Yukon, get himself a wilderness cabin and be a trapper. Only he didn't know anything about trapping, and he didn't much care for the cold. South maybe—Brazil, say—go up the Amazon and be a big game hunter like you saw on the TV. Unless that was Africa. Anyway, he'd never once held a gun in his hands (Mom didn't approve of them), and with his feeble vision, he'd probably shoot himself in the foot. Or get captured by a tribe of headhunters, end up cannibal stew.

Finally he had to conclude, however dismally, there was nowhere to go, no place to hide, and no way to escape the grim fate closing in on him fast. To take his mind off it he switched on the television; and as that capricious fate would have it, there appeared on the screen one of those infomericals plugging the amazing results of those persons open-minded enough to avail themselves of the services of something called a Psychic Hotline; which gushy testimonials sparked in Leon the memory of something he'd come across in the mail just last night, something about the possibility of communicating with the dead; which notion in turn revived a yearning ache to consult once more with Mom, get her wise advice on this terrible dilemma, and which prompted him to hop off the bed, dig through his bag, find the mail, find the flyer in question, re-read it with care and with a churning, feverish sensation he identified as nothing other than hope and, when he was finished, to dial the number cited at the bottom of the sheet.

Jim had succeeded in erasing all those idle, valueless speculations from his head, replacing them with a pragmatic tally whose numbers buoyed his spirits and went a long way toward quieting the worst of his fears. Numbers could have that effect on him, particularly when they added up right, and these did, or almost did. Put his sister's twenty-eight thou together with the thirteen, tack on whatever he could sling in the pot from his Reno account, and they were as good as home free. Well, maybe, depending on how much was actually in that account. Because he had the numbers juggler's passion for precision (matters like this, you'd better be precise) and because he had to arrange to tap that fund anyway, put the whole bundle together, he swung over to Northlake and pulled in at the first bank he saw.

The news there was good, too. So good, in fact, he had to restrain an impulse to release a joyous whoop, give the prim banker lady a spirited high-five. Turned out he had thirty-seven hundred and change in the account; and yes, they'd be happy (for a fee) to help him close it out, wire the money down here, and make it available by noon tomorrow. How he'd come by that much, Jim couldn't say. Prudence, was it? The mousey caution of middle age? A dawning awareness of the years slipping away with nothing to show for the slippage? Didn't seem likely. Didn't matter. It was enough to bring them three bills shy of the magic 45K, and if between them they couldn't put that puny amount together, then they'd by God hock their clothes if they had to, go home in a barrel. Whatever it took.

He thanked the kind lady and left the bank with a widening smile. Now all they had to do was stay down for twenty-four hours, collect the loot, lay it off, and duck out gracefully. Beyond that he didn't care to think. All those other nagging issues—the accelerating interest on the debt, the accumulating medical and "cleanup" (in the elegant argot of undertakers) bills, the generally precarious future of a dipstick nephew—his censors mercifully veiled. For the moment.

One of them, however, chanced to penetrate that flimsy curtain in the familiar shape of a funeral chapel located directly across the street, same one that had torched the remains of his sister. Also for a fee. Also unpaid. Fuck 'em, let them wait their turn in line. He nosed his 13K worth of Caddie into the stream of traffic, but as he pulled away, it occurred to him that as long as he was in the neighborhood anyway, he might as well drop by, concoct a tale of good intentions throttled by frozen assets, legal wrangles, probate gridlock—all that smoke you use to stall. Stalling he was experienced at, stalling he knew how to do. But it never hurt to keep in practice.

He turned at the next intersection, drove back, and parked alongside a sleek black Jaguar in the chapel lot. And coming through the door into a lobby resonant with lugubrious music oozing from concealed speakers like some cloying aural perfume, Jim caught a trace of an authentic scent, fragrant but subdued, and he heard a silky voice murmur, "So, Mr. Merriman, we meet again," the easy greeting of which inclined him to believe that perhaps he led a charmed life after all. For there, sitting quietly in a corner, hands demurely folded in her lap, legs fetchingly crossed, was a smiling Billie Swett, and she was smiling at him.

Leon was also the grateful recipient of an assortment of smiles that afternoon. The first was a warm, welcoming one from a paunchy guy in a black suit, who said his name was Bott, Reverend Bryce Bott. Gradually it folded into an expression of kindly pity as Leon told him about Mom and a little about why he desperately needed to talk to her again. Then there was sometimes a trace of one—more pained twitch than smile—on the pale lips of that poor dying lady while she searched the rolls of the dead 'til she located Mom, carried Leon's message over to her, and brought back a faint reply. And last of all, when Leon peeled ten bills off a fat roll and dropped them in the plate on the counter, a watery, faraway smile crossed the reverend's baggy face as he explained how Miss Waneta tired quickly, but now that she'd connected with Mom, they could expect next time some conclusive answers to his urgent plea for help. That next time could be as early as tomorrow, but only (and here the smile took on a stiffly pious cast) if Leon were persuaded of the gravity of their mission, its noble sanctity.

He was. Or said he was, since he hadn't the slightest idea what the guy was running on about, something about parallel realities and colors outside our fields of vision and voices beyond the range of ordinary ears. All Leon knew for sure was Mom was trying to reach him through that Waneta lady's voice—faint, whispery, and anything but ordinary—and if he came back tomorrow, she'd find him a way out of this dog-flop scrape he'd gotten himself into. She might be pissed with him, but she'd know the way.

"Tomorrow then," said Reverend Bott, ushering him out into the dazzling light of day.

And that's about how Leon felt, dazzled by the mystery of everything he'd just experienced and heartened by the promise of a deliverance soon to come. The Surf and Shore was only a few blocks south of the motel he and Jim had checked into last night, but he had no desire to return to that silent, stuffy room. Not yet. So instead he walked to the Ocean Mall and took a table in the same tavern where only yesterday a traitorous uncle had pledged to stand by him. Yesterday. Might as well be a thousand years ago; so much had happened between then and now.

Leon showered his dry mouth with cold beer. A swarm of images buzzed behind his eyes, some lifted from the day's eventful blur, others wholly imagined visions of himself embarking on a voyage to a new and different and secure place (for hadn't Mom, speaking through Miss Waneta, assured him he was soon to take a trip, its destination not yet clear, tomorrow maybe?). But persistent among those fanciful visions was another, not quite so agreeable: Uncle Jim in a fury on discovering how much money he had spent today and probably would again tomorrow. *Fuck him*, was Leon's bitter thought. Was his money—he'd do with it whatever he pleased. If he wanted to donate a couple thousand to those good people willing to help him out when nobody else would and who had trouble enough of their own—worst kind of trouble, death kind—well, then that was his business. Way he looked at it, wasn't so much a donation as an investment in his future. Sound one too, once Mom came through.

So Leon let him storm there, Uncle Jim, off in a corner of his eye. Served him right. By scooting out the way he did, he'd forfeited any claim on that rosy future.

They were standing, at Jim's invitation, outside the chapel's entrance, nicotine conspirators puffing cigarettes and picking up remembered threads of a conversation abbreviated but, to his recollection, full of promising undertones. "So what brings you to this house of darkness?" he began casually, his own errand there forgotten in the tingle of anticipation.

"I'm here with my girlfriend."

Jim, seeing no one, made an exaggerated visual sweep of the grounds.

"She's inside," Billie explained. "Taking care of bills. See, her mother passed over last week. Services were yesterday."

"There's a coincidence. We buried my sister yesterday too. Scattered her actually."

"Sorry to hear that. And these same funeral people did the arrangements?"

"The very same."

"That *is* a coincidence."

"Maybe it's fate," he said with mock solemnity.

"Fate? Why's that?"

"Well, after our little chat, I looked all over the hospital for you the next few days. Scoured the premises. No luck. After a while I gave up, figured it for another of those ships-in-the-night things. Yet here we are."

"And you think that's fate?"

"What else?" he said, turning over helpless palms as if to display destiny's incontrovertible evidence.

Billie looked at him curiously and with just a flicker of that impish coquettery he'd detected once before in those cool blue eyes. Just enough for him to catch. "If it is," she said, "and I'm not saying it is—but if it is, what do you suppose it means, Mr. Merriman?"

"You could call me 'Jim.'"

"Same question, Jim."

A history of easy flirtations and casual seductions had taught him to step nimbly, make haste with delicate deliberation. "Maybe nothing," he said, all practiced easy charm and lightness. "Or, on the other hand, maybe it means a couple of Dakotans like ourselves were intended to know each other better."

"Which one do you think it is?"

"My money's on the second one. If you'd consider joining me for a drink, we could find out for sure."

"A drink? Now?"

"No better time."

"I'd like to," she said, adding quickly and before he could respond, "except I can't."

"Any particular reason?" he asked, unwilling to plead but not yet ready to let it go either.

"Couple of them. For one thing I've got Courtney—she's that friend I mentioned—with me."

"Bring her along. We can all be friends."

"There's another problem. Bigger one. You may remember I'm married."

"So? Married folks make new friends too, I'm told."

"Not this marriage," she said ruefully.

It was a clear opening, and since he had nothing at stake here, nothing really to lose, he gave it a beat then drawled, "The big doolie wouldn't approve?"

"Who?"

"The doolie. That's what you called your husband, remember? That and your worse half. Your words, not mine." To them he could have added "asshole" but thought better of it.

"I said that?"

"That's how I heard it."

"Oh. Well, probably we'd had a little, uh, disagreement that day. You know how that goes."

"Matter of fact I don't. Never been married."

She looked dubious. "Never?"

"Never."

"That's a switch."

"Why do you say that?"

"Because most of the men coming on to me," she said, watching him steadily, "which is what we both know you're doing here, Mr. Jim Merriman—most of them got a wife waiting in the wings."

"But not me. No wife anyway. You see, already we're learning things about each other. Sure you won't reconsider that drink?"

"I wish I could..." she said, faintest of murmurs, as if she were speaking less to him than herself, the wish trailing away.

"But you can't," he finished for her.

"No."

"Another time?"

She had smoked her Luxury Length Capri down to the tiniest of stubs, but she brought what was left of it to her lips and managed a final drag, prolonging the moment. "I don't think so," she said, and in her voice, there was an unmistakable regret.

Jim generated a smile, gave a good-sport shrug. "Well, you have yourself a good life, Billie Swett."

"You too, Jim Merriman."

Some of them always get away, he reminded himself, driving in the direction of Singer Island. *Some you're bound to lose.* Another of those hard lessons experience taught. Was crazy anyway, chasing your dick when the sky was falling and critical business remained unfinished. Was doubtless for the best.

Except there was something about this one that sharpened the melancholy of the loss. Innocence you couldn't call it. Certainly not artlessness. Nothing artless about Billie Swett. But behind all that moneyed, worldly flash were the lingering traces of the Dakota girl, the heartland waif with the giveaway width of eye open to all the wonder of life's abundant mysteries and its infinite scope of possibilities. Easy for him to spot. He carried the same burden himself, same taint. Some things even experience couldn't rid you of.

So Jim came through the door of the motel room weighted with emotions vague and conflicting, all of which evaporated instantly when he discovered the room empty, Leon surely gone.

"Fuck you been?" Jim demanded furiously when, two hours later, a decidedly swacked nephew wobbled through that same door and stood blinking him into focus with the startled expression of an amiable if slightly fuddled sheep, at last bleating joyously, "Uncle Jim! You came back!"

"I'm asking where you been, Leon."

Some dim signal, more instinct than thought, penetrated the kid's beer-sloshed head and warned him now was maybe not the best time to bring up that Mom business (particularly the donation part of it), so to salvage something, he said defensively, "Well, when I figured you took off on me, I—"

"Took off on you!" Jim burst in on him. "Who the fuck took off? Didn't you read my note?"

"Which note's that?"

"The one I left you. Right there on the nightstand. Told you to stay down. Go nowhere. Wait for me to get back."

Leon lifted a corner of his mouth, half a guilty grin. "Musta missed that one."

"So you naturally assumed I'd booked."

"You wasn't here when I woke up. Car was gone. Kinda looked that way."

"So where'd you go?"

"Well, first I walked over to Riviera Beach. Branch of Mom's bank's over there. I'm almost busted, so I got some money."

"Some? How much is 'some'?"

Leon studied the patterns in the mustard-colored carpet at his feet. "All of it," he said finally.

"All? The CD and the checking account, you emptied them both?"

"Figured I was gonna need it, Uncle Jim, thinkin' you were gone and those guys comin' after me, like you said. Didn't know what else to do."

"Then where?"

"Huh?"

"You said the bank *first.* Where after that?"

"Oh, lemme see. Come back here a while and tried to think up a plan, but nothin' come to me. Was gettin', y'know, pretty nervous, so I went over to the mall there and had a couple brews," he said, omitting any mention of the Surf and Shore stop along the way. Be plenty time to talk about that later, was his thought, when he got his head screwed on straight again.

"A couple?"

"Might've been more."

"And all this time you're carrying the cash."

"Well, yeah. Safer'n leavin' it here."

Jim sank onto a chair, laid his brow in the palm of a hand. "Jesus," was all he could think to say.

Leon, correctly sensing that words were only digging this pit he was in deeper than it already was, offered no reply.

A tight silence opened between them and hung there 'til it was abruptly shattered by a heavy hammering at the door.

ELEVEN

JUNIOR AND HECTOR GOT OFF TO A BRISK START that Monday morning, and by the middle of the afternoon, they had successfully completed three more of their business calls, one in Lake Worth, the other two over in Greenacres City. The next names on the list would take them down to Lantana and points south, but Junior, always an orderly man, figured he'd cut this Cody boy enough mourning slack, so they backtracked to Palm Beach Gardens, tried the apartment again, and came up zip. Again.

Very annoying.

In addition to a methodical turn of mind, Junior also possessed a stubborn streak. Remembering the helpful little old lady from across the hall, he assembled as much of a deferential face as he could muster under these vexing circumstances, tapped gently on her door, and when she appeared, explained the problem and had a friendly chat with her. She was plainly flattered to be in on the action and generously volunteered everything she'd seen and heard over the past twenty-four hours, which wasn't much but just enough to encourage them in the search.

Junior anyway. Hector, he wasn't so persuaded. It was his thought they bag it for now, catch up to the stiffer on their way back. And if they lost one, so what? Nobody wins them all. Even Mr. B said they had to learn to calm their expectations, direct their energies, balance effort against reward. Shrewd fella, Mr. B.

Only Junior wasn't having any of it. By now it had become a matter of professional pride. Grief was one thing, coming to the window another. You buy the ticket, you take the ride. That's how it worked, this business. Even if it was your mom who croaked on you.

Required a shitload of phone calls—damn near every motel this corner of the Treasure Coast—the two of them standing at adjacent phones outside a gas station, pecking out numbers under a blistering sun, Hector grumbling how the tip of his index finger was going numb on him ("Be glad it ain't Mr. Stink," Junior advised him. "Keep dialin'."), but eventually their persistence was rewarded. Eventually they bingoed.

And so it was that by the time they arrived at the door of a seedy Singer Island lodging, Junior was feeling nowhere near so charitable toward this suckwad looking to slip him the dodge—*him*, Junior Biggs, your top-gun stalker whole state of Florida, bar no one. He was in fact seriously pissed, kick-ass pumped. Had nothing to do with the Miami Jew boy who paid the rent, everything to do with Junior's sense of who he was, his anointed station in this world. So when that door swung back (for on the other side Leon, standing nearest it, mistook his uncle's flagging arm for the go-ahead signal and, with the inebriate's reckless incaution, opened it wide), the first thing Junior did was lay a flat hand in the punker's face and send him reeling across the room. Next he planted himself in the entry, motioned his greaseball partner to get the door, raked the pair of peckerheads, one young, one not so young, with a venomous squint and demanded, "OK, which one of you's Leon Cody?"

The kid, skinny little wimp standing with his spine nailed to the wall, raised a quivery hand like a schoolboy answering roll call. Behind the goggle glasses, his eyes swam in a stricken daze, and on his face was a goofy, pointless grin. See who'd be doing the grinning once Junior Biggs was done with him.

But now that Junior had them boxed, some of his irritation was fading, and he was starting to feel good again, part charged, part mellow, all cool, like a showman who knows his act so well he could do it catching Zs. You got the natural rhythm, you do the dance. Another of those axioms to live by. To the other one, he said, pitching it in a tone of affable curiosity, "And who'd you be?"

"I'm his uncle," the guy said, flat and neutral, like he was maybe looking for the high ground. Lotsa luck.

"Uncle," Junior repeated thoughtfully. "That's good, families stickin' together. Comes trouble time, who ya gonna count on, it ain't family?"

Neither of them had any opinion on that, so Junior said, "Wouldn't be your name's Jim Merriman? Am I right, Uncle?"

That got his attention. Face went from stunned to baffled to bummed, like it just was coming to him how they'd gotten tracked.

"Yeah," Junior confirmed, "was your nice neighbor lady there filled us in. You want a word a' advice, Uncle? Free for nothin'?"

"Odds are I'm going to get it."

Little too sass ass for Junior's tastes. Oh, yeah, he was thinking, *You're gonna get it all right, Uncle Wisefuck, slingin' attitude when you oughta be stainin' your Jockeys. Gonna be a real pleasure, thumpin' this melon.* All in good time. Foreplay first. So he said patiently, "Next time you lookin' to help your relation here, duckin' out on his financial obligations, don't go checkin' into motels under your own name. 'Specially when you been spillin' it out, every sweet old lady asks."

Wisefuck there, he came right back with, "Appreciate the good advice, but I already had that one figured out. Nobody's ducking on you. You see anybody ducking? We've got your money."

"That a fact?"

"True fact."

"Hear that, *chico*? Uncle says they ready to step up. Must be these boys got one a' them magic wands pulls bills outta the hat 'stead a' rabbits."

"Maybe we oughta—" Hector started to say, but Junior quieted him with a curt gesture, and to the uncle, he said, "So you just hangin' out, hopin' we'd stop by so's you could fork over the loot. That it?"

"Something like that," said Uncle Cool.

Junior allowed a smile, slow and indulgent, into his face. "OK, whyn't you show us your magic act?"

The uncle elbowed the kid, who gave a startled lurch, like he was coming up out of a deep snooze, but then goddamn if he didn't produce from out his pockets, all of them, fore and aft, wad after wad of banded bills. Junior gaped at them, wonder-struck. More green there than he'd ever seen turned up, any collection he'd ever been on. Make that more than he had seen in a good long while. A crafty notion, too murky yet to be called a scheme, too ragged at the edges, stirred in a back corner of his head. All that green. Then, remembering himself, he snapped at the kid, "Lay it on the bed."

Kid done like he was told.

"*Chico*, you total it up."

Hector, banjo eyed himself at the sight of all that sugar, hurried over and plopped on the bed and started flipping bills.

"I can spare him the trouble," the uncle said. "What you'll find is twenty-eight large there."

"Actually—" the kid tried to say, but the uncle there cut him off with a hard look.

Junior's smile, which never really had departed, had in fact and against his will widened, shifted abruptly to a dangerous scowl. "Figure we talkin' here is forty-five. Not includin' juice."

"You'll have the balance by noon tomorrow."

"Oh, now it's tomorrow, is it? Hear that, *chico*? Man say he gonna kick in the balance tomorrow."

Hector was too occupied with his tally to comment.

"It's hard money," the uncle said. "I've got a buyer for that Caddie you saw out front. Rest is being wired to a bank."

"No shit. That's real enterprisin'. Only pro'lum is, you hear that tune all'a time, our line a' work. Never does play right."

"This one will."

"You make it sound like a gimme, Uncle."

"That's what it is. Come along tomorrow, and see for yourself. Collect on the spot."

Junior released a derisive snort that passed for a laugh. Like he was gonna buy into that poot. Nobody ran a game on your Junior Biggs. But he took a moment to ponder it anyway. No getting around the fact they were already sitting on top of a handsome take, incontestable evidence lying all over the bed there. And there was just enough bet-the-farm swagger in this slicker's voice to make you wonder if it wasn't the straight goods he was peddling. Also, and most persuasive, was the notion gradually enlarging in Junior's head, taking on the unmistakable shape of a plan. Finally he said, "Hey, that's mighty white a' you, Uncle, invitin' us to tag along that way. Whadda you think, *chico*?"

Hector put down the last band of bills, glanced up at him, and said, "I count twenty-seven."

Uncle's jaw fell. "Twenty-seven!" That's not right. You made a mistake."

"Comes to money," Hector drawled, "I don't make mistakes."

"Count it again. You're a dime off."

"You the one off. There's twenty-seven thou here."

Now he was looking snakebit, Uncle was. Seriously shaken. And not so cool anymore either. So Junior stepped over to him and poked his face in close and asked, kind of sad-like, like he was really let down, "See? How we gonna trust you, you can't even get your arithmetic right?"

He got no answer to that, so Junior went on, "Look to me like you tryin' to lipstick our lollyholes here. How 'bout you, *chico*?"

"Lookin' that way," Hector agreed.

Was a struggle for him, but Uncle found the voice to say, "Look, you'll have your money tomorrow. By noon."

"All of it?" Junior asked.

"All."

"Missin' dime too?"

"That too."

"You promise?"

"Yes."

"Hand to God?"

"Yes."

"Let's see it then. You too, boy."

Both of them put pledge hands in the air.

"Say you promise."

They said it.

Junior balled a fist and drove it into the uncle's middle, an inch or so beneath the belt. Then he did the same to the kid. They expelled consecutive gasps, dropped to their knees. Looked like a couple of choirboys there, kneeling, heads bowed, trying to spit out prayers. They'd better pray. "Tell ya what," Junior said, "I'm feelin' extra generous today. Dunno why. Must be it's you boys promisin' like that. Kinda gives you back your faith in your fellow man. So what I'm gonna give you is 'til tomorrow, noon sharp, come up with the rest a' that feed. 'Course, you thinkin' to bolt, hang noodles in our ears, you wanna get that thought right outta your head. You hearin' me, Uncle?"

He lifted smeary eyes and in a hoarse whisper said, "I hear."

Junior put a cupping hand to an ear. "Say what?"

"Hear."

"That's good, you hearin'. 'Cuz ain't no place to run we can't find you. And you ain't never gonna know where the next hurt's comin' from. Or when. Look over your shoulder, we'll be there. You follow?"

"Follow."

"OK, you boys enjoy the rest a' your evening. Be talkin' to ya."

He motioned at Hector, and they gathered the money and started for the door. But as if another thought had just occurred to him, Junior paused, turned, fashioned a gun out of a hand, sighted down its forefinger barrel, squeezed off a silent round with a slow depression of the thumb trigger, and delivered a parting line he'd always been partial to: "Meantime I wouldn't go buyin' no green bananas, I was you."

Out in the van, Junior fitted the key in the ignition but didn't turn it. Instead he stuck a plug of tobacco in his mouth and worked his jaws around it vigorously. For a while he didn't speak. Nor did Hector, who puffed thoughtfully on a cigarette. Some of the day's torrid, muggy heat was lifting, and the sky, still a livid pink off in the west, steadily blackened over the ocean. At last Junior said, "You thinkin' what I'm thinkin', *chico*?"

"Depends," said Hector guardedly.

"On what?"

"On what you thinkin'."

"You wanna hear it?"

"No reason not," Hector said, even though he could think of a number of them.

"Lemme ask you somethin'. In your wide experience, this employment, you ever know a stiffer to come up with this kinda cush?"

"Nope. Never."

"Ever come this close?"

"Not even. Had one once come across with a couple thou, but that was against a twenty-long marker, so I still hadda talk some smack at him."

"That two thou, what'd you do with it?"

"Turn it over to Mr. B like you do. Why?"

"S'posin' we was to skip that last part this time out."

Hector looked at him warily. "What're you s'posin' here?"

Junior rolled down his window and ejected a miniature galaxy of blackened spittle, sent it spinning through a shrunken cosmos to splatter ingloriously on the parking-lot tar. With the back of a hand, he swiped its moist residue off his lips and said, "Well, s'posin' them two jag-offs was to produce the rest a' that gelt tomorrow."

"Ah, no way. They shuckin' us, man."

"Maybe, maybe not. That twenty-seven large ain't no shuck."

"You sayin' you think they'll come through with the rest?"

"Ain't likely. But for the sake a' s'posin', let's say they do."

"OK, they do…then what?"

"Then we'd have a fat roll ridin' our hip. Both of us."

"Yeah, and all of it belongin' to Mr. B."

"But what if the jag-offs was to, y'know, evaporate, like. Answer me that, long as we s'posin' here."

"How you mean, evaporate?"

"Oh, like end up facedown out in the Glades someplace. Crocodile bait."

"That's alligators," Hector corrected him.

"Huh?"

"Crocodiles over in Africa. In Florida we got alligators."

Junior spat, sighed. Getting through to a spic, it wasn't easy. "Crocodiles, alligators—either one, they'd be outta the picture, right? Off the map?"

Very slowly, very carefully, Hector said, "Lemme see if I got this straight. You talkin' a smokin' here?"

Junior shrugged helplessly, like a victim of forces outside of his power to control. "Been known to happen," he said with a crimp of a smile.

"I dunno. Mr. B ain't all that big on the heavy hittin', never mind smokin'."

"Yeah, but if somethin' like that was to happen, how's he gonna know? Sure as fuck ain't gonna be me tellin' him. You?"

Junior's smile was always a tricky proposition, sometimes projecting a roguish mirth, sometimes ugly menace, their borders blurry and never easy to read. But there was little doubt in Hector's mind he had this one right, so he said quickly, "Me neither, man."

"There you are," said Junior, displaying the conclusion's self-evidence with upturned palms.

"That's *if* what you sayin' here happened. Big if."

"S'posin' we was to make it happen. All that dinero buy you a pile a burritos, *chico*."

"Also buy me pile a grief, Mr. B ever find out. You too."

"Except Mr. Yid ain't gonna find out, seein' there's nobody to tell him. Like we just said."

Hector made an oval of his lips, blew a perfect smoke ring, watched it float in the air and slowly dissolve. "Sound like you been givin' this some hard thought," he said.

"It crossed my head, inside there."

"Think we could swing it?"

"Can't see nothin' blockin' the road. Not from where I'm sittin'."

"How'd we do it? The whack, I mean."

"Oh, that part's easy. Worry about that tomorrow, after we see if they gonna step up to the pay window. Like they promised."

"They don't, maybe we just forget it, huh? Cuff 'em around and give Mr. B his loot?"

"Sure thing, *chico*. However you want it. First let's see how it plays tomorrow."

"How 'bout for tonight?"

"What about it?"

"Where we gonna crash?"

"Crash? Why, right here, 'course. Where else? Got to keep a close scope on our investment, right?"

Hector had a pretty good figure on who was going to be doing the scoping, who the crashing, but he said anyway, "S'pose I'm the one gets to do the eyeballin'."

"See," Junior said, climbing over the seat and settling onto a filthy mattress in the back of the van, "already you gettin' good at that s'posin'."

TWELVE

On the morning of the following day, there was speculation of a similar, guardedly buoyant nature going on in the busy mind of the Reverend Bott as he hurriedly tidied up the apartment in anticipation of the first of a pair of most promising clients. And with good reason. Hadn't they scored sixteen hundred and change in the mere thirty-six hours since the launching of this venture? Nothing shabby about those numbers. And hadn't his homework on the magnanimous Mrs. Swett uncovered the exhilarating intelligence that she was bound by wedlock to a fortune of staggering proportions, thereby vindicating his intuition and entrancing him with visions of a bottomless well of lovely lucre? What about the credulous woodchuck, young Mr. Cody, whose compelling need for "Mom's" advice was fueled by as thick a wad of bills as Bryce had laid eyes on in the proverbial coon's age? That well, while perhaps not without bottom, visibly ran deep and cried out for tapping. As swindles go, this was shaping up as one of his more inspired conceptions.

Of course there was a worrisome downside too. A couple of other marks had appeared yesterday: cranky, querulous seniors so plainly near the end of their own respective ropes they'd have been better advised to give it a feeble heartbeat or two, deliver and receive their messages in person. After prolonged and energy-depleting huddles with the gifted Waneta (and gifted at this game she surely was, improvising startling, ambiguous dispatches of her own invention like some divinely touched oracle), these nickel nursers each had dropped a skimpy double saw in the pot and grudgingly at that. Which accounted for the chump change and could hardly be called cost-effective time management. Still it *was* money, however niggardly, and all money spent the same.

So it wasn't that troubling him so much as the increasingly aberrant behavior of his mercurial partner, the source of which Bryce could neither fathom nor comprehend. Mostly she kept to her bed, all but immobilized by a sluggish, melancholic torpor. She seemed to have given up on food, subsisting exclusively on the occasional Wheat Thin and a jug of cheap, belly-vengeance wine, as if to hasten her dramatized demise. As if the occult mystery of the role had overtaken her, swamped her psyche and routed her will.

Not to mention her focus. Yesterday, after he had collected the turnip seed's extraordinary donation, he had found himself fairly skipping back to her room to display the munificent fruits of their labor, fanning out the bills and announcing joyously, "Ten of the big Ben Franklins! A full thousand! Waneta, my dear, I can see it now: Our future is in death, or more accurately, death's bountiful other side."

Ignoring the money she had fastened him with her gaze (and she had it down perfectly now, that zombie-eyed stare, quite unnerving) and in a voice faint and whispery said, "That kid's in bad trouble."

Bryce, more than a little puzzled by this curious and altogether irrelevant remark, humored her with, "And your message to him was entirely appropriate. The only way to dodge trouble is to show it your heels. As who should know better than ourselves?"

"Maybe I can tell him where."

"Where?"

"Where it's safe he can go."

"Why, of course you can," Bryce assured her. "All in good time. My sense of the situation is that it will require a number of consultations with the redoubtable mom before she can be persuaded to reveal a sheltering harbor for the lad. And," he added with a snap of the bills and a conspiratorial wink, "more of his kind benevolence. Considerably more."

"But he needs to know *now,*" she protested.

"Patience, as the old saw has it, is its own reward. And in this case, Waneta, ours as well."

"Maybe it'll come to me."

"Patience?"

"No. Where he's suppose to go."

"Come now, my dear. Does it really matter what we tell him?"

"Matters to me."

Waneta worried about a mark? That didn't compute. "Yes, well, you get some rest now," Bryce had said, fashioning an indulgent smile and backing out the door. "We can discuss the details of his destination tomorrow."

But they hadn't discussed those details this morning. Nor any other of the multitude of contingencies that could arise in a scam as slippery as this one. She'd simply stonewalled him, insisting again, "It'll come to me."

But what was coming to Bryce, for his part of it, was the reluctant conclusion something odd was going on in that scrambled head of hers. Surely she wasn't buying any of this preposterous banana oil. Certainly she couldn't actually believe herself capable of communing with that celestial swamp gas the dupes of this world were pleased to call the human soul.

Or could she? This wasn't the crude, crafty, cantankerous Waneta he knew. Something decidedly odd was going on here. Something almost spooky.

Most disquieting. And most unpropitious timing. For how often did a whimsical fate present you with back-to-back dupes, born victims handsomely heeled and breathlessly eager to part with the large dollar? Not often, in his experience. Which meant it fell to him to hold this teetery act together long enough to scoop up all the plunder he could pocket. After that, well, who could predict?

Bryce stationed himself at a window, anxiously awaiting the arrival of the first of those victims. After what seemed an interminable vigil, a black Jaguar pulled up outside the building, and he flung open the door and greeted its driver with his most sumptuous teeth-master smile. "Mrs. Swett, what a pleasure to see you again. My niece and I have been looking forward impatiently to your visit. Do come in."

Like Bryce, Billie Swett had begun her morning on a note of keen, if somewhat jittery, expectancy, the latter sensation predominating as her husband dawdled over coffee and half a pack of cigarettes while he watched the televised market report, serving up windy pronouncements on that bewildering stream of letters and numbers trailing hypnotically across the bottom of the screen. Taking his own sweet time. Maddeningly.

Though he was officially retired, a man like Big Lonnie, conditioned by a lifetime of habit, needed a place to go, somewhere to remind himself of the ponderous fiscal weight he carried. Somewhere to strut. Accordingly he created a company to oversee his investments (christened "Swett Equities" in another of those featherlight puns on his infelicitous name) and maintained a suite of offices down in Jupiter, equipped with a dazzling array of computers and staffed by two full-time secretaries, a manager, and a spineless son whose business acumen was dismissed, in his father's uncharitable judgment, as "not worth a bucket of warm spit." On a typical weekday morning, Lonnie sauntered in shortly after the market opened and hung around 'til it closed. Neither time, however, could be reliably clocked, for his arrival turned on how long he chose to steam his amplitude of flesh in the Jacuzzi, and his departure on whatever whim seized him.

This particular morning that ritualistic steaming had been especially prolonged, which accounted for Billie's rapidly mounting distress. And though there had been no visible disturbance in her show of interest as he'd babbled on, her thoughts had been elsewhere, calculating routes, distances, travel times, and sifting through a variety of cover stories, testing each for maximal plausibility in the likely event one of them had to be produced. She had told this Bott fellow she'd for certain be there Tuesday morning (exactly when, she couldn't say), which left only a narrow window of time to get from Stuart to Singer Island; confer with the expiring niece; possibly, with any luck, reach the anguished spirit of a slaughtered child (to say what, she wasn't sure: "Sorry I murdered you"? Endless apologies? Maybe something would come to her); then get herself home again in advance of the castle dragon, sidestep a spat. It was going to be tight.

At last, mercifully, he yawned, burped, got to his feet, broke a gust of toxic wind, and as though propelled by it, made for the door. Billie followed along dutifully, laid a wifely peck on a paunchy jowl, and advised him to have a good day. A morning grouch, he grumbled something about a stock skidding, and with that as farewell, the tycoon of trash, incongruously clad in polo shirt and short pants, was gone.

The instant the gate closed behind his Porsche, Billie was out of her own shorts and tank top and into a skirt and plain silk blouse suitable to the occasion. Ten minutes later her Jag was pointed south on 95, tooling along as fast as she dared push it, which wasn't a whole lot faster than the posted limit. Last thing she needed now was a ticket. Try and explain that one.

But the longer Billie drove, the more her anxieties cooled, and her thoughts, sprung loose by fluid motion and the freedom of the open road, flitted over a widening range of issues and images: the upcoming encounter of course, but that was out of her hands, outside her control, nothing to think about there; glimpses of her girlhood lifted from the dusty attic of memory, gladdening and mildly diverting, but apropos of nothing; grimmer flash-forwards to an arid future, herself stooped and withered, grown old in a gilded cage. And finally, unaccountably, they came to rest, these fitful thoughts of hers, on a vivid mind picture of that curious man from the hospital and funeral chapel, his lean used face and neutral eyes and thin mouth and, as if in contradiction to his name, only slightly amused. Also his curious talk of fate. Billie wasn't in the habit of questioning the course her life had taken, that aimless drift people liked to call destiny, but now it occurred to her she hadn't lived that life so much as allowed it to live her. Now she wondered what she might have missed, and if there really was such a thing as fate after all. And now she'd never know.

Gradually the picture faded, and as she neared the Blue Heron exit, the last lingering traces of these airy ruminations abruptly scattered at the rattle of the cell phone. Uh-oh. Dodge-and-weave time. She picked up the phone and murmured an absent greeting, like someone preoccupied with pressing business. Like she'd rehearsed it earlier, in her head.

The reply—"Fuck you at?"—was about what she expected, including the audible "gotcha" in it. No surprises out of your Big Chimichanga. But she said anyway. "Lonnie? That you?"

"Yeah, it's me. Askin' where you at."

"On my way to the Gardens Mall. Do some shopping."

"Shoppin' for what?"

"Those towels we were talking about? For the guest bathrooms? Remember?" The subject of the towels she'd been careful to introduce last night. For just this contingency. With him you had to cover every base.

"Oh, them," he grunted. "How come you didn't say nothin' about it this morning?"

"Didn't I?" Billie said innocently. "Must have slipped my mind." And then, to steer the talk in another direction, she asked, "What's up, hon?"

"You mean how come I'm callin'?" he countered suspiciously.

She held off a sigh. "No, I mean how's your day going so far?"

"Goin' good. Better'n good. That stock I was sayin', it's turned around. Soon's it hits fifty-two, I'm dumpin' it, walk off with a nice bundle a coin."

The topic of money always had a way of lubricating his normally dry, wheezy voice, softening its natural belligerence, and she said worshipfully and on cue, "That's terrific, honey."

"Oughta keep ya in towels awhile. Maybe even a new dress, you're good."

"You know I know how to be good," said Billie in the slinkiest of tones, refining her designated role. It was what you did to earn your keep.

"Don't I, though? Listen, honey, I gotta run, keep an eye on them numbers. Don't be long, huh? Things keep on goin' right here, I'll prolly pack it in early."

Not good, this last piece of news. Not good at all. Nevertheless she chirped brightly, "See you soon, hon," ringing off with the sound of a simulated wet kiss but thinking, as she put down the customized electronic tether, *Move smartly, Billie.*

So when, not so many minutes later, she stepped inside the Surf and Shore apartment, Billie was understandably impatient with the gushy reverend, all oily smiles and simpers and wash of words, but then immensely relieved when, back in that airless shuttered room, the wasted girl fixed her in a parched, feverish stare and said, softly but firmly, "Enough, Bryce. Leave us now. We'll want to speak alone."

"You did *what*?"

Leon, slumped in a chair, a faintly cornered expression on his pale, pinched face, mumbled, "What I told you last night."

Very slowly, very gingerly, Jim creased himself into sitting posture, braced his back against the headboard, and swung his legs over the side of the bed, testing them like some creaky octogenarian. It was nothing like the movies, getting clubbed in the gut by a swag-bellied brute with a fist as heavy as a wrecking ball and about as pulverizing. In the movies your hero was maybe stunned a little, staggered even, but he came storming right back in a blur of karate kicks, dazzling the bad guys with his blinding footwork. Or maybe he just threw your reliable old American right cross. Either one invariably carried the day. Of course in the movies you could always distinguish villain from hero, friend from foe. In this bizarre and increasingly bughouse drama, he wasn't so sure anymore.

Last night, after the goons were gone and after he'd somehow managed an all-fours creep across the floor and torturous climb onto the bed, Jim croaked out (for his nephew had crawled the opposite direction and was noisily retching in the john), "That thou, Leon. What happened to it? Where'd it go?"

What he heard—might have heard—hoped the fuck he hadn't heard—was something about a "message from Mom," too sloshy to understand. And Jim, groaning himself, was too punished to try to follow it. Too centered on his own raw, thrumming pain. Been enough for one day. More than plenty. So he just let it all go and slept the redeeming sleep that comes from flight from aches and woes. Sort it out in the morning.

Only now morning had arrived, and nothing had gone away in the night, and interrogating nephew fuzznuts here, Jim was only now beginning to grasp the weight of that loopy, gurgly reply, get his mind around its full import. In a voice glazed with frost, he demanded, "Tell me again."

"Again?"

"Yeah. Again."

"Well, I heard about this lady can maybe talk to people who, y'know, passed over to the other side. Like Mom. So I thought I'd see if she could get to her, tell her about this jam I'm in, find out what she got to suggest. Mom, I mean."

"Advice from the dead," Jim said tonelessly.

"Sorta like that. I figured it was worth a shot. Figured you was gone. Didn't know what else to do."

"And what did she tell you, this lady with the hotline to your mother?"

"Said Mom said I oughta go on a trip someplace. Get away."

"A little vacation."

"Guess y'could call it that."

"She say where?"

"That part wasn't real clear. She said—this is the lady I'm talkin' about here, one tryin' to get in touch with Mom—said she thinks maybe she could find out where exactly if I was to come back again."

"And pay another thousand dollars."

"Wasn't like they charged you, Uncle Jim. See, she's dyin' herself, this lady. And her uncle there—he's a minister—he asks can you spare something to help out on their doctor bills. Was more a donation, like. Like in church."

"Oh, yeah," Jim said, all the seething fury bottled up through this confounding recital unstoppered now and erupting in a geyser of monumental disgust, "church of the sacrificial lamb. Church of the holy scam. And you 'donate' a dime of the money I'm busting my ass to scratch together to save *your* miserable ass."

"What else was I gonna do?" Leon whined. "I needed help."

"What you need is professional help. Where the fuck's your head at? Are you well? You got a death wish? Whose side are you on, for chrissake?"

Leon merely gazed at him, destitute of answers, the sad appeal of a whipped, worthless hound in his myopic, violently batting eyes.

Jim looked at his watch. Deliberated. There was still time. Not much but maybe enough. Maybe, if he got moving right now, caught a break or two, just maybe he could still bring it in under the wire. Salvage the day. Like one of those movie heroes. It was a struggle, but he got to his feet and stood there for a moment, steadying himself. And once he was persuaded all the parts of his spanked body still worked, more or less, he said grimly, "All right, whereabouts these skinners located?"

"You mean the lady and her uncle?"

"Come on, Leon. Clock's ticking. Where are they?"

"Right here on the island. Some apartments just around the corner past the mall and down a couple blocks. Place called Surf and Shore."

"Which apartment?"

"Last one on the end."

"Names?"

"Preacher's name is Bott. Bryce, I think he said. Lady's Waneta."

"OK," Jim said, "now I want you to pay attention, listen carefully. I'm talking at you now, right?"

Leon looked baffled.

"These are words coming out of my mouth, right? Not written down on a sheet of paper somewhere, not a note. Right?"

"Right."

"What they're saying is, 'Stay here.' Telling you don't leave the room, don't get any more good ideas. You hear these words, Leon?"

"Yeah, I hear 'em."

"You understand them?"

" 'Course I do."

"That's comforting," Jim said, and started for the door.

"Where you goin'?"

Jim paused, turned, glared at him. "Where? To get back that money you pissed away. See if it's not too late to wiggle out of this Super Glue you got us into. That answer your 'where' question?"

"Uncle Jim?"

"What?"

"You comin' back?"

"Yeah, Leon," he said with a beaten sigh. "I'll be back."

Judas Quincy Priest, it's a sorry world when you can't even trust your own partner anymore. And after all he'd done, too: rescued her from Dogpatch, patiently coached her, shared the hard-earned wisdom of his vast experience, passed along everything he knew (which was anything worth knowing). But in light of the skewed direction this otherwise sweet swindle seemed to be taking, it was, for Bryce (banished to the outer room, where he sat, doughy tummy resting on loamy thighs, palms cupping baggy face, silently fuming), a conclusion sad but inescapable. What else could account for all that soppy emoting and that summary dismissal back there? "Speak alone" indeed! Waneta was no seminal thinker, but she was nobody's biscuit either. She recognized a ripe mark when she saw one (schooled by him, why wouldn't she?). Hers was a mind of low, if limited, animal cunning, and where the moneyed Mrs. Swett was concerned, it had to be busily at work right now, crafting an agenda of its own. Hell in a handcart, that's where it was headed, this deceitful world, when an upstart pupil tries to lay a sting on a selfless mentor.

Well, he'd see about that. See who was the stinger, who the stingee. Bryce Bott still had a few reality-check aces up his sleeve. Not for nothing was he the supple survivor of six decades on the hustle.

So intense were these pouty ruminations, so indignant, it required a piercing squeal of braking tires directly outside the apartment to intrude on them. Startled, he went over to a window and peeked through the blind. Curious sight, most puzzling (for the Cody turnip seed wasn't expected until later in the day, and no one else had phoned to arrange an audience with the sainted messenger). Yet pulled between the Swett Jaguar and his own venerable Cadillac was a vehicle of similar make but of truly antediluvian vintage, from which emerged a fierce-eyed man in a seriously rumpled suit. Clearly come to call.

Had another mark heard the buzz somewhere and arrived unannounced? Possible, but Bryce didn't think so. There was something in the determined stride and grim set of jaw that raised a distant alarm in his head, and he hurried to the door, got there first, swung it open, and planted himself in the entrance. Just in case he was mistaken, his suspicions groundless (with this one-oar clientele, you never could be certain, and you never wanted to pass up a bit of change, even of the chump variety), he flashed his greeter smile and said affably, "Good morning, sir. What can I do for you?"

The caller came to a stop a foot or so from him. Took his measure slowly, top to bottom. Wordlessly. His face was stony, shadowed in stubble. Mouth a thin truculent line, tightened by grievance. Definitely not smiling. And Bryce knew his first instinct had been right. He hadn't been mistaken. A conclusion sealed by the challenging pitch in the caller's voice when finally he said, "You'd be Pastor Bott, right?"

"I am that person," Bryce affirmed stiffly. "And you are?"

"My name's Merriman. Jim Merriman."

"Merriman, Merriman..." Bryce tapped a temple, as if to shake loose a trifling nugget of memory lodged there.

"Leon Cody's uncle. That ding any chimes for you?"

It was old hat to Bryce, the irate relative appearing at the door, demanding restitution. He'd played this scene before, many a time. Knew all its variations. Patiently he said, "And how may I assist you, Mr. Merriman?"

"Oh, that's easy. Just hand over that dime you skinned off the kid, and that's all the assistance I'll be needing."

"I beg your pardon?"

"Spare me the waltz, Pastor."

Bryce composed his face in an attitude of bewilderment. "I'm sorry to say I haven't the foggiest notion what it is you refer to, sir."

"What part don't you understand?"

"All of it, I'm afraid."

"OK. Try this. Bones, green, gelt, poke, sugar, cush. Billies, Pastor. A thousand of them. Scammed off him. By you and your partner. Give it back."

Bryce squared his shoulders and elevated his chin in a histrionic display of wounded dignity. "Are you alluding to Mr. Cody's contribution of yesterday?"

"That's a solid bingo."

"May I gently remind you, sir, that all our donations are free-will offerings? Freely given, gratefully received."

"Yeah, well, we had a little chat about it, that 'donation.' Seems he's changed his mind."

"And he deputized *you* to retrieve it?"

"That's about the size of it, Pastor. So if you'll just cough it up, I'll be on my way, let you get on with your heavenly messenger service."

While each of these scenes had its own nuances and rhythms, the common thread linking them all was, from Bryce's peculiar perspective, the boldly executed bluff. Possession, after all, was nine-tenths of the law. Not to speak of your extralegal swindles. And so with a look compounded of pity and distaste, equal parts, he said coolly, "Consider, Mr.…ah—Merriman, is it?"

"Correct."

"Consider then, an individual of rather slovenly appearance, to put the kindest construction on it…" Here Bryce paused a beat, pinched his nostrils like a man downwind of a disagreeable odor. "This person arrives unannounced at your door, demanding money on the flimsy basis of a dubious and, I must add, utterly unsubstantiated claim to kinship with a relative curiously absent. Nowhere in evidence. Nowhere to be seen." Coming down off this crescendo of elegant logic, Bryce slowed the tempo, scanned the horizon, and discovering no one present but themselves, concluded with a patronizing smirk, "Perhaps even you might agree it all looks a trifle suspect."

Timing, gesture, expression, the elocution of bluster—all the harmonic elements of a stonewall symphony, and Bryce was the self-confessed virtuoso of them all. The obstinate Mr. Merriman, however, appeared unmoved. Glaring at Bryce, eyes smoldering pools of righteous wrath, voice risen a decibel or two, he said, "What I agree to, Bott, is you owe me money. And you'd better produce it. Now."

"Come now, Mr. Merriman," said Bryce, still riding his bluff but no longer quite so confidently. "What do you take me for?"

"Take you for the sleazeball grifter we both know you are. So you can save your smoke and mirrors. You're not talking to the kid here."

The faint alarm Bryce had heard before had escalated to a strident siren's wail. This wasn't your ordinary mark, witless, sapless, a knock-over for the fast jabberjack. This one, by his combative bearing and, more revealing, command of street vernacular, was plainly not unacquainted with the life. Been around the dipsy-doodle block before. Bryce retreated a step, put up a shushing hand. "Please, lower your voice. My niece is gravely ill."

"Not half as ill as you're going to be if you don't come up with that dime."

"I'm afraid I have no more time for you, sir," Bryce said and, moving nimbly for a man of his bulk, backpedaled into the apartment, where, from behind the security of a slammed and bolted door, he called, toughly as he could pitch it, consistent with his persona, "And if you persist in this outrageous disturbance, I shall be obliged to summon the police."

No response.

So Bryce threatened the door, "I'm warning you. I won't tolerate any more of this boorish behavior."

Silence.

Maybe the threat of the heat was enough to back him off. Buy some time. Right now that was what he desperately needed, time to frame a plan to hold together this estimable swindle, perhaps his finest creation, unjustly unraveling before his eyes.

No time. For as if to compound his woes, just then a voice behind him inquired, "What is it, Reverend Bott? What's wrong?"

He wheeled around, and there stood the stellar money pump, gazing at him puzzledly. Holy Haggai!—what else could go wrong? "Mrs. Swett," he said with a sickly smile.

"We heard shouting," she said in that flat tone that demands explanation.

"A minor misunderstanding," Bryce extemporized. "Some repairman, plumber I believe, misdirected to this residence. A bit of an oaf, I'm afraid, as those people often are. Quite belligerent. But it's all been satisfactorily resolved."

"You're sure?" she said doubtfully.

"Oh, absolutely. There's nothing to fret yourself over."

"It's not me. It's your niece I'm worried about. She got awfully upset."

"Yes, well, I'll attend to her shortly. Comfort her as best I'm able, under these trying circumstances."

"You better. Poor girl needs it."

The last thing Bryce needed was for this one to happen on that other one who might, or might not, still be lurking outside the door. Lord only knew what might come of that untimely encounter. Certainly nothing good. So he assembled a wistful face and, stalling, said, "Yes, she suffers terribly, our Waneta. The price, I fear, of her unique gift. I do hope she was able to be of some small help to you."

"*Very* helpful," she declared emphatically.

"Sometimes her mind drifts, you know," Bryce said, trolling for details.

"Not today."

"Experiences of this sort can be emotionally draining," he cautioned. "I believe you would find it useful, therapeutic even, to share yours with a sympathetic listener. Which I like to believe I am."

"No, that won't be necessary," she said dismissively.

Squashed again. Discarded like a worn-out suit of clothes. Whatever game that traitorous twit was running back there, it appeared to be working, and without benefit of his wise counsel and direction. More than merely working, spinning away at a dizzying velocity, leaving him stranded in its dust. This wasn't the way he'd envisioned it. This wouldn't do. Outwardly composed, inwardly seething, but ever mindful of the more immediate danger just beyond the door, Bryce said, "As you wish. But please allow me to offer you a spot of tea, Mrs. Swett."

"Thanks, but I really have to get going."

"A bit of relaxation would do you a world of good," he coaxed.

"No, thanks."

So much for stalling. "I trust we'll be seeing you again," he said.

"Oh, you can count on that. I can't say when exactly, but I'll definitely be back." Almost as an afterthought, she fished through her purse, extracted some bills, dropped them on the plate set conspicuously on the counter, and made for the door.

"We're humble people," Bryce intoned unctuously, with an effort to avert his eyes from what looked to be another substantial take, "and we humbly thank you for your generous support in our hour of need."

"It's worth it" was all she said, and with that ungracious farewell, she was gone. A lady in a hurry.

No less hurried was Bryce's rush to the window, from which he observed his worst fear actualized. There they stood, Swett and Merriman, opposite poles of his once auspicious and now rapidly crumbling scheme, hopelessly magnetized. Yet, astonishingly, bewilderingly, there was nothing in what he could see of their huddle to suggest imminent disaster, no agitated finger jabbing on his part, no shocked dismay on hers. Rather they seemed to be chatting quietly, exchanging smiles and fond glances. Decidedly not the dialogue of strangers. Which added yet another murky dimension to an already shadowy game.

He watched a while longer, 'til they climbed into their respective vehicles and sped away, quite unaware of the other eyes watching them, all of them, himself not excluded, from a rusted van parked just up the street.

"Fuck you make a' this, man?"

"Dunno yet."

"You think he tryin' to catch the breeze?"

"Hard to tell."

"Maybe they lookin' to run in different directions."

"Maybe."

"Then we oughta be crowdin' the kid. He the one carryin' the marker."

"Kid don't know dick. It's the uncle drivin' this train."

"So whaddya we *do*, man?"

Do? Junior was fucked if he knew. He'd been rudely snatched out of a deep crash by a squawking spic ("Hey, Biggs, wake the fuck up. Somethin' shakin'."), and it was enough to do just to get his sleep-fogged head together, steer the van through the maze of traffic around the mall, and keep the time-warp Caddie in sight. "I ain't sure," he mumbled.

"Got to do *somethin'*."

"How 'bout we start by you stuffin' a rag in your tortilla hole?" Junior growled at him. He wasn't yet in a humor to listen to a spooked beaner.

Who, when the Caddie swung off the street and parked outside some apartments called the Surf and Shore, went ahead and said anyway, "One thing sure, that ain't no goddamn bank."

Junior pulled up along the curb half a block down, let the engine idle, and squinted through the blaze of sunlight glinting off the hood. "They was gonna hock that buzz buggy," he speculated. "Could be this is where the buyer's at."

"*Could*'s a long way off," Hector said worriedly. "What if he was to duck and run?"

Junior deliberated, weighed real risks against imagined rewards, arrived at a decision. “Some heavy loot on the line here, cholo. We’ll give it a minute, see what he’s up to.”

So they watched. Watched Uncle pop out of the car and march right up to one of the apartment doors. Watched that door swing open before he got there, geezer in a black suit filling it, shit-eater grin all over his face, like he can’t wait to see Uncle. “What’d I tell ya?” Junior said. “That gotta be the buyer.”

Only the next thing they watched was a lot of chin music accompanied by some heated arm flagging, like a couple of guys not reading off the same page, and then the geezer hopped back inside and slammed the door, leaving Uncle standing there scowling, fists pumping air.

“That look like a sale to you?” Hector said disgustedly.

“Least we still got him in our crosshairs. Ain’t a total loss.”

“Will be, we don’t lean on him. And quick.”

“S’pose you right,” Junior conceded sourly, visions of that anticipated eighteen large and all the good times it could have bought dissolving behind his eyes. “For a change.”

“So let’s do it, huh?”

“Awright, awright.”

Only before they could make their move, the apartment door opened again, and out came this pound-cake cooze, real smashing looker, and goddamn if she didn’t step on over to Uncle, and the chin-’n’-grin symphony band was at it again, only now it was all nicey-nice music, nothing like with the fossil, who Junior spotted peeking out a corner of a window, looking just as baffled as Junior was feeling right about now, and which prompted him to mutter rhetorically, “Fuck’s goin’ down here, anyways?”

“Be me goin’ down on that furburger, I ever get the chance,” Hector declared, staring bug-eyed at the twat out there.

“Talkin’ about Uncle.”

“Me, I’m talkin’ ’bout that skeezer. Lookit her, man. All that yellow hair, ripe ass. She pure stone fox. Eatin’ stuff.”

"Burrito boy like you got about as much chance eatin' at that lunch counter as at the Breakers."

"Tha's where you wrong. Down Miami they call me the 'Ass Bandito.' Steal their honeypots and make 'em squeal."

"Bandito," Junior snorted. "Be more like that Gay Caballero," he added, sounding the Ls. "Rump ranger ridin' the bunghole trail."

"Yeah, well, put me next to that slit an' you see. An' that's *yerro*. Cob-a-*yerro*."

"Yerro your ass, you don't get your mind off your nuts and back on business."

"Sure as fuck hope she gonna be part a' that business."

Didn't look too promising, though, Hector's hope. Now she was climbing into a zazzy Jag, giving Uncle a sugary smile and finger-waggle farewell. Off she went.

"Where you think she fit in, all this?" Hector asked.

"You see me packin' a crystal ball? Fuck would I know?"

"Think she's his squeeze?"

"Don't know and don't give a rat's red ass. It's him we're trackin'."

Uncle stood there a minute, fuddled look on his face. He glanced back and forth between the apartment and her Jag speeding away. If he saw the eyes at the window or their eyes watching him, it didn't show.

"Maybe we oughta just bag it," Hector suggested. "Tune him up, call Mr. B, an' tell him where it stands. Twenty-seven long ain't worth gettin' ourselves snuffed over. Which is what would happen, he ever find out."

"How 'bout that forty-five we was sayin' last night? That worth it to you?"

Hector had to think about that, and as he did, Uncle seemed to get his shit together, enough anyway to sprint over to the Caddie, back it into the street, and point it toward the mall. Junior pulled away from the curb and followed behind, cutting him a little space, not much. "Tell ya what, cholo," he said, "let's see where he's headed. He still got some time yet. We give him 'til noon to come up with that balance. Remember? And a man's only as good as his word, right?"

A fury powerless and paralytic seized him. Rendered him mute. His feet seemed to grip the earth. Breath came in quick, jerky pants. What felt like a shifting of tectonic plates rumbled ominously inside his skull. Outside it a fierce sun slicked his brow, spiked his eyes. His mouth twisted wordlessly, framing unuttered curses. Stiffed by a bogus preacher. And after all those years of elbow rubbing with jackleg chiselers. So much for worldly experience.

Time was ticking. Yet here he stood, glowering impotently at a door banged shut in his face and from behind which dire warnings had been issued, among them something about the police. The law he knew he didn't need. Peril enough without them nosing around, botching an already botched agenda. What he needed was to regroup, start thinking straight, get past this profitless and time-whittling storm, get his thumb out of his ass and get cracking, gather the tribute and orchestrate the happy ending in a dramatic thirteenth-hour deliverance. Like that cinematic hero he was supposed to be, a role thrust upon him by puckish fate.

By an act of will, he centered himself, uprooted his feet, and took a halting, decidedly unheroic step toward the car. Only to be stalled again, only this time by a honeyed voice lifting up behind him. "We've got to stop meeting this way, Jim Merriman."

He turned, and there she was, about the last person he'd expected to see again. And that was about what he said. "Mrs. Swett. And here I thought we'd said our last good-byes."

"Not quite yet, it seems," she said with a dreamy smile. "So you might as well call me 'Billie.' "

He smiled back, perversely buoyed by the sight of her standing there drenched in sunlight, cool and poised, like someone who'd just emerged from a cleansing sleep.

She regarded him curiously. "Looks like you had a hard night."

Jim was suddenly aware of his slept-in clothes. Rest of him too. He ran a hand through his tangled hair, swiped at a bristly cheek. "Fact is," he allowed, "it wasn't one of my better ones."

"Is something wrong? You seem awfully, well, jittery."

"Couple things on my mind."

"Am I holding you up?"

"Not at all," he lied.

"So what are you doing here?"

"I was about to ask you the same."

She gestured at the apartment door. "There's someone inside there. A girl. Very sick. Very...gifted. She's helping me get through some things," she said vaguely. Like that somehow told it all.

"No doubt," he said, voice dipped in irony.

Lost on her, it appeared, for she asked, "Is that why you're here? To see her?"

"Not exactly."

"Why then?"

Wasn't his place to disabuse her of these loopy notions. Nobody had appointed him chief scams inspector, Palm Beach County. "It's a long story," he said.

"I'd like to hear it."

"Maybe you should. Sometime."

"When?"

"When? *You're* asking *me* when?"

"Yes."

He looked at her skeptically. Like there was a joke in the making here, him the butt, punch line coming right up. "Let me see if I got this right. Now you're accepting my invitation?"

"Looking that way, isn't it?" she said, gazing at him steadily, eyes brimming with…what? Mischief? Pleasure? Promise? Some kind of tranced joy? They were unreadable even to him, who once had made his living reading eyes.

"Seems like we had this conversation before, Mrs. Swett, and—"

"Billie."

Jim started over. "OK. What I remember of that conversation, Billie, is hearing something about a husband in there."

"And what I remember most is just one word."

"Which one's that?"

"*Fate.*"

"*I* said that?" In the turmoil of the past twenty-four hours, he'd long since forgotten whatever cagey line he'd pitched her. "Fate" sounded as likely as any.

"Yes, you did. And I think it's maybe trying to tell us something, that fate. Why else would two Dakotans keep running into each other down here in the land of perpetual sunshine?"

"Maybe you're right. And I'm flattered you'd think so. Make that honored. Only I'm afraid I can't do anything about it today. Some business to attend to."

"Me either," she said with a quick glance at a jeweled Rolie on her slender wrist. "What about, oh, say, Thursday?"

"Thursday sounds good," he said, wondering if he'd be in a wheelchair by then. Or even have a pulse.

"There's a place in North Palm. Decesare's. You know where it's at?"

"I'll find it."

"Say about noon?"

"Noon it is."

"I've got to get going now. But I'm really glad our paths crossed again, Jim."

"Same here, Billie."

"And I really do want to see you Thursday," she said earnestly. "I'll try my absolute best to be there, but I can't, you know, exactly guarantee it."

"Neither can I."

He watched the Jaguar shrink to a black smudge at the end of the street, vanish altogether. Almost dazedly he watched, wondering if it had been nothing more than a hallucination, this improbable encounter, a product of his fertile imagination. Rejecting that notion (yes, she was there; yes, their antipodal orbits had in fact intersected yet again), he was put in mind of the loser's lament: "A day late and a dollar short." Story of his life. More likely its epitaph if he didn't get these maudlin, moonstruck sentiments out of his head and get moving on that short dollar.

He climbed into the Caddie, drove directly to the motel, came through the door, and discovered the dipstick sprawled on a bed, absorbed in a *Gilligan's Island* rerun, its laugh-track cackle filling the room.

Leon greeted him with a startled grin. "Uncle Jim? You're back already? What's up?"

"Looks like I'm going to need you after all. C'mon with me. Now."

In the car Leon inquired timidly, "You have any luck with that, uh, donation?"

"Not yet I didn't."

"So where we headed?"

Flying in the face of all sound numerical sense and fueled by a compelling, irrational need to trump that shit-sack charlatan, Jim pointed the Caddie back to the Surf and Shore. "You'll see," he said.

Steering north, oblivious to the world outside her head—its rushing traffic, blurred landscapes, highway stretching out ahead of her—Billie lifted from the riot of fragmented thoughts and emotions teeming behind her eyes an image vivid and stark in its clarity. Waneta, that sparsely fleshed girl with the piercing gaze, fragile as a maimed child yet desperately searching the hosts of the unquiet dead out there in the lonely dark, sorting through their wretched groans and cries 'til at last she'd made fleeting contact with another child, also a girl, a forsaken infant girl, wailing for an absent, murderous mother. But struggling, it seemed, with the vocabulary of forgiveness. "I've reached her," was what Waneta had said, slumping back on the bed, thoroughly drained, voice little more than a whisper. "Delivered your message. She's trying to understand. In time she will."

A second image emerged, not so much superimposed on the first as materialized beside it, like two congruent photographs set side by side. And visualizing the curiously anxiety-struck face of this Jim Merriman, this perfect stranger, was for Billie like staring into a motionless pond whose surface gave back a ripply reflection of herself. What were they, after all, but two Dakota fugitives linked by common geography and destiny's mysterious gravity?

She was a confirmed believer now, Billie was, or decided she was. What else could you be after so extraordinary a morning as this one? Vast, limitless horizons seemed to open onto the future and the past, auguring deliverance in one direction, redemption in the other. And even as the Jaguar hurtled her back to the arid luxury and money-insulated security of her lockstep life, Billie recognized she was arrived at a crossing. Suddenly panicked by that alarming recognition, she felt an urgent need to talk to somebody, confide in someone. Impulsively she picked up the cell phone and tapped out a familiar number.

"Hair Affair," announced a prickly female voice on the other end of the line.

"Dori? That you?"

"Yeah. Who's this?"

"Billie."

"Hey, the jackpot girl. How's things in the land of the big bucks?"

"Good. Listen, put Courtney on, will you?"

"She's with a client. Doin' a perm, I think. Some of us still gotta make a living, y'know."

"Come on, Dori. This is important."

"Hold on. I'll see what she says."

A moment later another voice, considerably less spiteful, said, "Billie? What's going on?"

"Court," she said breathlessly, "you won't believe what all's going on."

Neither could Bryce fully believe the remarkable conjunction of improbable events yet to transpire that morning. Even after the bargain was sealed, his stroke of genius scheme agreed upon by as unlikely—not to say unsavory—a band of confederates as ever he'd teamed with, he still found it difficult to believe in his potentially prodigious good fortune. Like Billie, he too had come to a crossing, one he could never in his most extravagant imaginings have foreseen.

As soon as the Merriman-Swett dialogue was finished and their respective vehicles out of sight, Bryce had fallen to the agreeable task of counting the take. And handsome it was: ten big Benjamins plus a curious assortment of smaller bills—fifties, twenties, the odd sawbuck—as if she'd offhandedly emptied the contents of her wallet. Tangible, spendable testimony to the brilliance of his inventive swindle and, he supposed grudgingly, to be fair about it, Waneta's Cinderella talent. Whatever means she had contrived to gull the credulous Mrs. Swett, he held in his hands the incontestable evidence of its power to mint money.

This sunny thought, however, had been clouded by another issue momentarily shelved in the noisy upset of the Merriman face-off and the subsequent riddle of his connection with Billie Swett. Bryce knew that sooner or later he was going to have to come to terms with his mutinous partner and the certainty of a double-dealing plot hatching in that crafty hillbilly head. Question was when. Was it better to confront her now or go along with the theatric dissembling, secure a substantial nut, and vanish in the night? Somehow the idea of abandoning this sweet scam—going solo again, a man of his advancing years and sociable temperament alone on the road again—seemed distressingly bleak.

The teetery balance of avarice and misgiving unsettled him, pleated his brow and moiled his belly. It was that thorny issue he wrestled with when a pounding at the door abruptly suspended all these fretful reveries.

Had anyone apprised him in advance, Jim would have been no less astonished than Bryce by the bizarre outcome of his return visit to the Surf and Shore. Unlike either Bryce or Billie, he entertained no romantic notions of clearly defined turning points in his life, critical decisions of his own making that dramatically altered its course. Within an hour he no longer would be quite so sure.

When they arrived at the apartment, Jim cut the engine, drew in a steadying breath, turned to his nephew, and said, "OK, here's the drill. We're going to have a word with your pastor there. Only inside this time. No more locked doors. And when we're done with it, we're going to walk out with that dime you let yourself be skunked out of."

"You sayin' I should come along?" Leon asked. His voice was trembly, and behind the thick lenses, a nerve visibly danced under one eye.

"Goddamn right, you're coming along. That's why you're here."

"What do I got to do?"

"Tell me something," Jim said evenly and in a tone patient, near to tutorial. Leon's obvious dread had the curious counteractive effect of calming him, clearing his head. "You know how to say the word *yes*?"

"'Course I do."

"Say it for me."

"Why?"

"Call it a rehearsal. I want to be sure you can spit it out. Go ahead. Say it."

Leon said yes.

"That's good. Now I'm going to be asking you a couple questions in there. Answers will always be yes. I'll ask; you'll say yes. Nothing more, nothing less. Think you can manage that?"

"Y'know, I *did* give it to 'em, Uncle Jim. That money, I mean."

"See, you're not listening. What I just said, that was one of those questions. 'Til I tell you different, the only word I want to hear out of you is *yes*. Got that?"

"Yes."

"There you are. See how easy it is? Try it again."

"Yes."

"OK, let's do it."

Though the reverend stiffened at the sight of them and tried to put up a restraining hand, Jim shouldered past him, Leon in tow, the instant the door fell open. "Nice crib you got here," he drawled, glancing around the small, tidy room. "But then a thou buys some fine accommodations. Right, Pastor?"

"I believe I told you once before—" Bryce sputtered, but now it was Jim elevating a palm and taking over the telling. "You see this young fellow here?" he said with a backward nod at Leon, who slunk behind him, examining the floor.

"I do."

"You recognize him?"

"Mr. Cody of course. Now if you're quite finished—"

"Not quite. Want you to hear what he has to say. Listen close." Addressing Leon, but with eyes leveled coldly on the pastor, Jim asked, "Am I your uncle?"

Answer was a reedy yes. Barely audible.

"Speak up."

Leon repeated it.

"Did this skaggy piece of dog shit spin you out of a thousand bucks?"

Another reluctant affirmative.

"You change your mind? Want it back?"

"Yes."

"You heard it, Pastor. Still want to call in the heat?"

"No need to involve the authorities," Bryce said with a treacly twist of a smile. "I'm confident we can, through reason and compromise, work out an arrangement satisfactory to all parties."

"Sure we can. All you got to do is hand over that loot you lifted, and we'll be satisfied."

"I'm sorry to say—" Bryce started to say but got no further, for just then a thuggish-looking pair burst through the unlatched door, and it was at just that moment that one of destiny's more antic collaborations, undreamed of by any of those five persons present, was about to commence.

Neither Junior nor Hector, however, were strangers to the peculiar, often prankish workings of chance, disinclined as they both were to introspection, and with the time horizons of callow adolescents, neither had given the subject much thought. Blown and buffeted by the fickle winds, their lives had been, up until now, a series of disjointed episodes outside their respective abilities to comprehend or control: a job today, joint tomorrow; a score here, bust there.

Hector, of course, liked to maintain the pretense of an orderly, directed life. He was, by his estimate, pretty much a grounded guy. Take this gig they were onto now, one he'd let himself get talked into against his better judgment. Wasn't like they actually put the burn on Mr. B yet, popped the vics and pocketed the take. So far it was all just talk. Nothing that couldn't still be turned around.

Small comfort, though, he thought, as he cut a sideways glance at brain-dead there scowling through the windshield, agitatedly drumming the wheel, and muttering baffledly, "Fuck they up to, comin' back *here*?"

"Got me, man."

"You think they lookin' to get small?"

"Fucked if I know. All's I know for sure is it'll be us in the deep shit, we don't crank ass."

"Ain't quite noon. Could give it another tick'r two. Least now we got 'em both under one roof."

"They got windows up where you come from?" said a thoroughly exasperated Hector. "That ain't a goddamn cave, y'know. They could be skatin' right now."

Still Junior hesitated. "Jesus, I hate to see the rest a' that loot flushin' down the crapper."

"You learn to hate it big time, explainin' to Mr. B what happen here."

"Fuck Mr. Yid," Junior snapped, but evidently swayed by his partner's logic, he added grudgingly, "Maybe you right again, cholo. OK, let's go do some serious punishin'."

"Well, wouldya lookit what we got here," Junior began, as he always liked to begin, slow and easy, smiling, taking in the room, taking his time, having some fun with it. "Whaddya s'pose goin' on, *chico?*"

"Look like three ladies humpin' their gums," Hector opined.

"Or a tea party," Junior chortled. "Only there ain't no tea."

"May I ask," Bryce said indignantly, "who you gentlemen are, and what exactly you're doing in my living room? Uninvited, I might add."

Junior passed his eyes over him as if he were a bug he was idly considering squashing. "Sure, you can ask. Ask anything you want. Don't mean you gonna get answers."

"In that case I must insist you leave. All of you. There's a critically ill woman here."

"Yeah, where she at? I don't see nobody sick. You, *chico?*"

"Them two not lookin' so hot," said Hector with a nod at Jim and Leon, who had retreated to a comer of the room.

"Yeah, sorta seasick, all right."

"She's in the back," Bryce said but not nearly so stoutly. With this hulking troglodyte and his sinister Latino straight man, whoever they were, prudence dictated caution.

"Well," Junior allowed clemently, "we prolly won't have to be troublin' her none, this sick lady. You either, you do what I'm recommendin' you do, which is to butt that fat ass a' yours out while we tend to business with these other two fellas here. You follow what I'm tellin' you?"

Bryce pinched his lips together. Said no more.

Junior, still smiling, though not quite as amiably anymore, turned his attention to Jim. "OK, Uncle, it's piper-payin' time. Us the piper. You got our scratch or not?"

"Not."

Junior leaned in toward him, did a deafy gesture with an ear. "Not? I hear you say *not*?"

"You heard right. But you'll have it inside an hour."

"Oh, 'nother hour now, is it? Know what I think, Uncle? Think you tryin' to rainmake us here." With his eyes, no longer much amused, still locked on Jim, he inquired of his partner, who had stationed himself at the door, "What's your thought, *chico*?"

"Same one. His mouth's writin' checks his ass can't cover."

"Maybe the boy got it," Junior suggested, getting the last bit of mileage out of it, glaring at the kid cowering behind Uncle, tic-ridden face gone the color of curdled milk. "Whaddya say, boy? You got our money?"

"He doesn't have it either," Jim answered for him. "But *you* will. If you'll listen."

"Done listenin'," Junior said, and seized him by the collar and slammed him against a wall. "You run a nice bluff, Uncle, but this time it ain't gonna wash."

Jim fired out a desperate, accusing arm at Bryce. "He skinned a dime of your money off us. You want the first installment, talk to him."

"It's you I'm talkin' to."

Always a quick study, Bryce had been watching this exchange warily and listening with an ear seasoned equally by calamity and opportunity. Fragments of thoughts, inklings, ideas, estimations, interpretations buzzed in his busy head; began to coalesce into the genesis of what was to become his most visionary scheme in a lifetime of scheming. Emboldened by its promise, he stepped into the middle of the room, clapped his hands together like a fussy schoolmarm restoring order to an unruly class, and, in a lordly voice, commanded, "People, people—control yourselves. Exercise restraint. Behave in a civilized fashion."

Junior released his grip on Jim and turned and gaped at Bryce, fish mouthed. No one had ever had the nuts to challenge him before, and for an instant, his repertoire of snappy comebacks edged with ugly menace failed him. Same with Hector, who merely looked back and forth between them, stunned into silence. Jim, grateful for even a nanosecond's reprieve from certain pain, also said nothing; and Leon was by then reduced to something approaching catatonia.

Bryce, center stage now, steepled the clapping hands and, addressing Junior, said, "Let me see if I understand the issue here. I gather *these* two owe *you* two money."

Junior recovered enough to mutter, "Yeah? So? What's that to you?"

"In what amount?"

"None your fuckin' business."

"Please. Hear me out. You might be pleasantly surprised. How much?"

"Eighteen long. Plus some late charges we ain't calculated into the total yet."

Jim, like Bryce, had been watching and listening, doing his own calculations of the mounting odds against survival. Now he took a calculated risk, broke his silence. "A dime of which he's holding. Shake him down, you don't believe me."

Junior's deepening scowl fell on him then swung to Bryce. "That the goods, old man? You packin' a thou belongs to us?"

"Quite true," said Bryce airily. "But also beside the point."

"Next thing I hear outta you better be that point."

Bryce arranged his features in an owlish, wise expression. "The point," he declared, "is that I have the solution to our common problem. And I'm confident you'll agree it's an inspired one."

"Fuck you woofin' about, solutions?"

"I speak of money, sir. Sums beyond your wildest dreams. And ours for the simple lifting. Unless I'm mistaken," he went on in the tones of a man satisfied, which he seldom was, "what we have here, in our several persons and talents, are the chemical ingredients, so to say, for that most splendid alchemy, the minting of pure gold."

"You gonna talk to me," Junior rumbled at him, "talk American. That's what I understand."

"Better yet, let me invoke a tongue even more universal. Numbers."

"What kinda numbers we talkin' here?" Junior demanded, his interest picking up some, thinking maybe they could still bail a couple bills out of this yet.

"How does, oh, say, five million strike you?"

Junior squinted at him. "I hear you say 'mil'?"

"You hear correctly."

"Five?"

"Five," Bryce echoed, adding, "against which a thousand—or even eighteen, for that matter—is paltry indeed. Pocket change."

Junior snorted skeptically. "Where you gonna come up with five big balloons?"

"C'mon, Biggs," the heretofore silent Hector interposed. "All this freeze-dry doin' is blowin' ass gas. We got business."

Junior put a staying hand in the air. "Askin' a question here. Wanna hear what he got to say."

"If you'll allow me to explain," Bryce said patiently, "you'll find it well worth a moment of your valuable time."

"That's about what you got," Junior growled, his own patience, never in abundant supply, rapidly dwindling, "one more a' them moments. Then you lookin' at a trip to the same gimp ward these two headed for."

Blithely ignoring the threat, Bryce turned to Jim. "It appears, Mr. Merriman, that you're acquainted with Mrs. Swett."

"I know her," Jim said carefully. "Why?"

"Would it be fair to say intimately?"

"No, it wouldn't be. We've spoken a couple of times. That's it."

"And perhaps will 'speak,' as you delicately put it, again soon. Am I correct in that assumption?"

"It could happen," Jim said. He wasn't sure where this was going, but wherever it was, he didn't much like it.

Junior evidently had the same problem. "Hold the fuck up," he broke in. "Who's this Swett you yappin' about?"

"A client of mine," Bryce told him. "And happily for our purposes, a friend of Mr. Merriman's, it seems."

"She the cunt we seen this dick eye rappin' with outside there?"

"That would be one way to describe her. Another would be the fortuitous solution I alluded to earlier."

"What'd I just say? 'Bout talkin' American?"

"Plainly then. That five million? She's the source."

"She got that kinda gelt?"

"Her husband does. His fortune, I've learned, is estimated at upward of fifty million. Ten percent of which I feel certain he'd be more than eager to exchange for a spouse of such obvious charms. A sort of marital tithing, one might say. With ourselves as the pious recipients."

"Lemme see I got this straight. You talkin' a snatchin' here?"

"I prefer to think of it as a sequestration. A detention, if you will."

"Wait a minute," Jim put in. "This is your idea of a stall, right? You're making a little joke?"

"That amount of money is hardly a joking matter," Bryce said.

"This is squirrely, you know, what you're planning."

"Nobody askin' your opinion, Uncle," Junior silenced him. But then, seriously in need of another himself, he turned to Hector. "*Chico*, what's yours?"

"Be a sweet snatch to be snatchin'" was Hector's considered opinion.

"Also be a heavy jolt, somethin' go wrong. Like an all-day and all-nighter. Or worse."

"Nothing will go wrong," Bryce was quick to assure him, "if we can all of us set aside our minor differences and work in harmonious concert."

"All?" Junior said with a jerk of his head in Jim's direction. "You sayin' these two weenies in on it?"

"Indeed they are."

"Fuck we need them for?"

"Mrs. Swett has consulted with me and my companion before," Bryce explained, slipping easily into didactic gear.

"Unfortunately with a friend. And there must be no incriminating link between myself and her brief—and that's all it will be, brief and absolutely harmless—ah, absence. Now, I suspect Mr. Merriman's relationship with the lady has been considerably more discreet. Is that accurate, sir?"

"I already told you," Jim told him. "I barely know her."

"So you've protested. Yet by your own testimony, you know her well enough to arrange a tryst."

Jim hesitated, weighing the substantive differences between immediate and deferred pain. He chose deferral. "Yes."

"There you are!" Bryce exclaimed triumphantly, and like a water witcher drawn unerringly to a subterranean pool, or a tranced spirit writer effortlessly scribbling a masterwork, he unfolded his plan, sketching in its details as they came to him, which they did as if by magic, wondrous and unbidden. In the long, empty pause that followed its summation, the five conspirators simply measured each other, and themselves, and breathed. 'Til Bryce, spraying the room with his acrylic smile, said in peroration, "We're all of us players here, of one sort or another. And this, my friends, promises to be our most spectacular, not to say profitable, game."

Before he dispatched Hector to stand watch over the weenies, Junior took him aside and said, "So where you really at with this, cholo?"

"Really?"

"Yeah. No shucks, really."

"Dunno for sure."

"Could be the big piñata."

"Maybe. But how we gonna keep Mr. B off our ass while this big score goin' down?"

"Goes down, who's gonna need that sheeny?"

"And if it don't?"

"It don't, we still collect something off Uncle. That flapjaw too. Don't see how we can lose."

"Can always lose, man. You oughta know that. We both done bids."

"Yeah, that's a fact. Still five mil buys a whole lotta kickin'."

"That part ain't no bad thing," Hector conceded, his head suddenly awash in extravagant visions: himself at the helm of his own business (of what sort was unclear yet, something like Mr. B had), crisply snapping orders at employees, meeting payrolls, paying taxes same as the citizens do, porking whatever foxy blond gash he pleased—that one they talkin' about snatchin' came readily to mind), generally larging it. 'Til a simple numeric reality intruded, and he said, "Only it be more like one each, after it's cut."

"Who said anything about cuttin'?" Junior replied with a wicked smirk. " 'Cept maybe the shank kind."

While the lout (who had given his name as "Junior' and peremptorily insisted on, in his words, "campin' out here") lounged in the living room, helping himself to the Jack Daniels, Bryce looked in on Waneta, all but forgotten in the flurry of scheme conjuring. Exactly where she fit into his ingenious scenario he wasn't yet prepared to say. Insurance, possibly, should anything go awry. It was always prudent to keep an option waiting in the wings, and in the past few days, she had demonstrated an indisputable aptitude for producing plunder, albeit of the skimpy variety in contrast to the princely sums he now envisioned.

He found her sitting rather unsteadily on the edge of the bed, staring vacantly at the floor, seemingly undisturbed by all the activity outside the narrow confines of her room. "And how are you feeling, my dear?" he inquired solicitously.

"I dunno, Bryce. Dunno no more."

"Is something troubling you?"

"Yeah."

"Tell me."

"It's Billie."

Oho, Billie now, was it? She moved smartly, this one, wasted no time ferreting out the long loot and tightening her grip on it. "And what do you perceive to be the problem?" he asked coolly.

"It's her baby. A little girl. Never got born. I reached her, but she can't talk. Got no words."

"Perhaps you could, ah, supply some for her?" he suggested slyly.

"I'm tryin'. But something's happening to me, Bryce." She lifted her hands, wiggled their fingers as if to assure herself they were actually there. Then she looked imploringly at him, eyes welling with tears, and moaned, "I think I'm really hearin' 'em."

"Hearing what, exactly?"

"Voices. In my head."

Either she was going for an Oscar or was truly coming unzipped. So persuasive was her performance, if that's what it was, Bryce could no longer be sure which. In either case he didn't need this kind of vexing distraction, not now, with his own head swarming with agendas and programs and fabulous dreams through which, if realized, he'd wag the world by the tail of this final masterly swindle. So he gathered her in his arms and eased her back on the bed and, in a gentle cooing voice, said ambiguously (for he was uncertain himself what he intended), "There, there, I'm sure it's nothing. Fatigue most likely. It's been a difficult time, but I promise you it will all soon be over."

In the kitchen of his sister's apartment (*late* sister, for somewhere among all this hash, she'd gone to her reward), Jim sat chaining smokes and reflecting dourly and with only a desolate relief at this latest dodged bullet. Sitting opposite him like some malignant shadow was his numbnuts nephew, agent of this worm bag he'd found himself snared in, agent at least in part, for in Jim's experience, folly was mostly a matter of choice, and he'd made nothing but scramble-brained choices ever since he'd set foot in this bad-news state.

Uttering his first intelligible words since the narrow crunch at the Surf and Shore, but carefully avoiding Jim's eyes as he did so, Leon asked solicitously, "You OK, Uncle Jim?"

"No."

"You want a beer? Oughta be some left in the fridge."

"No."

"S'pose you're, uh, little hacked off at me, huh?"

Jim glared at him stonily. "More than a little."

"Least we didn't get our legs broke, like you said. That's something."

"Not yet we didn't. Give it time."

"What happened back there, anyways?"

"Keep it down," Jim said, nodding in the direction of the living room, where the Mexican slouched on the sofa, gawking at the television, a cigarette hung between his moist lips. A band of late-afternoon sunlight slanted through a window, glittered on his black-as-boot-polish hair.

"Oh. Yeah. Sorry."

"You want to know what happened?" Jim said in a voice reduced by nerves and nicotine to a bitter, hissy rasp. "We—no, strike that—*me*...I just got snookered into the loopiest fucking scam ever hatched in the history of scamming."

"Something to do with that lady they was talkin' about? Rich one?"

"Yeah, Leon. Something to do with her. Like in kidnapping her."

Behind the glasses Leon's eyes steepened. "No kiddin'. That could get us in deep shit."

"Yeah, I already arrived at that conclusion."

"So what're we gonna do?"

Jim had to think about it for a minute. Conditioned to small catastrophes, he recognized how woefully equipped he was to deal with anything of this magnitude. "I don't know," he said truthfully.

"If you do it, will they, y'know, let us go?"

"Not in this lifetime, I think."

PART THREE

THIRTEEN

WHEN HE WAS TEN YEARS OLD, JIM MERRIMAN discovered he possessed two talents that set him apart from his schoolmates: Out on the playground, he could run faster than any of them, and in the classroom, he was quicker with numbers than they were. The latter of these gifts he'd probably inherited from his father, a timid bookkeeper employed by a Sioux Falls, South Dakota, meat-packing plant. Jim's fleetness of foot was genetically untraceable, though in later years he came to associate it vaguely with a neurotic mother whose abiding melancholia manifested itself in a hasty retreat from life and all its baffling, messy quandaries.

By the time he was fifteen, he had earned the first of his four varsity letters in track. He also had earned a reputation as the luckiest player in a small circle of poker-playing friends, routinely and consistently relieving them of their allowances and hard-come-by wages from after-school jobs. Luck, of course, had nothing to do with it. Early on he'd discovered that success in cards turned on a keen grasp of their strictly numeric relationships, and he exploited an easy mastery of those relationships to the felicitous degree that he always had a plentiful supply of money in his pocket without the inconvenience and energy-squandering drudgery of work. So remarkable was this discovery for a Dakota boy, so empowering, it infected him with the virus of extravagant dreams and fixed the course of his life forever.

When he was eighteen, he put Sioux Falls behind him for good. Off he went to the University of Minnesota on a track scholarship, ostensibly to study accounting (at his father's solemn urging: "CPA can always get a good paying job, good benefits, good pension, anyplace, any industry.") but secretly to test his demonstrated skills with cards at a higher level. Which he did, graduating quickly from dorm-room games, where he swamped the competition, to invitation-only contests in the dingy back rooms of Lake Street bars and bowling alleys.

It took him a year and a half to flunk out of college, but he didn't go slinking home to South Dakota. Didn't have to, ever again. By now, age twenty, he had been initiated into that shadowy fraternity of streetwise hustlers who made a living—sometimes comfortable, sometimes not—off the tables and assorted other wagers. He adopted their slick vernacular and loose swagger, cultivated the hard-rock player's studied neutrality of expression, cool distancing in the eyes. Inside of four more years, he was recognized as a major player, a force in the Twin Cities' gaming circles. Name your game: draw, stud, seven-card, five, lowball, high-low, hold 'em, even the garbage games—Jim Merriman excelled at them all. Now and then a particularly canny opponent with a flair for the blindsiding bluff ran him through the wash, but for the most part, his facility with numbers rarely failed him. His wallet bulged with bills, more than he'd ever conceived of acquiring. He rented a swank furnished apartment near Lake Calhoun, dressed fashionably, drove a leased Corvette, ran through a procession of flashy Nordic blondes dazzled by the sinister glamour of his life. He was on top of the world. This corner of it anyway.

It occurred to him, when he was twenty-four, he'd reached a plateau in his career; and it was time, in his considered judgment, to expand his professional horizons, scale new heights. Having so decided, he one day disencumbered himself of the few possessions he actually owned, packed a bag, and caught a plane to Las Vegas, that Everest of his chosen vocation. His arrival was timed to coincide with the World Series of Poker hosted annually by that city. He'd squirreled away the nut, by his measure, insubstantial sum required for the buy-in, and it was his secret ambition to become, in a single lightning-lethal stroke, a name in the tight, exclusionary, cutthroat world of gambling's elite. The mysterious stranger appearing out of nowhere to topple the fabled titans of the game—that was how he envisioned it, with himself emerging the instant celebrity, welcomed, deferred to, his prodigious talent hailed and sought after wherever he traveled.

And it was during that tournament Jim made the startling, deflating discovery that he was a good player, better than most, but not a great one. Mastery of the numbers, he learned to his dismay, could take you only so far, no further. What he lacked, pitted against leathery, sleepy-eyed men with tags like Tex and Bones and Doc and Squint, was that elusive, indefinable, unteachable quality that separates stars from also-rans, headliners from opening acts, them from him. Call it intuition, or instinct, or clairvoyance, or the lowly hunch raised to the power of omniscient perception. Maybe it was nothing more than an elemental grasp of human nature as reflected in the lineaments and giveaway kinesics of the human face. Whatever it was, he didn't have it. Worse yet he recognized it would remain forever outside his reach. Worst of all, and most humiliating, he never made the first-round cut.

But for all the humbling experience of the tournament, the glitz of Vegas, its torrid heat and shimmery neon promise still entranced him. A return to the Midwest, where in his mind it was always gray, always winter, was unthinkable. With the skimpy remains of his nut, he took to playing in the sawdust casinos downtown, five-and-dime action but enough to get him back on his feet and restore his confidence, or a share of it anyway. A stake horse, impressed by his mechanical, workmanlike play, offered to bank him in private games, and soon he became a fixture in the Strip hotels, one of those competent, colorless second-stringers who got by fleecing the endless parade of visiting marks convinced they were up to the challenge of the big leagues (even as he once had been so persuaded). What they failed to realize was that this was still the sandlot, for all its gaudy trappings, and they were still out of their depth.

And what Jim failed to recognize, after achieving a small prosperity and smaller localized notoriety, was the insidious, addictive nature of his calling. The cards defined him: What he did was who he was. He had a life away from the tables but not much of one. He had a mob of acquaintances, no friends. He had women, but no lovers. A series of places to crash, never a home.

The years passed. Fourteen of them. And then the storm hit.

In gambling parlance a storm is a protracted run of evil luck, a losing streak that won't let up. Like the lightning bolt descended out of a cloudless sky, it has your name on it, stalks you like a vengeance. For Jim it began innocuously enough with—of all your unlikely pigeons—some dentists in town on a convention. Inside of four hours, they methodically stripped him of seven large, easy as extracting decayed molars. He shrugged it off, and so did his stake. Nobody wins all the time, even with dentists.

Except the next night he fared no better, or the next, or the ones after that. The numbers, once so coldly austere, so reliable, seemed to take on a malevolent will of their own, turned on him, deserted him. The stake, sensing a contagion, got into the wind. He went back to the sawdust joints and got trashed by scrubs and pitiless old ladies risking their social security checks. He tried switching games: blackjack, craps, finally even the Sominex spin of the roulette wheel. He'd play red; up came black.

Maybe it was the venue. He took his rapidly dwindling nut down to Laughlin. But the hex still dogged him. Back in Vegas he recklessly agreed to make shade for a couple of small-time scufflers with a set of gaffed cubes and a surefire scheme to skin the casinos. He should have known better, but for the first time in his life, he was panicky, desperate. Desperate times, desperate measures.

Inept at dice palming, the scufflers got themselves nailed on the first pass. Toy cops materialized at a boxman's scowly nod and hustled them off; God only knew where. While the house had nothing incriminating on Jim, his transparent role as ratchet-mouth drunk hadn't gone unnoticed. A security chief with the face and charm of a pit bull took him aside and advised him of his new persona in this establishment. Which was non grata.

News travels fast in the clannish world of gaming, and Jim Merriman was suddenly news. Of the bad variety. He was barred from every casino in town, couldn't scare up a pretzel-bet game if his life turned on it. Which it did. *Fuck 'em* was his thought. *Who needs them?* So with a certain bitterness of heart (for Vegas was the nearest he knew to home), he packed up and headed north, to Reno. Same story there. To stroll casually through a casino door was to bring the rent-a-heat instantly out of the woodwork and a restraining hand on the shoulder and the admonition, polite but firm, "Sorry, sir. Management says no." Overnight he was become a marked man. A leper.

Now his back was truly to the wall. A paralysis had set in. He took a room in a low-rent, damp-sheets hotel, locked the door, and waited for an inspiration. None came. He had a bottle sent up, drank himself senseless. The next morning he woke with a poison headache and seventeen dollars and loose change in his pocket. No miracles had arrived in the night. He sat on the edge of the bed with his throbbing skull cradled in his hands, learning the meaning of despair.

Tardy lesson. Jim never had troubled himself to examine or question the pattern of his life, never mind its meaning. When you're winning you don't have to. Now, age thirty-seven, cashed, drowned, rootless, he did. It was an instructive exercise, if not a particularly cheering one. And while he couldn't call it revelatory, no high drama to it, no "Never again, O Lord!" breast beating, he could, if he cared to, date a new direction—not necessarily more desirable or virtuous, just new to him, different—from that precise moment.

He recalled passing a store a few blocks away with a HELP WANTED sign in the window. Sold books, or something like that. Whatever. He showered, shaved, put on his last clean outfit and an eager face, and marched over there for his first-ever job interview. Amazingly he got himself hired. Didn't pay much, but anything beat nothing. Peddling books wasn't brain surgery, and before too many months elapsed, they promoted him, put him in charge of sports and games. He discovered that building a nut citizen style takes time, but eventually he was able to move out of the hotel and into a tiny studio apartment. He put a down payment on a used car (an Escort, long slide from the Corvettes he'd once piloted), opened a bank account. For something to do, he took up running again, slow jogging, more accurately, in deference to two decades of lung-charring smoke. He even read some of the books in the store, histories mostly and the lives of great men, heroes. The fraudulent gambling primers he presided over no longer held interest for him.

For two years now he'd been clean. Hadn't booked a bet or dropped a single coin in the bandits at the mom-and-pop grocery where he shopped. But like a dry drunk, he still carried a deck, played endless games of solitaire, and he still studied the Vegas sports line in the newspaper, calculating what he might have won had he beat the spreads. Whenever he passed a casino, he was overtaken by an odd, vaporous feeling, like a ghost without a house to haunt.

It was just those last two clean years of his sorry, soiled history Jim chose to reveal (sitting opposite an unsuspecting Billie Swett in a North Palm lounge two days after the spontaneous scheme had been hatched, the ding-dong bargain—and his small but pivotal role in it—sealed), and then only in oblique answer to that routine leading question by which casual flirtations routinely blossom into casual affairs: "So tell me about yourself, Mr. Jim Merriman."

"What would you like to know?"

"Who are you?"

Who am I? Heavy question. He had to think about it for a minute, and while he did, a veiled expectancy seemed to kindle her eyes, animate her lovely lacquered features, shrink the narrow distance between them. A noontime crowd jammed the spacious room. Chattery voices braided with ribbons of tinsel laughter and rose on a haze of blue smoke over the big circular bar. At adjacent booths males stole covert peeks at Billie, quick glances full of lust and longing, as if they were powerless to keep their eyes off her, couldn't help themselves. If she were conscious of the attention her person excited, she was much too self-possessed ever to let it show. Awaiting his reply, she watched him steadily. Was it amusement he detected in her expression? Sincerity? Genuine curiosity? Impossible to tell. Finally he said, lightly but only half in jest, "Just another Dakota boy, I suppose. Who never quite made good."

"And who lives now in Reno, right? What do you do out there?"

"I work in a bookstore. I'm a clerk."

"C'mon. Be serious."

"'Fraid it's a true fact." Given what was about to happen, he could think of no good reason to embroider it. Better to maintain some of that distance now. There'd be a yawning chasm opened between them soon enough.

"A *clerk*? You?"

"You were expecting maybe a Howard Hughes?"

A flicker of disbelief—or maybe it was disappointment, or pity—dampened some of the luster in her eyes. Lowering them, she said, in stumbly search of something generous to say, "Well, that's...uh...that must be nice. Being around all those books."

"Yeah, well, it's a living," he said ruefully.

Maybe a little too rueful. For now she turned a puzzled gaze on him and asked, "What's the matter, Jim? What's bothering you?"

"Bothering me? Nothing's bothering me."

"Second thoughts?"

"About what?"

"Being here."

"Why do you say that?"

"I don't know. It's just you seem jumpy. Like the other day, over on Singer Island."

"The company of gorgeous women always makes me jumpy. Makes my palms sweat."

"Oh, wow! There's a smooth pitch."

Jim shrugged. "Just another of those facts, ma'am. Nothing smooth about it. Anyway, what's a clerk got to pitch?"

"Himself maybe?" she said with a teasing arch of a perfectly plucked brow.

Chilled by a knowledge of the certain perils directly ahead of her—of both of them—he dared say only, "Maybe."

Billie, slipping seamlessly between what was plainly open invitation and what appeared to be idle, directionless patter, remarked, "You know, in a way I envy you."

"You? Envy *me*?"

"Yes."

"Why's that?"

"Myself, I don't get to read much anymore."

"No? Why not?"

"Lonnie—that's my husband—he likes TV."

"And you don't?"

"Try it night and day. See what you think."

"But sometimes you read. First time we met, at the hospital there, you told me about some centering book. Something like that."

"You remember that?"

"I remember all our conversations. All three of them."

"Keeping count, are you?"

"It's a habit."

"What else do you remember?"

"For one thing, you wanted to be a nurse, didn't make it. Why not?"

"I got sidetracked."

"How?"

Now she was the one to shrug. "Being a nurse was never anything more than a dream. The way kids do. We were a big family, Catholic, dirt poor. What I really wanted—or thought I wanted—was to get out of North Dakota. Nothing for me there."

"I can appreciate that," he said.

"So right out of high school, I came down here. Thought it would change my luck."

Jim could identify with that one too, but he said simply, "And did it?"

"Oh, yeah. It changed all right. But not for the better."

"What happened?"

She hesitated, gazed at him curiously and with a trace of doubt. "You sure you want to hear all this?"

"I asked."

"I know you did," she said, almost timidly. "It's just I'm not, well, used to anybody listening to me."

It was a side of her he hadn't expected to see. Unless it was an act, more of those games that got played. Oddly, for nothing could ever come of it but grief, he caught himself hoping it wasn't. "I'm listening," he said. "Tell me. I'd really like to know."

"A guy," she sighed. "Always it's a guy..."

As Billie launched her tale in the air-conditioned comfort of the lounge, Morris Biggs sat behind the wheel of his van, strategically parked in a file of cars directly behind the black Jaguar in the lot out back. Sweltering in the clutch of the sultry midday heat; faintly scowling at nothing in particular; jaws methodically grinding a plug of tobacco, periodically ejecting an inky spray of it through the open window, he waited with the stolid gravity of a thinker weaving an abstruse system of metaphysics from a firm grasp of a single truth. Stark in its simplicity, the essence of that self-evident, inarguable truth was that only one person was truly deserving of five million big chippers, and that person was manifestly none other than himself. Not some phony Reverend and his ding-dong squeeze. Certainly not the two welsher weenies. Not even a sometime partner (what's a spic gonna do with all that green?). Which left only Morris Junior Biggs.

Accordingly, for the past forty-eight hours, he'd been uncharacteristically compliant, watching and listening as the fat-mouth preacher ironed out the wrinkles in his plot. Figured himself for a slick plotter, Bott did, all them big words, big ideas. Fuck would a flapjaw flammer like that know about fast-step, high-risk, long-loot action? Dick is what he'd know. Let him sling all the dribble shit he wanted. OK by Junior, who was busy evolving a plot of his own, more or less parallel to the one he was hearing, right on up to the push-and-shove hour, anyway. Way he saw it, there were two flash points here: the snatching and the collecting. In between was just keeping down, fucking the dog, and watching the paint peel. Come crunch time, though, that's when they'd see who was the deep thinker.

Meantime all he could do was sit and squirm and tug at the Jockeys riding up the old south gorge. Holy fuck, was it hot. Sweat glistened his brow, pooled in his pits and along the meaty ridges of his back. A bush of hair, wiry and damp, burst from the open collar of his shirt, raised a ripe stink. An itchy blue-black stubble, two days' growth, shadowed his heavy jaw. Behind a pair of BluBockers, his eyes were dull as swamp water. Shades and whiskers were as much of a concession to Bott's insistence on a disguise as he was willing to make. Fucking amateur. Seen too many movies. Junior, he'd never seen a stiff yet who could pick a face out of a lineup. Of course he wasn't about to tell the lard bucket that. Humor him along, let him think he was calling the shots. Until the time came for him to take one himself, right behind the ear.

But for now time seemed motionless, locked in a fist of fiery heat. To get his mind off his misery, settle his wired nerves, Junior allowed his thoughts to drift. Dreamy, if somewhat sketchy, visions of all that sugar romped through his head. What he'd do with it he wasn't just sure yet. Big on the list was putting this skanky hotbox state in the rearview. Whole fucking South, for that matter—let the spooks keep it. Scoot on up to Michigan, prolly, where you could still draw a cool breath. Maybe look in on some old Brotherhood road dogs, set them up with sauce and snow all around. Like a conquering hero returned from the wars with a potful of plunder. Then he'd hire himself some boss gash, dime-a-night kind. Bunch of 'em maybe, make a pile. Oh, and he'd for sure get a big monument for Mom's grave, which he'd never had the cush to do before, all them years. Angel or something, he'd get her. Something with style, class.

A lizard scurrying across the parking-lot tar brought Junior's head back to where it had been. Until he had the loot in hand, all that other was just tooters in the wind. "First things first" was another of Junior's mottos. Except that first thing waited on Uncle Weenie, taking his own sweet time with the twat in there. Better be some action here, and Pfuckin'Dfuckin'Q, or he'd goddamn know the reason why.

Eventually there was. Uncle and the chickabiddy came sashaying out the back door, making straight for the Jag. Had the old fuck-eye look, like it was pipe-laying time for sure coming right up. Watching her, Junior was thinking this was some slinky chunk of meat under that peekaboo blouse and skirt barely clearing the honeypot. Thinking how maybe he'd have to do a little ham slamming himself before it was all done. Little perk, like. Only now what he had to do was keep his mind on business, so he turned the key in the ignition and eased the van in behind them, giving them some space but not much.

Billie's first marriage, age nineteen, was to a Pratt & Whitney engineer who perceived the world and all its inhabitants as a mesh of levers, belts, and gears to be analyzed and measured and controlled. Kermit was his name, but she preferred to remember him as Mr. Warmth. Remote, moody, a world-class skinflint, he made a decent enough salary but insisted on living like they were on the public dole. After four years of garage-sale nickel nursing, she'd had her fill, figured life was too short, and the union was summarily dissolved.

She took her meager settlement and went down to Miami and enrolled in the Academy of Nails, graduating third in her class. Too much crime down there and too many foreigners for a Dakota girl, so she returned to North Palm and got on with the Hair Affair, where she met Courtney, who would become her dearest friend. Also was it there she met husband number two, Claude (straying from the chronicle here to advise Jim, "Never marry anybody named Claude," to which he replied dryly, "I'll be sure and keep that in mind.")

Claude was a prosperous attorney, fifteen years her senior. A handsome man, regally slim, charming, and generous. What Billie remembered best about him was his hands: exquisitely soft and delicate as a child's. Should have been her first clue, but it wasn't. During their brief marriage, those hands never touched her except to present themselves for beautifying, and after she learned the score, she didn't like to think where they'd been. Turned out Claude's carnal appetites ran to junior partners in his all-male law firm (with the occasional excursion into rough trade), and he needed a wife for cover. He had no objection to her taking lovers, so long (as he was careful to insist) as it was done discreetly and with proper prudence. Fair was fair.

Billie, for her part of it, enjoyed the creature comforts that came from living with Claude (after a stretch with Kermit, who wouldn't?), but she found the arrangement a little too kinky for her heartland tastes, never mind constricting, and inside of a year, they split. Without acrimony but without much to show for it either, divorces being among Claude's lawyerly specialties. That year of idleness had cost Billie her station at the Hair Affair, so she had to scramble for work, finally landing at a place with Get Nailed, where she'd been ever since. That is, right on up to the time Lonnie Swett swaggered through the door and plunked himself down at her table, fingers demandingly extended (nothing swishy about *those* big knob-knuckled hands).

Up to then, Billie had been reasonably content with her lot. Two strikeouts at the happily-ever-after plate had made her understandably leery of marriage, though she "did a lot of dating" (as she obliquely chose to put it to Jim, who, true to his word, seemed to be intently listening, as though he found everything she had to say not just interesting but spellbinding). She joined a health club, kept herself fit. Took a Caribbean cruise and, with Courtney, trips to Aspen and Vegas. After a few years, she scraped together the down payment on a condo. Her job was secure, the money, if nothing sensational, plentiful enough to satisfy all her needs.

At least it seemed that way until she met Lonnie and got an awed glimpse of real money and what it could do. On their first date, he pulled up in a Lincoln whose tape deck was unaccountably on the blink. Irritated (for he wanted her to hear some Barry Manilow tunes, get her in the mood), he swung into a dealership, struck a deal on the spot, and emerged with a glittery new Town Car, Barry's saccharine voice echoing through its interior.

This was impressive. This upended every standard of monetary measure Billie ever had known: a body of wealth so mysterious and vast it could only be guessed at, never tallied. After she saw his Stuart mansion, all her own hard-scrambled-for possessions seemed paltry and mean. And after a courtship of the kind they like to call whirlwind, she consented, without too much persuasion, to become the next Mrs. Swett, the prenup agreement making her an instant millionaire, with the unspoken promise of more to come, considerably more, if she could stay the course.

Which concluded her recital. She sipped the last of her Chardonnay, leaned back in the booth, treated Jim to a wry smile, and said, “So there you have it. Story of my life.”

It was not, of course, or at least not the full story. Chronologies, venues, selective memories of faces and events could not, of themselves, capture the essence of a life or reveal its infinite discoveries. Then too, like Jim, she hadn’t been entirely forthcoming. Among those events she neglected to mention was her first sexual adventure, at age fifteen, conducted with a Bismark banker (fortyish at the time, married, president of the Rotary, something of a stiffly pompous prig, but with a hot eye for nubile baton twirlers, which she was), its upshot the familiar tale of pregnancy hastily terminated, an eminently sensible solution, except that termination (performed in a back room by a sotted quack of the banker’s acquaintance, a year before *Roe v. Wade* and nearly botched) would leave her barren and shadow the remainder of her days with a wistful, guilty melancholy. Nor did she speak of all the other men whoo followed, troops and troops of them, a blurry procession passing casually in and out of her flesh and her life, evanescent and inconsequential as dust motes stirring in a drafty room. Also omitted from her account (more by necessity than design, for she hadn’t the words to snare it) was the peculiar paradoxical sensation an inexhaustible supply of money inspired in her, a kind of weighted lightness, like a zeppelin freely floating on a cushion of placid air but bound to a cragged earth by gravity's relentless tug. How do you explain *that*?

She didn't have to, for in response to her summation line he said simply, "Well, you've come a long way from Bismark."

"It's been quite a trip."

"This last marriage, when was that?"

"Twenty-one months and—let me see—three weeks ago, next Sunday."

"Now who's keeping count?"

"With Lonnie Swett, you better."

"But you hit the jackpot this time out."

"I guess you could say that."

"Wouldn't you?"

She tilted her chin reflectively. "What I'd say," she said, "is after all those years of living on the cheap, I feel like I deserve it."

Jim, staring into his empty brandy glass, said, "Live long enough, and most of us get just about what we've got coming."

"You think so? I wonder sometimes."

He lifted his gaze, fixed it on her. "Something still missing, huh?"

"If it is, I've no idea *what* it is."

"What about kids, these many marriages?"

"What about them?" she said, withdrawing from his gaze.

"You have any?"

"No," she murmured but in a tone that unmistakably said, "Leave it alone. Let it be."

So he tried a different route. "Maybe it's what took you over to Bott's."

"What do you mean?"

"He's a scammer, you know," Jim found himself telling her. "Kind of man attracts people who believe something's missing."

She looked startled. "No, I *don't* know that," she said, a little defensively. "Anyway, that was a personal thing. I'd really rather not talk about it."

Jim rolled over his palms in the helpless gesture of the man who's made an effort, done his best. "OK. Then why do you suppose you're here?"

The gleam of mischief that habitually ignited her eyes was suddenly gone, displaced by urgency and need. "Maybe it's that fate you said."

He shook his head slowly, defeatedly. "Maybe you're right."

Moments later they were pointed toward the Palm Beach Gardens apartment, Billie at the Jaguar's wheel. Except for his occasional directions—"Left at the light," "Hang a right up ahead"—they rode in silence, as if an unvoiced pact between them had been firmly sealed. Until she felt compelled to remark, "You know, I don't do this with just anybody."

Declaration, was it? Pledge? Another of those claims on his feeble, feckless service? Glancing from this singular, extraordinary woman, so dazzling she could tempt the devil, to the van looming ominous as a dark funnel cloud in the mirror over the dash, Jim had to wonder whether he'd been chosen by some droll gods as the butt of a devilish practical joke. "Neither do I" was all he could manage to say.

FOURTEEN

"YEAH, I'M SURE GONNA MISS THAT OLD BEATER," Leon was saying, winding down an uncommonly windy, for him, panegyric to his forfeited vehicle, surrendered in partial redress of his long overdue obligation. "Was getting kind of, y'know, attached to it."

Hector shrugged. "Shoulda thought a' that before you come up lame, that marker a' yours."

"S'pose you're right," Leon agreed, ever eager to please but adding, more in the way of conversation than complaint, "Just I put a lot of work in it."

"Why'd you wanna do that?" Hector asked, genuinely curious over what struck him as a bonehead activity, something only an Anglo would do. "Heap like that."

"See, that's the fun of it, right there. Find yourself a rust bucket everybody says is nothing but scrapyard then restore it with your own two hands, good as new. Better even, sometimes."

"That what you do for a livin'?"

"Pretty much," Leon said vaguely.

"Any money in it?"

"Oh, yeah. Take that Caddie of mine. I'd've ever got around to spiffing up the body and interior, it'd gone for an easy, oh, thirty thousand, I bet."

Hector snorted skeptically. "C'mon. Nobody'd pay that."

"You'd be surprised. Collectors, they'll pay top dollar for an ark. 'Course it's the dealers make all the money, not us grease rats."

"Wha's that? Ark?"

"Real oldie. I'm talkin' thirty, forty years and up. Got to be restored hundred percent, though. Mint shape."

"Me, I like 'em bran' new. Fresh off the lot. Drivin' a Mustang right now."

"You like Mustangs," Leon said, warming to the topic, "you'd *really* get pumped off this bomber we got in the shop a while back. Jeez, you should've seen it," he rhapsodized, gesturing excitedly, seeing it again in his mind's eye. "Impala Super Sport, sixty-three, bone-white convertible, big as a tank but with a rocket under the lid. God, that was a sweet machine! I was working on it before I got in all this, y'know..."

The thought trailed away on a helpless toss of a hand. "Dog shit?" Hector finished for him.

"Yeah, that's it. Dog shit."

"How that happen anyways?" Hector asked, damn if he knew why. None of his business, not his problem.

"Making bets. I was thinking I could maybe raise the money to buy that Impala myself."

"Dumb fuckin' way go about it."

"I can see that now. The time, though, seemed like a good idea. Maybe it's something in my blood."

Hector's eyes strayed to the floor. "Ah, whaddya you talkin', blood?" he said, batting the air.

"No, I mean something, like, inherited. My Uncle Jim, he's a professional gambler. Played in that World Series they got for poker, out in Las Vegas."

"That a fact."

"Yeah, he's really good at cards. Made a pile of money off them."

"He so good, how come he only got three long from over that bank, kick in on your debt?"

"Guess he's not been playing that much lately."

"Yeah, well, he in a game now, like it or not. An' he better pull a hand a' aces."

"You, uh, think he will?"

"Your sake," Hector said darkly, remembering his charge, "he better."

"Sure hope so," Leon murmured, his voice, clotted with dread, sinking to a whisper.

Though he was by nature and temperament an easygoing, social kind of guy, Hector took no great pleasure in batting the breeze with a dead man. Which was what this kid was going to be, if not today then for sure before the whole loopy caper got wrapped. Yet here they were, sitting at the kitchen table in his croaked mama's apartment, pot of coffee and plate of bagels between them, little ass wart woofing on about his wheels they hocked yesterday to come up with some coin against that marker he still had out ("Plan B" Biggs called it: "Case somethin' go scatty, the snatchin', we still got us forty-plus large to cut up."), chitchatting away like a couple of long-bid cellies passing the time of day. Instead of how it was supposed to be, him doing the strong-arm number, striking terror into the heart of their weenie hostage, while Biggs kept a tail on Uncle to protect their newest business venture.

So here you had this kid with the crop of wild hair and Magoo glasses and dippy grin, scarfing up a bagel slathered with cream cheese, humping his gums, without a clue he was crowbait, and here was your badass Hector Pasadena who got to baby-sit him, snubby Colt trey-eight (supplied courtesy of Biggs from the arsenal he kept in the back of the van) ominously stuck in his belt, slopping coffee and slinging his own share of the shit, but the whole time thinking how he never had done a waxing in his life. Never even come close. The thought of which stirred another nagging worry. Fuck, make that fear—call it what it is.

Earlier that morning, after Biggs and Uncle had left, Hector had put in a call to Mr. B, figuring to stall him until he got his head around everything that was coming down. Mr. B just listened while Hector spun some good-news smoke about how they maybe were going to collect the Cody marker, full bundle or pretty close. Then Mr. B said, distant and cool, the way only he could, "That would be most gratifying, Hector."

"May take a few more days," Hector cautioned.

"Perfectly all right. Take all the time you need."

Hector was thinking he was home free, until Mr. B put in, "By the way, I've another assignment I'd like you to attend to while you're up there."

"Wha's that one?"

"You recall my mentioning we'd have to reevaluate our situation? Regarding Mr. Biggs?"

"Yeah," Hector said carefully, "I 'member you sayin' somethin' like that."

"Well, I've come to the conclusion the time has arrived to terminate our business association with him."

"You sayin' you want me to—"

"Do whatever you feel is necessary," Mr. B broke in on him, "to effect that termination."

Dumbstruck at this abrupt, altogether untimely turn of events in an already snarled life, Hector could only breathe into the phone, quickened and evidently audible breaths, as Mr. B said, "You're all right with this, Hector?"

"Yeah, sure."

"You're certain now? If not, I can send in someone else."

"Nah, I'm good with it."

"Excellent. Let me know, will you, when the, ah, severance is complete."

"We lookin' at any special timelines here?"

"The sooner the better. No profit in delaying these unpleasant matters. Wouldn't you agree?"

Hector mumbled something that passed for agreement.

"Oh, and Hector, there'll be a handsome bonus in it for you."

"Bonus be good too," he said glumly, and they rang off, leaving him wondering about things he'd never thought to wonder about before, forces without names, blocking doors and backing you into corners, squeezing in on you and sucking your guiltless lifeblood like vampire bats in the shriek flicks do, and...A voice across the table brought him back to where he was, which was where he'd been ever since he'd put down the phone. Not a good place to be. He glanced over and saw the kid holding up the coffeepot. "You say somethin'?" Hector asked him.

"Said, 'Do you want me to make some more?' "

"Nah, don't bother. They oughta be here any time now."

"It's no trouble."

Hector flapped a hand, an impatient "whatever" gesture.

Kid set down the pot, gave him a funny crossways squint. "Anything wrong?"

"Ain't nothin' wrong."

"Then you mind if I ask you something?"

"You can ask," Hector said noncommittally.

"What should I call you?"

"Whaddya mean?"

"For a name. Your friend there, he calls you '*chico*,' but that's not really your name, is it?"

"No. An' he ain't no friend. We workin' together is all. Not friends."

"So what should I call you?"

"Name's Hector."

"Mine's Leon," the kid said, sticking out a hand as if to seal the formal introductions.

"Yeah, I already know that," Hector drawled, but he took the offered hand anyway, immediately regretting it, not because he was giving away something that someday would come back and bite him in the ass, but because it just didn't feel right, like pressing palms with a stiff. Too late now. He released his grip and got up out of the chair, saying, "Think I'll go watch the TV. Pass some time."

"Good idea," said the kid, trailing Hector into the living room like a shadow he couldn't shake.

So now they were sitting either end of the sofa, Hector clutching the remote, idly grazing the channels until he settled finally on a midday exercise show, troop of fluff with the cooze in charge, one of them big Amazon ladies, warheads out to here, python thighs, muscles in her shit, the kind that could fuck your brains right outta your skull and wanna know who was next on the boink list. It was an image diverting and welcome; only right away it got blurred by a casual remark coming off the kid: "You hear about that hurricane?"

Sounded like the opener to a gag, and Hector was in no mood for humor. "This a joke?" he said sourly.

"It's no joke. They're saying it's out in the ocean now but maybe headed our way. Could hit by early next week. You can probably catch it on the Weather Channel, you want."

Holy mother of fuck, now it gotta be a fucking hurricane blowing in? Like he didn't already have enough on his grief plate. "We'll stay with the jiggle butts," Hector said, but for all his best efforts at attention to the peppy display of wholesome sexuality on the screen, the lickerish image was lost to him for good.

Half an hour later, Jim swung open the door and ushered Billie into his sister's apartment. She took a tentative step inside and, discovering this unlikely pair slouched on the sofa and gaping blankly at the television, turned a puzzled look on him and said, "You didn't mention any roommates."

In his head, Jim had rehearsed a speech of quieting reassurance, but before he could deliver even its opening line, a guttural voice rose up behind him, upstaged him. "Couple other things he forgot to mention, I betcha." He spun around, and there stood Biggs, jeery smirk on his face, looming like a roadblock in the entrance.

"Whyn't you folks just mosey on in there?" Junior said, phrasing it more as cordial invitation than command, but at the same time, pulling the door shut and turning the lock. "Make yourselves at home."

For an instant Billie, baffled, was unable to move. "Jim?" she said.

And he, unable to meet the cluster of shifting emotions in her eyes—doubt, anger, confusion, disbelief, dismay, a dawning panic—could only respond to the plea in her voice with the feeble advice, "Better do what he says."

Junior, still smirking, made a brushing motion with the back of a hand, urging them on. In a kind of halting, invalid shuffle, Billie stepped into the living room. Leon and Hector came to their feet, and Junior, playing at mein host, clearly relishing the role, boomed, "Boys, want you to say hello to Mrs. Swett. She gonna be our guest awhile." Neither of them spoke. Both studied the carpet uneasily and a little shamefacedly, awkward sand kickers destitute either of words or sand.

When Billie saw the butt of a gun protruding from Hector's belt, her face went ashen under its layers of paints and powders, and her eyes began to moisten and her shoulders tremble. To Jim, flanking her, watching her, she said, "What is it? What's going on?"

"Like I just tol' these two dummies here," Junior answered for him, "we gonna have to ask you to be our guest."

"You're kidding," Billie said with that uncertain twitch of a smile of someone who's missed the joke.

Junior elevated his thick shoulders in a stagy, helpless shrug. "'Fraid not."

"You mean I'm being *kidnapped*?"

"That's about the size of it. Only more like a—what'd that shit sack call it, Uncle?"

"Detention," Jim mumbled.

"There ya go. Detention."

Billie shot an accusatory glance at Jim. "This was your idea?"

"Not mine," he protested from behind uplifted disclaimer palms.

"But you're in on it?"

"Well...sort of...in a way," he stammered then gave up. "It's hard to explain."

"With *them*?" she demanded, teary eyes shuttling among the other figures in the room, her expression a blend of revulsion and incredulity and disenchantment, equal parts.

"Look," Jim said, grasping after some scattered remnants of his prepared speech, "you're in no danger here. Nobody's going to hurt you." He could have cut it off right there, should have, but astonishingly and almost against his will, certainly his better judgment, he heard himself invoking the dreaded "p" word once again, declaring stoutly, "That much I promise you."

Junior, unwilling to surrender the spotlight for long, produced a big chortling laugh, not a scintilla of mirth in it. "You heard it," he announced, playing to the room. "Straight from the horse's ass's mouth. She got herself a he-man. Uncle Weenie here gonna protect her, case one a' you boys, ain't sayin' which"—pause here for a broad, lewd wink Hector's way—"get the ol' itch, take it in your head to do the dirty hula with this fine lady."

Billie shuddered.

"You know the agreement," Jim reminded him, not quite as firm as before.

Junior snapped a theatrically recollective finger by an ear. "Seem to me I do remember somethin' along them lines," he allowed, adding in vocalized sneer, "Good thing we got you to keep our mind on business, Mr. He-fuck."

"Why don't you get to it then?"

"Gonna do just that, soon's you people got yourselves cozied in. *Chico*, you watch out for these folks now, y'hear. Make sure they comfy while I put in that call."

Hector grunted something unintelligible and stayed on his feet, one hand resting on the gun butt. Junior picked up a cell phone and shambled off to the privacy of a bedroom. Leon sank back onto the sofa, and Jim joined him, still watching Billie, who, like Hector, remained standing. “Might as well sit,” Jim said, indicating a chair.

Dazedly she sat.

For a time no one had anything to say. On the television screen, muted at their arrival, the assemblage of female fitness freaks bounced and wriggled and kicked, bursting with pure mindless vigor. Finally it was Jim who broke the silence. Addressing Billie, he said quietly, “Listen, I’m sorry about all this. I didn’t want it to happen, but there was nothing I could do. For what it’s worth, I apologize.”

“What you said before,” she asked him, “did you mean it?”

“Which part?”

“About the danger. Am I going to be, you know, safe here?”

“I meant it,” he said, not unaware of the equivocation in his reply. Meaning it was one thing, bringing it off quite another.

But for Billie, hearing it uttered was enough. She was suddenly conscious of a wetness in her eyes; realized she was crying, only now not so much from the sheer terror of this as from a kind of elusive, heady excitement; and composed herself and simply stopped. “Wow!” she exclaimed in a voice full of wonder and the squirmy elation of a child on the way to her first circus. “If this isn’t something! I’ve never been kidnapped before.”

“You, uh, want something to eat?” Leon volunteered with a shy, jerky grin. “We got cold cuts in the fridge.”

“Shut up, Leon,” Jim snapped.

“No, that’s OK,” she said, faintly smiling. “Sounds good. Really. Believe it or not, I think I’m hungry.”

FIFTEEN

BRIMMING WITH EXPECTANCY AND ENERGIZED BY resolution, Bryce had wakened early that morning, slipped noiselessly out of bed, and in that coy, tiptoe way of walking he lately had adopted out of deference to his partner's frailty, real or feigned, crossed the narrow hall and peeked into her room. Sleep seemed to lend her gaunt, splendid features an almost ethereal beauty, as though discourse with the community of the dead had sanctified her, washed away all her trifling sins. For an instant he experienced a twinge of some emotion alien to his nature, something on the order of guilt, but he was much too charged to allow it to dampen his exuberance for whatever lay immediately ahead this day.

After his morning ablutions, he took a moment to regard his own features in the bathroom mirror, more or less approvingly: eyes clear, even sparkly, some might say; cheeks, under their doggie folds and fissures, ruddy still; chin admittedly a tad plumpish and, viewed in profile, slightly saggy but nothing a bit of gastronomic restraint couldn't remedy; hair utterly devoid of color, true, but with a springtime abundance and sheen remarkable in a man of his years. And twilighting though they undeniably were, those years remaining to him held out every promise of a sufficiency of time and vitality (for mirrors, after all, never lie) to savor the succulent fruits of this bold enterprise, once he successfully saw it through to its lofty conclusion.

Following this somewhat preening self-inspection, Bryce dressed in casual wear, prepared and consumed a substantial breakfast of waffles, eggs, sausage, and assorted pastries (time enough for that restraint later—everything in its time, if the Good Book had it right); stepped out the front door to examine the morning; and stifling a rising dyspeptic burp, pronounced it good. Sunlight seeped through a curtain of orange mist, gradually burning it away. Gulls wheeled across the sky. Sounds of a gently lapping surf reached his ears, and as though tugged by the ocean's subdued, rhythmic heartbeat, he set out, on impulse, for the beach. No reason not. A leisurely stroll, he reasoned, would do him good, sweep away any lingering nocturnal cobwebs, ease the self-inflicted weight on a seriously burdened gastrointestinal tract. Perhaps even settle his twitchy nerves.

Soon he was planted in the white sand that fronted the mall, its shops and beach deserted at this early hour. A salty breeze lifted off the water, deepened the pink in his already rosy cheeks. He gazed out at the grandeur and immensity of the sea, swamped by those feelings of awe that sometimes will overtake even the crassest of men, which he, while many things, surely was not. The filtered light cast gorgeous mosaic patterns of color on the ocean's ripply surface, which to Bryce seemed to reach like a sheet of stained glass to the very end of the earth, boundless as his dreams. And in that reverent moment, he found himself reflecting on a lifetime of dreams, summoning images long buried and blurred by time.

There was the boy he once had been, pathetic child of poverty, trudging the grim Depression-era streets of Cleveland, lugging a bag of *Plain Dealers* in his first legitimate job. Also his last, as it turned out. Customers along his route were kind enough to alert him to a suspension of delivery (and thus of desperately needed income) during their planned vacations, and it occurred to this clever boy that the lost revenues could be recovered by a selective looting of those empty dwellings. His first B & E netted him something under thirty amateurishly hidden dollars, a princely sum in those days, and it dawned on him he never would have to work again.

There he was, grown to adolescence but crafty beyond his years, teamed now with a corrupt postman who delivered mail to the prosperous citizens of Shaker Heights. Essentially the scheme was the same: suspended postal service for a conveniently specified period of time signaling a target residence. While the hazards in such a privileged and security-conscious a community were considerable, the rewards were commensurately greater than anything he'd experienced in his newsboy days. Until, that is, a platoon of postal inspectors collared his luckless partner, and Bryce was obliged to decamp in the night, the first of many hurried flights.

Next his memory served up a portrait of a dapper young man, slender, well dressed, quiet-spoken, projecting an air of substance as he toured, in the company of a gushy realtor, a selection of costly homes offered for sale in the affluent Chicago suburb of Winnetka, mentally cataloging those items that would turn a handsome profit following a later, unscheduled visit.

The man outfitted in drab institutional gray (lodged in a Stateville Prison cell after one of those return visits proved to be egregiously ill timed) was less clear to him, muddied by time's merciful censors. Yet his recollections of that five-year stretch, while dim, weren't entirely melancholy. Defeats are also opportunities, and with typical industry, he seized this one to embark on what would become a lifelong program of self-improvement, refining scamming skills that were by then as mechanical and thoughtless as breathing, and emerging as a free worlder armed with the liberating knowledge that there were easier ways to turn a bill than burglary.

Most of those gainful formulas had been lost in the lengthening shadows of the years, but some of the more ingenious among them came back to him now, sparking a fond, nostalgic chuckle. There was that poetry contest sponsored by the prestigious Society of Prairie Poets (the distinguished body of which consisted of himself). Modest sawbuck entry fee bought you a chance to win a guaranteed thousand-dollar first prize, publication in a soon-to-be forthcoming volume titled, *Best of the Prairie Poets,* and not least of all, the accolades of your fellow sensitive wordsmiths. A swarm of would-be bards responded to a few well-placed ads, crammed the society's Omaha PO box with mountains of atrocious doggerel, and stuffed Bryce's pockets with lucre. A week or so after the submissions deadline (for even those stragglers suffering from writer's block must be served), he prudently packed up his tent and moved on.

How about that "Save a Child" venture! That one could bring a smile to his face even now. That swindle operated out of Salt Lake City, with its geographic implications of Mormonesque endorsement, and expanded to regional publications with a full-page plea (complete with graphic photo of piteously malnourished waif) to rescue a starving tot in whatever far-off land was visited by calamity that year; he could vividly recall the intensity of his glee at the veritable avalanche of monetary mercy triggered by that inspired hustle. 'Til those irksome postal inspectors swooped down on him, and he was once again compelled in unseemly haste to search out new venues and ventures.

Never easy to trace (for Bryce Bott was quite possibly the last person in the republic to be without benefit of a social security number), he landed in LA. Its proliferation of lunatic fringe religious cults prompted him to obtain his divinity credentials (at the economical cost of one hundred dollars plus a small shipping and handling fee for the framed diploma) from an institute specializing in mail-order degrees. Soon he was launched on a career in applied theology, the pious applications of which resulted in a most comfortable living, thereby certifying the truth of that homespun homily that promises the Lord will provide, now and then even munificently.

Sadly, if inevitably, some problems developed out there, something to do with a too generous skimming of offertory plates, and under the sheltering cover of night, he was pointed next in a southeasterly direction. Reasoning that a fascination with the mystery of death was at the nub of all religion, he plunged into the tombstone business, traveling the back roads of that steamy, God-intoxicated Bible Belt designed by heaven for a man of his widening experience (not to speak of thickening flesh) and enlarging talents. Along the way he acquired a confederate, the hardmouthed but malleable Waneta Jean Pease, whose cranky presence and irascible disposition seemed perversely to fill the emptiness of his advancing years.

Looking back on it all, or all the fragments his crowded memory could retrieve, Bryce recognized his had been a life lived in a maze of plots and schemes, tawdry perhaps, but shaping him into the man he had become and drawing him predestinedly to this place where now he stood, a solitary figure on a lonely beach, hatching a last-hurrah swindle of daring and staggering dimension. Not for nothing was it called the Treasure Coast, this muggy, glitzy swamp where only good things happen to patient, deserving souls not unlike himself, and all worthy dreams ultimately come true.

The sky's thin veil of mist was gone now, melted away, and the sun's fierce slanted fingers of light beat in his eyes like a cosmic blessing. A reverie-annulling glance at his watch restored him to the then and there, the practical business at hand. He turned his back on the sea and plodded through the loose sand in the direction of the Surf and Shore, latest in a numberless succession of transient forgeries of home, sustained by the thought that if the gods were kind and if things went as planned, waiting for him somewhere at the end of this long labyrinthine road was a place of permanence and tranquility faithful to his vision of an authentic home.

While it was something of a surprise to come through the door and discover his partner out of her bed, if not her shapeless sack of a nightie, and perched on a stool at the kitchen counter, Bryce prided himself on an unflappable composure, and the sick-room ebullience of his greeting was only partly induced. "Waneta, my dear, what a pleasure to see you up and about. Warms this old heart."

"Huh?" she said, addressing not him but the wall on which her gaze was leveled, head slightly tilted, as though eaves-dropping on conversations outside the range of ordinary ears. Withered, skeletonic, Dachau-eyed, skin the color of dried paste, she seemed day by day to be shriveling before his very eyes, like one of those cinematic dissolves: a dizzying swirl, a poof, and there goes Ms. Pease. The manifest physical wasting Bryce knew could not be faked, but as for the rest of it, the ghostly-seeming trance, hard experience cautioned him, a man of earthly pursuits, to withhold judgment. "I was remarking on your visibly improved condition," he lied.

"Improved," she repeated dully. "Yes, improved."

"Would you care for a bite to eat? A light breakfast perhaps?"

Now she turned the vacant gaze on him. "Food?"

"I beg your pardon?" he was obliged to ask. Lately her voice never rose above the faintest of whispers.

"You're sayin' food?"

Bryce cleared his throat. "Yes. Food."

She moved her head slowly, negatively.

"Some coffee then?"

"OK."

"Coffee it is," he declared with a heartiness by now entirely forced, conscious of her hollow eyes trailing him around the counter and into the tiny galley and through the busy motions of brewing, the acuteness of his discomfort growing in proportion to the intensity of that zombied stare, probing but blank, giving away nothing. To put something, anything, into the silence, he said, "Sure you won't change your mind about that breakfast? A tasty poached egg? Some dry toast?"

"No."

"Plenty of time before our first clients arrive," he coaxed and, trolling, added, "And our larder is abundantly stocked, thanks to your stellar performances."

But she wasn't taking the bait, not even a nibble, though his slyly appended verbal bouquet was inarguably true. The trickle of other-side marks (at her insistence no longer referred to as such but rather by the softer "clients") had in the span of five short days swollen to a steady stream, validating testimony to his unerring swindler instincts. Coots, most of them, fugitives from the boneyard, with the dazed look of infants that seems to ask, "What's going to happen?"—or in their case, "What *did* happen? Where did it all go?" Hunched, buckled, clinging to crumpling puddings of flesh with gnarly claws desperately grasping after any wispy evidence of anything beyond the approaching darkness—their nasty presence reminded Bryce of his own mortality and rekindled his sense of urgency. And though he accepted their modest donations with an enameled churchy smile, they were side action now, nothing more, pregame calisthenics to the play-offs dead ahead.

He filled two cups, set one of them before Waneta, and declared, "Nothing like hot coffee to fortify one against the rigors of the day. Drink up, my dear."

She complied, trembly blue hand elevating the cup to blue lips, but swallowing no more than a droplet before returning it, like some enormously weighty burden, to the counter. The vaguely unsettling emotion Bryce had experienced earlier, spying on her sleep, surfaced again, unbidden, unwelcome, and in a voice that seemed to belong to someone else, he heard himself say, "You really must take better care of yourself, Waneta. I worry about you, you know."

She lifted a bony shoulder, half a shrug. Her eyes strayed from him to the toaster by the sink, and she seemed to scrutinize her image, weirdly distorted on its polished metal, not from some dimly remembered vanity but out of a compelling need to be sure she was still there. And watching it, this bizarre, revealing display, Bryce was almost persuaded she had in truth tumbled over the edge, truly believed she communed with a world more marvelous and dangerously seductive than the one we thought we knew.

Until she murmured, "Whatever happened to Billie?"; and then the alarm that more times than a few had delivered him from disaster sounded again in a distant vault of his head, and very carefully he said, "The generous Mrs. Swett, you mean?" Question for a question.

"She said she'd come back. Never did. What happened?"

Was that a hint of a canny shimmer Bryce detected in those ice-green eyes? His swindle radar was on full alert now, picking up the tiniest blips on its wide screen. Yet what could she actually know? Over the past forty-eight hours, the several tactical sessions with his new, if purely ad hoc, partners had been conducted elsewhere or, if here, late at night, after he was certain Waneta had fallen into an exhausted sleep. He decided she was the one doing the fishing now, so he said, "I have no idea. A woman of her status and means doubtless has many demands on her precious time. Or possibly someone got to her," he added with the deliberate ambiguity of a private joke.

The point of which she either missed or ignored, for she sighed dolefully and said, "I could've helped her."

"Really," he said, smothering a dubious smile. "And how exactly is that?"

"With that baby. I was so close. The words were coming to me."

"I'm sure they were. But as you may recall, in our profession even the most witless of, ah, clients will sometimes get away."

For an instant, no more than a frozen beat, she seemed to glare at him, then said, "When's the next one?"

"Client?"

"Yeah."

"Not for a while yet. No hurry. Finish your coffee."

"No," she said, climbing wearily off the stool. "I better get myself ready."

"But you *are* ready," Bryce protested with a sweeping, slightly distasteful glance that took in the whole of her frowzy, emaciated person, head to toe, and said it all.

She gave her temple a sly finger tap, and in that dementia voice she had mastered—hushed, superior, entranced—said knowingly, "*In here* ready," and shuffled off to her room.

Leaving him to ponder the riddle of her baffling metamorphosis, sudden as a flash flood, or a cyclone descended out of a bland sky. Real, was it? Cunningly dissembled? Bryce couldn't be sure. Circles inside of circles, games within games.

The morning crawled by. Punctually at nine the first in the day's procession of marks, a wobbly blue head (orange, more accurately, given the improbable tint in the frizzy hair) with clown spots of rouge on her collapsed cheeks, appeared at the door, oozing anticipation and that potent mix of dusting powders and vile colognes and musty old-lady odors. Nevertheless Bryce, outfitted now in his reverend costume and ever the consummate professional, double gripped her quivery claw with that clasp that conveys a double dose of pious warmth, and escorted her back to the celestial messenger girl. He waited in the living room (for long since had Waneta made it plain his presence at these séances was neither required nor particularly welcome), periodically wandering into the kitchen 'til finally he'd emptied the coffeepot and inhaled the remaining pastries. After an hour the fossil emerged, filmy eyed and subdued but not too numbed to forget to drop a nifty fifty in the plate.

Others followed, and as noon neared and passed, the hands on the dial of his watch creeping toward one o'clock, then two, then later than two, Bryce's patience began to dwindle and his confidence to crumble, pendulating between caffeinated agitation and chilling dread. Had something gone wrong? Could the cretinous Biggs somehow have botched it? Bryce had encountered his kind before, in the keep: raw, festering boils of violence waiting to erupt. Kidnapping, maybe even homicide—these were not your sidewalk-spitting bids. Grim visions of iron bars slamming shut behind him, or worse, himself strapped to a gurney, a needle pumping state-sanctioned vengeance into a bulging vein, flickered behind his eyes like scenes from a grainy black-and-white movie. He paced the floor, circled the stubbornly silent phone tacked to the kitchen wall, as though daring it to ring.

At last it did.

"Bott?" demanded the rude voice on the other end of the line, a growly response to a greeting deliberately muffled by a cupped hand.

"Speaking."

"Biggs."

"Yes?"

"OK. That treasure? We got it."

Bryce, with the natural showman's flair for the dramatic, had insisted they refer to the targeted Mrs. Swett as "the treasure," a cryptic code that, given the score's venue, not to say anticipated take, seemed altogether appropriate. "Without any, uh, complications, I trust," he said, with an effort to contain the tremor in his voice.

"Nah. Was cake."

"Swell," said Bryce, in one of those quaint anachronisms that sprang spontaneously to his lips. "That's just swell."

"Better'n swell. We're talkin' uptown ticket here. First-class ride."

"And how is our treasure taking it?"

"Not bad so far. No kickin' and screamin'. Not even much in the way a' your basic waterworks."

"Splendid. That should make the downtime easier. For all parties."

"Could at that."

"Our other associates? How are they holding up?"

"You talkin' about the weenie boys?"

"Yes."

"Good. Uncle, he done good. Took him a while, but he bagged her."

"I was confident he would," Bryce said, a trifle smugly now that a share of his own confidence was back.

"Y'know, speakin' a' them, the weenies, I'm thinkin' now we got our strut on, maybe it's time to lose 'em."

"Lose? I'm not sure I follow you."

"Oh, I think you do."

Which of course he did, followed it only too clearly to its logical, bloody conclusion, his earlier death-house visions displaced now by an image, stark and vivid, of this brutish lout and his sinister spic sidekick closing in on him, painfully dispatching him to the ranks of the conveniently "lost" and absconding with the loot. Merriman, for all his finicky scruples, was the only cannon in the lot not loose, and Bryce was keen enough to recognize what he needed in the white-knuckle days ahead was an ally, albeit temporarily. How to put it persuasively to Biggs was another matter. After a hesitation he settled on a decisive, "That would be very unwise."

"Yeah? Why's that?"

"By your own testimony he 'did good.' And he can do us even more good during that waiting period I mentioned. Obviously there's some sort of bond between the treasure and him. His presence will keep her calm, pacified. I'm sure you'll agree," Bryce concluded, praying sweet reason would penetrate that granite skull, prevail, "that we want no resistance or undue upset."

A silence, breath-catching in its menace, filled the line. Bryce clenched and unclenched his free hand, squeezing fresh dreads from the air. Finally, in a husky drawl, faintly amused, Biggs said,

"S'pose you're right. Couple more days ain't gonna matter none anyways."

Bryce's clenching hand went suddenly limp. "I'm pleased you see it my way."

"Your way or the highway, that how it is, Reverend?"

Bryce didn't much care for the insolent tone, but he wasn't prepared to challenge it either. "Not at all," he said mildly. "This is a collaborative venture. Has been from the start."

"Yeah, that's real good to know. So how's about we button 'er up here, and you collaborate us up a call to Big Daddy. Get that money ball rollin'."

"I was about to suggest the same."

"Couple great minds, huh? OK, you lemme know what you hear."

"You'll be the first."

Bryce put down the phone, released a prodigious sigh, removed from an inner pocket a scrap of paper covered with meticulously penned prompts, and softly tested the timbre of his voice on one of them, reaching after a tonal conception of the low, louring resonances of intimidation, Biggs fashion. It was a long way from perfect but the best he could do. He braced himself, picked up the phone again, and with a slightly trembly finger, pecked out the Swett number.

SIXTEEN

AN UNSEASONABLE SUMMER COLD BROUGHT BIG Lonnie home from his Swett Equities offices earlier than usual that afternoon. Manifesting itself in ominous bronchial rattles and spasmed seizures of hacking, accompanied by bursts of sneezing that fired gooey missiles of phlegm, this distressing ailment seemed to him like a personal affront, unaccountable and entirely unjust, and rendered his at best surly temper all the more dour. Nor was it improved when he stalked through the door, looking for the kind of wifely commiseration a man had a right to expect, and discovered no wife to be found. A snappish interrogation of the cowed housekeeper produced nothing more than the vague intelligence that Mrs. Swett had gone to lunch with someone, a friend, that Courtney, maybe it was, exactly where not known. Thoroughly disgusted, Big Lonnie told her to fix him a triple-decker club sandwich, heavy on the mayo, and a Bloody Mary and bring them to the Jacuzzi out by the pool.

And that's where he'd been for the past hour or better, soothing his aching flesh and looking, with his flushed face and grizzled torso projecting from the foaming water, remarkably like a side of human beef boiling in a cannibal pot, nursing clogged nasal passages and a fuming grudge when the omnipresent cell phone, strategically placed on the tray beside the crumbly remnants of the vanished triple-decker, rattled.

"Yeah," he barked into it in that itching-for-trouble tone of a man unaccustomed either to insubordination or neglect.

But to his considerable disappointment, the voice hurling back at him was not his wife's, cooing some sorry-ass excuse, as he fully expected and was fully primed to reject (no more Mr. Nice Guy) but rather a scratchy rasp demanding, "Lon Swett?"

"Yeah? Who's this?"

"None of your business who. From now on the only business concerns you is what I have to tell you. Got that?"

To Big Lonnie it sounded like some dink doing a bad impression of a mafia don, a sissified Marlon Brando. For an instant he wondered whether it was a joke, and that's what he said, "This some kinda joke? It is, I ain't in no haw-hawin' mood."

"See how much you're laughing when I'm done. You got any idea where your wife is right about now?"

"Huh?" Big Lonnie grunted, startled despite himself.

"Got your attention, did it? You listening now, Swett? I'm asking if you know where your wife's at."

"Fuck're you, talkin' about my wife?"

"I'm the one who's got her is who I am. You want her back in one piece, you better talk to me."

For perhaps the first time in his long life, Big Lonnie found himself strapped for words. Strained as the gravelly menace in this stagy voice might be, and undermined as it was by a distinctly limp-dick edge, its hardball message was nonetheless slowly getting through to him, tuning up the calculator that ran incessantly inside his head. "Swett?" it was demanding now, a little shrilly. "You there? Swett?"

"I'm here."

"Good, good. All right, now—"

"You sayin' Billie's been kidnapped?"

"That's exactly what I'm saying."

"She OK?"

"She's fine. Now if we can—"

"Put her on."

A pause on the line, followed by the uncertain, "She's not, uh, available just now."

"Then how'm I suppose to know this ain't some dog-shit hoax?" Big Lonnie shot back in his best "gotcha" pitch. "Huh? Answer me that one."

"Because I'm telling you is how," came the exasperated reply, all pretense of toughness erased on a prissy sigh. "Do you see her there? Heard from her today? Would I be calling you if I didn't have her? Use your God-given intelligence."

"God? What're you talkin', God?"

"Very well then, your head. Use your head, man."

"OK, s'posin' it's true, what you're sayin'. Fuck you want off me?"

"If you'll stop interrupting, I'll tell you."

"So spit it out."

"Five million dollars."

Now it was Big Lonnie's turn to expel a labored breath, more on the order of incredulous snort than sigh, and nothing prissy about it.

"Are you still with me, Mr. Swett?"

"You're kiddin', right? This really *is* a joke."

"Believe me, it's no joke. Five million. By Monday. Or she comes home in one of those, ah, bodybags."

"Monday!" Big Lonnie squawked. "That ain't possible."

"If you want her back badly enough, anything's possible."

"Today's Thursday, f'chris'fuckin'sake. You got any idea how long it takes to put together that kinda money?"

"I'm confident you'll find a way."

"You got shit in your ear? I'm sayin' it can't be done."

"You'll do it. I've got faith in you. Oh, and Swett, one other thing. No cops. Bring them in, and she's a dead woman. Are we clear on that point?"

"Yeah, it's clear."

"Splendid. You'll hear from me next on Saturday. And I'll expect to hear from you a progress update on that five million."

"An' what I'm tellin' *you* is—" Big Lonnie tried to tell, but he was telling it to a dial tone. He put the phone back on the tray and, half seething, half stunned, settled deeper—chin deep—into the frothy water, its bubbly heat a welcome anodyne for the staggering news, arrived out of nowhere, like this nagging fucking head cold, to rupture the rightful tranquility of his day. *His* day. And *his* wife. And *his* jack, five mil of it. Some sissy thought he was gonna lift five extra large off Big Lonnie Swett, he had another thing coming right at him, full steam. What kind of thug talked like that anyway, saying, "splendid" and "progress update," *scheize* like that? None he ever knew, and he'd known his share in his time. Something fishy was going on here, and he was going get to the bottom of it. Only how, that part he didn't know yet.

What he decided he needed was an audience, someone to run his thoughts by, help him find a way out of this worm can. Had to be someone you could trust, someone with a cool head, someone who could keep his lips zipped. Trouble was, among his wide circle of acquaintances, no one with those qualifications came readily to mind, and so by default, his jag-off son got elected. He picked up the phone and called the office and commanded a secretary to command Howard to shag his ass over here, double time, pronto Tonto. Then he hauled himself out of the water, hurried inside, dressed, dismissed the housekeeper for the day, and sank into his throne chair, waiting other than patiently, occasionally honking into a hankie and gazing fixedly at the gluey mess as if perhaps it held the solution to this confounding—and potentially costly—dilemma.

It didn't, but that's what he was doing when, some thirty minutes later, he heard the front door swing open. When he lifted his gaze, what he saw was not one but two approaching figures, his summoned son and the uninvited Troy Kroll, both their faces carefully knotted in attitudes of solicitous concern. Big Lonnie's ungracious greeting—"Fuck's he doin' here?"—was growled at a son so light up top that if there were a way to fuck up a wet dream, he'd be the one to find it.

"Troy dropped by right after you left," Howard lamely explained. "We were just, uh, chatting. About business and...things when you called. She said—secretary, I mean—you sounded real upset, so I thought maybe he ought to come along, in case—"

"Case what? Case I croaked?"

"C'mon, Dad."

Troy put his palms in the air, retreated a step. "Listen, if this is a private matter, I'll be glad to wait outside. It's just we were worried about you, Lon. Both of us. I'm relieved to see you're OK."

Big Lonnie didn't bother to acknowledge the relief. He continued to glower at his son, whose expression was rapidly shifting to that of a kid who'd gotten caught dipping his fingers in the jam jar, old enough to know better but powerless to control his urges. And now Lonnie had to wonder where the fuck his own head was, thinking this helpless pud, who'd come into the world on a dick-dribble afterthought, had anything to bring to the puzzle board. Kroll was a slippery customer, no two ways about it, but at least he wasn't brain-dead. So Big Lonnie made a snap decision: "No, you can stay. But what I'm gonna tell you here, it don't leave this house. Y'got that?"

"Hey, Lon, you can count on me."

"What is it, Dad?" Howard asked. "What's up?"

"Both you sit down there," Big Lonnie directed, indicating a facing sofa.

They sat, and he told them what was up, reconstructing the phone conversation in loose paraphrase and concluding with a swipe of a hand across pink-veined eyes and under a leaky nose whose reddened tip glowed like a neon bulb stuck in the middle of a shapeless lump of dough. Howard, mistaking the motion for a display of sorrow over the abducted spouse, said, "Jeez, Dad, don't cry. It'll be OK. We'll get her back."

"Nobody bawlin', you idiot. It's the goddamn cold."

"Oh," said humbled Howard. "Sorry."

"So whaddya think?" Big Lonnie said, opening the topic to serious discussion.

"We should call the police," Howard opined. "Or the FBI maybe."

"An' run the risk of her gettin' whacked?"

"But they're the kidnapping experts, Dad. They'd know what to do."

Big Lonnie sniffed, whether from nasal distress or contempt it was difficult to tell. He turned his gaze on Troy. "You got anything to contribute?"

"Well," he replied, pulling thoughtfully at his squared-off jaw, "I'm not sure I agree with Howie here. I think it's a little early to bring in the law."

"Yeah, that was my thought too."

"This person said Billie was all right?"

"That's what he said."

"But he wouldn't let her talk to you?"

"No."

"And he's asking for five million?"

"That's the figure."

Troy gave a low, significant whistle. "Lot of money."

"Don't I fuckin' know."

"You said his voice sounded funny. Can you say how exactly?"

"Like a wimp is how. Or a faggot."

"Or an amateur?"

"Yeah. Right. Amateur."

"So maybe that's what we're dealing with here," Troy said, with a superior slant of a smile. "Amateurs."

"So?"

Troy let go of the smile and made a ruminant humming sound. "I wonder," he said.

"Fuck's there to wonder about? Amateurs or not, they still got her."

"Do they?"

Big Lonnie fastened his eyes on him, a narrowing squint. "What're you gettin' at?"

"Well, I don't know quite how to say this, Lon. Or even if I should."

"Am I askin' for your thoughts here or what?"

"OK. Let's talk about Billie. You've been married to her how long now?"

"Goin' on two years. Why?"

"Why?" Troy echoed with the logician's quiet, measured patience. "Because I think you have to ask yourself some hard questions."

"Like what?"

"Oh, like what do you know about her? *Really* know?"

It was Howard, head swiveling back and forth between father and friend, forgotten in this Socratic dialogue, who arrived first at its inescapable conclusion, blurting, "She's in on it!"

Troy arranged a brow in enigmatic arch but volunteered nothing more.

"You wanna gimme that again?" Big Lonnie said, more demand than request, couched in ominous rumble and directed at his son.

Instantly Howard recognized his blunder, but under his father's baleful glare, he could only squeak out the feeble disclaimer, "It's *his* theory, Dad. Not mine."

Big Lonnie transferred the glare to Troy. "That right? That your theory?"

"That's not what I said, Lon."

"But that's what you *think*. Thinkin' it's my wife tryin' to nick me for five mil. Am I right?"

"All I'm suggesting here, Lon, is that we explore every possibility."

"That's your suggestion, is it?"

"Well, yes," Troy conceded, visibly less comfortable with this inversion of the Socratic drill. "More or less."

"OK. Now I got a suggestion for you. Both of you. Get the fuck outta my house before I pound the livin' shit right out your backstabbin', double-dealin' bungholes."

Howard and Troy protested, in chorus:

"Dad—"

"Lon—"

But that was as far as either got, for Big Lonnie, energized by a choking rage, bounded to his feet, thrust a pointing arm at the door, and bawled, "Out!"

Out they went, trailed by the boomed warning, "You spill a word a' this—even a word—an' you'll by God both be feedin' at the nearest soup kitchen, an' that's a Lon Swett iron-fuckin'-clad warranty, life-fuckin'-time guarantee."

OK, supposing there *was* something to it (Big Lonnie finally had to ask himself after the storm subsided, and he settled back in his throne in the oppressive silence of his opulent empty house, confused, exhausted, plagued by worms of doubt squirming through the damp loam of his stuffed, fevered head, sick with conflicting visions of betrayal and loss), what that prick lick Kroll was dancing around, too chickenshit to put it plain. What in fact did he know about her, this wife of his? Knew she was a nail buffer by trade. Hailed from the Dakota boonies. Couple of hubs and a pack of boyfriends under—make that below—her belt (which was OK by him, seeing as he wasn't in the market for no cherries). World-class in the knob-polishing department, sure, but he'd had so many wives and hookers and willing strangers that anymore, in the dark, he couldn't distinguish among them. Beaver was beaver. Except in the daylight, Billie was different, or seemed different: watched out for him, took care of him, listened when he talked, was low on the ball-busting scale.

Outside of that, though, there wasn't a whole lot he really did know. And Big Lonnie took his sense of the real from things, tangible objects: baubles, toys, houses, cars, cash, wives, women.

Things. And the thought of their absence or loss, even if he'd tired of them, was profoundly disturbing, for it raised the dreadful, unthinkable proposition that maybe they were, after all, unreal, insubstantial, and transient as smoke or dreams. All of them, himself included.

An antique clock on a mantle behind him ticked out the fractional segments of time that, beat by beat, consumed the dwindling hours and days and years of his life. Moment by moment, light faded from the capacious room, 'til at last he sat in the dark, dueling with hosts of phantoms, outnumbered, outgunned, and utterly alone.

Or was he? Years ago, in another marriage, another life, he'd engaged a man to dig up the goods on a treacherous, cheating slut of a then-wife. A fuzzy image of that man returned to him now. McReedy was his name, Don McReedy, but everybody called him "Cheetah" on account of his goofy-looking face. Not a handsome man, Cheetah. Did confidential investigations but only for a select, pricy clientele. Came with top-drawer references, Palm Beach kind. Had a rep for being thorough, diligent, discreet, a real pro. Didn't say much, was how Big Lonnie remembered him, but he got the job done. Smoother than a baby's oiled backside when he wanted to be, stomp-ass tough when he had to be. Tough enough to slap that dink on the phone there up against a wall and administer a thumping he wouldn't soon forget. And slick enough to get the straight skinny on whoever was the shit heel trying to hold him up for five mil worth of wampum. No matter who it turned out to be.

Good old Cheetah. Worked out of Delray or Boca, someplace like that. Big Lonnie still kept his card, two wives later. You never knew.

He'd call Cheetah.

SEVENTEEN

WEIRD. IF HE'D HAD TO PUT A WORD TO IT, JIM could come up with only one that properly did justice to the remainder of that increasingly bizarre day. Weird.

And how do you count the ways of weird? Start with that midafternoon spread of horse-cock sandwiches garnished with tortilla chips and pickle spears, and washed down with a beverage choice of Mountain Dew, beer, or bitter black coffee. The sum of their comestibles, prepared by that celebrated chef Leon Cody under Billie's watchful supervision and critical eye.

So there they were, the five of them squeezed around the kitchen table like some improbable family gathered for an impromptu feed. Junior, first to finish, swilled the last of a beer, sagged back in his chair, gave his belly a contented thump, and allowed, "Good nosh."

"You call this good?" Billie recklessly challenged him.

"Somethin' wrong with it? Don't meet your high standards?"

"As a matter of fact, it doesn't. One thing's sure, what we're going to need here is a radical change of diet. Starting with some nourishing food."

"Where you gettin' this *we*? I'm the one calls the plays, lady. An' don't you forget it."

"Oh, I haven't forgotten. But I'm also assuming wholesome meals come with the kidnapping."

"Don't worry. You'll get fed."

"Good. I'll make a list."

"You'll do *what*?"

"Make a shopping list. Maybe you didn't notice, but your refrigerator's almost empty. Same with the cupboards. What were you planning to do if that hurricane hits? Live on chips?"

"Hurricane?" said a fuddled Junior. "Fuck're you talkin', hurricane?"

"You don't know about it? Where've you been? It's all over the news."

"She got that right," Hector confirmed. "Kid here sayin' he seen it on the TV."

"When's it comin', this hurricane?"

"Next week sometime," Hector told him. "If it comes our way. Maybe it won't."

"It does, could fuck things up."

"Yeah, my thought too."

"I ain't never been in one a' them before," Junior said, a detectable uneasiness rippling the flat growl of his voice.

"And I've never been kidnapped before either," Billie remarked, more than a trace of crowing in it. "So we're both in for a treat."

"Nobody askin' your opinion here, lady."

"My name is Billie."

"Yeah, we got that one figured out."

"And you two are?" she asked, the query directed at Hector and Junior.

They traded looks. Junior shrugged. And they divulged their names.

"This gentleman I already know," she said with a cool flick of a wrist in Jim's direction.

Leon, seated to her left, thrust out a belatedly welcoming hand. "I'm Leon."

She grasped the offered hand, said, "Nice to meet you, Leon."

"He's my nephew," Jim clarified in irrelevant contribution, his first, to this incongruous, wandering dialogue.

"Really," she said, but with no eye contact whatsoever.

Thusly were introductions completed all around. *Talk about your weird developments*, Jim was thinking, but he prudently kept it to himself.

But Billie, not one to be sidetracked, closed the conversational circle by saying to Junior, "Now, if it meets with your approval, Mr. Biggs, I'll get started on that list."

"Yeah, yeah, yeah. Make your fuckin' list."

She turned to Leon and said sweetly and in pointed contrast to the chilly tone reserved for Jim, "Could you please get me a pen and paper, Leon?"

"You bet, ma'am."

"Call me 'Billie.' "

"OK," he said and, shyly grinning, eyes fluttering, hopped out of his chair and disappeared into one of the bedrooms. In a moment he was back, bearing notepad and ballpoint.

"Thank you, Leon," she said, and fell immediately to compiling her list, filling a sheet with two neatly printed columns of items plucked from some invisible inventory stored in her head.

Jim, covertly watching, couldn't help being impressed by her brisk efficiency. A real take-charge lady, to all appearances utterly absent of fear. More sides to her than he'd imagined, this Billie Swett, and he felt a tug of regret that now he'd never get a chance to explore them. Banished as he plainly was to the deep freeze in punishment for the betrayal of trust, that opportunity had been forfeited forever the moment he'd gotten himself mired in the quicksand of this buggy scheme.

When Billie was finished, she set down the pen and pushed the sheet across the table to Junior, who leaned forward and ran his eyes over it, lips moving as he read, brow gradually crimping into a frown. "Fuck's all this?" he demanded.

"All what?" she said innocently.

He stabbed a finger at one of the columns. "This."

"Those? Those are personal items, cosmetics, some outfit changes, things like that. If I'm going to be here a while, I'll need them."

"I ain't payin' for none a' this shit."

"Nobody's asking you to pay. I have money."

"You better, looks a' this slate."

"And I will. But it's only fair that you buy the groceries. You're the kidnappers."

Junior's lips tightened, and then, astonishingly, opened in a slow smile. "Lady," he drawled, "you must be sportin' a set a' brass balls under them drawers."

"Does that mean you're buying the groceries?"

"Yeah, fuck, why not? We'll buy. Right, *chico*?"

"S'pose it's fair," Hector agreed. "We all got to eat."

"So there ya go," Junior said, handing him the sheet. "On your horse."

"Me? How come I get tagged?"

" 'Cuz you the shopper in this band a' desperados we got here. Besides, I'm waitin' on that call outta you-know-who."

Hector scanned the list, groaning, "There's *underwear* on here. How'm I gonna buy ladies' underwear?"

"Play like you a fag. Senor Swish, just floated in from old Me-he-co."

"C'mon, Biggs."

"C'mon where? I got heavier shit on my mind. Work somethin' out."

"Wha's there to work out? I'm either buyin' this stuff or I ain't."

Junior swatted the air exasperatedly. "Awright, awright. Take nephew weenie along. Let him do it. Only keep a close peep on him, case he get to thinkin' to hit the hump. Y'got that?"

Hector, visibly relieved, assured him he understood. Billie fished through her purse, removed some money, and gave it to

Leon, along with some parting instructions and advice. And then, after the two shoppers were gone, it got weirder yet.

"Now we've got to do something about this place," she announced boldly.

Junior looked mystified. "Whaddya mean? Fuck's wrong with it?"

Jim cautiously said nothing. He had an idea what she meant.

Billie rolled her eyes so far back in their sockets there was nothing but a sliver of milky blue left beneath the lids. "What's *wrong*?" she repeated in an incredulous echo. "It's filthy is what's wrong. Look at it."

A thoroughly disgusted sweep of a hand directed their gaze around the slandered kitchen. An Alps of unwashed plates and saucers and bowls ascended from the sink. Grease crusted the stove burners. An assortment of emptied cans, bottles, and pizza cartons littered the counter. Prominent among them was a Styrofoam cup containing a deepening pool of Junior's blackened spittle, on the surface of which floated an armada of slowly disintegrating butts.

"So maybe it's a little grungy," Junior conceded sullenly. "Whaddya expect? Goddamn Ritz?"

"What I expect is if I'm going to be held against my will, it can at least be in halfway decent surroundings. Instead of a pigsty."

"You don't like it, clean 'er up."

"That's exactly what I've got in mind." She turned a quick, wintry glance on Jim. "Where's the cleaning things?"

"You got me. Think I saw a vacuum in the front closet there. Could be a mop and some dustcloths in the one back by the john."

"OK. You do the kitchen. I'll take the bedrooms and bath, and you"—indicating Junior—"get the living room."

"Me? You sayin' me? Do cleanin'?"

"Yes. You."

"Forget that good idea. I got a important call comin' in."

"You can still do your share while you're waiting. If everybody pitches in, we'll be done in no time at all."

With that bit of homely wisdom, she came to her feet and swept out of the room. For a long moment, Jim and Junior gaped at each other. Finally it was Junior who said, "Y'know somethin', Uncle?"

"What's that?"

"You got a real talent for cunt pickin'."

In they pitched, all of them, even Junior. Carpets were vacuumed, furniture dusted, floors mopped, dishes scrubbed, sinks and toilet bowls scoured, mirrors polished, bedsheets stripped and laundered. Somewhere in the middle of all this purposeful bustle, the phone sounded, and from his appointed station at the kitchen sink, Jim saw Biggs nodding and muttering into the speaker, voice pitched too low to be audible. That would be Bott on the other end, delivering the buzz on how the first contact had gone down. And as he stood there, arms sunk elbow deep in dishwater, it struck him with the force of a revelation that now there was no going back, no undoing what had been done. For any of them. No matter how seismic the consequences.

Some two hours later—the promised "no time at all"—the apartment was spotless. All but unrecognizable, as the stupefied expressions on the faces of the two laggard shoppers confirmed. Laden with bags, they stood in the entry and glanced about bewilderedly. "Jesus," Hector said. "Wha' happen here?"

"Fuck's it look like?" Junior answered for the exhausted threesome, sprawled on the living-room chairs and couch in various attitudes of fatigue. "Cleanin's what happen."

"You? Cleanin' house?"

"Yeah, me," Junior grouched. "While you whack-offs drivin' around pullin' your puds, I'm bustin' ass. Coulda used some help around here."

"Shoppin' ain't so hot either."

"Better'n bein' on the wrong end of a vacuum machine. I ain't done this much hard labor since the can."

"Sure looks nice in here," Leon volunteered. "Just like Mom used to keep it."

A grin, wickedly sly, worked its way across Hector's brown face. "Kid's right. You do good work, Biggs. Oughta hire out."

Junior seized his crotch. "Hire this."

Chuckling softly, Hector lugged his grocery bags into the kitchen.

"I got all your stuff, Billie," Leon told her proudly. "Took a while, but we found everything on the list."

She replied wearily, "That's nice, Leon. You want to take them into a bedroom?"

"Which one?" he asked, glancing from her to Jim to Junior.

Billie, following the circuit of his anxious eyes, gave Junior a hard stare. "I'm expecting a room of my own," she said, coldly now. "Privacy."

Junior, too trashed to argue, said, "I don't give a shit. Whatever."

"I'd take the one in the back," Leon suggested. "It's bigger, got a TV. Used to be Mom's."

"That'll be fine," Billie told him.

Bundled with packages like some shrunken Santa, he started for the bedroom, paused, said, "Oh, you got some change coming too."

"You keep it, Leon."

A sunburst smile, pure devotion, lit his face, and he tottered off down the narrow hall.

Hector sauntered into the living room, a cigarette pasted to his lips. Seeing it, Billie said, "Did you get my Capris?"

Rather sheepishly, he reported, "Uh, them we couldn't turn up no place."

"That's my brand!"

"Sorry. We sure tried. Got you some a' them ladies' smokes instead."

"Virginia Slims?"

"That's the ones."

"Figures," she said petulantly. "I seem to have come a long way today, baby."

Hector looked blank.

"Never mind."

Cigarettes, Jim was thinking. *A spat over cigarettes.* A sardonic spectator inside his head, witnessing this scatty exchange, mockingly concluded that lurking at the bottom of every plot, scheme, act, deed, emotion, intention, feeling—at the bottom there had to be something profoundly irrational, something farcical, absurd.

Hector settled into a chair opposite Junior. "That call come through?" he asked.

"Yeah, it come through."

"So?"

"So we talk about it later," Junior said with a significant glance at Billie.

Who was keen enough to catch it. "You gentlemen have business to discuss," she said, pushing herself up off the couch.

"It'll keep," said Junior.

"No, that privacy goes both ways. Besides, I'm beat myself."

"You wanna leave the keys to your vehicle?"

"Why?"

"Just leave 'em, OK? Don't gimme no grief."

She dug the keys out of her purse, tossed them insolently on an end table, and stalked away.

As soon as she was out of the room, Hector resumed his questioning. "So wha'd he say, this Bott dude?"

Junior looked over at Jim, who hadn't moved. "Thinkin' to get an earful, are you, Uncle?"

"Why not? I'm in this too."

"You in it long as I say you're in it an' not a shaved minute longer. You got that?"

"It's not all that hard to grasp," Jim said, and stubbornly didn't budge.

"Fuckin' wise-fuck weenie," Junior rumbled ominously, but he didn't move either.

"C'mon, Biggs," Hector put in. "Wha's the damage, he hears?"

"Yeah, s'pose you right. Don't mean dick."

"So wha'd he say?" Hector persisted.

"Said he connected with the twat's old man."

"Yeah? What else?"

"Told him the terms is what else."

"So what's his take on it? Bott's, I mean."

Junior probed a bristly nostril with a forefinger, examined the find, and flicked it across the room. "That part ain't clear yet."

"What're you tellin' me here?"

"What I just said. Ain't clear."

"How?"

"Sound to me like the hubby maybe thinkin' a' doin' some wafflin'," Junior said, assaulting the other nostril.

"He is," Hector said, a rising, decidedly worried skirl in his voice, "fuck we gonna do?"

"What you're gonna do is sit tight right here. Make sure our company's bedded down for the night."

"That ain't what I'm askin'."

"But that's what *I'm* tellin'."

"OK. OK. How 'bout you?"

"What I'm gonna do is run the bitch's Jag over to a chop shop I heard about in Lake Park. Oughta get a nice dollar for it."

"I'm talkin' this wafflin' shit. How 'bout that?"

"Way ahead a you, *chico*. I'm thinkin' to pay our preacher partner a visit, have a word with him. Make sure he got this drill down. He don't, I'll be takin' over the negotiatin'."

"When?"

"When what?"

"When you gonna do this visit?"

"Soon's I can get my achin' bones movin'."

Which wasn't to be for another hour or more, most of it spent dozing, raising great spluttery snores. One of which eventually roused him, and he hauled himself stiffly to his feet, scratched his pits, instructed Hector to "Hold down the fort," and then was gone. During Junior's slumber, Leon had tiptoed back into the room, and he and Hector and Jim sat in deferential silence, each occupied with his own teeming, troubled mind life. Now, with Biggs out of there, Hector seemed to loosen up some. "Gonna pop me a brewbie," he said. "You boys want one?"

"Don't mind," said Jim.

Leon made a negative gesture. "Think I'll turn in. That shopping takes a lot out of you."

"Hey, you got that correct," Hector affirmed.

"So where you want me to sleep?"

Hector had to think about that a minute. Finally he said, "Guess you two bunk down the other bedroom. Me 'n' the honcho'll take turns on the couch. One of us be up all night standin' watch anyways," he added in a resigned tone that implied a knowledge of who that one likely would be.

Leon told them good night and padded off to bed. Hector went into the kitchen, returned with two cans of beer, handed one to Jim, and slumped back in his chair. Sipping, smoking, gazing into their laps, they extended the earlier silence a while longer. 'Til Hector glanced over at him and remarked conversationally, "Kid say you play cards for a livin'."

"Used to. Not anymore."

"How come?"

"They turned on me."

"Had a run a' bad luck, did ya?"

"You might say."

"Can happen," Hector observed thoughtfully.

"It did. Still going on."

"How y'mean?"

"I'm here, aren't I?"

"Yeah, you here all right."

"I'd call that pretty deadly luck. Poison kind."

"Y'know," Hector said, his eyes straying from floor to walls to ceiling, anywhere but Jim's, "wha's goin' on here, it ain't, like, personal."

"I know that."

"It's just a line a' work. Everybody gotta be employed."

"I know."

"You, uh, wanna watch some tube?"

"Might as well."

Hector switched it on and surfed the channels 'til he found a comedy: some happy, zany family beset by wacky happy problems; exciting whoops of mirth from a phantom audience. The light beyond the window gradually softened, faded. And so this strange, singular day wound slowly down on peals of tinny, packaged laughter.

But it wasn't over yet. Still to come was, from Jim's perspective, the weirdest part of all.

He soon tired of the hilarious clowning on the screen and told Hector he was calling it a night. Got a sluggish grunt in reply. In the darkened hall that fronted the two bedrooms, he saw a splinter of light under Billie's door and, on a reasonless impulse, stepped over and tapped on it softly. The response was instantaneous, alert, anything but sluggish: "Who's there?"

"Me," he said, locating his voice somewhere between librarian hiss and thin whisper. "Jim."

"Who?"

He repeated his name.

"What do *you* want?"

"You OK?"

"What?"

He repeated the question.

"I can barely hear you. Suppose you might as well come in."

He did, quickly getting the door behind him and standing with his spine pressed to it. Across the room she sat with her back braced against the headboard of the bed, a sheet pulled over her lap, hands serenely folded in it. She had on a floppy T-shirt, evidently one of the day's purchases. A lamp on the nightstand supplied the only light. "Well?" she demanded haughtily.

"Just checking to see if you're OK."

"I'm all right. No thanks to you."

"Yeah, well, sorry if I woke you."

"You didn't."

"I thought you were tired."

"I am."

"No wonder, all that work today."

"It's not the work," she said, laying a frosty stare on him.

Jim, looking to lighten this stiff conversation, said, "I didn't know you ladies of privilege did cleaning."

"I know how to work. I grew up in a big family, seven kids. Remember me telling you that? In the bar today? Were you listening to *anything* I said?"

"I was listening."

"Sure you were. Thinking all the time how you were going to kidnap me."

"Look, Billie, I told you. It's a long story."

"And stories are your strong suit, right? You're real good with the stories."

"All right." Jim sighed. "Have it however you will. But let me give you a word of advice."

"Advice? From you?"

"Yes. From me."

"And what would it be, this good advice?"

"Those two goons may seem like a couple of slapstick comedians, dumb but harmless. But trust me, they're not your friends."

"But *you* are?"

"Believe me when I tell you Leon and I are as much at risk here as you. Maybe more."

"From what I've seen so far," she murmured, almost leniently, "that much I think I can believe."

"Well, just so you know," he said, and reached for the doorknob.

"Wait a minute."

He waited.

"I trusted you, you know. Thought you were somehow different. Special. It was an instinct I had. Or thought I had."

"Looks like your instinct was wrong."

"Was it?"

"Not for me to judge."

She pondered him. Then, folding back the sheet, beckoning, lips parting in a small, rueful smile, she said, "I shouldn't forgive you. But I do."

Gently he used her supple, articulate body, and she his, tenderly. And later, watching this sleeping woman nestled against him, this stranger, their fates and flesh so bizarrely linked, Jim tried to sort through the tangle of his tarnished emotions. But with no success. So he stored them in one of the few remaining empty compartments in his head and joined her in sated, dreamless sleep.

PART FOUR

EIGHTEEN

BY SOME QUIRKY ACCIDENT OF GENETIC REGRESsion, Donald Peter McReedy bore an unfortunate but almost uncanny resemblance to an ape. Actually it was more the chimpanzee species he favored, which doubtless accounted for the tag laid on him at a tender and impressionable age. Once, as a young boy, he and a group of chums had attended a Tarzan double bill. As they came out of the theater, one of the alleged friends scrutinized him closely then delightedly exclaimed, "Jeez, McReedy looks just like Cheetah!" (a reference to the ape man's mischievous simian companion). The others, with all the sadistic cruelty of children, picked up the squawky chant: "Cheetah, Cheetah, Cheetah!" He grinned weakly and, smoldering inside, endured their taunts. It was a lesson in friendship.

The name stuck. He carried it with him through public school, a year at Miami-Dade, a tour in Vietnam (where he logged a body count of fourteen confirmed kills, emerging with a Bronze Star), twenty years with the Miami PD (narcotics, missing persons, homicide, with three sanctioned shootings to his credit, one of which resulted in a perpetrator's death and, for him, a departmental commendation), and a dozen more spent in private investigations of a confidential nature (a lucrative solo practice that required the occasional tune-up but, to date, no waxings). Now, at age fifty-four, the physical characteristics that had earned him that other-than-flattering sobriquet had settled into an even more pronounced facsimile of our arboreal ancestors. A squat, chunk-chested man, he moved with a kind of hunched, slouching gait, as if in confirmation of the uncharitable appellation. His facial features, in maturity, seemed only to reinforce it further: bristly crew cut sprouting from a precipitous slope of brow; flat, blunt nose; thickish lips downturned at the corners; prognathic jaw; cheeks rubbery as a deflated party balloon. Yet out of those deep, loose, sad creases and from under that bony morainal rim peered eyes of such vigilant cunning that they seemed to have telescoped all the instincts of predation and survival acquired over evolutionary eons and deposited them intact, like a compensatory gift, in the cranium of this late twentieth-century man. So in a curious way, the name he'd gone by and lived with for the better part of a lifetime, born out of youthful malice, was perhaps not so unsuitable after all.

Now, seated in the magnificent living room of the Swett mansion on the morning of the day following the abduction (or whatever scam it might turn out to be), Cheetah commenced with the same terse line by which he opened all his investigations: "What seems to be the problem here?"

In excessive detail the seriously agitated Lonnie revealed the problem. Cheetah listened impassively, now and then interposing a query designed to move the distressed, digressive account along, but mostly just allowing it to unfold. Its subtext of nagging doubt wasn't lost on him. As he attended to the windy recital, he was doing what he always did at the outset of an assignment, mentally sorting through the client's conflicting, often contradictory motives, winnowing out the extraneous ones and narrowing in on the compelling ones. Swett's were transparent. What he plainly wanted (but couldn't bring himself to say) was to recover the missing wife, if only for the satisfaction of scrapping her should the unuttered suspicions prove to be true. What he *didn't* want was to squander any loot on what amounted to a readily replaceable toy. Fine with Cheetah. Judgments, slippery moral distinctions—these weren't included among his pricy services.

"So whaddya think?" Lonnie concluded, run finally out of breath.

"Hmm..." hmmed Cheetah, trailing off musingly. A taciturn man, he often communicated by silences.

"So you don't think we should call in the cops then?" Lonnie asked, putting his own interpretation on this one.

"Not yet. Let's find her first. See where that takes us."

"But can you do that? Find her?"

"Oh, yeah," said Cheetah in the practiced drawl that, as much as any words he spoke, evoked the infallible reliability of planets in their fixed and timeless orbits. "I always find 'em."

"Good ol' Cheetah," Lonnie burbled. "Knew I could count on you."

"Got a photo of Mrs. Swett you could spare?"

"You bet."

Lonnie produced a snapshot from his wallet and handed it over. Cheetah inspected it, allowing, "Handsome woman."

"Yeah, she's a looker, Billie. Your cocksmen all'a time tryin' to hit on her. 'Course," he added quickly, if none too confidently, "she never give 'em the time a' day."

Cheetah let another of his silences speak to that.

"So where you gonna start?" Lonnie wanted to know.

"Last person to see her—last we know of so far—was the housekeeper?"

"Correct."

"Suppose we could have a word with her?"

"Fayola!" Lonnie bawled. "Get in here!"

The improbably named housekeeper, a drab, painfully skinny drudge of a woman of indeterminate middle years, appeared instantly. She stood before them, a broom trembling in her hands, eyes bright with dread. Cheetah sized her up, decided on the gentle path. In a voice to match the quivery hands, she did her dull best to respond to all his questions, spilling everything she knew. Which wasn't much. Nothing more, in fact, than he'd already gleaned from Swett's tiresome monologue. "Thanks, Fayola," he said, politely dismissive. "You been a big help."

Gratefully she fled.

Once she was out of earshot, Lonnie said slyly, "Know what I think, Cheetah?"

"What's that?"

"I think she's holdin' something back."

"No."

"No? How come you so sure?"

"Practice," Cheetah said flatly, thinking, *Deliver me from the amateur sleuth.*

As nearly as Lonnie could ever look humbled, that's about how he looked. "OK. You the gumshoe. So what's next?"

"That friend of your wife's?" Cheetah said, phrasing it as question.

"Courtney? What about her?"

"Pretty tight were they?"

"Tighter'n they needed to be," Lonnie said with ill-concealed disgust. "They go back a ways. Why you ask?"

"She's what's next."

"You thinkin' she's in on it?"

"Thinking nothing yet. Except maybe to have a chat with her. You tell me where she might be located?"

"Works in an ugly shop down in North Palm, name of the Hair Affair. I can look up the address, you want."

"I'll find it," Cheetah said, and abruptly got to his feet and shuffled toward the door. Over his shoulder, he advised, in parting, "You better hang by the phone today. I'll be in touch."

Lonnie managed a pinch of a smile, feeble and uncertain. "Go get 'em, Cheetah," he called after him.

"Yeah, I'll do that," Cheetah drawled without returning the smile.

"Wonder if you could help me out" was how he began, another of his standard opening lines.

Courtney, who had appeared at last, ran appraising, cartoon button eyes drenched in violet shadow over his anachronistic buzz cut and anthropoidal features, arrived at a quick judgment, and replied archly, "I don't take walk-ins."

For well over an hour, he'd been waiting, sitting stolid and motionless as a brass monkey in the Hair Affair's reception area, inhaling the powerful odors of scented sprays and acrid chemicals, watching the traffic whiz down PGA Boulevard, watching the fashionable women and men come and go. Girl at the desk had told him Courtney was real swamped today, it being a Friday, and suggested he make an appointment. Cheetah said no, he'd wait, and the girl just gave him an "It's your funeral" look, airily indifferent, and went back to doing whatever it was they do in places like this. Cheetah, he didn't mind. Long since had he mastered the ugly man's stoic, stony dispassion. It was one of those things you had to learn. Now, to Courtney he said, "Not looking to get a haircut. This a matter regarding—"

"Look," she broke in peevishly, "I got two perms going and a—"

"Regarding your good friend, Mrs. Swett," he finished, returning the rudeness.

"Billie?" she said, cautiously now. "What about her?"

"Place we could talk private?"

"Is something wrong? Something happen to her?"

"Private be better, Miss Cleland," he said mysteriously.

She hesitated.

"Won't take but a minute."

"OK," she said, beckoning. "C'mon."

Mysterious did it every time. He followed her down a narrow aisle flanked by partitioned booths and through a rear entrance opening onto a blacktopped back alley studded with Dumpsters and running the length of the strip mall. A small canvas awning over the door partly shielded them from the brutal midday sun. "So what about Billie?" she started right in.

"Maybe ought to introduce myself first," Cheetah said. "Name's Don McReedy, but everybody calls me 'Cheetah.'" With a wink and a big, toothy, self-deprecating grin from which any warmth was entirely lacking, he added, "Never could figure why."

"I'm asking about Billie," she said, one sandaled foot beating an irritable tattoo. "She OK?"

She was a flashy woman, this Courtney Cleland, striking, some might say, fortyish by his keen measure, stack of hair a bottle-induced platinum, deepening facial fissures camouflaged beneath layers of makeup applied by trowel, Slimfast- and spa-slenderized figure under a tarty outfit of sheer pink tittie-flaunter blouse and skirt that barely cleared the twat. Came machine-stamped off the Florida assembly line. Looked not at but through guys like him, invisible men, eyesores, blights on the beautiful-people landscape. "Don't know for sure," said Cheetah, master of indirection.

"What're you sayin'? Where's she at?"

"Don't know that either. Which is why I was hoping you could maybe help me out."

"How?"

"Thought you might have some ideas, where she could be located."

"Me? Why would I know?"

"Well," he said, slipping into his cultivated drawl, "folks say you're her best friend."

"Who said that?"

"Some folks I been talking to."

"You a cop?"

Now, finally, she was looking at him but warily and with a suspicion of doubt in the weirdly purpled eyes. Or maybe it was fear. Too early to tell. "Oh no," he said easily. "Just a regular citizen. Like yourself."

"Yeah, right. So how come you askin' around about Billie, Mr. Regular Citizen?"

"Doing a favor."

"Who for?"

"Fella I know."

"This *fella*," she said shrewdly, "he wouldn't happen to be Lonnie Swett?"

Cheetah invoked one of his silences.

"Figures. And that'd make you one of them private detectives. Checkin' up on her. Right?"

He said nothing.

"I got no more time for this," she said, and made a move for the door.

Cheetah shifted his bulk just enough to block it. On a hunch he said, "Tell me something, Miss Cleland. You into the goofy dust? Like to do a little sniffing?"

"What're you talkin' about? I don't do drugs."

"Sauce?"

"I hardly ever drink. Bad for your health. Where you get off, askin' me these questions? You got no right."

"Men then?" he went blithely on, ignoring her protest. "Everybody got to have a hobby."

"I got a boyfriend. Any law against that?"

"None I heard of. How about your friend Billie? She got one? On the side, like?"

"Billie's married."

"Yeah, I heard. But that's not what I'm asking."

"Well, I wouldn't know anything about that."

Cheetah pinched his eyes into a gaze so baleful and spiky it could have etched glass. His "Congo glare" was what he called it and came accompanied by a throaty rumble in the voice, elemental as the sound of thunder, distant but gathering. "You're sure?"

"I don't," she said, retreating a step. "Honest."

"Think hard."

"OK, OK. There was this guy she met over at the hospital."

"Hospital?"

"When my mom was dying. Billie was helping me get through it."

"This was when?"

"Last week."

"Name?"

"What? The hospital?"

"The guy."

"I dunno. She never said."

"What'd he look like?"

"Dunno that either. I never seen him."

"She balling him?"

"C'mon. How would I know that?"

"Lot you don't seem to know, Miss Cleland, for being a best friend."

"Even best friends don't share everything. I had to guess, I'd say no. Lonnie, he keeps her on a tight leash. Look, I gotta get back to those perms."

Cheetah didn't budge. "Perms'll wait. We're almost done."

"Nothing left to tell," she said pleadingly.

"Except when you last saw Mrs. Swett," he corrected her.

"Lemme see. Was Monday, I think. Yeah, Monday, at the funeral home. She come along while I was settling some bills. Oh, and she ran into him there too, this guy."

"At a funeral home?"

"Yeah."

"But you didn't see him?"

"I was inside."

"And you haven't seen her since Monday?"

"No," she said, but her eyes sought a spot just slightly to the left of his shoulder, and in her voice was a falter so slight only a trained ear could have caught it.

One like Cheetah's. "You're sure?" he said, repeating his intimidator line. Mysterious, it seldom failed him.

"That's the last time I *seen* her. But she called the next day."

"About what?"

"Said she was gonna have lunch with him. Sounded like she was, y'know, excited about it, like she was sort of, well, attracted to him. But that's no big yank. Don't mean she was sleepin' with him."

"She give you the where and when?"

"Thursday, I think it was. Yesterday. Where, she didn't say."

"Any place special you ladies like to meet your men friends for lunch?"

"Billie's always liked Decesare's."

Every interrogation was a collaboration, and each had its own unique measures and inflections and rhythms. Was just a matter of knowing how to listen for them. Cheetah knew how. It was another of those things you learned. This one seemed to strike most of, if not quite all, the right chords, but it also was rapidly running down. He had an instinct that way; he could tell. So he shifted abruptly back into affable drawl and said, "Be obliged if you could give me the names of that hospital and funeral home."

She gave him names and directions for both. "We done now?"

"Think we are. For now anyway. I need any more of your helpful information, we'll talk again."

"Can I go?"

He removed himself from the door, swept an arm toward it. "Why sure, Miss Cleland. You can go."

Again she hesitated.

"Better hurry," he advised her, reviving the mirthless grin. "Don't want to gum up those perms."

"I ask you something?"

"Anything you like."

"What's goin' on?"

"Well, see, that's what I'm trying to find out."

"For this fella you said?"

"For him, yeah. Mrs. Swett too."

An expression of alarm, genuine and unmistakable, emerged from beneath the strata of powders and paint. "Nothing bad's happened to Billie, has it?"

"Like I say, that's what I'm looking to find out."

"Could you maybe let me know when you do?"

"Oh, you can count on that. You're on my short list."

Her directions were good. Couple of winding blocks off Prosperity, and there was the Palm Beach Gardens Medical Center, just like she'd said. He went inside, stepped up to the nurses' station, made some polite inquiries, and ran square into his first glitch. Turned out the day nurse who had cared for the late Mother Cleland was gone on vacation, and the night one wouldn't be on 'til eleven. Nobody else knew shit. Cheetah thanked them, said he'd stop by later, have a word with the night shift.

Next he drove down to Northlake and found the funeral home. No luck there either, even after he showed Billie's picture around and made the connection with Courtney. Miss Cleland they remembered, of course, but no one could place the other lady, never mind some guy with neither name nor face.

So he swung over to Decesare's on Federal and took a booth in the bar. By now it was going on six, so he ordered a vodka martini, straight up, and something off the menu. Made nice with the waitress (or nice as anybody who looked like him could ever hope to make) and learned that, yes, Mrs. Swett came by sometimes and, yes, she could have been in yesterday. Who she was with, though, or what he looked like, the hasher couldn't remember: Always a big lunch crowd in here, hard to keep everybody straight. He thanked her anyway, finished his dinner, and left a big-spender tip. Nothing to him. You were on the clock, everything was expenses. He took a stool up at the bar but switched to ginger ale to keep his head clear. Day wasn't over yet; he wasn't discouraged. It required patience, this line of work. So he sat there, quietly killing time.

Shortly before eleven he drove back to the hospital, and this trip he struck pure gold. It took the form of the nurse he'd come to see, big horsey broad named Eleanor, beat with the ugly stick as bad as he was but couldn't have been more forthcoming. Sure, she remembered Mrs. Swett, kind of a kook, that lady, filling poor Mrs. Cleland's head with some crazy notions about death. Also did Eleanor react instantly to his casual question about a gentleman Mrs. Swett might have encountered here. Oh, yeah, she was happy to report, that'd be Ms. Cody's—she was another terminal, Ms. Cody—brother, always asking about Mrs. Swett, like he was, y'know, sniffing around, which seemed a little out of place, his own sister dying and all. Name? Jim, it was; last one she didn't catch. Description she could supply and in abundant detail. Whereabouts? That she couldn't help him with, but she suggested he might try Ms. Cody's son, Leon his name, lived someplace here in the Gardens; she could probably find the address if he wanted.

He did. She got it for him. He heaped on the gratitude.

"You in insurance?" she asked as he was departing.

"Yeah, you might say that. In a manner of speaking."

"I knew it! I can always spot an insurance man."

"You got a good eye, Eleanor. Thanks."

It was close to midnight before he got out of there, too late for any moves tonight, though he did a quick drive-by of the Cody apartment in a complex off Military Trail. Little recon, against tomorrow. You always want to know your terrain. No lights on inside, no sign of the Jag Billie Swett had been driving. Which was about what he expected. Victim, was she? Accomplice? From everything he'd gathered so far, it looked to him to be a toss-up, could go either way.

But that's not what he told his client when, forty-five minutes later, he put in a call to Swett from the room he'd taken at the Singer Island Embassy Suites.

"Yeah?" was the greeting, groggy, heavily nasalized.

"Cheetah," he said, by way of identification.

"Cheet? What's up?"

"You sleeping?"

"Nah, just dozin'. Too wired to sleep. Plus I got this goddamn cold, stuffy nose."

"Try some NyQuil."

"Yeah, yeah, but tell me what's goin' on. You got anything?"

"Think maybe I turned up a lead," Cheetah said, deliberately vague.

"Already? Sensational."

"Nothing solid yet, you understand."

"Yeah. Sure. Right. But how's it lookin'?"

"Which 'it' is that?"

"The shakedown. Billie. Whole thing."

"Too early to tell."

"You, uh, got any idea who they might be?"

"Which 'they'?"

"Ones behind this, Cheetah. Who else we talkin' about?"

Some serious fishing going on here. Cheetah, he wasn't nibbling. "No," he said.

"No? No what?"

"No ideas. Yet."

"When you think you might?"

"Tomorrow maybe. Speaking of which, there's something I want you to do for me."

"Name it and you got it."

"When that call comes through tomorrow, want you to stall on the money end. Say you need another business day to put it all together."

"Fuck, that'll be easy. Be close to the fuckin' truth."

"Tell this guy to call again on Monday; you'll have a better fix on it then."

"What if he wants to nail down a time?"

"Tell him you'll have it for him Tuesday. That'll give me some breathing space, case I need any."

"Think it'll be wrapped by then?"

"Hard to say. I'll know more tomorrow. Check in with you then."

Anybody else, be a clear signal to ring off, call it a night after a long day. Not Swett. "Cheet?"

"Yeah?"

"How about Billie?"

So finally he got to it, the question eating at him all along, right from the get-go. "What about her?" Cheetah said.

"Any thoughts on where she's at?"

"Located at? Or where in this clip she's at?"

"Either. Both."

"No thoughts yet, Lon."

"I, y'know, worry about her."

Sure you do, Cheetah was thinking, distant second place behind that five-mil-rivets worry, but he let a silence convey that particular thought.

"So I'll be hearin' from you tomorrow, right?"

"Right."

"Talk to ya then."

"Oh, Lon?"

"Yeah?"

"Don't forget to try that NyQuil. Works for me every time."

NINETEEN

WITH MORE THAN THIRTY-SIX HOURS OF COMMUNAL togetherness behind them, this peculiar *ménage à cinq* had settled into an affiliation that could be likened to only a cozy, if guarded, domesticity. Perhaps it was due to the close quarters; perhaps in some small part to the sleeping arrangements, which hadn't gone unnoticed or occasionally, by Junior, lewdly unremarked on; but mostly it could be traced to the captive herself, who, with a kind of resolute maternal authority, somehow had contrived to impose a semblance of order on an otherwise disastrously untidy household.

This morning, following the supervision of laundry, a general straightening up, and a nourishing breakfast of unsugared oat bran, unbuttered wheat toast, freshly squeezed orange juice, and gourmet blend coffee (no more fatty bacon and greasy fried eggs served in *this* kitchen), Billie, outfitted in jeans and crayon-colored lime-green blouse (Leon's well-intentioned but inexpert off-the-rack choices), turned her attention and considerable energies to the appearance of her captors. Specifically their nails. Yesterday she'd noticed their uniformly deplorable condition and determined something had to be done about it. Over Junior's rapidly limpening objections, she dispatched Leon and Hector on another shopping excursion, this time to an establishment devoted exclusively to the arcane arts of beauty. And now, with some rudimentary tools of her former vocation laid out on the table, along with four bowls of warm soapy water, she summoned them from the living room: “All right, you can all come in now. We’re ready to start.”

Three of them came to their feet and, somewhat sheepishly, sidled into the kitchen.

“You too, Mr. Biggs,” she called to the recalcitrant Junior.

Who called back, “I ain’t gettin’ no fuckin’ manicure. That’s for punkers.”

“Well now, there’s an enlightened attitude.”

“Maybe, but it’s the one I got.”

“Your nails are in terrible shape. Do you want to look like a common laborer? Or a lout?”

“Lout’s better’n a sissy.”

“All rich men have presentable hands. And you expect to get rich off this crime, don’t you?”

“Goddamn right, rich.”

“Well?”

To this inarguable syllogistic logic he had no reply. Billie interpreted the silence as consent and said to Hector, “Take him a bowl.”

Hector obediently carried one of the sudsy bowls into the living room and set it on the coffee table. “There ya go, man.”

“Fuck’m I suppose to do with this?”

Hector shrugged helplessly.

“Soak your hands in it,” Billie directed from the kitchen.

“Why?” Junior demanded.

“To soften the nails and cuticles,” she explained but with a rising exasperation edging her voice. “Just do it.”

Grudgingly, muttering some dark curses, he dunked his knobby paws in the water, while Hector, suppressing a giggle, retreated to the relative security of the kitchen.

“Rest of you too,” she instructed, indicating the three remaining bowls.

Four soaked minutes later, Billie glanced around the table and said, “OK, who’s first?”

No one volunteered, but Leon gave her one of his shy, expectant, infinitely guileless grins, so she said, “Leon? How about you?”

“Sure. I’ll go first.”

He pulled his chair in close, extended compliant, dripping hands. Billie toweled them dry and set to work. Gripping his left hand, she shaped the ragged nails with the coarse side of an emery board, moving with assembly-line efficiency from pinkie to thumb. Under her expert touch, his hand trembled slightly. “You nervous, hon?” she asked him, slipping easily back into working-girl persona and vernacular.

“I’m OK,” he said, but his voice was reedy, unconfident.

“No, what I mean is are you a nervous kind of person?”

Now he looked flustered. “Nervous? Me? Don’t think so.”

“Reason I ask is it looks like you chew your nails. Which is why they’re so rough. That right? You bite them?”

“Well, maybe sometimes,” Leon owned up.

“What’s your occupation?”

“Job, you mean?”

“Yes.”

“I work on cars. Restorin’ ’em. Y’know, engines mostly,” he stumbled, the nervous man’s giving up of more answer than there was question, “sometimes bodies. Once in a while, interiors. Depends on the vehicle.”

“What you’ll want to do,” Billie counseled, “is keep your nails clipped real short. And clean them thoroughly every day after work, to get all the dirt and grease out.”

“Yeah, I’ll be sure ’n’ do that,” Leon said earnestly, as though taking an oath.

“Now your cuticles,” she announced, after the tenth nail was planed and smoothed to her satisfaction.

Leon winced at the sight of the next instrument she produced from the abbreviated lineup of tools. “What’s that thing?”

“Cuticle nipper.”

"Looks sorta like a needle nose for a midget," he said with an uneasy snicker. "What's it for?"

"Trims your cuticles. That's the dead skin that grows over the nails."

"Maybe I, uh, don't need that part done."

"Just relax, hon. It won't hurt," she said soothingly and, asserting her professional prerogative, grasped one of his hands and snipped away the thin layers of expired epidermis haloing his nails.

She was right. It didn't hurt. Leon's tightened shoulders sagged, and he looked on worshipfully as Billie, bent like a microsurgeon to her task, eyes intently focused, moved skillfully and with a masterful touch from one digit to the next.

From across the table, Hector, his hands still immersed in the sudsy bowl, inquired diffidently, "Can we take 'em outta the water yet?"

"No," she said without glancing up.

"Could use a smoke."

"You can wait. I'm almost done here. You'll be next."

Hector grimaced but said nothing. Nor did he remove his hands from the bowl. And Jim, watching them all, taking in the whole bizarre scene, hands also soaking, could only shake his head and smile.

Once Billie was finished with the nipper, she set it aside, took a bottle of creamy lotion, poured some into a palm, and massaged it into Leon's hands, stroking each in its turn with gently caressing motions, wrist to fingertips. Behind the thick glasses, his lustered eyes glazed over, and an expression of almost seraphic bliss appeared on his heated face. "This is another thing you ought to do regularly," she advised him matter-of-factly. "Keeps the skin soft and supple."

"Yeah, I'll do that one too," Leon vowed.

Like all good things must, the sensuous stroking came finally to an end. "Now a little polish on the nails, and you're done," she said brightly.

His hands recoiled as though snakebit. "You mean paint 'em?"

"No, no. This is just a clear polish. It'll protect them, add a nice healthy sheen."

"Jeez, I dunno..."

"Contrary to what Mr. Biggs thinks," she assured him, deliberately projecting her voice, "there's nothing 'sissy' about it. Men of style and class have it done all the time. You want to be in style, don't you?"

"S'pose so."

"All right then. Give me your hands."

Nail by nail she applied a coating of colorless gloss. During the process Junior, hearing his name, lumbered into the room. He stood leaning against the refrigerator, watching, and his habitual scowl shaded over into sneer as Hector took Leon's vacated seat and offered up slim brown hands. "Better be careful," he chortled. "Never can tell what chili them mitts been into."

Everyone ignored him. Billie picked up her emery board and sanded the jagged nails. "Looks like we've got another nervous Nellie," she said.

Hector didn't know how to respond to that, so he grinned weakly and said nothing. It was confusing to him, being all day around this smashing woman who seemed astonishingly to have a will and personality and thoughts and ideas all her own. What it did was scatter all his preconceptions (derived as they were mostly from girlie shows and triple-X films and unrequited fantasies) of your fur-burger Anglo blondes, leaving him with the inescapable conclusion that beneath that vavoom bod lurked a living, breathing human being with fears and hopes and dreams and aspirations independent of her cooch. It was a revelation startling in its novelty, perplexing, and for Hector just a little dismaying.

When she got to the middle finger of his right hand, the observant Junior remarked, "Better get Senor Stink there filed down good. That's how he keeps the senoritas happy."

Hector did not acknowledge the jeering comment. Nor did Billie, who kept moving steadily through her structured routine. At its massaging step, Junior, persuaded of his comedic talents, tried again: "You get them hands a' his all oiled up, he ain't never gonna two-time 'em again. Wear ol' Mistress Five Fingers right down to the bone."

Billie fixed him with a chilly stare and, spacing her words to extract their maximum disdain, said, "You are a crude, nasty, vulgar man, Mr. Biggs."

Junior looked stunned, even a little hurt. "Me? You callin' *me* nasty?"

"I just did."

"Well, lemme give you the straight poop. Ain't me who's nasty. It's your beaners, like *chico* here, the nasty ones."

"No. It's you. Hector can be a gentleman when he wants to be."

Hector beamed at this unexpected endorsement but prudently stayed out of the debate.

"Listen," Junior said heatedly, "you want a 'for instance,' I'll give ya one. Just the other day I was readin'—*Enquirer*, think it was—how they caught this greaser, worked in a Kmart's kitchen someplace, spankin' his monkey into a mayonnaise jar. That nasty or what?"

"What it is is the most ridiculous story I've heard in my life."

"Yeah, well, next time you go orderin' a BLT, one a' them Kmart's lunchrooms, I was you, I'd tell 'em hold the mayo."

Even Hector had to chuckle at that.

"Don't encourage him," Billie said primly, and resumed her work.

Jim remained watchful and silent. Leon drifted into the living room and switched on the TV. Junior sulked. And so the flash point appeared to have passed.

A few moments later, Billie released Hector's beautified hands and said, in dismissal, "There you are. That's it."

Unable to meet her eyes, he stood, mumbling a thanks.

"You're very welcome. Mr. Biggs, you're next."

Junior looked uneasy. "Me?"

"Yes. You."

"Whyn't you do Uncle first?"

"No. You."

"Ah, I dunno about this shit."

"Just sit down."

"OK," he said, settling into the chair and plunking his huge, coarsened hands onto the table. "But let's make it quick."

"Quick in your case could mean the rest of the day."

"Take more like rest a' his natural life, them meat hooks," Hector chimed in, catching the spirit.

"What you better be takin' is that skinny spic ass a' yours outta here," Junior snapped. "Before I take it in my head to carve you a new one."

Sniggering to himself, Hector sauntered into the living room.

Which left only the three of them: self-assured artisan, supremely discomfited subject, and bemused onlooker.

"I guess I don't have to ask your occupation," Billie said, inspecting the snagged Biggs nails.

"Whaddya mean by that?"

"You *are* a kidnapper, aren't you?"

"Yeah? So?"

"So that tells me something about you already."

"Like what?"

"Well, you're the first kidnapper I've ever worked on, but going by the condition of your hands—which isn't good at all, by the way—I'd have to say it's not your best profession to be in, nail-wise."

"Fuck's wrong with 'em?"

"What's *wrong*! Look at them. All those hangnails. You're lucky you don't have some awful disease."

"Disease," Junior snorted skeptically. "Fingernails don't get no diseases."

"Oh, but they do. Fungal infections are quite common. Isn't that right, Jim?"

"Oh, yeah," he affirmed. "Very dangerous, your fungal infections."

Like most bullies, Junior was understandably suspicious of any humor not his own, on the entirely reasonable grounds that sooner or later the joke was bound to be on him. Now he looked back and forth between them, scowling. "You two honeymooners puttin' me on?"

"Not at all," Billie said innocently. "Just trying to let you know some of the risks."

"Better be all it is."

"Look at the color of the skin around your nails," Billie said in further evidence of her professional concern. "See how yellow it is? That means you've got too much nicotine in your system, probably from all that disgusting tobacco chewing."

"Both a' you two smoke," he said defensively.

"But in moderation."

"Yeah, sound a' them bedsprings squeakin' the last couple of nights, you ain't nobody to be talkin' about moderation."

"That, Mr. Biggs," she said haughtily, "is none of your business."

"No, you got that wrong. Everything goes on here's my business. I'm the one callin' the shots. Remember? Me. Junior Biggs."

"Not at this table."

Junior shook his head vigorously, like a hound shaking water from its fur. "What's that? What'd you just say?"

"You heard me."

"All she's talking about is nails," Jim put in with a studied neutrality. "Just nails."

"Shut the fuck up, Uncle."

"He's right," Billie said. "What do you know about nails?"

The question seemed to stump him. “You askin’ what I know about ’em?”

“Not a whole lot, I’d say, from the looks of yours.”

“That’s what you’d say, is it?”

“Yes.”

“OK,” Junior said, fairly spluttering now. “OK. Tell ya what I know. Know it’s your pansy-ass pussywhips, like Uncle here, worry about ’em. And cunts like you make an easy buck off ’em. Which is all any real man needs to know.”

Having so declared, he jerked his hands away, heaved himself up from the chair, and stalked out of the room. “You’ll regret it,” Billie called after him.

In oblique, ominous warning, he called back, “Man packin’ the piece don’t got no regrets.”

And now there were only two of them.

“You know,” Jim said, voice carefully lowered, “it may not be such a slick idea, baiting him.”

“Who’s baiting? All I was doing was telling him the truth.”

“Evidently he’s not ready for it.”

“Well, that’s his problem, not mine. You ready here?”

“You still want to keep on with this?”

“Of course. Why wouldn’t I?”

“Didn’t shake you up just a little, that face-off?”

“Certainly not. Let’s see your hands.”

Jim presented them.

“Not too bad,” she allowed, commencing with the emery board.

“We clerks don’t count nails among our heavier problems.”

“Looks to me like this clerk has had his done before.”

“Right you are. But it’s been a while.”

“You shouldn’t neglect them.”

“Kind of low on my financial priority sheet lately. There was a time, though, believe it or not, when I had money. Not in your league but enough for the occasional small luxury. Like this.”

"But now you don't?"

"If I did, I wouldn't be here. Neither would you."

"Well, maybe we'll both get lucky," Billie said, treating him to an ambiguous smile, partly mocking but with a trace of tenderness in it. "Meantime think of this one as free."

Sitting up close this way, Jim saw that her skin, innocent of paint this morning, had the tautened look of a lift, as though it were secured by invisible wires under the roots of her hair. Doubtless she was older than he'd first estimated. But that was OK. Older or not, scalpel enhanced or not, she had an indwelling, incorruptible quality about her, an ageless freshness lovelier than a morning sky. And when it came time for the hand massage, it struck him suddenly, and with a kind of premonitory foreshadowing, that this was one of those singular moments in life a man never forgets, recalls vividly long after his vision is blurred and flesh withered and bones brittle and bent; and whatever it was, this curious bond between them, however tenuously forged, it had emerged from some mysterious facet of themselves neither had ever acknowledged or understood. But also, as she expertly manipulated the joints and tendons of his hands, her secret smile not quite discarded, was he overtaken by a dizzying sensation of guilt, like a future grief disremembered in advance, or a chilly omen of something soon to happen to her, to both of them, something unspecific but terrible and outside his power to forestall.

A thumping at the door, soft but insistent, abruptly canceled all these slippery emotions and dreads, launching new, more immediate ones. Out in the living room, Junior leaped to his feet and in a hissy voice demanded of no one in particular, all of them, "Who the fuck's that?"

No one presumed to venture a guess.

The knocking continued. Whoever it was wasn't going away. Junior made an executive decision. "OK, I'll field it. *Chico*, get 'em in the back."

"C'mon, you people," Hector said, hailing the other three.

"Your piece, fucknuts. Use your piece. One word outta 'em—even one—and you blow 'em away. Got that?"

"I got it."

Reluctantly, almost apologetically, Hector removed the .38 from his belt and, motioning with its barrel, guided them into a bedroom.

With the kitchen and living room clear, Junior eased his Colt Banker's Special .22 out of its hip holster, held it partially concealed behind him, stepped over to the door, opened it no more than the length of the chain, and peering through the tiny notch, saw just about the ugliest fucker he'd ever laid eyes on. Looked like a goddamn circus monkey duded out in suit, tie, the works, gonna do some tricks. "Yeah?" he said.

"This the Cody residence?"

Monkey can talk. And the minute he opened his chimp mouth, Junior made him for heat. What brand—fed, local, private—he don't know for sure, only that it was heat. No mistaking that bad-news rumble in the voice. Junior, he'd heard it before, many a time. He knew. "Yeah, it is," he said.

"Would you be Mr. Cody?"

"No, he ain't in right now."

"Don't suppose you'd be his uncle?"

"No, he's out too. You wanna leave a message, I'll see they get it."

"Be a big help."

Behind the door Junior slowly elevated his piece hand. "Shoot," he said.

"Name's McReedy," the monkey told him, parting those thick lips in heat's idea of a cheery citizen smile. "I'm an insurance adjuster. With the hospital. Where Miz Cody passed away recently."

Insurance. Sure. Acting lessons is what they all of 'em need, Junior was thinking, but he said, "So what's the message?"

"Good news. Looks like they got a nice refund check coming. On the hospital bill."

"That a fact?"

"It's a fact," he said, hanging on to the smile but letting it turn up slightly at one corner so it ended up more like a sneer. Or a challenge.

"You wanna leave it, this check, I'll be sure they get it."

"Like the message?"

"Yeah. Like that."

"Wish I could. Spare me some shoe leather. But company says no. We got to deliver it in person. Some paperwork too."

Junior wasn't biting on that; he said nothing.

"You got any thoughts on when they'll be back?"

"Prolly be late," he extemporized. "They went fishin'."

"No kidding? Deep sea?"

"It was out a ways."

"Lucky them. Nothing like fishing to relax you."

"Yeah, they pretty lucky."

"Maybe tonight?"

"Huh?"

"They'll be back? Like we were saying?"

"Maybe. I was you, I'd try tomorrow."

"Tomorrow's Sunday."

"So?"

" 'Six days shalt thou labor.' Find that in your Bible."

Fuck's he talkin', Bible? "Tomorrow's when I'd try," Junior repeated.

"I'll do that. Thanks for your time."

"Nothin'," Junior said, and started to push the door shut, but before he could, the monkey wiggled a finger in the air and said, "Oh, one other thing. Can you tell me Miz Cody's brother's name? Need it for that paperwork."

"Can't help you out there. Just met the gentleman myself."

"Friend of the boy, are you?"

"We go back a ways."

"You're not an angler, though."

Piece poised, Junior squinted at him narrowly. "Ain't sure I follow."

"Angler. Fisherman. You didn't go on the fishing trip today."

"No," is all Junior could think to say.

"Next time maybe."

"Yeah. Next time."

"Well, nice talking to you."

"Same here."

Junior bolted the door and holstered his iron, thinking, *Yeah, real fuckin' pleasure, better'n getting' your wick dipped.* He ran a hand over his damp brow, plucked at the fabric of his shirt where it clung wetly to his skin. Air on high, and he was still sweating like a blue gummer. Feeling like he always felt after a sparring session with the heat: wired, spooked, fucked over.

If that wasn't bad enough, the phone had to pick just that minute to rattle. About sent him through the ceiling. He steadied himself, picked it up, and said his surly, wary, "Yeah?"

"Bott here. I have some news to report."

"So report it."

He listened. As he did, the reliable scowl settled over his broad, scarred face. When the report was finished, he said grimly, "That's it?"

"I'm afraid so."

"OK, now I got some buzz to pass along. Ain't no better'n what I'm hearing outta you."

Junior told him about the baboon man. During the telling, Hector peeked out from behind the bedroom door, discovered everything was clear, signaled his charges, and the four of them came into the living room just as the phone conversation was winding down, Junior saying, "OK, but I'm gonna give it a while, make sure nobody trackin' me," then recradling the phone.

"Wha's goin' on?" Hector wanted to know.

"Goin' on?" Junior repeated sourly. "Slickerin' goin' on."

"What kinda slickerin'?"

"Like the five-miles-a'-pothole-road kind, cholo. An' we ain't light on our feet, we gonna be dust."

"What're you sayin', dust?"

"History. Dust."

"Who's that at the door?"

"A flic was who."

"Law?"

"Am I lyin'?"

"Uniform?"

"Suit."

"So how you sure he's the law?"

"'Cuz I know heat."

Some of the color drained out of Hector's brown face, paling it the shade of dry clay. "Fuck we gonna do?"

"Go DL."

"Them too?" Hector said, tossing his head in the direction of the three silent spectators.

"'Course them, dick brain. They the treasure. Least the twat is."

"Five of us, I dunno. Where we gonna find to get down low?"

"Bott. That was him on the horn there. He gettin' us a crib over where he's at. Right next door."

Thoroughly baffled, Billie had been attending closely to this impenetrable dialogue. Now, at the giveaway mention of the pastor's name, she turned to Jim and said, "Bott? *Reverend* Bott?"

"The very same," Jim said.

"*He's* in this?"

"Remember what I told you?"

"Scammer, you called him."

"Well, this is the scam."

She looked stunned. Behind the sea-blue eyes, a doubt seemed to be circling inside her head. "But not the girl?"

Jim shrugged.

It was Junior who supplied an answer. "That dizzy slit too lunched to be in on anything."

"I suppose that's some small comfort," Billie said.

"Gonna get smaller, your old man keeps stallin'."

"I haven't the slightest idea what you're talking about."

"Talkin' 'bout loot, lady. Long green. Five mil of it, goin' rate for that box lunch a' yours. He don't come up with it, you lookin' at a dirt nap."

Again she turned a bewildered face to Jim.

For an instant Jim hesitated then took a halting step forward, positioned himself between them, and said boldly, considerably bolder than he felt, "Why don't you give it a rest?"

"That your thought, is it?" Junior snorted contemptuously.

"One of them."

"Try another."

"All right. The money then."

"What about it?"

"You want it, don't you?"

"Doin' more'n wantin', Uncle. Gonna get it. Or somebody be feelin' the heavy hurts."

"And she's the key to the treasure, right?"

"You oughta know. You the one bumpin' her fuzz."

"But *you've* still got her, haven't you?" Jim said, letting the lewd remark go by.

"Bet your ass, I got her."

"So where's the problem?"

"Pro'lum is her hub's tellin' shit-sack Bott he can't raise the cash 'til Tuesday now," Junior grouched, sounding more than a little worried.

"So what's another day?" Jim said, pitching it like the voice of reason.

"Yeah," Hector seconded. "One more day can't hurt none."

"With heat sniffin' around?" Junior said, disgusted now. "Like I just got done tellin' you? Ah, fuck'm I doin', talkin' to a beaner and a weenie? All's I know for sure is we sailin' close to the wind here."

"Not if we're moving over to the island," Jim reminded him.

With a kind of dull resignation, he conceded, "Yeah, that's today's plan."

Jim held in a sigh. Another flash point—second one today, and far more perilous than the first—skirted, however temporarily. "When are we leaving?" he asked.

Reasserting his authority, Junior snapped, "Soon's I say when."

Which wasn't until seven hours later, under the cover of falling light and only after he had combed the entire complex, scouted all its parking lots, and satisfied himself the baboon man (or any of his kind) was nowhere in sight.

Junior drove, the others huddled in the seatless rear of the van: Leon and Hector (his gun brandished, at Junior's command) on one side; Billie and Jim the other; all their bags on the rancid, sweat-and-semen-stained mattress between them.

"You OK?" Jim asked her.

"I've had more comfortable rides. Otherwise I'm fine."

Amazingly it seemed to be true. Her own nails done during the long wait, hair carefully styled, face lacquered, she looked (except for the dog-rack outfit) like an elegant lady on her way to the governor's ball: radiant, excited, eager to make the grand entrance. Whatever doubts or fears she may have entertained through the course of that earlier rambling exchange (or may not, given its murky street idiom) seemed to have trickled right out of her, evaporated, and a breezy, sportive energy, bordering on the manic, took their place. Like an adventuress, she was supremely confident hers was a charmed life.

Jim felt suddenly very weary, very old. "What day is it?" he said.

"Saturday."

"No. Date, I mean."

"Let me see," she said. "Sixteenth, I think. Yes, August sixteenth. Why?"

"Tomorrow's my birthday."

"No shit," Hector said. "Mine's the twentieth."

Billie clapped her hands delightedly. "*Two* birthday boys!" she squealed. "We've got to have us a party!"

TWENTY

IF THERE WAS ONE THING CHEETAH PRIDED HIMSELF on, it was his ability to spot a hard case. Maybe it was working the trades that put an identifiable stamp on them. Or maybe it was because they were always wearing it, couldn't seem to help themselves that way, even if they'd wanted to try, 'til at last the pose became the man. Whatever the reason, he could make one in a heartbeat, pick him out of a jam of citizens instantly and without fail. For them, even as for himself, physiognomy (a word he'd acquired long ago, when the full dismal weight of his own appalling features first sank in on him) was destiny.

Like this family "friend" he just got done dancing with. Classic knuckle dragger. Dumb as a sack of dirt but with just enough street and joint savvy to be dangerous (to be fair about it, never mind cautious). Where exactly he fit into this widening burn wasn't clear yet, but Cheetah wasn't worried. He had the scent now; was only a matter of time 'til he circled his prey and moved in for the kill. Everything in its time.

Two hours of which he spent sitting patiently in his inconspicuous Olds parked at the far end of the lot outside the building that housed the Cody apartment, scoping its entrance in the unlikely event the dragger was stupid enough to try and bolt. No such luck. He gave it another thirty minutes. Still no action. If the victim (or accomplice, if that's what she was) was inside, she was keeping (or being kept) down. By himself he had no authority, forget about hard evidence, to toss the place, and anyway the client clearly wanted everything done on mute, spare himself the humiliation of a public scandal, if that's how it was going to fall out.

So Cheetah figured what he'd better do was go to a backup plan. What he needed was some small incriminating link between victim/accomplice and goon. Anything would do. Her vehicle, say. He picked up his cell phone, dialed the number of a snitch he knew up this way, called in a favor, and rang off with the names of half a dozen choppers in the vicinity. Then he set out in search of the missing Jag.

The shops were spread all over the area, and each required its own special access code, some kicked-back, others kick-ass. So this maneuver ate up the time. It was, in fact, half past six before he finally struck oil, at a place called Fixit Fred's Body Shop located off Old Dixie Highway in Lake Park. COLLISION PROS, the sign outside a windowless pole-barn garage announced, Cheetah thinking as he read it, *Yeah, right, like the melt-down-and-vanish variety collision.* But what he said, starting off easy, agreeable, with the gearhead sitting with his feet on the desk in the grimy front office was, "Wonder if you could help me out."

"Depends," was the cagey reply coming out from behind a squinty stare, part puzzled, part amused, like a visitor to the monkey house at a zoo will sometimes get.

Nothing new to Cheetah: That's how most people, seeing him for the first time, looked. "Would you be Fixit Fred?" he asked.

"That's what they call me," he said, tilting his chair back at a jauntily precarious angle, feet still propped on the desk. He was a scrawny little runt, this gearhead, with the sharp, sniffy features of an aging rodent and beady pinprick eyes of a bird feeding on roadkill. Not so handsome himself.

"Well, Fixit," said Cheetah amiably, "I got a problem you may be just the man to fix."

"Kinda problem we talkin'?"

"Well, suppose I had a vehicle I wanted to make, y'know, disappear."

"How you mean, disappear?"

"Oh, you know, exit, go south. Vanish without a trace."

"Wouldn't know nothin' about that."

"Yeah, well, humor me anyway. Suppose this vehicle was a Jag. Nice, shiny black one. Parade piece. New."

"What you're supposin' here, friend, is against the law."

"Yeah, I heard that."

"You heard correct."

"Also heard you could make it happen, though, this disappearing act. Even if it was bending the law a little."

Fixit stuck a cigarette in his mouth, lit it, sneered out some smoke. "That part you heard wrong. So maybe you oughta take a hike, gruesome. Before you scare any my customers might drop in."

Agreeable, Cheetah decided, wasn't going to get the job done here. So he reached across the desk, seized the bonebag by the ankles, gave a yank, and sent him sprawling onto the concrete floor. Then he came around and grasped him by the collar, jerked him to his feet, shoved him against a wall, and pinned him to it with the flat of a hand. "Sign out front says you're the collision pro," he said mildly, like a man searching for a small-talk topic.

"Cocksucker," Fixit wheezed, shaking the daze out of his gearbox head.

"Reason I mention it, see, is I give good collision too. Smashmouth kind, sample of which you just experienced."

"What you jammin' me for, man? You steam?"

"I was steam, you'd be in lockup by now, getting your fudge packed by a gang of boogies."

"Fuck you want then, you ain't steam?"

"Just some help is all. Everybody needs help now and then. Even you."

To demonstrate this universal human need, Cheetah made a blade of his free hand and brought it down across the Fixit nose, shattering bone, squirting blood, and exciting an astonished, yelping cry that Cheetah had to muffle with the blade hand. Little extreme, maybe, but it always gave him a certain satisfaction, demonstrating this particular point. Made up in small part for all the taunts and revolted looks he'd endured all these years. "See," he drawled, removing his hand once the yipping slacked off, "without help all kinds of bad things can happen to a man."

"My nose! You fuckin' ape, you broke my *nose*!"

"I do necks too. So you better listen up, what I'm going to ask you here. Only got a couple questions. Think you can handle that?"

The bloodied Fixit head move compliantly up and down.

"OK, you get a black ninety-seven Jag XK8 in here past forty-eight hours?"

The head moved again, same direction.

"That a yes?"

"Yeah."

"Gentleman brought it in, was he one of your regular clientele?"

Now the head moved horizontally.

"Let's use words, Fixit."

"No."

"You sure about that?"

"Honest, man. Never seen him before."

"This gentleman," Cheetah inquired, plugging in descriptive details picked up and memory filed from the brief encounter at the barely cracked apartment door, "was he a big fella, six three or better, heavyset? Thin hair, kind of a square face, pits in it? Bad teeth?" Deliberately he neglected to include the distinguishing facial scar. Little test for Fixit.

"Yeah, that's him."

"You sure now? You're not just curving me here?"

"Tellin' ya, man, that's the guy. I remember the teeth, all yellow, from chaw. He was spittin' juice all'a time he was here."

"Anything else you remember? Think real hard now."

"Yeah, there was this zipper alongside his mouth. Forget which side. But it was there."

"Congratulations," Cheetah said. "You just got promoted to songbird, first class." He removed the pinning hand from the frail Fixit chest and, on his way out the door added, in genial farewell, "Sure hope you can find it in your heart to think kindly of me. 'Specially every time you try and take a deep breath."

The problem with working solo was you couldn't be in two places at the same time. Ordinarily that wasn't a major pinch. The nature of Cheetah's work was, for the most part, sequential: point A to B to C, and so on, to the jackpot. This instance, though, it was proving to be something of an aggravation, as he was discovering, doggedly banging on the Cody apartment door and getting zip in response. He could, of course, jimmy the lock if he had to—plenty of experience along those lines—but that, like the artillery strapped under an armpit, was always a fallback for Cheetah, court of last resort. Tone of voice, Congo glare, now and again the bladed hand—individually or in concert, these generally were enough to take care of business. So he kept pounding for a while, in case whoever might be inside there was hunkered down, praying he'd go away. Fat chance.

"You don't hold it down," a voice behind him suddenly shrilled, "I'm callin' the manager."

Startled, Cheetah wheeled around and faced an antique little toad of a woman, Granny Time, who had materialized in the doorway directly across the hall. Like some mothballed battle wagon, she stood there, draped in an ankle-length flannel robe, vein-roped hands belligerently planted on bony hips, pink-rimmed eyes rheumy and fierce. "Sorry about the commotion, ma'am," he said, penitently as he could.

"Person entitled to expect some peace and quiet," she fired back in a volume calculated to inspire neither.

Cheetah had no thoughts on that particular entitlement, so he said nothing.

"Wastin' your time anyway. They all of 'em packed up and left. Thank the Lord for small mercies."

"Left?"

"Couldn't been ten minutes. You just missed 'em."

"'They,' you say?"

"I did. You deef?"

"Don't suppose you'd happen to know who they were?"

"Why you askin'?" she parried suspiciously.

"Need to get in touch with Miz Cody's brother."

"What about?"

"It's a business thing," Cheetah said vaguely.

"Well, he was one of 'em. And there was Leon too, her boy."

"Anybody else?"

"Couple other fellas, one a Mexican. And the woman."

"Woman?"

"You got this hearin' problem, young man, you oughta get yourself one a' them Miracle Ears."

"Yeah, I'll look into that," Cheetah pledged. "But you say there was a woman with them?"

"Said it once, say it again. Use to be this was a respectable place to live. They got no right, sneakin' in chippies. Goes against common decency. Why, Mrs. Cody, she'd turn over in her grave, she knew about it."

During this outburst of sanctimony, Cheetah had fished the Billie Swett snapshot out of his wallet. He presented it to her, asking, "Wouldn't be this was the lady?"

She thrust her wizened head in close, studied the photo, and arrived at the inconclusive judgment, "Could be, could be not."

"That mean you don't know?"

"Means what it means. Looks little like her, but I wouldn't swear to it. Only seen her once, couple days back."

"Not since then?"

"What'd I just say?"

"So it could be she never left the apartment?"

"Wouldn't know anything about that. Tell ya this, though, been some funny things goin' on, that place."

"How, funny?"

"Comin' and goin' all hours the day and night, that's how. Lord only knows what they up to. No good, you want my opinion."

"Think maybe you're right," Cheetah agreed dryly.

"Y'darn right I'm right. And now I got something to ask you."

"What'd that be?"

"You got business with Mr. Merriman, how come you snoopin' around askin' about these other folks?"

"Business with who?"

"Jim Merriman. Mrs. Cody's brother. Who you think I'm talkin' about?"

"That's his name, is it?"

"'Course it's his name. You doin' business with a man, and you don't even know his name? Who are you anyway?"

Shrewd customer, this old dreadnought. Everybody into shrewd these days. Must be the TV. Cheetah leaned over toward her, lowered his voice to confidential whisper. "You keep a secret, ma'am?"

The watery eyes batted expectantly. "What kinda secret?"

"Top kind."

"I can keep it."

"OK, I'm with the government. CIA. This business I got with Mr. Merriman, it's real hush-hush. Can't go into any details except to tell you it's of grave national importance. Which is why I got to ask you all these questions."

"He's a *spy*?" she exclaimed.

Cheetah let a silence serve as answer.

"Who'd've ever thought?" she said, dumbfounded now.

"Ask you one more?"

"Why sure. Anything to help."

"You notice what kind of vehicle these people driving?"

"Sure did," she declared proudly. "Was one of them vans, you see, like they use to make deliveries with, no windows on the sides. Green, it was, or maybe blue. Pretty old, beat up."

"Didn't catch the license, did you?"

"'Fraid I didn't."

"Well, that's OK," Cheetah drawled tolerantly. "Most folks don't."

"My name's Gath," she told him, as though in anticipation of a framed certificate of commendation. "Irma Gath."

"Been a real service you done here today, Miz Gath," Cheetah said, starting away. "Your government thanks you."

"I ask you to do something for me?"

"Name it."

"Couple days after Mrs. Cody passed on, I took over a nice casserole for Leon. That's how I met his uncle, Mr. Merriman. When you catch him, will you get my casserole dish back for me?"

"Deliver it to you in person. Word of honor."

If you got a name, you got a trail, and if you got a trail, you got a destination. And now that he had a name, Cheetah had a hunch the destination was almost in sight, even if he seemed to be temporarily stalled. Hunch also told him it was Miss Courtney who was going to lead him there. Yesterday he'd figured her for holding a little something back. Today he'd spring the Merriman name on her, see if she blinked.

So when he left the apartments, he swung over to PGA and pulled up outside the Hair Affair. Featherhead reception girl gave him the gnarly news that Court and her boyfriend took off for the weekend; where, she didn't know; be back Monday morning, though, first thing.

Cheetah decided to pack it in. Nothing more of any substance to be done tonight. Tomorrow he'd check all the motels in the vicinity, but he didn't expect to turn up anything from that.

Nobody was dumb enough to go by his own name on the register, not even these single baggers.

He drove back to his place at the Embassy Suites, ordered a room-service dinner, and while he was waiting, put in a call to Swett, last burden of the day. Had to suffer through a breathless account of the morning call from the contact man and how stalwart Swett had cleverly laid him off 'til Tuesday, just like Cheetah had said to do.

"Nice work," Cheetah stroked him, once the wheeze at last expired.

"Asshole's callin' again Monday morning. To finalize, he says. What'll I tell him?"

"Tell him you need 'til late in the day on Tuesday."

There was a silence on the line.

"Lon?"

"Late now?"

"Yeah. Late."

"You, uh, run into a snag, that lead you was sayin'?"

"Nothing serious. Just I may need a little more time. May not too."

"Jesus, Cheet, I dunno. I kinda made it sound like Tuesday morning. I was, y'know, countin' on you to come through."

"I always come through, Lon."

"You gettin' close then?"

"Practically in the can. Better I don't trouble you with the details yet."

"Billie, though. She OK?"

"Think it's safe to say she's doing just fine," Cheetah said ambiguously.

Seemed to be as much as he wanted to know, for the next question was, "You got any ideas how I'm gonna sell that stall?"

"Tell him bankers get skittish, all that cash. Require another working day to put it together in unmarked bills. You'll have it ready for him Tuesday night, for sure."

"You think he'll buy it?"

"Trust me, he'll buy. We're not dealing with your deep thinkers here."

"OK, do my best."

"You'll do fine."

"Anything breaks, you let me know, huh?"

"You're the client, Lon. Client always gets to know first."

Later, after his dinner and a couple of loosener brandies, Cheetah strolled over to the window and gazed pensively out across the Singer Island rooftops, watching the sun sink like a stone beneath the western horizon and thinking, *I know you're out there, and I'm right behind you, nipping at your collective asses.* Had he glanced down and a little to his left, he would have seen a battered van, not unlike the one described by the observant Irma Gath, parked behind a row of tourist apartments on the street below him.

TWENTY-ONE

"WHO WOULD CARE TO OFFER A GRACE?" SAID the Reverend Bott, spraying a mushy, churchy smile around the table.

Jim cocked a puzzled eye, wondering if it could be intended as a joke.

Biggs must have felt the same way, for he said, "Only grace I know's a broad brings her own meat with her to dinner," punctuating his witticism with a huge guffaw.

Bryce gave him a look of withering pity. Evidently no joke. No one else volunteered, so he said, "Very well, then. Allow me. Let us bow our heads, please."

Six heads, his own among them, obediently dropped.

"Dear Lord," he began, and in pious drone petitioned God's blessings on the abundant feast awaiting them; on the health and prosperity of the two honorees specifically, the assembled company generally; and, in afterthought, perhaps as an appeal for a kind of heavenly endorsement, on the success of this bold enterprise they were embarked upon.

It was windier than a simple grace needed to be, more on the order of an abridged sermon; and as it wore on, Jim snuck a peek at the supplicant and was convinced he caught a brief glimpse of the mischief-maker child, naughty prankster, behind the baggy features of the aging man. As with most men whose lives are a perpetual performance, his true identity was forever cloaked in the guise of the moment, but the irrepressible imp within seemed to be sniggering a contrapuntal refrain: *Oh, but there is indeed a joke here, my very good friends, and it's on all of you.*

Like the crack of a starter's gun, the murmured amen set the diners in motion, Junior well out in front, clutching his tableware like weaponry and plunging headlong into the spinach-salad first course. He chomped a generous mouthful, washed it down with an Adam's-apple-bobbling gulp of wine, made a doubtful face, turned to Billie, and demanded, "Kinda dressing you got on here?"

"It's a light vinaigrette. Brings out the flavor of the greens."

"I like Thousand Island. Y'got any Thousand Island?"

"Of course not," she said archly. "That stuff's loaded with fat, terrible for you. Not to mention what it does to a salad."

"Yeah, well, it's what I like."

"Well, we don't have any."

"How about Eye-talian. Got any that?"

"No. Eat your salad."

Grumbling something about "goddamn rabbit chow," he nevertheless cleaned up his bowl.

They were arranged around a small table carted from kitchen to living room and lengthened enough to accommodate the six of them by a leaf Billie had come across in a closet. She and Bryce anchored either end; Leon and Jim sat on one side facing Hector and Junior on the other. Absent only was the frail Waneta, asleep in the apartment next door, too exhausted by the daily procession of credulous seekers of tidings from beyond the shades to attend the party.

It was all Billie's doing, this birthday celebration, testament to her singular gift for salvaging the merely preposterous from the truly absurd. First thing that morning, she'd rousted everyone out and set them to work cleaning the shabby Surf and Shore apartment (Bryce, occupied in overseeing the duping of the marks, exempted). Its tasteless decor—tangerine drapes at the windows; some hideous seascapes along with a framed portrait of two saucer-eyed puppies adorning walls the color of curdled lemon custard; a sofa pillow embroidered with a likeness of a haloed Elvis, garish costume and all, clasping hands with a welcoming St. Peter—was beyond any hope of redemption, but she was nevertheless determined to make the place as presentable as it could ever be. Next she dispatched those two veteran shoppers, Leon and Hector, to an upscale market in the area, armed with a formidable list of victuals and beverages essential to her meticulously planned menu. During the afternoon Leon, Jim, and Junior napped the naps of physical fatigue, while the luckless Hector, nominal sentry, was impressed into kitchen duty as Billie busily prepared the banquet.

And now, eight o'clock on a Sunday evening, exactly forty years to the day Jim Merriman came naked and squalling into this perilous world, and approximately seventy-two hours short of the thirtieth anniversary of the arrival of the infant Jesus Morales (as he was then known), this unlikely band of celebrants was gathered to commemorate those two gladsome occasions. Dress was necessarily, given the circumstances, casual, though Bryce wore his all-purpose funereal black suit, and Hector, in dazzling contrast, a spiffy ensemble of tasseled burgundy loafers, salmon-colored slacks, lavender sport coat over pastel pink shirt and narrow midnight-blue tie (sneeringly referred to by Junior as his "spigger suit"—"spigger" an inventive blend of "spic" and "nigger"). Manners, however, were, at Billie's insistence, formal, or as formal as she could hope to impose upon this unpolished company. On that score she was ably assisted by Bryce, who kept up a steady stream of sociable patter; a bubbly, beaming tub of ebullience. A smatterer, he had a scrap of knowledge on most every topic and an opinion on all of them. Just then he was remarking on the wine. "Excellent Chardonnay, Mrs. Swett," he pronounced, elevating his glass and sniffing it expertly. "Superb bouquet."

Billie, by now more or less reconciled to his duplicity, said simply, "Thank you," though she was clearly pleased with the flattery.

"Veritable nectar of the gods," he gushed on.

"I don't know about that, but I think it should go well with the dinner."

"Which we await impatiently," he said in gentle prompting.

"Everyone finished with your salads?" she asked, and received in reply affirmative grunts and nods from either side of the table. "Leon, will you give me a hand?"

"Sure thing," said the reliably cheery Leon, and the two of them stepped into the kitchen and returned bearing large serving bowls of wild rice and a mysterious steamy broth, reddish and thick. Another trip produced a loaf of sourdough bread and a fresh bottle of wine.

"Shrimp Creole," Billie announced, identifying the main course.

"That what you call that goop?" Junior inquired dubiously.

"It's hardly goop," Billie said.

"Looks like that gut-bomb stew they got in the joint. Give ya the ol' Aztec two-step, right, *chico*?"

"Nah," Hector said diplomatically, "look real good to me."

"Fuck would a homey know?"

"I fear our Mr. Biggs's gastronomic tastes were unfortunately stranded somewhere at the peasant level," Bryce put in with amused tolerance.

"Maybe so," Junior said. "But you gimme a slab a' steak cooked to a char and a mound a' mash spuds sunk in that brown gravy—that's my idea of a feed."

"Well, that's *not* what you're eating tonight," Billie haughtily reminded him, effectively arresting that line of conversation.

Bowls were passed, plates heaped, and dinner was underway.

Jim, nibbling at his food, glancing uneasily around the table, taking in the several strands of amiable prattle, had the dizzying sense of a man suspended in a bubble of hallucination. To his left sat a nephew sporting the dazed grin of a child for whom each new day comes as a bewildering surprise. Across from him a pair of ruthless thugs traded anecdotes of adventures in prison dining, a showy exercise in outrageous one-upmanship. To his right a bogus preacher, born to the gritting arts, delivered a nonstop encomium on the main course, its piquant seasonings, delicate blending of flavors, exquisite textures; while the hostess, his entirely unforeseen bedmate, as accomplished there as she was in the kitchen, glowed under the effusion of praise. It had all the giddy, goofy ambiance of a madhouse, lunatics dancing on their own graves. Everyone seemed to have forgotten the sinister conjunction of accidents that had conspired to bring them together; no one seemed even remotely concerned over the violent collision inescapably in store for them all. Maybe Jim was missing something, some subtle undertone outside the range of his perception. Maybe he was the lunatic after all.

"I 'member this one inmate up to Jacktown, name a' Henspecker," Junior was reminiscing, capturing the attention of the table with a booming, wine-charged voice, chewing noisily as he spoke and thereby setting each rapidly liquefying mouthful on display. "'Chicken Dick,' we called him. Skinny little pissant, but man, could that fucker put away the nosh. Worked mess, cleanup crew, just so's he could eat the leavings off the trays."

"How come you call him 'Chicken Dick'?" Hector wanted to know.

"Henspecker, retard," said Junior peevishly. "Hen's. Pecker. Get it?"

"Don't make no sense."

"Whaddya mean, no sense?"

"Hen's a female chicken."

"So?"

"So females got no dicks on 'em, last I checked. So it don't make sense, what you called him."

"That ain't the point," Junior said, thoroughly exasperated. "Point I'm tryin' to make here is how much he could scarf. I tell ya, that geek eat the dingleberries off your bunghole, you let him.

"'Course, he was a spook," he added, as though the racial identification explained it all.

"I don't see what that has to do with it," Billie said.

Junior looked baffled. "What got to do with what?"

"This person being black."

"Got everything to do with it. Them people eat anything don't bite back first."

"*That's* what you learned in prison?" she said scathingly.

"That 'n' a whole lot more. You locked up with 'em, you learn quick. Ninety percent a' your offenders are spades, y'know."

"That I seriously doubt."

"Listen, lady," Junior declared, rising to the challenge, "that's a statistics fact. Look it up. Ninety percent. With your beaners, like *chico* here, runnin' a close second. Which is why you gotta have organizations like your Brotherhood, you wanna stay above ground in there."

"Brotherhood? What's that?"

"Aryan Brotherhood," Junior said with fraternal pride. "Bunch a regular white guys hangin' together 'gainst your mud people and your taco benders."

Billie turned a puzzled gaze on Hector. "Why do you put up with that?"

"Ah, don't mean nothin'," Hector said, giving the air a feeble swipe.

Throughout this exchange Bryce had remained uncharacteristically silent. Now he cleared his throat, preface to a pronouncement, and directing it at Billie, said, "You must forgive Mr. Biggs. Tact and the elementary social graces are, I fear, not a large part of his repertoire."

Junior looked at him narrowly. "Fuck you sayin' about me?"

"Merely that you are a product of the earth, my friend. Earthy. Which accounts for your boundless wit and ingenuous charm."

"Say it in American."

"You must indulge me. I confess to a weakness for the elegant turn of phrase."

"Yeah, you be confessin' to a world a hurts," Junior rumbled, "you don't start talkin' plain."

"Very well," said Bryce, nimble dodger. "Plainly then. I propose a toast—no, strike that—a series of toasts. The first to our lovely hostess, in appreciation for her peerless culinary talents and tireless efforts, the results of which we have just been privileged to feast upon."

"You talkin' about the eats now?" Junior asked.

"Yes," Bryce sighed. "The eats."

"I'll go along with that one. Wasn't half bad at that."

"To Mrs. Swett, then, treasure of the Treasure Coast, who truly has outdone herself tonight."

Glasses were lifted and clinked. Billie's glow deepened. "Hector helped me," she said with becoming modesty.

From the pit of his throat to the very roots of his brilliantined hair, Hector's brown features turned the shade of iodine. "Didn't do much," he mumbled. "Peeled some shrimps is all."

"Yeah, ol' cholo," Junior hooted, "he a real hot rock in the kitchen. Gonna make some lucky guy a sensational wife one a' these days."

"Fuck you, Biggs."

"Whoa, beanbag gettin' touchy. Must be payin' Auntie Flo her monthly dues."

"You don't quit steppin' on my dick here, be payin' you off in blade."

"Gentlemen, please," Bryce interceded. "This is an occasion of camaraderie. Good fellowship. Not childish bickering."

Like chastened schoolboys, they lapsed into sullen silence.

"To proceed then," Bryce pressed doggedly on. "Let us now raise our glasses in homage to our two headliners of the evening, namely Hector Pasadena and James Merriman, on their milestone birthdays: thirty and forty, respectively, benchmark years. May the remainder of their allotted days be filled with physical vigor, spiritual harmony, and material abundance; their nights"—here a sly wink in Jim's direction—"with joy."

Glasses again were touched (even Junior's and Hector's, in guarded truce) and emptied, the bottle passed, more wine poured.

"And in conclusion," said Bryce, voice gone syrupy, enameled smile sweeping the table like a torch beam, "may fortune continue to smile on her favorite sons, and daughter of course"—the beam flashing on Billie—"each according to his just desserts, and may we all of us emerge from this splendid adventure the wiser and better persons for the experience."

"Don't forget richer too," Junior reminded him.

"For ourselves, yes, a reasonable compensation for our pains. And for Mrs. Swett a safe and speedy return to the sheltering comforts of home and family."

Billie joined in this final toast but limply and with some of the glow drained from her face.

"Speakin' a' dessert," Junior prompted her, "like I heard in there someplace, all that dribble shit, these two birthday dinks got a cake comin' or what?"

"I'll get it," she said, and hurried into the kitchen.

A moment later she was back, carrying a sheet cake illuminated by files of candles and bedecked with colorful swirls of frosting fashioned in the shapes of flowers. The traditional anthem was warbled, private wishes wished, candle flames dutifully extinguished by the two stars of the evening (Jim fully persuaded by now he was in the grip of a delirium), the cake carved and consumed, seconds all around (only Jim declining). Afterward coffee and liqueurs were served. Gradually the festivities wound down. Bryce, self-appointed master of ceremonies, settled back in his chair, tummy swag straining the buttons of his suit coat, a look of pure sated bliss on his paunchy drink-flushed face. "I can't recall a more delightful evening," he said with customary hyperbole. "Inarguably among the most memorable in my long life."

"It's a shame your niece couldn't join us," Billie remarked casually.

"Yes, well, she's a frail creature, you know, poor Waneta. Her energies are easily depleted."

"Tell me something, will you?"

"Whatever I can. Consistent, of course, with our unique circumstance."

"Is she really your niece?"

"There are bonds that transcend even blood" was his cryptic reply.

"Is she dying, or was that just another part of this plot?"

"Only the good die young, Mrs. Swett," he said wisely. "If the proverb tells true."

"There's some cake left. Why don't we take her a piece?"

"Most considerate of you, but I doubt she'd be receptive. Her appetite is delicate."

"Why not let her be the judge?" Billie persisted, and in her voice there was a clear challenge.

Bryce deliberated for a moment, seemed to be balancing the risks involved in this simple act of kindness against its potential revelations. "Well, if you insist," he decided, "I suppose no great harm could come of it. It might, in fact, prove to be instructive. For all parties."

Billie reached across the table, cut a generous wedge of cake, placed it on a clean plate, and surveyed the group. "Who's coming along?"

"I'll go," Leon eagerly volunteered.

"Me, I'm cashed," Hector said through a fly-catcher yawn. "Gonna get me a night's sleep, for a change." He stood, stretched his limbs, and flopped onto the couch.

"Jim?" she said.

"You sure you want to do this?"

"I'm sure."

"Changes nothing, you know."

"It will for me. Are you coming or not?"

"Think I'll pass on this one."

"You're not even a little curious?"

"Fresh out of that commodity."

"All right then. Leon, let's go."

Junior, forgotten in this conversation but watchful and silent through all its curious tangents, suspicious of its direction, meaning, suddenly burst in, "Hold on a fuckin' minute. You ain't goin' no place alone, lady." He leveled an accusatory stare on Bryce and, in a bewildering clash of metaphor, demanded, "Fuck's your head at, lettin' our ace in the hole shake her ass right out the door, maybe catch the wind on us, fly the coop?"

"Why don't you escort them," Bryce suggested mildly, "while I keep Mr. Merriman company?"

"Why me? That's your fluff next door, not mine."

"Because you are manifestly the most vigilant among us."

"Yeah, you got that part right. Good thing somebody still got his head screwed on straight."

"Plainly that someone is yourself."

Cornered by this logic, Junior jerked his head at the waiting pair. "OK, you two. Let's go deliver the squirrely bitch her goddamn cake."

After the missionary trio was gone, Bryce and Jim sat at the table for a time, quietly measuring each other, the remnants of the feast chilled on the plates before them. From the couch rose a cadence of snores, regular as a pulse. Finally Jim said, "You can leave if you like. It ought to be obvious by now I'm not about to bolt."

"I prefer to stay, if you don't object. I see quite enough of the dear girl during the course of a busy day. And I suspect it hasn't escaped you that intelligent company is hard to come by in this peculiar and, it pains me to say, rather shaky alliance."

"That would be me, this intelligent company?"

"Who else?"

"If I'm so smart, what am I doing here?"

"That question, my friend, is both irrelevant and tardy. The real one—only one actually—is how you intend to extricate yourself."

"Wish I knew."

"Perhaps we could chat about it."

"I'm listening."

Bryce nodded at the slumbering Hector. "Elsewhere might be prudent."

"C'mon," Jim said, beckoning.

Bryce followed him to the farthest removed of the apartment's two bedrooms, where at Jim's direction, he took the single chair. Over on the bed, Jim reflexively produced a deck of cards and laid out a hand of solitaire, waiting for the chat to begin, initiating nothing.

Obliquely was how it began. "Beautiful day today," Bryce said. "Warm and sunny but without an excess of the enervating Florida humidity."

"I wouldn't know. They don't let me out of here."

"Of course it may only be the proverbial calm before the storm," he went on, sidestepping the grievance. "You've heard about the threatened hurricane?"

"Yeah, I heard."

"They're saying now it could arrive as early as Tuesday. Or it may veer north, spare us altogether."

Weather? They were talking about the weather? Jim had nothing to contribute, so he kept silent.

"Could complicate things."

"Expect it could, at that," Jim allowed.

"Fascinating game, solitaire," Bryce said, indicating the lengthening columns of cards on the bed.

First weather, now cards. Jim wondered if there was a direction to any of this, or a destination. "Passes the time," he said.

"It has, I believe, a symbolic quality to it, in certain respects."

"Which?"

"Well, you strike me as something of a solitary man."

"Maybe not as solitary as you think. Billie sleeps back here too, you know."

"So I've been given to understand."

"You don't approve?"

"One takes comfort where one finds it. It's hardly my place to pass judgments."

"There's a relief."

"All that, however, is quite beside the point."

"Still waiting on that point."

Bryce laid a fat finger in a flesh fold alongside his nose, one of his bag of thoughtful gestures. "Let me put it this way, Mr. Merriman. While the mathematics of cards always has eluded me, I like to think of myself as a keen student of human nature. Keener than most, if you'll forgive the immodesty."

"You're forgiven."

"All my perceptions—instincts, if you prefer—compel me to believe that you and I would make a most effective team. Against two very formidable antagonists. In a game far more perilous than solitaire."

"Partners, you're proposing?"

"Precisely."

"You've already got a partner," Jim reminded him.

"You refer to Waneta?"

"Yeah."

"It's not beyond the realm of possibility that Miss Pease may have an agenda of her own."

"On her deathbed in there?" Jim said skeptically.

"Anymore, nothing about this undertaking seems too farfetched."

"On that much we agree."

"And on the other?"

Jim put down the cards, stroked his chin ruminantly. Gesture for a gesture. "I don't know," he said.

Bryce countered with a hands steeple. Peering over it he said, "Are you familiar with the science of phrenology, Mr. Merriman?"

"Can't say I am."

"Put simply, it's the study of the various protuberances found on the human skull, to the end of analyzing and revealing the character of the person within."

"That one I must have missed in school."

"Probably not. It's fallen out of fashion with the scientific community. Rather like bloodletting."

"You know, it's real educational, chatting with you, Reverend. But this time I'm afraid you've lost me."

"Allow me to explain. Among my several careers, I was once a practitioner of that arcane art. Quite rewarding it was too, but then that's another story. The reason I introduce the topic now is to inquire if, by chance, you've taken any notice of the Biggs skull."

"Only that it looks to be made out of cast iron."

Bryce permitted himself a small chuckle. "I invite you to scrutinize it closely sometime. Sometime soon. Observe the steep gradient of forehead, heavy ridge of bone above the brows, almost tumorous knobs behind the ears and over the crown."

Unsteepled now, his hands gestured broadly, as if capturing the shape and configuration of the Biggs cranium on a slate of air. "While naturally I've had no opportunity for a fingertip examination," he went on, "even a cursory visual inspection has persuaded me he is not all that far removed from our primordial ancestors. Cro-Magnon at the very least and to be charitable about it."

"Really. And the sleeper out there? What does your inspection tell you about him?"

"Sadly, under that carpet of hair, our Latino confederate displays essentially the same anatomical signals. A dangerous pair, those two, capable of who knows what mayhem or monstrous acts of depravity. Particularly given the proximity and obvious charms of our guest."

"What exactly do you mean by that?" Jim said, understanding full well what it meant but pitching his voice as steady as he could.

"You can't guess?"

"Help me out."

"Well, our Mrs. Swett is a very desirable woman—and who should know better than yourself. And thirty-six long hours stand between her and sanctuary. A not inconsiderable time in such close quarters."

"They're not going to hurt her. She's their bargaining chip."

"You may entertain that pretense if it gives you solace," Bryce said with a wicked smirk. "On the other hand, you may care to entertain my proposition."

"Where would she fit into it, this proposition?"

"Biggs tends to listen to me. Steps could be taken to ensure her safety during this critical waiting period. Once the transaction has been successfully completed, whatever arrangements you and she choose to make would be entirely up to yourselves, none of my affair. And the plunder, of course, would be cut evenly down the middle."

"That accounts for the before and after. How about the crunch hour? What happens then?"

"I'm working on that. Certain details remain to be ironed out."

"In other words you've got no plan."

"My imagination is fertile. It's taking shape."

"But you're not going to share it."

"Not without a commitment."

Jim lowered his eyes, arranged the cards in front of him. "I'll think about it," he said.

"Don't think too long, my friend. Time is short, and hesitation could be costly. Fatal, even. As the poet says, " 'Be wise with speed; a fool at forty is a fool indeed.' "

It was one of those nuggets of wisdom to be deliberated on, and Jim was doing just that as, an hour later, he lay in the dark, wide-awake, freshly turned forty, a curious gorgeous woman snuggled against him, and suspecting himself a fool.

"What are you thinking about?" Billie asked him.

"Nothing much."

"Tell me anyway."

"Well, among some other things, I was wondering if you discovered what you were after tonight."

"With Waneta?"

"Yes. With her."

"I think I did."

"Care to fill me in on your discovery?"

"It may be she's everything you said, or was at one time. But not anymore. She has a gift, Jim, a truly remarkable gift."

"And what was tonight's gift?"

"Now you're scoffing."

"No, tell me. I'd really like to know."

"Well, weak as she is—and I've been around enough sick people to know that's not faked—she found the strength to speak with each of us, and—"

"Wait a minute. All three of you?"

"Yes."

"Biggs too?"

"Him too. She had a message for him from his mother. He came out of that room all teary."

"Maybe she can deliver spankings from the other side."

Billie jabbed him in the ribs.

"Let me take a wild guess," he said. "Leon heard from his mom too."

"Yes, he did."

"And you? What message did the swamiette bring for you?"

"If you're just going to poke fun, I'm not telling you," she said, petulant and even a little hurt.

"OK, no more weak wit."

"Promise?"

"I promise. Talk to me."

"What she told me was I had a very serious problem to solve, but once I did, I'd find happiness."

Now there's a deep insight, Jim was tempted to say, but he restrained himself and asked instead, "Who was it from, this message?"

"That's not important," she said in a tone at once wistful and dismissive. "Doesn't matter."

"Any, uh, clues on the nature of the problem?"

"Nothing too clear. But I've got a pretty good idea what it is."

"What's your idea?"

"You."

"Me?"

"Yes. You. See, when I look back on it, my life's been one long problem. Then Lonnie came along, with all his money. And money solves everything, or at least I thought it did. 'Til I met you."

"Me?"

"I've known a lot of men in my life, Jim."

"Be surprised if you hadn't."

"You know what's different about you?"

"What would that be?"

"Everything."

"Only I'm the problem?"

"Yes."

"A clerk? Clerks can't cause problems. Or solve them either. We don't come with the baggage of money."

"You're no clerk, Jim."

"Who told you that? The message lady?"

"Leon told me."

"Leon's mistaken."

"I don't think so. He told me everything—about you, how the two of you got mixed up in this, how you tried to help him. Everything."

"You don't want to believe everything you hear from Leon. He's navigating without all his switches on."

"I know what I believe. And who."

"Look, Billie, you say your life's been nothing but problems. Take a number. All of mine, I've been kicking a can of beans down the road and calling it relocating."

"Maybe," she said softly, "after all this is over, I could come along with you."

"With me? *You* come with *me*?"

"We could take turns kicking."

Through the veil of darkness, he felt her smile on him, and it struck him suddenly how little he knew her and how powerless he was to arrange anyone else's happiness, never mind his own. "Maybe we will," he said.

For a while neither spoke, and the silence settling over the bed and the room seemed to take on a character of its own. Then, from out of a twilight of sleep, she murmured his name, and he said, "Yes?" and she asked if he liked his birthday party, and he told her, "It was a terrific party. Go to sleep now. You've had a long day."

"Jim?"

"Yes?"

"I'm sorry I couldn't get you a gift."

"You're the gift," he said, meaning it.

TWENTY-TWO

FIRST THING IN THE MORNING (WHICH IS WHAT that bubblehead receptionist had assured him) had to have a whole different meaning for your hair benders than it did for normal citizens. Two hours now Cheetah had been cooling his heels (make that heating them, and the rest of him too, under a fierce sun splashing out of a white sky, steaming the interior of his Olds) in the lot outside the Hair Affair, watching all the foxy people, both genders, come and go, and still no sign of the Cleland bimbo. Probably treating the boyfriend to an adios boink (Cheetah was thinking sourly and, if he was going to be honest about it, with just a trace of envy) to top off the weekend.

Ordinarily he was a patient man—you had to be, this business—but already he had pissed away one day and wasn't in a humor to let another go down the whizz drain. A Sunday-morning call to a badge he knew on the West Palm force had produced the unsurprising poop that neither the Merriman nor the Cody names were in the system, sheetless, which supported the evolving Cheetah theory that the whole number was an amateur-hour hustle (though where that hard case at the Cody apartment—no astrophysicist but certainly no stranger to the life—fit in he wasn't sure yet). Rest of the wheel-spinning day was spent combing motels in the vicinity, greasing sticky-palmed clerks with double saws, offering up descriptions and getting back—another big surprise—dick for his efforts and his (Swett's actually) coin.

Which left square one, Courtney. So she'd better be shaking her bootie in here quick time, or he'd by God know the reason why, even if it meant tracking her down and uncoupling the old two-backed beast, if that's what it came to.

Turned out he didn't have to do either. Five minutes shy of ten bells, a sleek 'Vette pulled up, studly dude at the wheel, Courtney ornamenting the passenger seat like a trophy, both of them wearing dreamy brains-fucked-out-of-their-skulls smiles. She planted a wet one on him, hopped out, wiggled her fingers bye-bye at the zoom-away 'Vette, and came tripping across the lot. Right into the Cheetah roadblock.

"'Mornin', Miss Cleland. Remember me?"

"You again?"

She flashed him a look compounded of dismay, distaste, and alarm. Long as that alarm was in there, Cheetah knew he was still on his game. "Have a good weekend, did you?" he inquired affably.

And she countered defiantly, "Yeah, I did. Sensational one, matter a fact."

"Little grieving getaway, was it? For your not-so-late mom?"

Now she gave him a pussy version of a frosty glare. "Look, if you got some news to tell me about Billie, that's cool, I'm all ears. But if you're here to snoop around in my private life, you're wastin' both our time."

"Actually was neither."

"What's *that* supposed to mean?"

"Means I got nothing solid yet on your absent friend, and like you say, what you do on your own time's no business of mine."

"Then I guess that about wraps up this conversation, right?"

"Busy day coming up at the hair factory?"

"Yeah, it's busy. I got a full book, first client at ten. So maybe you could step outta my way?"

Cheetah didn't move. But he said in a vocal pitch swung suddenly from affable to stomp ass, "Name 'Jim Merriman' mean anything to you?"

"No," Courtney declared, startled.

"You sure about that?"

"Never heard it before. Honest."

Blank expression on her face, blank on blank, said it was likely true, worse luck for him. "How about 'Cody'? 'Leon Cody'? Any bells there?"

"No. No whistles, no bells."

"OK, let's go back, start over."

"C'mon, it's after ten," she whined. "I'm already late."

"This'll only take another minute, your valuable time."

"So can we scoot past that minute? Before I'm lookin' for a new salon to work at?"

"Couple more questions is all. Last time you saw Mrs. Swett was at that funeral home, right?"

"Right."

"Monday that was? Week ago today?"

"Correct. Except for that phone call I already told you about. Which wasn't the same as *seeing* her."

"Before Monday when'd you see her last?"

"At Mom's funeral."

"Which was when?"

"Day before. Sunday."

"Anybody you didn't recognize show up at the services? Anybody she talk to?"

"Strangers, like?"

"Yeah, strangers."

"No, was just family, few a' Mom's friends."

"How about after?"

"After the services, you mean?"

There was that same slight catch in her voice he'd detected the first time around, and the same skittish gaze seeking a place to alight, anywhere but his eyes; and Cheetah knew he was on to something large here, maybe turn the corner for him, could feel it right down to the marrow of his intimidator bones. So he brought up the old Congo glare, authentic version, and said,

"Asking you a critical question here, Miss Cleland. Want you to think real hard."

"Well," she said, gaze having found the tar at her feet, "now you mention it, we did stop by to see some people afterward."

"Which people is that?"

"This preacher and his sick niece who could, y'know, take messages over to the other side."

"Other side of what?"

"Death."

Even Cheetah was a little wigged by that one, though he was careful not to let it show. "Messages to *dead* people?"

"It was Billie's idea, not mine. See, she has all these crazy notions about spirits, soul centering, hoke like that. Takes it real serious, which is why she insisted we go see them. Been up to me, I'd've never gone."

"But you did go, the two of you?"

"Yeah," she said sheepishly, "we went."

"Whyn't you tell me something about these messengers?"

"Like what?"

"Like everything you remember."

"Not much to tell. His name's Bott; he's old. Niece is young but got some rare disease, which I guess is why she can, y'know, do what she does."

"Take messages to the dead?"

"Bring 'em back too, sometimes."

"You have to pay for this delivery service?"

"Didn't *have* to, but you was sorta expected to leave a donation, like."

"You remember how much Mrs. Swett donated?"

"Couldn't say exactly, but it was quite a lot. Billie's always real generous, especially now she's got the big bucks."

"Bet she is at that," Cheetah said, thinking how this buzz could maybe put a whole new spin on his theory and wondering where it was going to take him.

Right back where he started out that morning was where, no more than half a block down from the hotel, right under his fucking nose. "One of those tourist apartments over on Singer Island," she said in response to his question regarding the whereabouts of these two ingenious grifters. "Place called the Surf and Shore."

With only a flake of irony, Cheetah thanked her for her cooperation and removed himself from her path. A moment later he swung his Olds out onto PGA Boulevard and pointed it back to Singer Island.

Where, in the claustrophobic rooms he'd come to regard as his own private cracker factory, the Reverend Bott was himself experiencing a most confounding, not to say unnerving, morning.

His multiplying catalog of woes began with the eagerly anticipated, meticulously rehearsed call to Lon Swett, the purpose of which was to unveil the details of his cunningly crafted plan (loosely adapted from a television drama he'd once seen) for the tricky exchange of loot and lady but whose upshot—yet another stall, 'til tomorrow night this time—was something less than cheering. But for all of Bryce's stammery protests (the studied lines tangled or forgotten altogether in a riot of confusion), Swett was adamant, unshakable: "You want unmarked bills, Tuesday night's best I can do."

"But we'd agreed—"

"Take it or leave it."

What choice did he have but to take it? He rang off humbled, wondering who was the perpetrator here, who the victim. Wondering also how he would summon the courage to break this deflating news to Biggs, hardly your most patient confederate to begin with. Downright chilling, that thought was, reviving as it did the grim specter of his visionary swindle violently unraveling before his very eyes.

As if that weren't distressing enough, no sooner had he put down the phone than a plaintive moan stung his already reversal-stung ears. He hurried back to the room of his erstwhile (and lately seriously neglected) partner and discovered her tossing fitfully in bed.

"Waneta, what is it? What's wrong?"

"Bryce? That you?"

A bit reluctantly (for he hadn't the slightest idea how one copes with bona fide madness, if indeed that's what this was), he approached the bed, laid a quieting hand on her fevered brow, and purred some wordless sounds of commiseration. In the dim light, the tautened flesh beneath the stark hollows of cheekbones looked almost phosphorescently pale, the mouth blue, eyes like green stones sunk in a pool of murky water and steepened now with wonder, as though they peered into a cosmos more magical than any star-studded sky and more terrifying. "Help me, Bryce," she whimpered. "Please help."

"Calm yourself, my dear. Of course I'll help. But you must tell me what it is that troubles you."

"I'm startin' to *see* them!"

"See who?"

"The ones on the other side. Their faces."

"Dreams," he said soothingly. "You've been dreaming."

Waneta gave the air a feeble cuff. "No, no, no—not dreamin'. They're in there."

"In where?"

"In my head. In my eyes. That man was here last night, the mean one, I seen his mother. And Billie's baby, her face come to me too."

"Perhaps it's your lively imagination, artistic sensibilities. The quest for the perfect performance."

"Not playactin' no more. Something's happening to me, Bryce. I'm scared. Will you help me?"

Her voice was little more than a whispered groan, and genuine tears leaked from the glassy, pleading eyes. This had to be,

Bryce was thinking, what schizophrenia was all about: voices echoing startlingly in the ears, shadows shaping themselves into faces behind the eyes. And on the night table, an untouched slice of birthday cake supplied even more compelling evidence of her dementia, the visible, tangible kind a pragmatist like himself required (for he knew her to possess an intemperate appetite for sugary treats, recalling how once, after a profitable score, she'd singlehandedly and at a single sitting devoured a two-pound box of Godiva chocolates). Now she had passed his final cagey test, and now he was at last persuaded she was not dissembling, was in fact a certifiable head case.

What to do about it was another matter, one that compounded the lengthening scroll of urgent issues. As a stopgap measure, he lowered his ample buttocks onto the bed and gathered her, weightless as a withering orchid petal, in his plump arms. "There, there, my dear," he intoned. "You've been under enormous stress, and your health is fragile. But I must ask you to bear with me one more day. Our work here is almost finished, and when it's over, I'll see that you get proper medical attention."

She clung to him piteously, trembling like a plucked harp string. "You won't leave me, Bryce?"

"I'll always be here for you," he said, wondering how—or if—he would ever make good on that guilt-driven pledge. Maybe he would. Given a few strokes of luck and a sufficiency of plunder, he could perhaps fund a stay in a comfortable psychiatric facility. He owed her that much. The genesis of this bold swindle could, after all, be traced indirectly to her. So maybe he would.

But there was no time this morning for idle speculation. At 9:00 a.m. the first in the day's parade of marks arrived at the door, an elderly couple with the kind of puckery vinegary features that seemed eroded more by chronic distemper than time. As he always did with twosomes, Bryce insisted, gently but firmly, on individual consultations, pleading the frailty of the poor expiring girl. Which was partly true, of course, but it also was a precaution against any stiffing at the offertory hour, two passes with the plate being better than one. And the take from this pretzel action—swollen now to well over three long—was not altogether trifling. Not by his former standards anyway. Mad money was how he thought of it now (certainly an apt designation), insurance against some unthinkable collapse of the primary swindle, and he kept the bulk of it hidden in a laundry basket in his room, neatly folded in a pair of soiled boxer shorts.

The wife elected to take the first plunge into weirdo world, so Bryce escorted her back, did his introductory dance, and returned to do host duty in the living room. The husband was a laconic coot, responding in grunts and monosyllables to his efforts at amiable pious prattle (fine with him, since his head was by now a humming hive of stratagems and revisions and schemes and rerevisions). Forty-five minutes later, the two dyspeptics traded places, and by ten thirty, he was ushering them out the door, their messages delivered and received, their net worth lightened by a bill, a not dissatisfying, if modest, take. Standing outside, finger poised on the bell, was an uncommonly ugly man who stepped politely out of their way, and once they were gone, turned to Bryce and said, "Wonder if I'd be able to see the lady who can talk with the people on the other side."

"Did you have an appointment?"

"No, but I was hoping she could maybe squeeze me in."

Bryce deliberated a moment. Next mark was due at eleven, and he could use some time to himself, get his thoughts ordered. On the other hand, the unscheduled appearance of another vic supplied an excuse to delay the inevitable bad-news disclosure to Biggs. And walk-ins, in his experience, could be generous at the plate. So he assembled his starched smile and said, "I believe we can accommodate you, sir. Do step in. My name is Bott, Reverend Bott."

"Mine's McReedy."

Junior had wakened early that morning, achy and stiff from a night of restless dozing in a recliner dragged across the room and positioned to block any passage through the door. His eyes were crusted and puffy, his mouth sulfureous, bladder sorely in need of a tap, all of which distresses were traceable to a near empty bottle of Ten High on the floor by the chair. Maybe to some other nagging vexations as well, but he was unable or unwilling to confront them just then. Instead he stumbled back to the crapper, pumped the bilge, and splashed cold water on his face. His reflection scowled back at him from the mirror above the sink, a coarse stubble sprouting over its pitted cheeks and neck and monumental jaw like a smear of soot. His sweated flesh and slept-in clothes raised a powerful stink, but right now he was too thrashed to run through the shit-shave-shower-shampoo drill. Later maybe, when his head got deflated.

Everybody else was still crashed, so he went outside and stood for a while in the narrow parking space in front, feeling sun-drenched and listless, and a little ornery too. Least there was a goddamn sun in the goddamn sky, which maybe meant the goddamn hurricane wasn't blowing in after all. Fucking air, though, that was a different story—so thick with humidity, it wrapped him like a wool blanket, damp and itchy, and beaded on his skin like spatters of rain. He spotted a lizard along the curb, motionless as a ceramic figurine except for the darting tongue. Stealthily he stuck a plug of tobacco in his mouth, ground it into juice, and fired off a round that caught the little bugger square between the eyes and sent him scampering. *Ol' sharpshooter still got the touch*, Junior thought smugly, though when he carried that thought further, remembering how the Swett cunt banned chewing inside the apartment on the grounds of it being gross, disgusting, and unsanitary—when he thought about *that*, it chapped his ass raw. *I tell ya* (he silently told himself), *goddamn good thing this fuckin'-the-dog, playin'-house time windin' down fast, or they be some hardball changes around here, Morris Junior Biggs brand a' hardball, your hardest kind.*

Timex read a little past seven gongs. Nothing was shaking here for a couple hours, so he decided to take a saunter, stretch the legs. First he went inside and shook the chili bean out of his sweet south-of-the-border dreams, telling him it was time to drop the burrito and grab the socks, his turn in the watch-standing barrel. Once he was sure Senor Dickeye got his head clear, Junior marched out the door and headed for the mall at the end of the street. Place was shut up tighter than a worm's twat at this hour, so he hoofed it all the way over the bridge and down a couple more blocks 'til he came upon a booze shop that opened up early to collar the pooch-hair trade. Since Junior was himself a firm believer in the curative powers of that canine fur, he stepped in and bought a pint of J.D., figuring, *Why not? Never too soon to get in the large-livin' habit.* He paid the gook behind the Jew piano with a bill peeled from the fat wad he carried lately, the loot collected off the weenies plus the take from the cunt's Jag. Come close to 50K, not much when you set it alongside the five mil that would be bulging his hip about this time tomorrow but still a nice cut of change. Enough that he wasn't about to let it out of his clutch. You never know.

All that hiking sapped him out, so he hailed a cab and directed the spear-chucker driver back across the bridge and around the mall 'til he spotted a bench in the shade that faced out to the ocean. Uppity spade balked at the short hop, so Junior paid him his fare and not a squeeze nickel more. Fuck him. Rich or not, he wasn't giving them people the steam off his shit.

He slouched on the bench, unsealed the pint, and took a healthy, start-up chug. Burned the pipes going down but that was OK; that was how you got well. He kept the bottle bagged, in case some mall toy cop came by looking for a pissing match. You come this close, you don't need any grief.

The sun hung like a gold coin in a spotless sky, and the ocean, flat and calm, seemed to shimmer under a brilliant light. If there were a storm out there, it sure as fuck was keeping its head down. A few people, not many yet, dotted the broad expanse of beach: rays addicts mostly, couple early-morning Frisbee freaks, the occasional jogger puffing by, some leathery freeze-drys who had no better place to pass their days 'til croaking time. Another three, four hours, the place would be crammed with oiled bodies frying in the midday heat, standing-room sand only. Which was the key to lard bucket Bott's plan. Swett would show up here alone, looking like just another sun soaker, carrying a cell phone and two big beach bags, half the loot in each. They'd scope him for a while, make sure nothing cute was going on, then send in someone to collect one of the bags and get small in the crowd. First pickup was what Bott called a good-faith pass: If no one nailed their man and the money was right, it would prove Swett had no pranking ideas. So they'd put in a call to him, tell him to look about a hundred yards down the beach, and he'd see his lost pussy waving at him. He'd hightail it off to get her while they hauled in the other bag then haul ass. Happy ending all around, except the Swett wallet a little lighter.

That's how it was supposed to go, and even Junior had to grudgingly admit it wasn't a half-bad plan, for coming from a pus-gut slicker. Their bag pickup man would be one of the weenies—that was Junior's own inspired contribution: Let somebody else run the heavy risks. He had some other ideas too, but they weren't the kind you shared with partners. Not yet anyway. Tomorrow would be soon enough for that. Like they say, no tomorrow for dead men. Dead ladies either.

Which thought, along with the sight of a blimp of an old lady waddling across the sand (Mom was a little on the chunky side too) called to mind last night's rap with the wacko broad next door. Of course he didn't actually believe any of that twitch-house shit she was peddling, just did it for a hoot. Still was kinda spooky, though, sitting back there in that dark room, candles on the dresser, shadows on the wall, listening to this warmed-over stiff tell him how Mom sends her boy her love and forgiveness (that forgiveness part after his apologizing for not getting around to put up a gravestone yet) and how she warns him to be extra careful, this job he's on, whole lot a danger in it for him (that being the *really* spooky part, her or Mom, whichever one was doing the talking, having an opinion on that). And thinking about it now, here in the harsh morning light, remembering Mom and her unconditional love for him, Junior experienced much the same sensation he had the night before, an unfamiliar prickling in his eyes, followed by a moistness there, followed by a flood of tears. He swiped at them with the back of a hand, and when his vision was clear, he discovered a child, little pickaninny girl in a ragged swimsuit, perched on the bench beside him like a peewee crow, gazing at him curiously.

"How come you bawlin'?" she asked in that chirpy, jungle-bunny voice they all had.

"Nobody bawlin'."

"Was too. I seen it."

"Got somethin' in my eye is all."

"You was bawlin'."

"Look, kid, whyn't you go get yourself an ice cream?"

He reached into a pocket, pulled a bill off the roll, and extended it to her. She stared at it, doubtful and wary. "That real?"

"It's real."

"For me?"

"Yeah. You. Free money. Take it."

She took it, saying, "You goin' be OK?"

"Be just fine now," Junior said, but watching that little black ass scooting away, he wondered if he maybe wasn't playing with your bad-luck fire here, breaking his own rule that way.

Maybe not. Maybe that's what Mom (or whoever) was trying to tell him: Do a good deed, and it'll come right back at you.

Which it just did, solved at least one of those vexations chewing at him, got him right past it. Shame to have to pop the bughouse messenger lady along with the rest of 'em, but what the fuck are you gonna do? Five mil was five mil, and business was business.

Like Junior, Jim had slept badly, though unlike him the source of his troubled slumber could be traced not to drink or communiqués from the dead but to the equally beguiling illusion of hope. Sparked as it was by Bott's ambiguous proposition of the night before, that deception had taken, for Jim, the form of a succession of fantastic dreams, the details of which he was unable to reconstruct on waking, only their conflicting themes of collision and flight countervailed by fragmentary scenes of almost paradisiacal peace gilded with blurry images, unsullied by lust, of Billie Swett. But when at last he surfaced from that stormy netherworld and reached over for the comforting feel of her flesh, his arm embraced only empty air. Alarmed, he pulled on some clothes and hurried into the living room, where to his immense relief, he found her busily occupied with the cleanup of last night's revel.

Considerably less reassuring was the outfit she had on: ribbon of a halter top and frayed cutoffs that exposed, respectively, the deep cleft between her breasts; smooth wings of her shoulder blades; a field of soft, white, navel-dimpled midriff; firm mounds of buttocks; and elegant legs that snapped like scissor blades as she bustled about the room, dustcloth in one hand, bottle of lemon Pledge in the other. Leon and Hector apparently had been assigned pots-and-pans duty in the kitchen, and if they noticed this shapely package of provocation, they were too discreet—or awed—to let on. Luckily the crotch-driven Biggs was nowhere in sight.

"There she is," he said, addressing the back of her head. "Homemaker of the year."

Billie spun around and yelped, "Jim…you scared me—sneaking up like that." Then a smile began in her eyes and spread slowly over the finely whittled bones of her face, and she added teasingly, "Sleeping Beauty's finally awake?"

"And without even the kiss of a princess."

"It's about time."

"Which is what, by the way?"

"After ten. We've been working for over an hour. Three of us anyway. Place was a mess."

From the kitchen Leon called, "'Mornin', Uncle Jim."

"Good morning, Leon. Hector."

Hector mumbled something in the way of a greeting, short of surly but less than chipper, due no doubt to the disagreeable nature of the chore.

"Where's the monster?" Jim asked Billie.

"Biggs, you mean?"

"He's the only monster in the house, last I looked."

"I don't know where he is. Wasn't here when I got up. Hector said he went out early, for a walk or something."

"Off a short pier, one can always hope."

"Oh, I don't know," she said mildly. "He's a lout, but he's not so bad."

Jim rolled his eyes at the ceiling.

"Well, he's not," she insisted. "Did I tell you how sad he was last night? About his mother?"

"Yeah, you already told me," he drawled, and took her by the elbow and led her around the corner and into the hall, out of earshot of the kitchen if you kept your voice down, and he did. "Look, you almost finished up here, this cleaning binge you're on?"

"Why?" Billie said, and now her smile was deft and knowing. "What did you have in mind?"

"Not what you're thinking. Not now anyway."

"What then?"

“Can I give you a word of advice?”

“You can give it. Whether I accept, I can’t say ’til I hear it.”

“Change your clothes,” he said bluntly.

“What? What’s wrong with my clothes?”

“Nothing’s *wrong* with them. Sensational threads. It’s just they’re maybe a little too, well, revealing. For this company.”

“You got to be kidding. What am I supposed to clean in? A cocktail dress, assuming I had one?”

He tossed his hands in the air. “I don’t know. How would I know? Whatever kidnapped cleaning women wear.”

Now she looked at him soberly, smile departing. “I sure hope you’re not one of those jealous kind of guys, like my husband. I’d be real disappointed with that, Jim.”

“Jealousy’s got nothing to do with it. It’s not jealousy. It’s caution.”

“Against what?”

“Not what. Who.”

“Tell me who then,” she said, a certain testy impatience seeping into her voice. “Those two dishwashers out there? Biggs? The reverend? Tell me.”

“How about number two on your list.”

“Biggs? I know his type. All talk. Trust me, doing nails you run into a lot of men like him.”

“And I’m asking you to trust me: This one’s worthy of your caution.”

“You say yes, I say no. What’s the point in arguing?”

“Point is…” “Survival” he was tempted to say, but he softened it to “…getting past the next twenty-four hours without a rumble.”

“It’s my understanding,” Billie said stubbornly, “that today’s going to be just another long day of waiting. Hanging out. And if that’s the case, I intend to at least be comfortable.”

Jim gave a defeated shrug. “I tried.”

And she gave him back a light, brushing kiss, murmuring, "It's nice to know you care about me. Been a while since anybody has." The smile restored, tender now, untroubled, she returned to her tireless pursuit of dust.

With nothing better to do, Jim seized the opportunity to appropriate their communal, boardinghouse bath, and thirty minutes later, he emerged, shaved and showered and feeling a little steadier, not much. Even less when he strolled into the living room and saw Biggs pacing the floor and heard him growling into a phone spliced to an ear, "Fuck's *that* suppose to mean?"

There was a pause. Jim searched the faces of the cleanup crew, discerned only a stricken vacancy there, all three.

"What're you talkin', 'slight delay,'" Junior went on, voice rising. "I don't wanna hear that word."

Another pause, shorter.

"What?" Junior bellowed. "What'd you just say? Hold *you* down and nail your nuts to the floor."

A final pause, briefest of all.

"Don't give a rat's ass who you got in there. You better close up shop and shag that blubber butt over here quick time, or you gonna find out what a Junior Biggs tune-up all about. And you ain't gonna like it."

He hurled the phone onto the couch. The furious pacing had brought him to the corner of the room where Jim stood, and he thrust out a clenched, bristly jaw and demanded, "Fuck're you lookin' at, Uncle?"

"To tell you the truth, I'm not quite sure."

"Maybe this help you figure it out."

This was an elevated, balled fist, big as a sledge. Erasing even the smallest trace of mockery from his voice, Jim said quickly, "I doubt it."

"Wha's up, man?" Hector asked from the relative safety of the other side of the room.

Junior resumed pacing. "No good, cholo," he said grimly. "No good is what's up."

Jim released a clutched breath. Saved by the Hector bell. For now saved.

Cheetah had them instantly made for a couple of five-and-dimers, the broad maybe a little slicker than the ersatz pastor, but both of them out of their depth, this burn. If in fact they were in on it. Certainly no evidence anywhere in the apartment, which looked like just another of those drab tourist cribs the snowbirds flock to, except for its musty, funeral parlor air, particularly in the bedroom Bott led him to after some opening remarks and a quick Q & A on who it was Cheetah hoped to contact over on the other side and, if the connection could be made, what he hoped to communicate.

"My brother," Cheetah had improvised, "passed away last month. Wanted to let him know I'm sorry I never took any time for him."

He really did have a brother, hadn't seen him in maybe a decade, alive and well and running a Dairy Cone over in Tampa, last Cheetah had heard. So part of it anyway was true. And that's how Bott presented him to the girl back in the cheerless room dimmed against the blaze of morning light by closed blinds at the window: "Waneta, my dear, this gentleman is Mr. McReedy. He seeks your assistance in reaching his brother only recently expired."

"I'll try" was the faint reply.

To Cheetah the reverend whispered, "I must ask you to be brief. She's very weak. Her time is short, I fear." That caution delivered, he guided him to a bedside chair and tiptoed out of the room.

Better than passable imitation of a soon-to-be stiff, she did, lying there like a figure made out of wax, inky hair splayed over the sheets, eyes pools of shadow in the ashen, sunken face. Was the mouth, though, Cheetah decided, that gave her away. It had, in repose, a kind of sullen quality to it, thin lipped and mean and relieved not at all when she broke the silence with a curt question: "His name?"

"My brother?"

"Yes."

"Chesney. Chet, we called him."

"When did he pass over?"

"'Bout a month back."

"Which day?"

"Was July fourth," Cheetah told her, picking a date at random. "Independence Day. His spirit's independence."

"Suppose that'd be one way to look at it."

"Older or younger?"

"Than me?"

"Yes, you."

"Younger."

"Let me see if I can find him."

For an easy ten minutes, maybe longer—hard to keep track of time in that oppressive gloom—she lay motionless as a cadaver except for the periodic stagy shudder, eyes wide-open but focused, it seemed, on nothing at all. 'Til she leveled them on him and said, "I can't seem to locate any Chet McReedy."

"Shame," Cheetah said, getting into his part. "I'd've liked to made my peace with him."

"Maybe he's still in passage."

"Where'd that be?"

"Between worlds."

"Sorta like in transit, huh?"

"Or maybe," she said shrewdly, "you're mistaken. Maybe he's not dead."

"Oh, he's dead all right."

"You're sure about that?"

"Absolutely," Cheetah averred, thinking, *Jesus, fleecer's using my own lines on me. Nobody's fool, this girl.*

"Well, if he is, I can't find him."

"That's OK. You tried. Maybe next time."

"Maybe," she said doubtfully.

Out in the living room, Cheetah found her partner standing at a window, fatty shoulders bunched, hand cupping a phone. Conversation was too muffled to catch much of it, but Cheetah picked up a "with a client" in there and a "Please hold your voice down," before the reverend's head snapped suddenly back, as though an unseen hand had reached down the wire and slapped him in the face. He hit the "off" button, turned, and seeing Cheetah, recovered enough composure to say, "Ah, Mr. McReedy, finished, are we?"

"Sure hope not," Cheetah said, arranging his mouth in a loose grin to show it was a joke, though his eyes weren't laughing.

"I refer, of course, to your consultation with my niece," Bott said stiffly.

"Yeah, we're finished. For today anyway."

"Any success in contacting your late brother?"

"Not yet. But she's working on it."

"These things can take time," the pastor murmured. "And time, sadly, is in short supply for the poor girl."

"She's not looking too good," Cheetah agreed.

"It's my fondest hope to ease the suffering of her final days and, when the time arrives, to mark her resting place with a suitable monument in commemoration of her unique gift."

"That's real thoughtful of you, Reverend. Both those good ideas."

"Both of which require a level of funding outside our humble reach," he said with a significant nod at the plate on the counter.

Great moments in scamming: laying on the touch. *About as subtle as a boot in the ass*, Cheetah was thinking, but he dug out his wallet and asked innocently, "How much do folks usually give?"

"We rely on the natural benevolence of the human heart," Bott said unctuously, but as if to put a floor under that benevolence, he added, "Some have favored us with a hundred dollars. Others more."

Cheetah extracted a pair of honeybees and laid them on the plate, figuring it was Swett's money well spent, whole lot cheaper than five extra long if this should turn out to be the breakthrough he was looking for.

"Most generous of you, sir," Bott purred.

Cheetah made an "Aw, shucks" gesture. "I ask you something, Reverend?"

"By all means."

"You really believe it's dead people your niece is talking to back there?"

"Oh, most profoundly do I believe," he declared, making this assertion the way a man might lay claim, soberly and in perfect deadpan, to a belief in elves or goblins. "The miraculous, my friend, is merely the other side of that impostor we're pleased to call the real."

"Funny, lady who put me on to you people said something like that too."

"Really. And who might this lady be?"

"Name's Swett. Billie Swett. Remember her?"

It's only in the movies that someone gives himself away with the startled double take or twitchy hand. In that real world Bott dismissed so lightly, the one Cheetah inhabited, it was the calculated gesture that betrayed you, or in the reverend's case, the studied facial expressions: knitted brows, to demonstrate the effort of recollection, followed by simpery smile, to display the effort's success. "Why, yes, I do seem to recall Mrs. Swett," he said carefully, "though it was some time ago she stopped by. Charming lady. Friend of yours?"

"You might say."

"You must pass along my well-wishes when you see her next."

"Yeah, I'll be sure and do that."

Cheetah was confident he'd turned the corner on this one, easy sprint now into the end zone. But if you wanted to survive in this business, you could never get too cocky. Or too impulsive. Man had a license to protect, had to think hard before he went breaking bad on citizens, even the scammer variety.

That's what he was doing, formulating a closure strategy, as he left the apartment and sauntered to his Olds and sped away, conscious of Bott's eyes following him from the window. Took him no more than an hour's aimless driving the streets of the island to come up with a simple, workable plan, and once he had it squared away in his head, he pulled into an IHOP lot, cut the engine, picked up the phone, and dialed Swett's number. "Cheetah," he said in response to the agitated greeting.

"Cheet! Whaddya hear?"

"Good notes, I think."

"So talk to me."

"You first. Wanna hear how your call went this morning."

"Not as bad as I thought it would. Cocksucker did some bitchin'—whinin' more like it—but he bought the stall. Just like you said."

"Remember how you told me, up at your place there, this fella sounds kind of funny?"

"Sure, I remember that. He does too."

"You say how exactly?"

"Voice, y'mean?"

"Voice, things he says, whole package. Whatever you remember."

"Sounds like a wimp to me. Y'know, five-dollar words, sissy voice on him. Why?"

"Just tracking a hunch," Cheetah said noncommittally, but in the privacy of the car, there was a smile on his face.

"So where's it takin' you, this hunch?"

"Any luck, your wife."

"No shit! When?"

"Soon."

"Today?"

"Could be today. Could take another. It does, I need you to do something for me."

"You don't even gotta ask, Cheet."

"Wait'll you hear it first."

"I'm listenin'."

"When's this fella calling you next?"

"Tomorrow morning. Gonna spell out the details of the swap, he says."

"OK. You don't hear from me before then, what I want you to do is tell him it'll be Wednesday now, that swap."

A groan came down the line.

"You got a problem with that, Lon?"

"Damn right, I got a pro'lum. I thought you said you had 'em good as nailed."

"Said I'm on their tails. This is what you call a contingency plan. May have a close for you before we have to use it."

"But if we do?"

"You got to trust me here, Lon."

"Ain't a matter a' trust. It's how I'm gonna sell another day."

"You'll think of something."

"Yeah, easy for you. I'm the one gotta come up with it."

"Maybe that hurricane they're talking about will blow in."

"Hope the fuck it does. That one he might buy."

"There you are."

"Where'bouts you at now, Cheet?"

"West Palm," he told him vaguely.

"S'posin' somethin' else happens today. How'm I gonna get in touch?"

"You got the number to my car phone, right?"

"Right."
"That's where I'll be."
"All day?"
"Maybe into the night too."

If he'd had to put a word to it, *flummoxed* might best have defined Bryce's emotional condition as he watched that suddenly sinister figure, whose misshapen features brought whole new dimensions of meaning to ugly, climb into his car and speed away. *Panicked* might have served as well, or even, contemplating the brutish confederate (a close runner-up in the sinister department) impatiently waiting next door, *terrified.* Of course it was always possible his fears and confusion were groundless. Both these mystifying developments—Swett's stonewalling delay and this McReedy's casual dropping of Mrs. Swett's name—could be quite innocuous too, mere coincidences empty of connection or threat. Unfortunately for Bryce, he hadn't the luxury of time either to ponder them or to concoct a nimble set of dodges, relying instead on his native wit and invincible powers of persuasion to see him through the rancorous scene he suspected was in store, directly ahead. And so, after stiffing the scheduled 11:00 a.m. mark, pleading Waneta's woefully sapped strength, he offered up a skyward prayer and exited the front door and took the few steps over to the adjacent apartment, where came through its door flashing his toothy smile in wide arc and announcing with determined cheeriness, "Good morning, people. Gorgeous day out there, wouldn't you say?"

"What *I* say. Fuck gorgeous" was the choleric Biggs's opinion of the day. Like a pugilist commanding the center of a ring, he dominated the room with an aggressive wide-legged stance and hammy fists belligerently planted on his hips. The others were scattered around the room's perimeter, occupying sofa and chairs and exhibiting various attitudes of misgiving. Awed by the wrath of a Neanderthal, they collectively chose to leave the day's beauty unremarked upon. No help there. So Bryce abandoned cheery in favor of an easy jocularity, saying with a small chuckle, to establish his humorous intent, "Spoken like a Pericles."

"Like a who?"

"Pericles. A wise Greek, renowned for his eloquence. Not unlike yourself."

"You callin' me a Greek?"

"I simply meant—"

But before Bryce could clarify his meaning, Biggs, swaying slightly, stepped over and seized him by the knot of his tie, elevating him to tiptoes in a gaspy effort to sustain his breathing. "Don't fuck with me, Bott. I ain't in a mood for any your wise-ass Greek boogaloo."

A wormy coil of veins insistently pulsing in a temple, coupled with the assaultive boozy breath, were sufficient nonverbal signals to persuade Bryce of the error of the jocular approach. "Just making a little joke," he sputtered.

"You shavin' the edge here, Reverend, and you better snap into my world or you gonna learn a whole new way to hurt."

"If you'll release me, perhaps we can talk rationally."

Biggs let go of the tie but remained looming over him, fixing him with a dark, flat stare. "So talk."

Flat-footed again, stroking the seriously wrinkled neckwear as though it were a tangible extension of his wounded dignity, Bryce rallied his wits and said, "As I tried to explain on the phone, Swett's problem isn't with the figure we've specified but rather in obtaining it in unmarked bills without arousing the suspicions of bankers. Evidently he has to tap a number of sources. Hence the brief delay."

"That's what he told you?"

"That was the substance of our conversation," Bryce said, omitting any mention of the bullying Swett tone or, for that matter, the enigmatic McReedy and his oblique reference to Billie Swett. One hurdle at a time, and this one was looking steep enough.

"And you bought that?"

"It seems eminently plausible to me."

"And to me," another voice seconded, Merriman's, from the sofa where he sat rigidly, a scantily clad Mrs. Swett clinging to his arm.

Biggs turned the cold stare on him. "What'd you say, Uncle?"

"Said I agree with the reverend. You can't just breeze into a bank and walk out with five big balloons in cash without setting off the alarm."

"Fuck do you know? You can't even raise the vig on that marker you got out. Dick is what you know."

"Have it your way. You're the honcho."

"Goddamn straight I'm the honcho here, and this honcho tellin' you to butt out before them hurts start comin' *your* way."

Jim shrugged, and Bryce, grateful for even a moment's respite, shot him a quick glance, and a look passed between them like a seal on a bargain, the terms of which remained to be struck.

"What he's doin'," Biggs declared, swinging his attention and fierce mongoloid eyes back to Bryce, "is runnin' a shell game on us. We say Monday, he say Tuesday in the a.m.; we say OK, he say, 'Oh, sorry, run into little snag. Now it gotta be Tuesday night.' "

"I fail to see how a few hours can make a significant difference in our plan."

"Yeah, well, how about that collectin'-the-take part a' your genius plan? Remember that part—daylight hours, crowd at the beach? How you gonna do any a' that in the dark? Answer me that one."

Recalling another heist movie he'd once seen, thinking at the outer limits of his capacity for speed, Bryce said, as boldly as he could couch his reply, "A minor adjustment is all that will be required. We'll move the collection site to the airport. One of those baggage lockers. The usual glut of traffic at an airport should reduce the risk factor measurably."

"Got an answer for everything, don'tcha?" Biggs sneered from a corner of his tight, bitter slash of mouth.

"I like to think so."

"OK. OK. When's your next chin wag with Swett?"

"Tomorrow morning."

"OK, here's what you tell him. We don't see our loot by six bells, he gonna get his old lady's wedding ring back, finger attached, express mail. Then for every stall hour after that, there'll be another present. Ear maybe, toe. Maybe a titty nipple. That's what you tell him. Got that?"

"I understand," Bryce said, understanding also, and perhaps for the first time, that he was in over his head. "Now if you'll excuse me, I must get to work on the details of our revised plan."

"Yeah, you do that. And they better be good. I ain't buyin' the needle or takin' a jolt off old sparky, whatever they got down here, on account a' any more your bumblefucks."

As he slogged back to the tenuous shelter of his apartment, Bryce felt, dazzling sunlight and prickly heat notwithstanding, an immense weariness, the corrosive rust of time on his brittle bones. And in that chamber of the head where images were shaped, he saw a dreadful vision of a casket slowly descending into the earth, and carved on the gravestone was his own name, and the recorded date of his death was tomorrow's. What he didn't see, in the here and now outside that chamber, was an Oldsmobile parked up the street, a figure behind its wheel, patiently waiting.

Apart from lechery and drink, Junior was a man without resources when it came to occupying idle hours. Denied the former (except as it gathered in his loins at the blurring sight of that jelly roll in her tool-teaser Daisy May getup), he was obliged to fall back on the latter, filling the past six of those empty hours pulling from a bottle, defiantly spewing viscous gobs of tobacco juice into a cup set on the floor alongside the recliner, but mostly just sitting there scowling into his lap. Given his morning head start, by dusk Junior was rapidly approaching that border that separates (in cases like his, by only the thinnest of margins) drunk from dangerous. Eventually he crossed it.

It was a chance, though monumentally incautious, remark by Billie that pushed him over. Like all the others, Hector included, she hadn't moved after the explosive scene with Bott. Petrified by the viciousness of Biggs's threat, she clutched Jim's arm as though grasping at a lifeline and shrank down on the couch, doing her best to keep outside the field of vision of that lumpish, brooding figure in the chair blocking the door. A progressive silence settled over the room, 'til at last Hector, mumbling something about killing time, switched on the television and swept the channels, settling finally on an ancient Abbott and Costello farce.

In the beginning Billie stared at the screen blankly, her mind flooded with terrifying images: a severed finger, a toe, worse. But fear, like pain, has a lifespan too, and as the long day creaked by and the light softened in the window and nothing more chilling than the odious splat of spittle issued from across the room, Billie decided that it had to have been the drink talking, that no one was capable of such savagery, that tomorrow everything would be normal again, or at least as she had come to define normal over the past five days. Finally persuaded, she found her vision gradually refocusing, even caught herself now and again snickering along with the other viewers at the slapstick antics on the screen (all but Jim, who sat gazing stonily into some private middle distance). When Junior lurched to his feet and announced in sloshy voice, "Gonna go dangle the hose," she heard herself say, "After you're finished, will you please remember to put the seat down?"

"Do *what*?"

"Put the toilet seat down."

A faint, nasty smile parted Junior's lips, displaying a row of stained teeth. "Now why'd I wanna do that? I ain't like Uncle there, don't gotta squat to pee."

The shaky camaraderie of this loony band of thieves always had troubled Jim's mathematical sense of probability, and the middle distance he'd been scanning held, for him, a mind's-eye peek—viewed as though through the wrong end of a telescope—of its violent crumbling. Now he shifted his gaze onto Biggs but said nothing. Over in a corner, Leon giggled, softly but audibly.

Junior glared at him. "Fuck're *you* laughin' at, weenie dog?"

"Nothing," Leon said, barely a whisper.

Hector made an exasperated wheel-rolling gesture around an ear, but it escaped Junior's attention, which was honed in again on Billie. "Tell ya what," he said, "whyn't you come on back there with me, walk me through this seat-droppin' drill?"

"I think you can handle it on your own," she murmured, seeming to recognize, too late, the colossal blunder of her remark.

"Come along anyways," Junior coaxed in a fraudulently wheedling tone. "Put a little lipstick on this dipstick for a change." To specify which, he gripped his genitalia with a meaty paw.

Billie shuddered.

"C'mon, man," Hector put in. "We got enough grief goin', way it is. Who needs more?"

"Nobody talkin' grief here, cholo. Talkin' hide the salami, like Uncle been doin', while we floggin' our budgies. 'Bout time to pass the candy box around is my thought. What's yours, Miz Billie?"

Her eyes desperately sought Jim's, but he kept his on Biggs and answered for her. "No."

Junior's smile, which never had really departed, widened, revealing a purplish tongue too thick for the cavity that contained it. "What's that? Gotta speak up here, Uncle, or, like they say in church, forever hold your peace. Only it won't be this piece you holdin' no more," he added with a nod at Billie and a chortle at his excellent pun.

For a sliver of an instant, Jim hesitated, thinking, unaccountably, of the cards, how all his life they'd built a fence around him, turned that life into a spectator sport. Up to now. Thinking also of the pain inevitable in any participation, pain suffered and pain delivered, and wondering whether the solitary life wasn't better after all. But a quick glance at Billie and another at his nephew, both of them paralytic with dread, reminded him he wasn't alone anymore, and he rose off the couch and stationed himself between it and Biggs and, in as firm a voice as he could produce, said, "Her thought is no."

"Hear that, cholo? Flea fucker found he got a set a nuts on him. Thinks he found 'em anyhow."

"Let it go, man," Hector muttered. "Leave the fuckin' seat up, you want."

"See, that ain't the point," Junior said, addressing Jim now. "Point is your cunts, they like to say yes after a little tussle. So I'm thinkin' you got her thought wrong, Uncle. An' recommendin' you step outta my way."

"No," Jim said.

Junior shook his head sadly, said, "Big mistake," and came rocking toward Jim, who ducked the first wild punch but took the second square in the face and, spurting blood, backpedaled under a hail of clubbing fists 'til he found himself pinned against a wall, arms crossed over his head, deflecting some of the blows, not all, and none of those that drove into his torso with the curious thumping sound of a rug being tirelessly beaten for what seemed like forever, 'til his legs went rubbery, and he sank to his knees. And through a smear of blood, he saw, or thought he saw, an afterimage on the lids of his closing eyes, Biggs drawing back a boot—looked about a size thirteen—and aiming it at his groin; and standing behind Biggs, gun leveled on him, the shape of a figure who resembled Hector. And in his closing ears, Jim heard, or hoped he heard, that figure saying, "Tha's enough, man. Back off."

Puffing a little from his exertions, Junior turned slowly and stared first at the weapon trained on him then into the grim brown face, a look of baffled disbelief spreading over his own. "You *drawin'* on me, cholo?"

"Tellin' you back the fuck off."

"Easy, easy. Them trey-eights open a wicked hole in a man. Maybe you wanna point it another direction."

"Soon's you back off," Hector said stubbornly.

"Whadda we got here? Bean dip in love? Gonna rescue the fair lady, like in the movies?"

Hector's face darkened. He jabbed the gun at him. "Gonna open up that hole, you don't do like I'm sayin'."

Junior put two flat palms in the air, took a compliant retreating step. "You got it."

"Take your shooter too."

"Huh?" Junior grunted incredulously.

"You heard it."

"You relievin' me a my ordnance?"

"Holdin' it for you. 'Til you got your head right."

"Nothin' wrong with my head."

"You mashed, man. Gimme the shooter. Two fingers, butt end first."

A storm gathered in Junior's eyes, smeared them, but he lifted his snubby out of its hip holster and handed it over, saying, "OK, cholo, you got that one too."

Hector stuck the Colt in his belt. And remembering all the taunts and slurs he'd endured these past many days, he said, "Name's Hector."

"So?"

"Try sayin' it."

"You sayin' say your name?"

"Tha's what I'm sayin'."

The narrow space between them crackled with hostility. Junior shrugged and slurred out the full inventive name, tacking to it a qualifier of his own coinage: "Hector Pasadena, the man with the cannon."

There followed a long silence broken only by the sounds of Jim's ragged breathing rising from the floor, and during which it occurred to Hector that if he was ever going to carry out Mr. B's directive to smoke this swaggery gringo, now was the time. Pump a round into the 'ole ticker and drop the shit sack where he stood. Walk away from this whole loco game, back into what once had been an orderly, predictable life. If he had the cojones to do it. If.

He wagged a thumb at Jim and to the two onlookers said, "Get him outta here."

Eyes glassy with fright, neither one moved.

"Do what I'm tellin' ya," Hector bawled. "Hop to!"

Now they hopped, both of them. Dragged Jim to his feet and wobbled him down the hall and into the bedroom in the back. As soon as they were gone, Junior said evenly, "OK, you wanna tell me what the pro'lum is here?"

"Pro'lum's you. Five-mil score, an' you got to go fuckin' things up."

"How's that?"

"How? Crowdin' the broad, thumpin' the dude. Tha's how. No good reason, either one."

"Just funnin' around is all. You know me, partner. Don't mean dick."

"Don't look like no funnin' to me."

"It's the sauce. You right—I'm blitzed. Need me a night's sleep."

"So whyn't you step over to your chair there, crash?"

"Good idea. Big day tomorrow. Payday."

He shambled across the room and lowered himself with inebriate caution into the recliner.

"You straight now?" Hector said.

"Yeah, I'm straight."

"'Bout fuckin' time."

In a voice surprisingly meek, Junior said, "Hector?"

"Yeah?"

"You, uh, gonna gimme back my piece?"

"In the mornin'."

"Then maybe you wanna holster yours?"

"Not yet, I think."

Like that murky, transitional voyage from wakefulness to sleep, there were spheres of sensation you one goes through, coming back into the world following a serious beating. One such zone, Jim was discovering, was outside yourself, a cushy softness beneath you, say, or a cool dampness on your brow: precise, tactile, soothing, welcome. Another was internal: a dispersive numbness that has no identifiable bodily venue and isn't so much pain as its grateful absence. And then there are other gradually emergent perceptions as well: clashing aromas of female fragrance and your own sour sweat; pale light flickering over the slits of your eyes; shadows that seemed to coil like serpents on a distant wall; a voice, gentle but urgent, summoning you. "Jim, are you awake? Jim?"

"Yeah," he said, not a little regretfully. "Awake."

"Are you all right?"

"Been better."

"Anything broken?"

He put a hand to his face, testing the bones in his jaw, nose, cheeks. "I don't think so," he said.

"You've got a bad cut over your eye. I tried to stop the bleeding with a wet towel, but it needs stitching."

Nurse Billie, he thought, had found her calling at last, even if it was too late. "How'd I get back here?" he asked.

"We helped you, Leon and me."

"Where's he now?"

"Leon?"

"Yes."

"In his room. I don't think he can stand the sight of blood."

"He OK otherwise?"

"He's scared, Jim. So am I."

"You see now the kind of world you're in here?"

She looked at him searchingly and as though for the first time. "*This* is your world?"

"Not mine," he protested and then amended it to "Not exactly anyway" and then admitted, "But I suppose I've been flirting with it all my life."

"What are we going to do, Jim?"

Very deliberately, very cautiously, he pulled himself into sitting posture, while Billie, in her best bedside manner, placed a pillow between his spine and the headboard. "Thanks," he said. "Do me another small favor?"

"Whatever I can."

"Get me a cigarette?"

"You think you should?"

"Right now death by nicotine is low on my list of worries."

She reached for a pack on the night table, lit one for each of them, handed Jim his, and dragged deeply on her own, anxiously awaiting his solution to their joint peril. And as he ransacked his bleary head to produce one, he was reminded, irrelevantly, of their first meeting, two outlaw smokers, and of the braided chain of accidents that had brought them here. "Tell me what happened out there," he said, stalling.

"Just now?"

"Yes."

"I thought he was going to kill you," she told him. "It's a miracle he didn't."

"Why didn't he?"

"Hector stopped him."

"Hector? How could he stop him?"

"With a gun."

"You mean—" he said, grasping after another of those thin strands of hope, elusive as the smoke settling over them.

"No. He didn't shoot him. Just made him quit beating on you."

"Pity. About the shooting part anyway."

"Don't I know? Did you hear what he threatened to do to me tomorrow?"

"I heard."

"You think he meant it?"

"Was just talk. He's swacked."

"But what if he did, Jim? What are we going to do?" she petitioned him, again in that insistent, inescapable plural but in a voice wavering this time on the edge of tears.

"There may be a way out yet," he said in a tone of guarded confidence he didn't feel at all.

"How?"

"Bott."

"He'll help us?"

"He might."

"But why should he?"

"To save himself."

"How do you know that, Jim?"

"We talked last night. While you were next door."

"Does he have a plan?"

"He didn't then. I'm betting he does now, after that Biggs wake-up call this morning. Trick will be to get to him tomorrow."

"Can you do that?"

"I'm not sure," Jim said truthfully. "I can try."

"Do you think we have a chance? Any at all?"

"Chance is always..." he started to say, but he had no idea where that thought was going and where it was supposed to end, so he let it drift away.

There seemed to be nothing left to say. They stubbed out their cigarettes, and Billie switched off the lamp and stretched out beside him. A breath of a wind, like the first hint of a threat of a warning, rattled the windows, and they clung together like the two frightened Dakota waifs they were, lost in an eerie woods, the night coming on.

TWENTY-THREE

DURING THE NIGHT, THE HURRICANE (LABELED A gender-neutral "Chris") taunted its trackers, pointing first this many degrees northwest then whimsically dipping just as many in a southwesterly direction, spinning like a child's erratically twirled top. By morning it seemed to have settled on that stretch of shore known as the Treasure Coast, and though the meteorologists had classified it as only a Category Two storm, police cruisers and fire trucks prowled the streets of Singer Island, squawking amplified alerts and urging residents to evacuate in expeditious, orderly fashion. Although a few didn't, most did, abandoning homes and condos and apartments and hotels and businesses for a presumed security inland.

By midmorning a wall of clouds had advanced across a low, sullen sky, gradually blotting the feeble sun and casting a strange amber light over this unlucky parcel of earth. The ocean rippled under a rising wind and, in the long distance, beaded with the first drops of rain, like water coming to a slow boil. On the shore the air seemed to vibrate under a rumor of wind, and then jointed shafts of lightning suddenly split the sky and the plump clouds unleashed a deluge of rain and the charging wind lifted it off the beach and swept it through the deserted streets of the island.

It wasn't a good day for swimming or surfing or soaking up the rays of the sun, but it was a good day for a storm and an even better one for death.

Among those who had elected not to leave that morning was Reverend Bott. He stood at a window of his Surf and Shore apartment, watching the rush of wind send trash cans dancing crazily down the street, listening to the hard rain drilling the roof, silently cursing whichever malignant gods governed the elements, and not least of all, debating what to do. The two principals in this internal dialectic were familiar antagonists: caution (fear, some might call it) versus greed, but their acquaintance didn't make the contest any less heated, or easier to resolve.

Only a moment before had he put up the phone, reeling from the confounding news after leaving the perfidious Swett with the ominous, entirely warranted thought: "Very well, if you insist on yet another delay, then I can't be responsible for the consequences."

He couldn't either. Even in the happiest of scenarios (caution/fear advised him), there was no way he could hope to reason with that imbecile Biggs or restrain his vengeful fury. Better to bolt for the car and beat a prudent retreat while you still can (caution further argued) and return for Waneta, much too frail to travel, when the coast was, quite literally, clear.

On the other hand (greed rebutted), there undeniably *was* a hurricane raging out there, and banks *were* certainly closed (Swett's not unpersuasive justifications for this latest stall). And given the covenantal look Bryce had seen, or believed he'd seen, on Merriman's face yesterday, there was at least a chance they could forge an alliance; perhaps, over the next twenty-four hours, lull Biggs with drink and extravagant dreams of wealth of that most alluring kind, the ill-gotten-gain variety; possibly spirit the lady away unharmed and intact for the trade. Exactly how all these fine feats of derring-do could be accomplished wasn't clear yet. Surely an opportunity would present itself. Something would come to him. You need only rely (greed reminded him) on your eloquence and guile and native wit, qualities that in the past have served you well and seen you through darker days than these, though when they were (caution cautioned) he couldn't quite place.

Eventually greed prevailed. He went back to the bedroom and offered a few comforting words to Waneta, assuring her (on no factual grounds whatsoever) there was absolutely nothing to fear from the storm. That obligation fulfilled, he steadied himself, stepped outside, and pelted by rain and pummeled by wind, staggered next door.

Another of the drawbacks of working solo was you had no one to relieve you on a lengthy stakeout. Minor inconvenience, no big deal for Cheetah, who had trained himself to slide into a kind of hypnotic trance, half dozing behind eyes and ears on hair-trigger alert. Was one of those survival skills you learned in the jungle and adapted to your profession. One job he'd stood a sixty-hour watch on a moonlighting wife holed up in a motel with her stud muffin, came away with all the goods his client required and a fat paycheck he didn't have to split with anyone. The virtue of which made up for a whole lot of discomfort.

So this was nothing, not even twenty-four hours' worth of scoping time in yet, though the hurricane added a unique dimension, not altogether bad, seeing how it cleared the terrain. And so he waited with a vulture's patience, the wind shuddering his vehicle and driving flattened sheets of rain down the emptied streets.

Everything broke at once. First came the jackleg preacher out his front door. Buckled by the force of the gale, fighting for every step, he wobbled over to the adjoining apartment. No sooner was he inside (Cheetah was thinking this could be the break he was looking for) than the phone got to rattle. Odds-on bet who was on the other end of the line.

"Cheet? Lon."

"What's up, Lon?"

"Just got off the horn with the wimp."

"And?"

"I done like you said. Told him he'd have to wait 'til tomorrow for his money, storm 'n' all."

"How'd he take it?"

"Not good. Pissed and moaned."

"Figures."

"He said somethin', though, got me little worried, Cheet. Thought I better call, run it by you."

"Bottom line, Lon," Cheetah said impatiently. He wasn't big on hand-holding and didn't want to be hanging on the goddamn phone, in case there was any more action coming on up the street.

"I sez to him, 'Look out your fuckin' window. Ain't nobody gonna be doin' no business 'til this hurricane blows over, tomorrow earliest,' and he sez, 'OK, but it ain't my fault for whatever happens.' Somethin' like that, anyway. You think that means they, uh, y'know, maybe gonna hurt Billie?"

"Think it means I better get moving," Cheetah said, and abruptly broke the connection, unholstered his piece, and tottered toward the Surf and Shore, floundering like a man caught in a field of wet cement and, with his simian features, cutting an almost comic figure: an ape in dress-up clothes, slogging through a storm with a gun in its paw.

"It serves no purpose...to become exercised over...matters outside one's power...to control," Bryce was stammering—squeaking, actually, his vocal cords (to say nothing of his breathing) seriously constricted by the bear claw tightening at his throat and nailing him to a wall.

Nothing wrong with Biggs's voice, though, if you count a flinty snarl as socially acceptable pitch. "You want exercise, I'll give ya a workout you won't forget."

Bryce was able to produce only a gurgly sound, no intelligible words in it. So much for eloquence.

"Fudgin' your undies are ya there, Reverend?"

Bryce's bulging eyes swept the room, found Merriman's but detected nothing there, nothing in the way of sympathy or support. Billie's were glassy, Hector's remote. The simpleton nephew was nowhere in sight. No support anywhere. He lifted a limp hand and sketched a gesture of supplication in the air.

With a sneery contortion of his face, Junior loosened his grip then released it altogether. "Now say again what he told you."

Bryce drew in a series of shallow hawking breaths. "Hurricane," he gasped. "Banks closed...impossible to travel...Tomorrow."

"OK, that tears it. Fuckin' around time's over. Gimme his number."

"If you'll only—"

"Gimme the goddamn number, or you gonna be suckin' air through your asshole."

Bryce told him the Swett number.

Junior snatched the cell phone and began to dial. He got no further than four digits when the door burst open, and standing there in a howl of wind and wash of rain, like a rabbit—or in his case a monkey—produced out of a magician's hat, was Donald Cheetah McReedy, smiling the thin smile of the man who holds the gun.

Bryce's jaw fell. "You!" he blurted.

"The fuckin' baboon man!" Junior exclaimed.

"Guess that'd be me, you boys referring to," Cheetah confirmed. He kicked the door shut behind him, did a quick scan of the room: A lady who was without a doubt Billie Swett huddled with some dude on one side of it; preacher and the hard rock on the other; spic in a chair in the middle, butt end of a piece sticking out his belt, another on an end table next to him. Not good deployment. Not good at all.

"Think maybe we better get organized here," Cheetah drawled. "First I'm gonna ask the gentleman in the chair there to put both his weapons on the floor. Real careful, like."

Hector complied.

"Be obliged if you'd drop that phone," Cheetah said, indicating Junior with a motion of his gun.

Junior let it fall.

"OK, now you and the pastor can join the lady and her friend over there. Mexican gentleman too."

The three of them stepped over and stood next to Jim and Billie. Five backs to the wall.

Cheetah moved into the center of the room. "So what do we got here?" he inquired cheerfully. "Little hurricane party?"

Nobody responded.

"Mrs. Swett?"

Billie, dumbstruck, uttered not a word.

"You *are* Mrs. Swett, aren't you?"

She moved her head up and down.

"Your husband's been awful worried about you. Maybe we oughta give him a buzz, tell him you're OK. That'd be right, wouldn't it? You *are* OK?"

Again her head moved affirmatively.

"That's real comforting to hear," Cheetah said, and gun leveled, he stooped down and, with his free hand, searched the floor for the phone. Never once did his eyes leave them.

Not, that is, until a figure appeared in the hallway to his hard left, whistling tunelessly and rubbing the sleep from his eyes. Cheetah dropped into a crouch, and in what would prove to be one of the few errors in his professional career, though easily the costliest, he pivoted slightly, not much, but enough for Junior to come lunging off the wall and slamming into him. Cheetah reflexively swung the gun in time to stagger him with a sidewinder blow to the skull but too late to dodge the spic's blade, which first came slashing across his face then plunged deep into his chest, opening a geyser of blood. He grunted once, toppled onto his back. For a while, not long, he lay there, twitching like a dying insect. His vision began to blur. Bloodied spittle bubbled from his mouth, which was set in a peculiar, slack smile, as if to say, "It's not so bad, this dying business, once you get the hang of it."

Neither was the killing end of it, Hector seemed to have decided, for he knelt over the fallen body, rocking back and forth, pumping a fist triumphantly, chanting, "Did it, did it, did it, did it!"

Junior heaved himself up into an all-fours posture and waggled his head like a dazed, baffled hound. "Ape got a mean wallop on him," he allowed to no one in particular.

"I *killed* him, man," Hector declared exultantly. "Took him out."

"Good thing you pack that shank. Coulda been us eatin' the worms."

Hector tugged the blade out of the punctured flesh. Didn't come easy. He held it up and gazed at it wondrously. "I killed him," he repeated, not quite so jubilant now.

"OK, OK. So you ain't a cherry that way no more."

"Not no more," Hector echoed, as though in confirmation of that irrefutable fact.

From behind them came a ragged whimpering, terror's shorthand, and from the hallway a nervous titter, soft but steady. "Shut the fuck up, both you," Junior bawled.

Both sounds instantly ceased.

Hector's gaze dropped to his blood-spattered shirt. "I gotta shower," he said dully.

"Shower? Now?"

"Lookit me. I'm all soaked. Gotta get this off me."

"Now ain't the—" Junior started to protest, but a thought seemed to occur to him, and he said instead, "Good idea, *chico*. You scoot on back there and get yourself ragged off. Take your time. I'll cover these weenies."

Simultaneously they scrambled to their feet. Hector shouldered past Leon and shuffled down the hall. Junior recovered all three weapons, holstered one, stuck another in his belt, and brandished the third. Three-gun Biggs, appraising the cowering foursome with eyes cold as tombs. Cunt held a trembly hand to her mouth, as if to bottle a scream. Kid grinned vacantly. Reverend chewed his underlip. Uncle merely stared back at him, his face empty of expression.

A silence opened, heavy with threat. Junior waited 'til he heard a splash of water coming from the crapper, and then he nodded at Bott and said, "OK, Reverend, I'm puttin' you in charge here, minute."

Bryce looked bewildered. "Me?"

"Yeah. You. Whole scam was your idea, correct?"

"Yes," he said ruefully. "I suppose it was."

"Which makes you a full partner, correct?"

"I'd certainly like to believe that."

"An' partners split a take right down the middle. Am I right on that one too?"

"That's the usual arrangement."

"OK, partner, what I want you to do is keep an eye on these people for me, case they get the bookin' notion. Ain't likely, that storm out there 'n' all, but if any one of 'em should, want you to sing out loud and clear. Think you can do that?"

"I could. But what are you—"

"Don't you trouble that snowflake head yours 'bout me. I'll be right down the hall there. Takin' care little business. Won't be but a minute."

The strength of Hector's vanity was such that the first thing he did was examine his face in the mirror to determine whether the act of execution had in any way reconfigured its features. Detecting nothing, he next rinsed off his stained blade and laid it across the top of the sink. Then he stripped, adjusted the water in the shower to a temperature just short of scalding, and stepped under it.

Hector stood in a spray of water, methodically scrubbing his wiry body, thinking how it's easy to kill someone if you had to. Nothing to it. Cake.

A cloud of steam saturated the tiny room. And materializing out of it like a photo developing in a pan of solution was the shadowy outline of a bulky figure, and gripped in its hand was Hector's very own blade, and it flung open the shower curtain and seized him by the knob of a ponytail and jerked his head up and back, presenting a brown column of throat that the blade hand neatly sliced, ear to ear. Hector slumped to his knees. The astonished wail that is a violent death's distinctive anthem rose from his mouth, lifting higher, falling, lifting again, like a trumpet muting and unmuting. Then the aggregation of cells that made up the person of Hector Pasadena began to spin away, death bound, and he sagged back in the tub, legs grotesquely twisted beneath him, but cleansed of the froth of blood draining from his neck by the steady splash of water.

Junior inspected him for a moment. A blank, pitiless stare. 'Til a recollective smile came into his face, and on a whimsical impulse, he squatted and stuck his head in close—drenching it in the process, but that was OK—and whispered, almost tenderly, in Hector's ear, "Remember that story I told you about Ramon? Santa? Well, cholo, look like Christmas come early for you this year. And I'm your Santa."

As soon as the bathroom door closed behind Biggs, Jim turned to Bott and said, "Now's our chance."

"For what? He's right, you know. How far could we get in a hurricane?"

"Farther than here."

"On foot? Impossible. Believe me, I've been out there."

"Make it to your car, and we're home free."

"My car's in the back."

"So we run for the back."

"We'd never make it."

"We can try."

Bryce hesitated, calculating, weighing his private options, those two lifelong disputants, fear and greed, squabbling inside his head. "I don't know," he said, the fear in ascendancy. "If we fail it will only, well, exacerbate an already delicate situation."

"Delicate!" Jim pointed at the corpse lying in a swamp of blood on the floor, its mouth gaping fishily. "Talk to that one about delicate. You're not buying any of that 'partners' shit? He's wasting one partner right now. We're next."

"Perhaps they're simply, uh, conferring," Bryce said, greed rationalizing for him.

At just that moment, Hector's death song came wafting down the hall. Jim said, "Now what do you think?"

"I think you're right."

Jim beckoned at Billie and Leon, who had remained silent throughout this debate, glazed with shock, both of them. Not protesting, they followed him to the door. He swung it open, and a fist of wind struck him, staggered him. He'd never seen a hurricane before or felt its force. Maybe Bott was right; maybe it was lunacy, this dream of flight. But then he heard a door opening at the back of the apartment, footsteps in the hall, and he shoved Billie and Leon out into the storm. Bott, frozen with fear, didn't move. "He's coming," Jim said. "We've got to run."

"Where? We'll never get to the car now."

"I don't know where. Away from here."

A runner once, Jim ran now, heart thundering in his chest, rain-washed breath scoring his tarred lungs. But it was like running underwater or in one of those nightmares where your legs refuse to take you where your mind desperately wants to go. He glanced over a shoulder and saw the three of them trailing him by a good ten yards, maybe more. There was something faintly comic in their labored motion: Leon's spindly legs pumping; Bott's scuttley waddle; Billie's arms wildly flailing, as if to ward off a horde of wasps. But there was nothing at all funny about the figure now coming through the apartment door, charging the wall of wind like a maddened bull, moving gracelessly and in what seemed to be slow motion, but coming on all the same, reliable as the death he carried in his hand. "Run, run!" Jim shouted, but his words were scattered on the storm.

Directly ahead was that dingy collection of weathered frame tourist traps that passed for a mall. Still, it was a shelter, of sorts, and if they could just reach it, maybe there'd be a place to get down. Maybe he'd find a weapon there or something that would serve as a weapon. Anything would do, however makeshift. Anything was better than what he had now, which was nothing.

A cry reached him, riding the strident voice of the wind. Still running he looked back, and there was Billie, fallen in the street, struggling to get to her feet. Without success. Something slowed him, braked him, something too elusive, too ambivalent to put a name to. It was the wind as much as his conscious will that spun him around, and he ran to her, passing the stupefied Leon and Bott, waving them on. He grasped her by the wrists and hauled her up. "My ankle," she said apologetically. "I twisted it."

"That's OK. We'll make it."

"How?"

"I'll help you."

Arms linked, straining for balance, they hobbled toward the mall. And in the shrinking distance behind them the bullish Biggs charged on.

Whole fuckin' thing's a bust, Junior had decided when he'd come into the living room and found the weenies gone, all of 'em. Took too much time with *chico* back there, but he'd figured the dickeye reverend was too nutless to bolt. Figured wrong. Least he still had that 50K, so it wasn't a total wash. Pop in the van, raise some dust, lay doggo a while. Up in Michigan, maybe. Someplace.

Except if he let them scooters scoot, they'd be nine-elevening him inside a Jew York minute. Steam would be all over him like flies on shit. Be lucky if he made it over the bridge. Next stop, Sparks City.

So he'd better just zap them, be done with it. Only when he looked at that wide-open door, wind whipping through it, sky pissing rain outside it, he was stricken with doubt. He'd never been in a fucking hurricane before. Solid and square as he was, maybe it would blow him over, blow him right away. And how about that wad of bills in his pocket? What if he lost that too? Then what? He had to do something, though, and speedier than quick.

An inspiration came to him. He pulled out the bills and bent down and stuffed them inside the baboon man's Jockeys. Last place any citizen would look was in a stiff's crotch. What he'd do is go on out there, take care of business, come back, get his loot, and maybe torch the place, seeing how his prints were on file, then get into some serious wind. Michigan, dead ahead. Home, or the closest he'd ever known to home. Where Mom was planted. Her memory stoked him. He checked his pieces, all three of them. Two stiffs down, four to go.

There'd been no time for Jim to search for a weapon and even if there had, what was he going to do? Deflect bullets with T-shirts and tanning lotions? As it was, they were lucky to have made it this far, groping down the shadowy interior passage between the two files of utterly abandoned shops. Open to the elements, that corridor supplied only flimsy shield against the wind hurtling in off the ocean and none whatsoever from the stinging rain.

That's where Jim had found Leon and Bott when at last he and Billie had come stumbling into the mall. Huddled against a wall, breathing the quick choppy breaths of hounds run too far, too long, they'd looked to him for direction, a frantic wordless appeal in their terror-stricken eyes. Billie's too. Like he was supposed to know. What did he know?

"C'mon," he said and led them down the passage, here and there testing a door along the way, none of which gave. At the extreme north end, there was nowhere left to go except back out into the open: empty parking lot to the left, empty beach to the right. Open targets.

One door remained, a sheet of solid glass. He tried the handle. Locked of course. He took a step back, drove a shoulder into it, the way they do in the movies. Door didn't budge. He tried kicking at the glass but, for his effort, received only a sharp pain in his sneakered foot. Everything was easier in the movies.

"Uncle Jim?"

Leon timidly tapped him on the shoulder.

"What? What? What?"

"Would that work?"

Jim followed the pointing arm to a twisted metal shaft that looked like the post of a traffic sign, uprooted and tossed into a corner of the passage by the vagrant wind. "Let's find out," he said.

Wielding it like a battering ram, they assaulted the glass, once, again, yet again. First it splintered, then shattered, opening a breach just wide enough for Jim to reach inside and release the lock.

And now they were hunkered down at the far end of one of the shop's three narrow aisles. Its shelves were draped in shadow; no way to tell what sort of merchandise was peddled here. More trinkets probably. Or maybe it was a pharmacy, judging from the dim outline of a flat counter behind them. Didn't matter anymore. Concealment was their only defense now, the counterfeit dark of the storm, and the wispy hope that somehow Biggs might miss the broken glass, pass them by.

"Are we safe here?" Billie whispered in his ear. "Will he find us, Jim?"

"Shh."

He waited, listening to the wind lashing the walls, the rain hammering the roof like the sound of nails sealing the lid of a coffin. Listening for other sounds as well: footfalls in the corridor, a door creaking.

Presently they came.

Holy fuck (Junior was thinking, back pressed to a wall in the skimpy shelter of the mall, snorting, wheezing, limbs aching right down to bone from the uneven contest with the storm), if this was a hurricane he'd take a goddamn Michigan blizzard any day of the week. At least you couldn't drown in snow or go sailing off like a popcorn fart in the wind.

Gradually his thumping heart slowed down. Chest quit heaving. Vision cleared. OK, he'd seen 'em slip into this entrance. So they had to be in here someplace. Hiding in the shadows probably, run out of places to run. Maybe thinking ambush. He'd give them an ambush.

Assuming the shooter's crouch, piece arm extended and braced at the wrist by a steadying hand, he came cautiously down the rain-slickened corridor, eyes nimbly darting, probing the murk, checking doors and windows for any sign of forced entry.

Eventually he found one, though he might have overlooked it but for the shards of glass crunching under his feet. Last one in the string of shops. Must be that the weenies liked suspense. He'd give them that too.

He grasped the handle, inched the door back slowly. Gave it a beat then ducked inside, arcing his piece across the empty space in front of him. Off to his left was a long aisle, too dark to make out much of anything at the end of it. Only two more aisles on other side of this one, all three of them flanked by chest-high shelves, the kind you could see over. Perfect.

Since he had them boxed now, he might as well have little fun with it. "Yoo-hoo," he crooned in neighborly singsong. "Anybody home? It's your partner, come to call."

Wind shook the outside wall. Rain pounded the roof. Inside there was only silence.

"You can come on out now, folks. I ain't mad. Honest. Ain't the kinda guy holds no grudge."

More of the silence. Like they were thinking he was going to give it up, go away. Junior Biggs never went away.

He stepped into the middle aisle and crept down it, senses on red alert. Coordinating arm and eye, he jabbed the piece over the top of shelf right, straight ahead, shelf left, back to forward, then right again, repeating the drill, a robotic cadence to his motions, taking in all three aisles in a single frugal sweep. The master of stealth, virtuoso of precision.

By now Jim's eyes had grown accustomed to the faint light. Enough, anyway, to distinguish object from shadow. Enough even to make out a display of charcoal lighter fluid and a stack of cook's aprons midway down the aisle. A thought occurred to him: *Lighter fluid lights; cloth burns. So does flesh.*

He made a keep-down gesture at the others and, on hands and knees, crawled over to the display. CLOSE-OUT SPECIAL, a sign above it proclaimed. FANTASTIC CLEARANCE PRICES! He reached up and softly, noiseless as an eyelid's blink, lifted one of the plastic bottles off the shelf and an apron off the pile. He peeled back the bottle's safety cap, saturated the apron with fluid, and wadded it into a tight ball. Then he placed both of them on the floor, rocked back onto his heels, and patted his pockets, searching for a cigarette lighter. No lighter. No lighter, no flame. No flame, no plan. No plan, no hope. For want of a Bic.

No time anymore either. He heard a sound of movement in the next aisle over. Saw a hand, gun in it, appear over the shelves, vanish, reappear a moment later, like the automated arm of a kinetic machine measuring its own steady advance. A choppy, five-count beat. There it came again. Vanished. He counted. Same rhythm, same beat. He gripped the bottle and waited with a terrible expectancy, counting. Numbers you could rely on; numbers never failed you.

The gun hand stabbed the air no more than a foot from where he crouched. On "three" Jim sprang to his feet, squeezed the bottle, and shot a spray at the half-turned figure, drenching its hair and neck and shoulders. Biggs swiveled, too slow by a finger snap. The fluid caught him full in the face, soaked his eyes. He clawed at them with one hand, swung the gun wildly with the other, jerking its trigger, firing scattershot, blind.

Jim dropped to the floor, flattened himself. Slugs tore through the shelves, pinged off the walls. He counted them: two, three, four...He saw the others hunched in a corner at the end of the aisle, all but forgotten in the melee. To Billie he called, "Lighter! Throw me your lighter!"

She gazed at him dumbly.

"Lighter! Now, now, now!"

She fumbled through the pockets of her jeans, slid a lighter across the floor. He snatched it, holding on to his count: five, six...a hollow clicking sound, instant's silence. He seized the wadded apron, ignited it, leaped up, and flung it into Biggs's face, igniting him. Ribbons of fire illuminated his head, crackled his hair, streaked down his shoulders. He howled like a devil sloshed in scalding holy water. Jim nourished the blaze with another splash of the lighter fluid, howling back, "Burn, you cocksucker! Burn, burn!"

Watching that thrashing, flailing, writhing clump of animated flame, soon to be reduced to a rubble of scorched cinders and blackened bone, hearing its sustained anguished shriek, Jim felt as though he'd been granted a privileged peek into the darkest recesses of his own heart and discovered a demon there.

He stood in the mall's passageway, gazing numbly out at the empty streets, emptied himself of any emotion, vacant of feeling.

Abruptly, miraculously, the rain stopped falling and the wind slackened, and an eerie light shimmered in the smudged sky like a tarnished benediction laid on the punished earth.

"What is it?" he said. "What's happening? Is it over?"

"It's the eye," Billie told him. "We're in the hurricane's eye."

"A window of opportunity," Bott said, "albeit narrow. We must hurry."

"He's right, Uncle Jim," Leon confirmed. "They don't last long."

He was conscious of Billie watching him curiously. He took her aside and said, "How's the ankle?"

"Sprained."

"Can you walk on it?"

She hesitated. "I'm not sure."

It was in that hesitation, as much as the words, that Jim recognized what she was trying to tell him. "Well, it's better you wait here. We can make a call, send somebody to get you."

"Jim?"

"Yes."

"It's just that…I don't think I could live this way."

"It's not always this way," he said, more explanation than plea.

"Even once is too much. What happened here today, I couldn't go through anything like it again. Can you understand that?"

"Yes."

"I wanted to come with you. You know that."

"I know."

"Where will you go?"

"I don't know. Only thing I do is we've got to put some geography between us and this body count."

"We?" she said doubtfully.

"Me. Leon. Bott. You'll be OK."

"I could say you had nothing to do with it. The kidnapping, I mean, and the killing. None of it."

"Appreciate the thought, but that might be a hard sell to the law."

From behind him came Bott's fretful voice: "Mr. Merriman. Please. Time is short."

"Yeah, I'm coming."

Billie gripped his hand. "After everything, you know, dies down, you could maybe call me. Or write."

"I'll do that."

"We could meet somewhere."

"Sure."

They fell silent, hands linked, unwilling to part, neither of them believing for a moment in these impossible pledges. Jim glanced up at the sky, a shrinking hole in heaven, circled by troops of gray-bellied clouds. When he looked at her again, there was a wetness in her eyes, a stinging sensation in his own.

"I've got no regrets," she said. "Not a one."

He moved his mouth into a wan smile. "Neither do I."

TWENTY-FOUR

BY THE TIME THEY EMERGED FROM THE SOUTH end of the mall, the wind was picking up again. Out over the ocean, lightning snapped like whips across the sky. Rain spattered the street. "Looks like intermission's over," Jim said, breaking into a sluggish trot. Most he could manage.

Leon had no trouble staying with him. Bott fell behind. "This old heart," he gasped, clutching his chest histrionically, struggling to hold the pace, "is unused to such stresses."

Jim slowed down. No other choice. Bott was the one with the wheels. They needed him. A while longer anyway. "Another block is all," he said by way of encouragement.

"God willing, I'll make it."

"You'd better."

They slogged on.

Once his breathing was restored to the level of a ragged pant, Bott said, "Allow me to express my deepest gratitude, Mr. Merriman."

"For what?"

"Saving our lives back there. I'm in your debt."

"Give us a lift out of here, and we'll call it even."

"Small recompense for your valor."

"Oh, yeah, that's me all right. Captain Valor."

"Perhaps you and your nephew would do me another kindness."

"What's that?" Jim said warily.

"Lend a hand with Waneta. She really is weak, you know."

"You're not thinking to stop for *her*? Lady with her own agenda? Remember you telling me that?"

"Indeed I do. Still she *is* my associate. I could hardly abandon her."

"There's no time."

"With your generous assistance, it would require only a moment."

"We could help out, Uncle Jim," Leon volunteered, unasked. "Go quicker if we did."

"And then there's the proceeds from our little cottage industry," Bott added, as though in afterthought. "Funding for our journey, wherever it may take us. I suspect you're both a bit short of the wherewithal."

Advice from a scammer and a doodle dick. Fact that it was inarguably right told Jim something about where he was, how far he'd fallen. "OK," he said. "Whatever'll get us on the road."

But when they came through the door of the apartment and hurried to the bedroom in the back, all they found was emptiness. Empty closet. Empty bed. No Waneta.

Bott looked baffled.

"Where you suppose she went?" Leon said.

"I confess I've no idea."

Jim stood in the doorway, tapping a foot urgently.

"This is most puzzling," Bott said.

Leon pointed at a scrap of paper on the pillow. "That a note?"

"Appears to be."

Bott went over and picked it up, his first written communication from Waneta in all their years of partnering. And this is how it read:

Deer Brice:

I new that pis ugly dood for heet soons I seen him. Look like your in the deep shit now. Time for me to say by by. Lots luck with them to stiffs next door.

—Waneta Jean Pease

p.s. You got to find better spot to stash the lute than your hershee squirt drawers

p.s.s—Dont bother look for that fifty long either. Dood keep it in his shorts same as you, car keys to.

p.s.s.s.—I left you the caddee for old time's sake.

Bott scanned the note once, brow pinching. Then he read it a second time, more carefully. Then he sank onto the bed, shaking his head slowly, side to side. Where before he had looked baffled, now it was stunned.

"Well?" Jim said.

"She's gone."

"Gone? Where?"

"Who knows? By now I expect as far off as the mountains of the moon. The money with her."

"She took the money?"

"So it seems."

"*All* of it?"

"To the last dollar, I fear."

"You mean," Leon asked Bott, voice stammery, stricken, "she really couldn't talk with people on, y'know, the other side? She was, like, faking all the time?"

"To put a benevolent construction on it," he confirmed with a crooked smile.

For a moment no one had anything to say. Jim watched the two of them, each miseried in his own way, each with a joy mislaid. When he thought about Billie, which until then he'd not allowed himself to do, he understood their grief. But because none of them could afford the luxury of sorrow just now, and because someone had to act, he said, almost gently, "If we want to get out ahead of this storm, we'd better get moving."

At Bott's request Leon did the driving. Jim sat up front, the reverend in the back. They wound through the deserted streets of West Palm, bearing west, the wind tracking them, rain beating the hood and roof of their chugging vehicle. As they neared the turnpike, Leon asked, "Which way?"

"I don't know," Jim said. "North maybe." He turned to Bott. "What do you think?"

"North is as good a direction as any."

They pointed north. Rode in silence. 'Til eventually Leon's natural cheeriness resurfaced, and he said to Bott, "Y'know, these old humpback Caddies were really something in their day. You wait—they're going to be classics someday. If I had the money, I'd buy this one off you."

"That seems to be our common problem."

"What one's that?"

"Money."

"Well," Jim put in, "'fraid we've got nothing to contribute there. I know for a fact Biggs was carrying that cush we raised. Which means it went up in smoke. Along with him."

Bryce didn't have the heart to tell him differently. "Money comes and goes," he remarked philosophically. "Like that wind out there."

Oddly this stoic pronouncement seemed to cheer him. A smile came into his face, and he chuckled softly.

"Something's funny?" Jim said.

"I was thinking about Waneta. Evidently she was a quicker study than I'd imagined."

"You're not bitter?"

"Not at all."

"You're sure about that?"

"Absolutely. Bitterness serves no useful purpose. Think about it. Who among us is without flaw? Why, even the saints had their small, forgivable blemishes. Take Aquinas for example. It's been said he was grossly overweight. Obese even. Hardly the appearance one would expect of a saint. Yet saintly he was."

What do you say to that? Jim had to wonder if this curious, windy scammer ever actually listened to the torrent of words spilling from his mouth. Maybe he simply drew from a bottomless well of gassy bromides. Whatever the case, he seemed to be genuinely at peace with himself. The sort of man who understood the wicked ways of this sorry, sinister world and had long since accommodated himself to them. Maybe his was the right idea after all.

The dwindling remnants of the storm followed them. The wind had tapered to brisk breeze, the rain to anemic drizzle. Off in the east, the sky gradually blackened. In the west a pinkish glow burnished the horizon. Hours passed, and no one spoke. To one degree or another, they were all in that fatigue- and motion-induced zone where time and distance meld, and the miles and minutes glide seamlessly by on the carpet of highway unspooling out ahead.

Jim sat with his eyes closed, watching the anarchic drift of images behind them. Now and then Billie Swett's appeared then was instantly gone, like a phantom ache in a severed limb. By now, of course, she would be reunited with the husband, back in the suffocating shelter of limitless wealth, the careless adventure over and no one the wiser. Except maybe for him. Maybe he was wiser by a fraction of a fragment of a particle. Or maybe not.

Maybe it was merely the melancholy creep of the accumulating years, all those bungled opportunities and ruinous choices that, glimpsed over the shoulder, pass for the wisdom of experience and age. Either way he was persuaded of the certitude of one simple truth: Wherever you travel there are places and persons you never leave behind, and that place back there and that woman would remain with him as long as images flickered and memory lasted.

A here-and-now voice intruded on these reveries. "Where are we?"

"Not exactly sure," Leon replied. "Saw a sign said Lake City couple miles back."

"Hmm, Lake City," said Bott. "That would mean the fine state of Georgia cannot be far off."

"That where we're headed? Georgia?"

Bott made another hmming sound.

"We probably oughta be deciding pretty quick," Leon suggested tentatively. "Don't you think?"

"Mr. Merriman, what are your thoughts?"

"Fresh out," Jim said.

"As am I, it seems."

Leon cleared his throat. "Y'know," he said, "last time I was talking with Miss Waneta there, I asked her where I should go. She said Mom said home, and I said, 'You mean back to the apartment?' and she said—guess that'd be Mom talking again—'No. Home.'"

Jim looked at him with the arid indifference one pays a familiar household pet. "So what's your point?"

"Well, I was thinking maybe she meant home like in South Dakota. Y'know, Sioux Falls."

"Sioux Falls," Jim snorted. "Fuck would we do in Sioux Falls?"

"That's what I thought too. Then I remembered this farmer I knew up there. Name of Emmitt Toliver. Little light up top but basically not a bad guy."

"Point, point."

"He got these three Edsels, stores 'em in a barn," Leon said, as though his point were now established.

"So there's a Dakota dillweed with three rust-bucket lemons parked in a barn. So what?"

"Oh, no, they're in mint condition, Uncle Jim. Never been drove. See, my idea was we'd zip on up there, buy 'em off him, do any work needs to be done, and sell 'em to a collector someplace. Three brand-new Edsels oughta go for some nice money. What do you think?"

"You want to know what I think?"

"Well, yeah, sure," Leon said, but hearing his uncle's caustic tone, he wasn't so sure he was sure.

"I think it's a brainless idea. Loopy. Right in there with kidnapping somebody. Close second."

Up to then, Bott had kept out of it, listening, weighing, evaluating, calculating. Now he said, "I'm not certain I'd agree with that assessment."

Jim swung around in the seat, regarded him coldly. "Who asked you?"

"Well," he said mildly, "it *is* my vehicle we're driving. I should think that would entitle me to an opinion."

"OK. Fine. But first let's review our circumstances here. We got between us...what? Thirty bucks? Forty? Be lucky to make it to the state line on that, never mind another couple thousand miles. But let's say, just for the sake of argument, we got there. What do we use to buy these heaps?"

"We must learn—" Bryce started to say, but Jim cut in on him.

"Wait, let me finish. Leon, when did you last see these cars?"

"It was a while back," he mumbled.

"So you don't know if they're even there still."

"No."

"Or even if this hayshaker's still alive."

"No."

"How about collectors up in that part of the world. You know any?"

"No."

To Bott, Jim said, "I rest my case. Let's hear yours."

"I was about to say," he said now, enigmatically, "we must learn to bend circumstance to our collective will."

"Oh, good. That's good. Not sure what it means, but it sounds real good."

"What it means, my friend, is that this venture seems not unworthy of further exploration. Tell me, young man—Leon, may I call you?"

"Yeah, sure, that's OK."

"As long as we're going to be traveling companions, we may as well address each other by Christian names. Mine, as you know, is Bryce." He turned to Jim. "Is that agreeable with you, sir?"

Jim shrugged. "Whatever."

"Now then, Leon," he resumed, "in your expert opinion, what kind of dollar would a mint-condition Edsel fetch these days?"

"Jeez, I dunno. Oughta be fifty thousand, easy. Maybe more."

"A hundred and fifty thousand," Bryce purred. "Possibly more. A tidy take."

"*If* you've got a buyer," Jim reminded him.

"As it happens," he said complacently, "I'm familiar with one."

"In South Dakota?"

"No. California. A gentleman I met in my ministerial days. A man of considerable substance and an avid collector of antique automobiles. Lived in Hollywood, if memory serves. Connected in some way with the motion picture industry."

"What about money?"

"To purchase the vehicles?"

"To get there first."

"Why, that should pose no great difficulty. In the trunk of this very car, you'll find a bundle of brochures featuring gravestones in a variety of tasteful designs. And between here and the heartland, there are persons departing this coil even as we speak. No, seed money will prove to be no problem whatsoever. Once we arrive..."

On he went, spinning grand strategies and fantastic schemes with the passionate ardor of the man for whom life without a swindle, or the dream of a swindle, was unthinkable, intolerable. No puzzle was too complex, no hurdle too high for his artful ingenuity, his rascally charm.

Leon, catching the spirit, said, "Bet I could get some work along the way. Garages, y'know, gas stations. Help out on the money end."

"A most generous offer, but I doubt we'll be in any one place that long. Better you handle the driving and lead us to this noble tiller of the soil. That will be contribution in plenty."

Even Jim found himself articulating a thought that had been stirring in his head for the past many hours. "Maybe, if we're able to put together a little nut, I could scare up some action."

"Action?"

"Yeah, cards. Poker. Action. Low-roller stuff, you understand."

"You thinking to start playing again, Uncle Jim?" Leon asked him.

"It could happen."

"There you are," Bryce said exuberantly. "Yet another potential source of income. How can we fail?"

Struck suddenly by the sheer lunacy of the preposterous scheme—gravestones, gambling, South Dakota, Edsels, California—Jim said, "How? How about what just happened back there? You forgetting Singer Island already? What do you call that?"

"A minor setback."

"Tell that to some of the people involved."

"No need to fret," Bryce observed, back again in philosophic gear. "If you'll think about it, I'm sure you'll agree that all parties concerned got exactly what they wanted, or richly deserved. Mr. Swett has his lovely wife back, and she the worldly comforts and security she so clearly covets. Waneta has her independence, a first-class education—if you'll pardon the seeming immodesty—and a handsome take. Hector, Biggs, and that other intrusive fellow the tranquility of death. So in every respect, it's a happy ending all around."

"And us?" Jim said with the flatness of a man unaccustomed to happy endings. "What about us?"

"We're still drawing breath, aren't we? Still partaking of the wondrous privilege of life. And with every prospect of a profitable new enterprise just over the horizon."

"Yeah. Dakota horizon."

"Destination and destiny, my friend, are not always the same."

"He's right, Uncle Jim," Leon seconded brightly. "We oughta do real good up there."

Jim looked at him, this man-child nephew who slouched and grinned and apologized his way through life, desperately in need of a guide. A champion. And he was the one elected. Some champion. He said, "You got a lot to learn, kid. We both do."

ABOUT THE AUTHOR

Tom Kakonis was born in California, squarely at the onset of the Depression, the offspring of a nomadic Greek immigrant and a South Dakota farm girl of Anglo-Saxon descent gone west on the single great adventure of her life. He has worked variously as a railroad section laborer, lifeguard, pool hall and beach idler, army officer, technical writer, and professor at several colleges in the Midwest. He published six crime novels before retiring for over a decade, then resumed fiction writing with the novel *Treasure Coast*. Currently he makes his home in Grand Rapids, Michigan.

Made in the USA
San Bernardino, CA
19 March 2017